BETWEEN BLOOD AND DARKNESS

BETWEEN BLOOD AND DARKNESS

Lili Mastronardi

BETWEEN BLOOD AND DARKNESS

This work was written entirely by a human author without the use of artificial intelligence.

Cover Art: Lili Mastronardi
Chapter Header and Scene Break Art: Lili Mastronardi

For Samantha, Sara, Stef, Jenny, and Giuliana. Thank you for believing in me when I had all but stopped believing in myself.

I would go to Hell and back for you.

THE NINE CIRCLES OF HELL

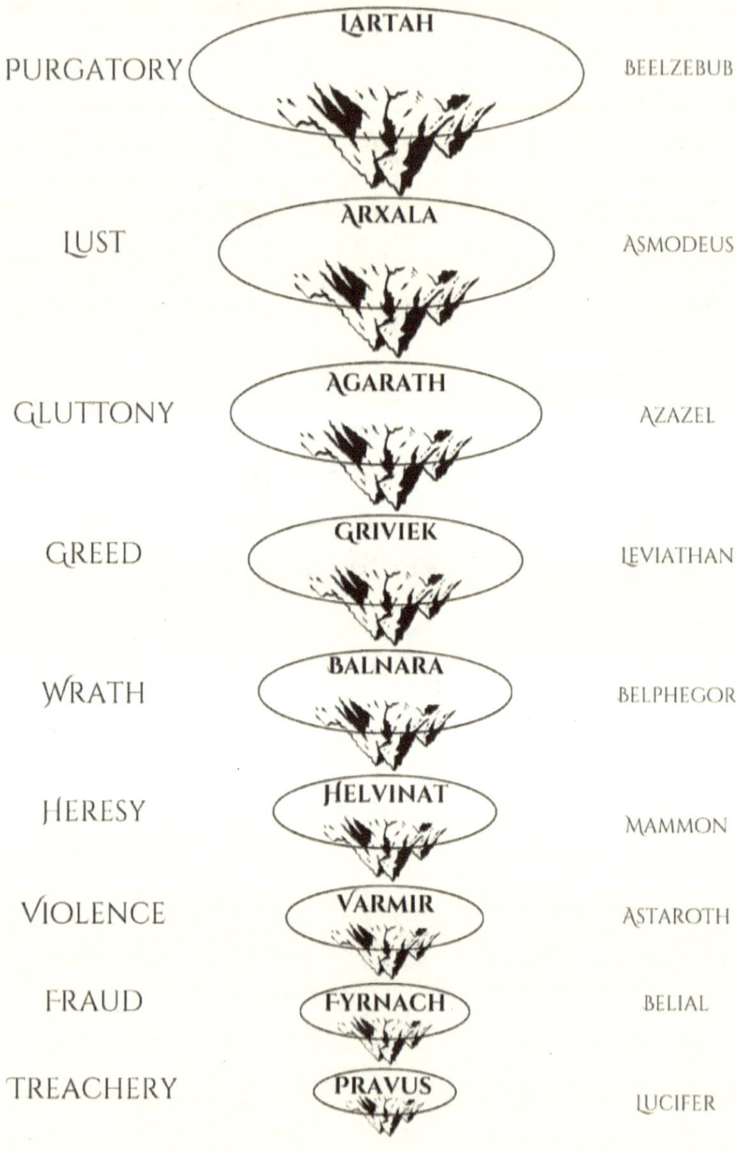

TABLE OF CONTENTS

Content Warning: explicit language; sexual content; mentions of suicide; scenes of blood, violence and death.

CANTO I

Good versus Evil? More Like Evil versus High School Mean Girl

A chill clung to the night air, dark and biting. Over the street lingered a sharp quiet, free from the howling winds of March, but deafening still. The slightest sound, it seemed, would most likely wake the dead.

That peaceful silence was immediately shattered when I stumbled over a loose stone while attempting to walk on the path to my front door. "*Shit!*" The word echoed, resulting in a cacophony of dog barks.

"Adara?" Frankie called after me. "You okay?"

"You'd think the booze would have worn off by now," I grumbled.

"Hold up. I'm coming." Frankie turned off his car, locked it, and came to help me with my keys.

I put a finger to my lips and let out a "Shhhhhhh!"

"You shh," he retorted in a whisper as we crossed the threshold. He gently closed the door after us, and we removed our shoes, placing them to the side.

"See," I said, starting up the staircase first, "I told you we wouldn't get"—the light in the living room turned on, revealing my dad sitting in his armchair, displeased as ever—"caught."

Frankie swore, also frozen like a deer in headlights. Reluctant, he descended the steps with me not far behind. "Nice to see you, Kamael—I mean Mr. Goodman, sir," he blurted. "Dara was just… uh…"

"Sleepwalking!" I offered, hoping that sounded somewhat sober and believable.

"Yes," Frankie said, nodding multiple times and hugging himself, "she was sleepwalking and I found her outside, all alone in the cold—"

"Francisco Suarti, cut the crap," my dad interrupted. Sleep had dishevelled his deep brown, almost black hair, and the bags under his eyes were visible, even from here. "I know you guys snuck out. Do I have 'born yesterday' tattooed on my forehead?"

Frankie's eyes dropped to the floor. "No, sir, you don't."

"Exactly. So, stop trying to pull a fast one on me. It won't work." He stood from his armchair and approached us. "I'd tell you to go home but I'm sure your mom would rip into you as soon as you got there."

Frankie glanced at me. Angela definitely would, which was why he had to stay here.

"Well… this was certainly a good talk." I pushed Frankie toward the stairs. "We're going to go to bed now. We're *really* tired."

"Woah, woah." My dad waved us back. "Not yet. I'm not finished." Frankie and I braced ourselves for a lecture. "As a parent, I should be reprimanding you two. You left the house without permission to go for a joyride in the middle of the damn night and engaged in underage drinking. That's against the law. You could have gotten caught and spent the night in jail. Both of your mothers would have gone ballistic, not just Angela."

"Are you going to tell Mama?" I asked, flashing him my puppy eyes—which I knew he couldn't resist—to get out of the situation.

Frankie joined in. "Are you going to tell mine, too?"

My dad rubbed a hand over his face, scratching his beard before eyeing the direction where my mom was sleeping. "No, I won't tell either of your mothers," he sighed. Frankie and I fist-bumped behind our backs. "I understand that you're young and you want to go out and do stuff but what you have to remember is—"

"We need to be more responsible and think about the consequences of our actions," Frankie said. I patted him on the back and he gave me a proud smile.

"What?" My dad's brows drew together. "That works fine, but I was going to say make sure you don't get caught."

My jaw nearly hit the ground. "Huh?" I elbowed Frankie to get him to stop gaping.

My dad looked around like I hadn't heard him. "Was I speaking another language?" he wondered. "Don't. Get. Caught. That's a life lesson. Now go to sleep, my little rebels."

Frankie and I sped up the staircase, still in shock from the conversation. "*What was that?*" he whispered when we got to my room. "I thought he'd tell on us."

I removed my jacket, hung it up on the rack by the door, then flopped onto my bed covered in pillows and released a long, relieved breath through a smile. "Yeah, me too."

Frankie came to lie down beside me, staring up at the slanted lilac ceiling. "Have I ever mentioned how cool your dad is? Because he is."

Less than a minute later, as if he'd been summoned, he appeared in the doorframe. "This isn't what I meant when I said, 'go to sleep,'" he drawled. "Frankie, get out of my daughter's bed and head over to the couch."

I rolled my eyes. "Let him stay, dad. The couch isn't comfortable. I told you we needed to go to Ikea for a new one."

"Yes, we will, but in the meantime, you two are both drunk, so I want you separated."

"Sir, I'm not drunk," Frankie said, a half-truth.

"Did I ask?" My dad snapped his fingers, and Frankie jumped out of my bed.

I followed suit, grabbed a blanket from my closet, and tossed it onto the floor with a bunch of pillows. "There. He can stay here and we'll be separated."

My dad wasn't satisfied. "Nope. He's going downstairs. Hop to it, Suarti."

Frankie shrugged in apology. "I'll see you in the morning, Dara."

Once he'd left with my dad, I changed into my pyjama bottoms but kept on the sweater he'd lent me earlier, hoping it might trick my mind into thinking he was still with me. I hated sleeping alone. I liked sleeping over at Frankie or Jess' places because their presence helped chase *it* away. Lying down as I was, in the eerie, almost suffocating, silence of my dark room, called back the vivid nightmare that made me wake up in the dead of night for years on end.

Every time, without fail, a man with one eye black and one eye gold, surrounded by flames and monsters, flashed in my mind. Although my parents and I had moved around a lot, one thing remained constant since I was six: the piercing screams echoing through the halls. At first, I was afraid of what my dreams meant, but my mom assured me they were nothing serious. She knew I'd ignored my dad's warnings when he told me not to go into his office to read his theology and myth books from work, saying they were most likely the cause of my nightmares. I couldn't help myself, though; when I got curious about something, I had to learn every detail or it would drive me insane. And so, the nightmares didn't stop; I just found ways to cope with them, hence Jess and Frankie.

The sudden knock on my door startled me, and I tossed in bed to see who was bothering me at five in the morning. Through the limited light, I spotted a head of sandy-blond hair enter and lower to the ground.

"So… your couch stabbed me in the side," Frankie whispered, wrapping himself in the blankets I'd provided.

I laughed as quietly as I could. "Was it the spring in the middle of the second cushion?"

"I hate that stupid couch. Kamael said we're going to Ikea when we wake up."

"You're coming?"

Frankie shuffled around to find a comfortable position. "Since I'm the one who usually sleeps on the couch, he said I should tag along."

"That's not the only reason, is it?"

Frankie was silent for a few seconds, which confirmed my suspicion. "I convinced him to let me come with you so I wouldn't get the third-degree from my mom."

"Yup, there it is. Now go to sleep, it's five in the morning."

Yawning, he said, "I'll be dreaming of Ikea's Swedish meatballs."

As I heard his breathing grow light and even, his presence clear in the room and in my mind, I knew I would be dreaming of something comforting as well. "Good night, Frankie."

"Night, Dara," came his mumbled response.

Returning to school after Spring Break was hard—no, strike that. Going back to school after *any* long break was hard. It had been brutal after I'd been kicked out of Sproul in Colorado, especially considering the years of homeschooling and then the move halfway across the country. In the three times I'd been expelled in my academic career, I maintained that not one of them had been my fault. Other kids could be real *assholes*, and it extended to their parents too. That fact didn't magically change when I started at Newton North, however having Jess and Frankie to rant with helped to ease the aggravation.

Michael helped a bit as well—a little crush to distract from the Hellscape called the 'American High School Experience.' Did I tend to turn in the opposite direction when I saw him in the halls? Sure, but who hadn't done the same in my position?

Jess' voice rang in my ear, telling me no one did.

When Senior year began, I was disappointed to find I had no classes with Michael, which meant I had to stick to only seeing him in the hallways (when I didn't avoid him) or on the field during P.E. I wouldn't complain about that last bit, though. I'd take seeing him practice over shared classes any day, and it seemed a decent number of girls and a handful of guys in my P.E group agreed with me. All they would do was sit on the bleachers and stare at him. As tempting as that sounded, I needed academic perfection, so I put aside what Jess dubbed my 'yearning-from-afar' and continued participating.

"*Ouch.* Do you mind?" I hissed when she nudged me in the ribs. "That hurts."

"He's looking over here," she whispered loudly, causing his other fans to glance at us.

"And? What's your point?" I asked, more concerned with rubbing my arms to warm up since the jog had been useless. Why in the Hell did P.E have to happen outside when it was 55 degrees? It should've been illegal to let students out in this weather.

"My point is," she began, heading across the patchy grass to the goal net, "you're obsessed with him and he's looking over here."

"I'm not 'obsessed' with him," I mimicked. Dribbling the soccer ball between my feet, I focused on lining it up with the goal. "Are you ready or not?"

Jess tightened her ponytail of golden-brown curls, put on the goalie gloves left by our teacher, and stretched and clapped her hands. "Are you?"

Taking a running start, I aimed for the top right corner of the net and kicked the ball hard with the inside portion of my foot. Jess threw herself to block it. The ball rolled over her fingertips into the exact corner I'd aimed for. I pointed at her. "*Ha!*"

Someone laughed from behind me. "You got one in. You're not exactly Messi."

I put my hand to my ear, ignoring the obvious identity of the girl who spoke, and took up a sarcastic, apathetic tone. "Is that you, Satan?" Having registered who it was as well, Jess left her post at the goal and jogged toward me. By the time she'd arrived, I had already turned around. "Oh… Lenia," I said with feigned disappointment. "Sorry, I thought you were somebody else."

Lenia Rivers' vibrant brown-green eyes flicked from her phone to me, smiling in that false way of hers. It was the same smile she'd worn when she'd introduced herself on my first day at Newton North and was also the reason I'd rejected becoming her friend. I figured she wasn't someone who was told 'no' very often; naturally, she resented me for it. In the end, my intuition had been right about her. Had she been genuine to start, had she used the privileges she flaunted for something better, I might've felt for her what I now felt for Michael. All that beauty and intelligence, yet she chose to act like this.

"You think you're so funny, don't you?" Lenia quipped.

"I'll forward you some reviews later for my one-woman show," I deadpanned, and flashed her a tight smile. "If you don't have anything else to say, you can move along."

Lenia pursed her lips and left with her friends to sit on the bleachers. She turned to Jasmine and Victoria to whisper something to them, resulting in a burst of barely-suppressed laughter. My hands balled into fists at my side, half from anger, half from the anxiety spreading through me at their judgement.

"You good, Dara?" Jess asked.

"Yeah. I'm fine."

Obviously I lied, but luckily, she didn't have a chance to mention it since our gym teacher, Mr. W., blew his whistle, signalling for the class to gather on the bleachers before the period ended. Jess and I sat at the very top, the place we'd usually eat our lunches if the weather was decent. Mr. W. gave us a rundown of the co-ed soccer tryouts he'd be hosting with Coach Joe and encouraged us to try out for the team before dismissing us, headed to see the Coach who was talking to Michael.

Jess and I had nearly reached the pavement when Lenia said from behind, "Maybe you should try out for goalie, Adara. I'd pay good money to see you get hit in the face with a ball."

"Sounds like your typical Saturday night, Lenia," I returned.

The remaining students on the bleachers snickered. Lenia silenced them with a glare and stood up. Almost an entire head of space separated us; it was hard to get intimidated by such a short person. "Do you want to repeat that?"

"Dara, come on. It's lunch. Let's go," Jess said, pulling at my arm. "There's a pizza with our names written all over it."

"Sounds good." I ignored Lenia's question, uninterested in spending another second around her.

"*Hey*," she snapped. "I was talking to you."

I shifted toward her. "Yes, you were talking, but were you saying anything?" I pouted. "I didn't think so."

Lenia's lips curled. "Who do you think you a—"

A voice I'd heard the whole of last year's English class interrupted her. "Hey, Adara?"

I stopped in my tracks, however my blood didn't. It raged through my body, constricted around my heart. My parents really made me win the genetic lottery with these anxiety and moderate panic disorders.

Jess tapped my arm. "*Dara.*"

Plastering a smile on my face, I veered in the direction of one Michael Lamont in his Newton North Tigers' captain's uniform. "Hi, Michael. What's up?"

"Smooth," Jess whispered from beside me.

"Shut the Hell up," I whispered back.

Michael's light brown, almost caramel eyes passed between the two of us, and he resumed no matter how puzzled he seemed. "Coach Joe and Mr.

W. are holding tryouts for the team and told me to come ask you if you would consider joining."

"Why didn't Mr. W. ask me himself?" I wondered.

Red flushed Michael's cheeks. "Um, because…" he brushed away a stray lock of hair from his forehead, and the sun's rays emphasized its chocolatey-brown colour, "I'm the team captain."

Oh. Right.

"It's a nice offer, but I'll pass. I'm not that good."

"I saw you when I was practising," he said, and the warmth in my chest flared. "You *are* good. Great, even."

"Yeah, Adara," Lenia taunted from behind. "Don't be modest."

"Len, do you mind?" Michael motioned between him and I. "We're kind of in the middle of something."

Jess shot Lenia a look, and the other girl raised her hands in playful surrender.

"I'm not cut out for soccer," I told Michael, already inching to join my class passing by us to make their way into the school. "I already have a lot on my plate with AP classes, and I feel like I'd be too competitive, anyways."

Michael laughed. "Competitive? With the guys?"

I frowned. "What's so funny about that? Is it because I'm a girl?"

He turned serious instantly. "No, no, it's just… I would fear for everyone's safety with those wicked shots of yours."

I raised a brow. "Nice save."

He continued to convince me: "We could use more talent on the team."

"Because there isn't enough with you as captain?"

"*Wow.*" The corner of his mouth tugged upwards, and he pressed a hand to his heart. "I don't know if that was supposed to be a compliment or an insult."

"Take it as both; one to boost your ego, the other to deflate it a bit," I responded. "As for your offer, I can't." As much as joining the team sounded like fun, the pressure would be overwhelming—hundreds of eyes weighing on me, judging or waiting for a screw up. Not to mention he'd be close to me too… It was a wonder I'd made it this long talking to him without blacking out.

"That's a shame. We needed a strong forward." Withdrawing to his teammates, Michael added with a wink, "And I would've liked to have seen you in our uniform."

I blinked at the interaction we'd had, confused and blushing.

Jess spun me toward her. "Dara, that was cra—"

"That was cute," Lenia interjected.

Every semblance of my fluster dissipated; I had no intention of letting her see me like this. "You're still here," I said, blunt. "Why? Go do something productive with your life."

My efforts were in vain, of course.

"I just find your crush on him adorable," she remarked, "and how pathetic you are about it."

Lenia had to be perceptive. After all, what better way was there to set an example, ensuring no one crossed her, than by collecting and hoarding information under the threat of releasing it to her own benefit? She'd done it multiple times before, these humiliation rituals, which explained why the rest of our grade flocked to her. The closer they were, the more they flew under her radar. I'd once been on its perimeter, not worth the trouble despite my rejection of her, but I might have just bought myself a ticket to its very centre.

I wasn't delusional to the point of being unable to recognize her remark as the threat it was. Even though I'd schooled my face into neutrality, worry ate away at me, preventing any possible reply.

Detecting a change I hardly realized I'd been displaying, Jess held my hand, coming to my defence. "What's truly pathetic is your mean-girl act," she told Lenia. "Is your life so violently boring because you're deprived of attention that you need to stir shit for no reason to keep yourself entertained? Act your fucking age, we're not ten anymore."

Lenia's jaw dropped. "My life is not—"

"That was a rhetorical question," Jess stated. "We're finished here." With that, she brought me with her, merging into the flow of students passing through the gate surrounding the field.

"Thanks for standing up for me back at that shit show," I said, regaining my voice. "I love how I managed to mostly avoid Lenia since Freshman year and she chooses to mess up my last few months here."

"She's harmless," Jess said. "All bark and no bite."

"That bark made Elena switch schools a year ago."

"Which sucks, yes," she acknowledged, "but *you* have bite, so there won't be any problems." She gave my hand a squeeze as a reminder which I had no energy to unpack. "Cheer up, Dara. Did you forget Michael wanted you on *his team*? He was practically begging you."

I said nothing about him, or about what she was insinuating. Instead, I removed the band from her hair, letting the curls loose and fall to her back. "So you don't get a headache later."

Jess' lips parted to argue with me for changing the subject, however, all she said was: "Thanks" and hid what she wanted to tell me under a smile. It'd been more comforting than her assurance that Lenia would leave me alone, even though they were both lies.

Lenia was after me for the rest of the week. Despite trying to avoid her to the best of my abilities, whenever she'd pass by me in the halls, she'd make a comment or an insult indirectly aimed at me like the coward she was.

The weekend finally gave me a break and a much-needed recharge; I'd spent it with Jess and Frankie, making my Monday morning bearable. Great, even. He and I had walked to school together since he'd slept over on the new couch we had chosen at Ikea a week ago—with my parents' approval, of course—and we got there early because he didn't need to stop by his place to grab his favourite sweater. It was already at my house, clean and warm from the dryer.

To make things infinitely better, right as we were entering the main building, Jess texted Frankie that she'd stopped by *Peet's* on her way to pick us up drinks and was waiting at our lockers.

Sure enough, we found her leaning on my locker, one of her vintage tennis shoes braced at the bottom, with our drinks in a cardboard holder in her ring covered hands, half hidden behind the sleeves of her fluffy beige jacket. She turned toward us when I called her, revealing her favourite Playboy T-shirt of Pamela Anderson, who we both had crushes on. "One iced coffee for you," Jess said, handing it to me when I arrived. "I made sure to ask for less ice because you think there's always too much."

"You got me a large?" I kissed her cheek, careful not to mess up her makeup or mine. "I love you with all of my heart, Jessica Torres, have I ever mentioned that?"

She beamed. "Only every single day, but I'll still accept it." She passed Frankie his order while I sipped on mine. "And take this dark roast—no milk, no sugar, no fun—you boring child."

"My day can never truly start without your wonderful insults, Jess." He took off the lid and sniffed his coffee. "*Perfect.* And I appreciate you."

"Yes, yes." She nodded, grabbed her drink, and tossed the cardboard into the recycling bin across the hall.

"What did you get?" I swiped the cup from Jess' hand before she could answer and tasted it. "*Ugh*, this is disgusting."

"What?" She took the cup back. "It's March and St. Patty's Day is coming up. Lucky Leprechaun frappé season."

"There is nothing '*lucky*' about that mix." I faked a retch and Frankie cackled.

"Yeah, well, keep this up and I'll never buy you coffee again," Jess threatened. "I'm going to my locker now. Dara, I'll meet you in class, and Frankie," she started leaving, "we'll see you during free period?"

"Yes, sir. I'll text you!" Frankie shouted down the hall after her.

I unlocked my locker with Frankie doing the same next to me. "*Tienes español ahora, ¿no?*" I asked.

'You have Spanish now, no?'

"I do?" He set his coffee down on the top shelf, swiping his schedule from between his books on the second. "Seems that I do. You have… Calculus now, right?"

"Do I?" I mirrored his actions, checking my phone for my schedule. "I love how we know each other's schedules better than our own." Once I confirmed my first period class was, in fact, Calculus, I shoved my textbook into my bag along with my spiral notebook and zipped it up. Beside me, Frankie struggled to find where he'd placed his Spanish workbook.

"*Dara*," he whined, rifling through his things.

I handed him my coffee, closed my locker, and hip-bumped him out of the way so I could help him. Frankie was always losing his things and calling me to find them, which I did. I lifted his gym clothes from the base of the locker. "I think it's here—"

"Your weekend looked interesting. I saw the Story you posted with Michael on Saturday."

I turned around to see who was talking. My fingers gripped onto the Spanish workbook I'd found. *My morning was going so well*, I internally groaned as I glimpsed Jasmine and Lenia standing outside of their class in similar skirt and legwarmer outfits.

"Yeah, he asked me out like… three times before I actually said yes," Lenia told Jasmine, speaking louder when she noticed my presence. "Turns out he's been into me since Junior year."

Irritated by Lenia's constant attempts to piss me off, I threw Frankie his book. "Sorry, I didn't mean to hit you." I retrieved my coffee from him and took a long sip, hoping the caffeine would magically fix my mood.

"I don't know what everyone sees in Lamont," Frankie mumbled, zipping up his backpack.

Lenia arched a brow at me. If I didn't get away from her soon, I might start swinging, and I couldn't afford to do that.

"Do you want me to walk you to class?" I offered to Frankie.

"I know what you're trying to do," he said, watching as Lenia whispered to Jasmine. "I don't understand why you don't just fight her. She'd leave you alone then."

"I'm not going to beat her up," I whispered. "I promised my mom I wouldn't do anything rash. It's bad enough I antagonized Regina George's cousin already. I don't want to make things worse."

Frankie scoffed. "Oh, screw that. She has it coming."

"I know, but I don't want to be the one who does it," I said over the ringing of the bell. "I don't want to risk getting kicked out of another school."

"You won't if it's an accident. Remember, 'as long as you don't get caught.'"

I gave a nod. "Yes, I'll 'accidentally' push her down the stairs and break her legs." Although I was joking, the scene that appeared in my mind had serious promise. A back-up plan, then.

"I'm telling you, Dara," he started, "she's going to get what she deserves eventually."

"That's not the way the world works, Frankie. Those kinds of people never have to deal with the consequences of their actions."

His head tipped from side to side. "That's not completely true." He held out his free hand so we could do our signature handshake before we parted. "Text me when you're in class. I'm going to be bored out of my mind."

I pointed at him. "Make sure Señora Fuentes doesn't catch you. I don't want detention again."

"That happened *one* time."

And thankfully, it didn't happen again when I was in Calculus. The class came and went in the blink of an eye, though not because math was fun. Math was never fun unless you genuinely knew what you were doing. Jess made the droning about differentials tolerable. Her talent for making a boring class entertaining had been responsible for bringing us together during my first days at Newton North to begin with. Time seemed to slip away whenever I was with her. The caffeine from the coffee she'd bought me kicked in right as I went into my Chemistry test, and I thanked her again through text after completing the 3-paged nomenclature early. Then, I messaged Frankie to prepare for a rant about Jeremy, the serial test-cheater, when we got to the lockers after the bell.

Usually, Frankie would've been there within a few minutes, but this time there was no sign of him. I stayed where I was, waiting for him, unpacking my books and repacking others.

"Hey, *Dara*."

A chorus of laughter followed.

Releasing an exaggerated sigh, I slammed my locker shut and turned. I'd been pissed off since I saw Lenia earlier in the morning, and the stunt Jeremy pulled in class hadn't helped. "What is it you want now, Lenia? I'm not in the mood for whatever sadistic shit you have planned for today. Maybe another time? The day after 'never 'suit you?"

She fiddled with the Tiffany necklace draping above her lacy shirt. "You know, I've heard some things about you."

"You've been asking around about me? I'm flattered."

"Did you say the same when you were being kicked out of your previous school?"

"Alright, Nancy Drew." I rolled my eyes. "You overheard me talking to Frankie this morning. Found your source."

She tapped a finger to her glossy lips. "Not exactly. See, I heard you got kicked out because you were crazy. Not even your shrink could figure out what was wrong with you."

A few students who'd overheard her stopped to watch our interaction unfold. And they weren't the only ones. People continued to join in until a giant group had amassed around us.

With each new pair of eyes that drew to me, the shallower my breathing became. The more my vision narrowed. "Seriously, Lenia. Stop it," I warned. "This isn't funny. You don't know what you're talking about."

"Don't I, though?"

This couldn't possibly get any worse.

"Len," someone interjected, "you should back off."

Of course, it got worse.

My eyes widened, and the familiar heat of panic rushed to my face when Michael pushed through the swarm of students to intervene. He stood a few feet from us in his uniform, having stopped on his way to the gym for resistance training.

"This keeps getting better." Lenia laughed, noting the way I looked at him. "You're worried he'll learn about how psycho you are and won't want you anymore? Newsflash," she stepped closer to me, "he never wanted you in the first place."

I wanted to shrink and disappear into nothingness. Lenia had not only told the entire student population about some of my past, however inaccurate it might have been, but also revealed the crush I had on Michael. *Right in front of him.*

The embarrassment had taken its toll on him too, seeing as how he'd turned red.

"Maybe it's your parents' fault you're so screwed up," Lenia said, continuing her assault. Bringing my parents into this argument was low, however what she said afterwards was lower. "Actually, I shouldn't even say that. I mean, you were probably adopted considering the fact you look nothing like them."

It was a hilariously juvenile insult, yet it still affected me. That was what she did, after all. She discovered others' insecurities and exploited them for her entertainment. She had found mine as well. A birth complication left a medium-sized streak of blonde hair at the front of my head, cutting through the rest of the light brown, and had made me extremely self-conscious over the years. As I got older, though, I grew to love it, no matter how many comments were made. My dark eyes had been another result of my birth complications, but the colour hadn't lasted long so she couldn't know about it unless she'd seen pictures of me as a kid. They had eventually lightened to a dark brown like my dad's, and it went without saying I had definitely inherited my mom's above-average height.

How desperate was Lenia to tear me down that she had to resort to this? Her statements were clearly the work of her own insecurities.

Once I regained a hold of myself, I said, "Adoption jokes? Is that the best you can come up with?"

"They're not jokes if they're true."

"Even if it was true, at least my parents actually wanted me. Your parents were stuck with you. I wonder how disappointed they are that you turned out this way." My retort earned me a chorus of laughs from the students around us.

Lenia bristled. "Disappointed like your birth parents must have been when they first saw you?" She retreated to her friends. "Or right after, when they decided they were better off without you weighing them down?"

The retort gripped my throat, and tears prickled my eyes, intensified by her smirk which stayed behind to taunt me even though she had left. It didn't matter if she'd gotten the details wrong when she'd gotten my fear, at its core, right. All this moving… I had put my parents through so much. Being a child didn't excuse it, and my inability to remember the majority of what I'd done didn't either. I must've looked half a child now too, in front of everyone surrounding my locker who continued to whisper and stare and judge thanks to Lenia's lies.

This *wasn't* fucking over.

I wasn't embarrassed anymore. I was angry—angry that Lenia had been constantly harping on me and that she'd humiliated me in front of the whole grade, Michael included. Mostly, though, I was angry at myself for not doing anything to stop it, for not pushing through my discomfort and fighting back using her own methods, but worse. I'd promised my mom I would be on my best behaviour, and I had kept that promise for the last three, almost four, years; I stayed out of trouble at school and didn't draw any unnecessary attention. As much as I had told myself I wouldn't let anything ruin this for me, enough was enough.

Maybe Jess and Frankie had been right.

Swallowing my tears and my mortification, I silenced the phone ringing in my pocket and followed after Lenia, avoiding eye contact with

Michael as I passed him. When I finally caught up, I grabbed her arm, forcing her to face me.

Lenia yelped, and Jasmine next to her jumped in surprise. "Don't touch me! What the Hell is the matter with you?" She recoiled and fixed her purse onto her shoulder.

I closed in on her. "If you're going to insult me, have the balls to say it to my face, bitch." The heat rampaging through my body, ravaging every coherent thought in my mind, carried into my eyes, no longer burning from sadness but from rage and retaliation.

Lenia's attention left her bag and landed on me. "What didn't you get the first time aro…" When her gaze met mine, she trailed off, and the colour drained from her face, replaced by unbridled horror. Her lips trembled, parting only to release a glass-shattering scream that pierced through the air. "*Get away from me, you monster!* What the fuck is wrong with you?" She stumbled backwards, frantically grasping at Jasmine. "Her eyes, Jaz, did you see her eyes? They turned *black*."

Jasmine stepped out of my way as I approached Lenia. If she was this scared now, I could make her wish *she* had never crossed *me*. The promise I'd made my mom whispered in my ear, advising I reconsider. In the end, I listened, choosing to walk away, to be the bigger person, and trusted Lenia would get what she deserved eventually. I only hoped that day would come sooner rather than later.

Just then, another scream sounded. Not Lenia's.

Jasmine's.

Everyone in the hall ran to the source of the noise and discovered Lenia at the bottom of the stairs, her legs twisted beneath her body, the bones visible where they'd snapped like twigs.

Jeremy, who'd copied off of me earlier this morning, vomited right then and there.

"*She pushed her!*" came Jasmine's tremulous cry.

"Who?" someone in the crowd asked.

From where she lay, Lenia raised a bloodied, shaking finger, pointing directly at where I stood. Her eyes rolled back, and her head lolled onto the tile.

A ghost of a smile came to my lips.

CANTO II

Man and Monster

The school called my mom to inform her of the incident and of my suspension for the day. "Ma, *honestly*." I threw my bag onto the floor when we entered the house. "I didn't do it. They suspended me without hearing my side of the story."

My mom hung her jacket on the wooden coat rack, removed her shoes, and came to the living room where I sank into the couch. "No need to shout," she said calmly, sitting behind the coffee table opposite me in the upholstered armchair. "Your dad is going to be here any minute; we can talk then."

As if on cue, the metal clang of jumbling keys rang and the door creaked open. My dad walked in and dropped his briefcase against the wall. "I got here as fast as I could," he said, loosening his tie. "What happened?"

"Nothing," I answered.

"Addie," my mom warned.

"I'm serious," I insisted.

"Tell us your side of the story," my dad said, gravitating toward my mom to kiss her temple and perch on her armrest. "In *detail*, preferably."

I did what they asked of me, launching into the events starting from the first interaction I'd had with Lenia up to her accident; I went so far as to mention the security footage that had been reviewed. In a half-second frame, it showed me, or *something* with my appearance, shove Lenia off those stairs, when I knew for a fact I hadn't touched her. I had turned around. Walked away. Nevertheless, the playback ended, frozen on a shadow, and Lenia lay on the floor, bloody and broken.

By the time I'd finished my story, my mom had paled, and her light blue eyes were fixated on me, almost worrisome. My dad's expression, however, gave nothing away.

"What?" I asked, concerned. "You don't actually think I did it, do you?"

No one believed me. None of the witnesses spoke up.

"No, sweetheart, it couldn't have been your fault," my mom assured. "There must have been an electrical malfunction in the cameras and they didn't catch the girl tripping; it could've overlapped the footage. Not uncommon."

"I tried not to let her get to me, even tried avoiding her. Today…" My nails dug into the sofa cushions. "I don't know what happened. I snapped. And I know what I promised you, but I swear I'm telling you the truth. My hands didn't so much as touch her when we were at the staircase. All I did was confront her."

"It's okay, Addie, darling. It's okay." My mom offered a comforting smile, with no traces of disappointment or anger. "Go lie down, love. Try to sleep your agitation off."

"We'll come get you for supper," my dad said, mirroring her expression. "Your mother and I will make you some lasagna. It'll make you feel better."

Springing from my seat, I contoured the coffee table and wrapped them in a tight, grateful hug, burying my head into their shoulders. The thought that I had disappointed them weighed on me heavily, and the relief of their understanding had come to wash it away. "I love you."

"We love you too," my dad said, patting the back of my head.

"More than anything," my mom added.

With a light smile, I grabbed my bag from where I'd tossed it and headed upstairs toward my room. I'd just reached the second floor, having turned the corner of the railing, when I picked up on their whispering.

"We have to tell her, Kamael. Look what she's done."

My stomach dropped.

"Samantha, we don't know it was her who did it. There's still a chance the Lenia girl did it on purpose."

"Why would she *willingly* injure herself, Kam?" my mom asked.

There was a moment of silence.

"For sympathy, maybe? I'm trying to keep an open mind."

"Kam, the school said Lenia and her friend Jasmine saw Addie's eyes turn black. What do you make of that?"

"Could be the friend is maintaining the story Lenia came up with," he suggested.

My mom considered the possibility. "Alright, you make a fair point."

"But even if it was Addie, Lenia deserved what she got."

"She's a high school girl," my mom scolded in a whisper.

"She's a *bully*," he corrected. "Addie put her in her place, and I'm proud of her for it."

"In the hospital, you mean?" A sigh followed my mom's amendment. "I'm not condoning what Lenia Rivers did to our daughter, and I'm certainly not upset with Addie for standing up for herself. It's *how* she did it. She's about to turn eighteen in a month, Kam. It's been getting worse and you can't deny it. First it was Alex in Seattle, then Eva's father in Colorado, now this?" Another moment of silence stretched. "We can only hide it for so long. We need to contact..." She fell into incomprehensibility, her voice dropping so low I couldn't hear what was being said.

I only caught part of my dad's answer. "He knows… sent... watching her... since Colorado… sending someone else..."

When I realized I couldn't make out any more information, I quietly headed to my room, shut the door, released my bag, and sat on the edge of my bed, facing the mirror of my vanity. The longer I stared at my reflection, the darker my eyes grew.

Rushing to the mirror, I glimpsed a shadow flit through my irises before they faded back to brown.

I wiped my face with my hands, laughing. "I am *not* crazy."

Determined to fall asleep, I grabbed one of Frankie's sweaters from my closet, however, it didn't help much. My mind was too preoccupied; I couldn't manage to stop thinking about what my mom said. As much as I tried, I couldn't fully remember the incidents she was talking about, couldn't recognize the names she'd listed. All I knew was that I'd done something to these people. Something bad enough to force us to move.

The phone in my pocket slipped out and I grabbed it, hesitant, recalling how I had silenced it at school. Although I didn't want to open it, I did so anyway. When the lock-screen lit up, two prominent words appeared:

Michael Lamont.

I frowned. "*What*… in the actual Hell?"

Sure enough, at the top of my Instagram inbox, there was a message accompanied by a small profile picture of Michael in his soccer uniform.

Why was he messaging me? How did he find my account? What did he want?

My hands stilled, and my phone slipped from them, bouncing on my bed where I soon threw myself to scream into a pillow. 'What did he want?' I'd wondered as if Lenia hadn't exposed and humiliated me in front of him. After taking three deep breaths and four reminders that I existed on a rock floating in space, I flipped over and opened the message.

hey adara, just checking in to see if ur ok.

I blinked a few times and brought the phone closer to my face to make sure I wasn't hallucinating. He messaged me to ask how I was. *Messaged* me? To ask how I was?

"What are you going to say, Adara?" I asked aloud. "Don't say anything stupid, play it cool. I mean, it's not like you can embarrass yourself any more after what happened today, right?"

Right?

"I live on a rock. I live on a rock." My fingers shook as I answered Michael, saying I was fine which, admittedly, wasn't the best response I could've sent. While I was waiting for his reply to my un-follow-up-able message, the screen flashed, and a picture of Jess and I popped up. I braced myself and slid the 'accept call.'

"You haven't been answering my texts!" Jess shouted through the line. "What happened? Lenia was taken to the hospital?"

I returned my ringing ear to the phone. "Yes, but calm down for a sec."

"I'm coming over. We have to talk about thi—"

"I'd rather not right now; I'm too agitated, I can't think right. I'll explain eventually, though."

"It better be good." She hummed at a distant male voice. "Yes, I'll tell her," she said to it. "Frankie says he hopes you're okay and he'll come to yours to walk with you tomorrow."

"I might not even come in," I said. "Tell him not to wait up."

Jess didn't push. "Alright, Dara. Rest up. Text us if you change your mind."

"Thanks, I will." I hung up and debated on whether or not I would go to school tomorrow. My suspension would be lifted by then, and I did have an important Physics test I had to be present for. Come to think of it, I should've probably started studying by now. And if I focussed enough on this, I'd focus less on the buzzing thoughts.

Hopping off my bed, I padded to my desk. Heaving my *Complete Works of William Shakespeare* aside next to Chaucer, I pulled out my Physics textbook from the shelf and collected loose sheets of paper for my practice problems. My lamp was on, my book was opened, I'd solved the first question and was finishing the calculations. Before I could get to the second, my phone lit up in my periphery.

"No," I said. "I'm going to study because I don't want to fail or have bad thoughts."

But what if it's Michael? my mind asked.

"Whose side are you on?"

Come on! Go see if it's him.

I drew my diagram. "What is the total voltage of this parallel circuit?"

It could be him!

"I don't have time to—okay, screw this."

My mind had been right. Michael had asked if I'd be going to school tomorrow, to which I responded I had no choice because of my test. In full honesty, I was suspicious of why he was talking to me, given what he'd heard today. What made it that much stranger was how, during the entirety of our exchange, the incident wasn't mentioned once; we didn't speak about Lenia at all. Our conversation fell into normalcy like nothing had ever happened, continuing through the evening and into the night like my Physics problems which were stuck to my cheek when I woke up at my desk in the morning.

A splitting headache greeted me, so I took a few pills to make it go away. They didn't help. My parents allowed me to stay home because of it (and because they suspected I'd be uncomfortable going to school after all the 'excitement' from the day before), but as much as I would've loved to rot in bed all day, I couldn't miss my test.

The headache was my body's way of warning me I should've stayed home.

At school, no one looked at me directly. No one spoke to me either, yet my name was still coming out of their mouths. The whispers originated from Jasmine, whose best friend was now in the hospital 'because of me.' She copied Lenia's last insult, calling me a monster under her breath whenever she'd cross paths with me. How original.

Jasmine faded, hidden by a head of loose, dark golden-brown curls bouncing down the hallway toward my locker. Students watched Jess approach me, their expressions uneasy, as if they believed I would hurt one of my best friends.

Jess wrapped me in a hug. "Hey, Dara. Are you okay? I swear, everyone at this school is stupid. They're treating you as if you're a murderer or something. It's not right."

Her arms didn't block the eyes. Hundreds of them, on us, filled with judgement and contempt and scrutiny. I wanted to yell at them that I didn't touch Lenia. She wasn't even here and they still took her side.

"Earth to Adara Goodman?" Jess waved a hand in front of my face. "You're not even paying attention."

"Sorry, I'm out of it today." I shook my head. "I know I said I'd tell you what happened, but can we do it later? During our break?"

Jess nodded, and we walked to our English class, in which I paid no attention to the teacher and focused all my energy on not crying. Was it the situation I was in? No, I didn't cry when I was anxious. I wouldn't normally be like this unless…

I checked my phone for the date.

Oh no.

I had to sprint to the bathroom before people started staring at me for a whole new reason. On the bright side, at least I wouldn't have to deal with my period for another few months, one of the perks my birth complications gave me.

On my break, after my Physics test, Jess met me at my locker and we headed outside to the bleachers, away from the suffocating atmosphere indoors. I sat at the top-most row, wrapped in a light jacket in case the grey clouds overhead decided to surprise us, facing the soccer players training on the field while Jess' back was toward them to pay attention to me. At her encouragement, I explained what happened yesterday, including the parts with Michael, but left out the strange conversation my parents had about me.

"Dara, I believe you didn't touch her," Jess repeated, "but the bitch deserved what she got. Now no one will mess with you."

Frankie and Dad said something similar, I thought, staring off into the distance.

"Except for Michael, apparently," Jess mentioned to lighten the mood. I buried my face in my hands. "See?" She poked my leg. "Silver linings."

I peeked at her through my fingers. "I just told you a story about a girl who got her legs broken and you're interested in a cute guy who texted me?" I laughed. "You have your priorities in order, that's for sure."

Jess pulled a face and hit me with her backpack. "*Excuse me* for being excited about the guy you've had a crush on since the moment you stepped foot in school and for not giving a crap about that Regina George wannabe. This is a big deal. Your last crush was, what, a million years ago? On that girl Erin, right?"

"Yes, Erin, and—hold up—it wasn't 'the moment I stepped foot in school.' You're exaggerating and making it sound like I'm in love with the kid. This isn't a fairy tale or a Jane Austen novel. I'm not going to fall in love with someone only by looking at them. I have to know them."

"You guys spoke, no? Which means you know stuff about him, so technically speaking—"

"'Technically speaking' I did what you asked and our conversation is finished. Say something else. How was Chem?"

Jess arched a brow at me, but answered regardless. "It was actually hilarious. I would've taken a video if Miss D. didn't yell at us to put our phones away…" She recounted how a student set his lab manual, and *shirt*, on fire with a Bunsen burner while they were supposed to be doing gravimetric analysis. As she spoke, my focus drifted across the field, only to snag on someone on the other side of the fence separating the school grounds from the street.

Considering he had no bag and dressed like an English or History major—his collared sweater, ironed slacks, long coat and sleek boots all devoid of colour—he didn't go here; and yet, the strangest feeling of familiarity settled over me. Where had I seen him before? Outside in the parking lot, waiting for one of his friends or siblings? My eyes narrowed on him. I couldn't place his face. Had he—

His gaze met mine, and a biting coldness infiltrated my bones.

"Hey, dumbasses!" Frankie shouted from my right.

I yelped, jumping in his direction; Jess patted my leg to calm me. "You little shit, you almost gave me a heart attack!"

He motioned to himself, grinning. "Have you seen this face? You wouldn't be the first."

I beamed. "I'll be the first to break your nose. Give me a medal, will you?"

He gaped, faking offence. "Glad to see your comebacks didn't take a blow from what happened yesterday."

"Nothing could ever stop me from humbling you."

When I looked back across the field, the man had disappeared. My seat on the bleachers turned cold, and I rubbed my temples in response to my returning headache.

"Does that equally mean nothing could stop you from coming over later too?" Frankie motioned between Jess and me. "*The Lord of the Rings* marathon, anyone?"

"I wish," Jess groaned. "I have a project to work on with that idiot Jeremy at five. You know I'd usually cancel to hang with you guys, but I don't want to fail. The kid isn't the sharpest crayon in the box, if you catch my drift."

A field of potatoes was sharper.

How is he still in advanced classes?

"What about you, Dara?" Frankie tapped my bench from where he stood, waggling his brows. "You're always down for a good *LOTR* marathon."

"You know me so well." After today's fiasco, I could use some quality time with my best friend. In any case, I'd been meaning to watch the movies again since I'd re-read the whole series throughout the Winter Break and finished it at the beginning of Spring Break.

"By the way," Frankie started, "did you guys hear about…"

My phone in my pocket drowned out what he meant to say, its buzz informing me that Michael had texted. Removing it from my jacket, I checked what he sent.

where r u?

outside

where outside?

why do you want to know?

God forbid i wanted to see u.

A smile came to my lips at that. Everyone always says you know you're screwed when you start smiling at someone's texts.

"Dara? YOO HOO! Did you not hear what I said?"

Looking up from my phone revealed Frankie giving me an accusatory stare. "Huh? No, sorry. Give us the line one more time?"

According to what he'd overheard from Victoria, Lenia would need to wear casts on her legs for months for her bones to heal, and she'd have to do physical therapy to learn to walk without crutches. And although I had nothing to do with what happened to her, this would be a teaching experience for her. It wouldn't be so easy walking all over whomever she wanted now, huh?

"Adara."

My eyes widened at the sound of my name, and I looked away from Frankie to find the source. Michael stood at the bottom of the bleachers, his hair tousled from the wind, curling around his ears and pushed from his forehead. Despite his soccer uniform hanging loose on his frame and the lack of sun, his athletic build was still discernible beneath.

"Michael," I replied, propping my elbows onto my knees. "You look good today."

I said that out loud. I want to die.

His smile was lopsided and teasing. "Only today?"

"Obviously only today," I lied to bury my fluster.

"*Oooookay.*" Swiping her bag from by my feet, Jess slid from the bleachers. "I just remembered I had a thing… that we *both* had to do.

Right, Frankie?" she said, not in the least bit inconspicuous. "Frankie?" She cleared her throat to grab his attention, honed on Michael and me.

"Yeah, I'm coming," he said, eyes never leaving us. "Wouldn't want to intrude on Dara's date."

I shot him a glare. "Frankie, that's not what this is. Don't be rude."

"Don't worry about it, Addie," Michael said, and I recoiled slightly at his use of my nickname. It felt unnatural.

"Don't call her that," Frankie told him. "Only her parents use it."

An apologetic air swept through Michael. "Oh, I'm sorry. I didn't know."

"My friends usually call me Dara," I informed him.

A smile curved the corner of his mouth. "Alright then, *Dara*." The way he'd said it made my stomach do at least ten flips. *Ridiculous*.

Frankie tapped my seat. "I'll wait for you after school, okay?"

I nodded and held out my hand for our handshake. Once we'd finished, he followed after Jess, leaving me with Michael. "I'm really sorry about Frankie," I said. "He's protective."

"It's cool, I get it," Michael replied. "I'm protective of my friends too whenever someone new shows up and flirts with them."

Was he flirting with me? Was that what this was? Why else would he have said it? No, I was reading too much into the situation. Or was I? "Look, Michael," I began, "I don't know what your deal is exactly, but just because you're here and we've been texting for a bit—"

"I don't know if a whole evening, almost a whole night, and the morning is 'a bit,'" he muttered in correction.

"That doesn't mean I'm falling for any of," I gestured in his general direction, "whatever *this* is."

He glanced at himself, almost amused. "And what exactly is this?"

"There's a catch here but I can't see it yet." Right then and there, the thought finally came to mind. My eyes narrowed on him. "If this is some kind of sick payback for your girlfriend, you can shove it up your fu—"

"Woah, hold up, hold up." He laughed, confused. "My girlfriend? I don't have—"

"That's not the impression Lenia gave." It sounded more childish than I expected. "She said you asked her out because you were into her since Junior year."

"She's the one who asked *me* out, not the other way around," Michael amended. "And honestly, it wasn't even 'asking out.' We had a project to do in Du Maurier's class."

Wow. I probably looked like an idiot right now.

"Is it true what she said?" Michael resumed. "When you guys were fighting in the hall?"

"No, I'm not a psychopath." I'd been tested for the disorder already.

"That's not exactly what I was talking about. She didn't exactly *say* say it; she just, sort of, made it sound…"

No. This wasn't happening.

"Do you like me?"

My stomach dropped. I could've died right then and there from embarrassment. My eyes darted around, searching for a path I could take to make a run for it. But my legs wouldn't move. I was stuck to my seat and had no choice but to say something. "'Like you?'" I echoed, putting on a clueless act. "I have no idea what you're talking about."

"Weird. I could've sworn I heard something about it."

"Right, right." I nodded once, pressing my indexes to my lips. "Have you had your ears checked recently?"

"My ears are fine, thanks for asking." He folded his arms across his chest, shrugging. "How come you never said anything, never told me?"

I gave a dry chuckle. "There are *ten thousand* different reasons."

"Like?"

"Well, for one"—I tapped my temple— "do you think I'd like to see you all over the place after being rejected? For two—"

His left eyebrow rose, accentuating the cut on its arch, as he interrupted me. "Who says you would've gotten rejected?"

"What do you…?"

"It's kind of obvious, don't you think?" He glanced at his cleats and played with the piercing on his left ear. "I've had a thing for you since last year, but you never noticed. You barely looked at me in English."

That was a *lie*. I looked at him every chance I got.

"And then this year, you had P.E at the same time as my practice so I was able to see you other than in the hallways." He paused and rephrased. "Actually, not in the hallways. For some reason it almost seemed like you were avoiding me."

Way to be subtle, Adara.

"Okay, this is a prank." I looked around. "Where's the camera?"

Michael's expression didn't shift. "Dara, I'm serious."

"*Sure*. You had to wait until our last year of high school to tell me you liked me." I eyed him, suspicious. "Why now?"

"I didn't say anything for the same reason you didn't," he confessed. "Because we didn't really know each other outside of class. I didn't think you saw me that way. I thought you would reject me."

"But you're *you*," I said. "Confident and outgoing, etcetera etcetera."

"How was I supposed to be 'outgoing' with you when you barely ever spoke to me?"

"I could ask you the same thing," I countered, locking us in a stalemate. My hands refused to stay still, grabbing a strand of my hair to twirl around my fingers.

"You don't have to be nervous."

"Who says I'm nervous?" I hid my surprise at his scarily accurate read of my emotions.

He pointed to the strand of hair around my fingers, and I dropped it immediately. "I kind of figured it out when we were in English together," he said, rubbing his nape. "You... you usually twirl your hair when you're bored. Or nervous, like before your presentation on Dante."

Did he really pay such close attention?

"Who says I'm not just bored of *you*?" My mind was unable to differentiate between actual flirting and plain insulting.

"Bored of me?" Michael's mouth opened, faking offense at my joke. "Pardon my Spanish, but I call bullshit." His answer won a laugh from me; not many people would've responded how he did. Michael smiled. "You have a cute laugh." Right after the words left his lips, he reddened. He coughed a few times, trying to cover up his comment, however it was useless. I had heard him.

"Maybe you're the nervous one," I suggested.

Michael rested a leg on the bleacher, preventing himself from toying with the rocks on the pavement. "And here I thought I was hiding it well."

"Aren't you nervous, though?" I inquired. "About what you're telling me? I'm not the best person for you to be seen talking to right now."

"You don't unde—"

"You heard what they're saying about me, Michael," I interrupted. "You should've seen how everyone was treating me earlier, avoiding me like I was a killer on the loose." At the emotions pooling in my eyes, I blinked and focused on my breathing. How had I managed to go from being a psychopath to a monster overnight? And why in the world would Michael want to associate himself with that?

"Hey, hey." In the next moment, he was at my side. "Adara, you're making it sound like I actually believe what everyone's saying. I saw what happened; you didn't touch her. I told the Principal."

I looked at him. "Y-you did?"

He nodded. "Yeah."

Coach Joe whistled. "*Lamont!*" he shouted. "What kind of example are you setting for your teammates?"

"I'm coming, Coach!" Michael yelled back. "Give me five minutes!"

A centre-forward answered: "Yeah, Lamont! Quit your cringey-ass flirting and set an example for your teammates!"

Michael laughed, flipping his friend the finger. "How's this, Nico?"

"Maybe you should go back," I said.

"But I'm not done talking to you yet," he replied, winking.

"Your friend was right." I scrunched my nose to hide my smile. "You do have a cringey way of flirting."

"It isn't that—"

Coach Joe interrupted us again from the middle of the huddle. "Lamont! I'm giving you three! If you're even *one* second late you're running an extra ten laps!"

Michael gave him a thumbs-up before returning to me. "Look, Adara, I know I've said this before, but I don't care what people are saying about you and I definitely wouldn't give a shit about what they'd say about me for liking you. Nico didn't say anything when I told him. And the bright side is that this whole misunderstanding," he motioned to the school, "means I'll have less competition for your attention."

My heart swelled in my chest. "Well, damn," I crossed my arms, "you're annoyingly persistent, aren't you?"

He grinned. "Oh, trust me, I'm aware."

'Trust me.' Should I have trusted the voice at the back of my mind warning this might not end well? The last thing I wanted was to fall for a trick.

As if he read my thoughts, Michael said, "You're still debating. You're probably worried I'll hurt you—"

Or the other way around, my mind said.

"—but I won't."

I almost laughed right in his face. Every guy on Earth had said something like that or a variation of it at least once in their lives and it ended up a lie. "Not possible," I said, shaking my head.

"Yes it is," he said, adamant.

"How are you so sure?"

"Because I'll promise it. I'll pinky swear if that's what it takes."

"Oh, this is serious." The sarcasm in my voice was unmistakable. "A *pinky swear*."

"If you want I can head to practice right now and leave you here," he teased, beginning to stand.

He wasn't actually going to leave.

I jumped to my feet regardless, sticking out my finger. “Promise? This is under pain of death, by the way.”

Another dazzling smile lit up his face as he held my pinky with his. “I promise.”

CANTO III

Instructions Unclear: Man *Dating* Monster?

Frankie had waited for me after school as promised, and since our movie marathon didn't start for another hour or so, I went home to drop off my things. The second I got into the house, I called Jess to invite her over before she went to Jeremy's to give her an update of the day's events. It amazed me how she couldn't contain herself for more than fifteen minutes when I told her about Michael.

Her voice rang throughout my house. "A pinky promise? No way."

"Can you lower your voice?" I urged. "My mom is home. She can hear everything you're screaming."

"Sorry, Samantha!" Jess called out.

My mom walked into my room, folding my snowman pyjama bottoms, a book clamped underneath her arm. "What happened? Where's the fire?"

"Fire?" Jess laughed. "There's no fire."

My mom shook her head, setting my pants on my bed. "Why do I always assume there's a fire?" She placed the book on my dresser and tucked a strand of honey-blonde hair that had escaped its bun behind her ear.

"Because Adara is a fire hazard?" Jess guessed. "Remember the time she tried to cook chicken cutlets and they caught on fire?"

My mom's face brightened. "Yes, in January! We couldn't open the frozen windows and the house smelled like burned chicken for days—"

"That was one occasion!" I clapped my hands a few times. "Alright, that's enough. *Comedy Network*'s 'Roast of Adara' is officially finished."

"We were just kidding, Addie. We're aware of how well you cook. Just like your dad." My mom kissed my head. "I'll be leaving you girls to it."

"Do you want some help folding the laundry?" I offered.

"No, I'm almost done," she assured, closing my door on the way out.

"Thanks! Love you, Mama!" I shouted after her.

Her voice sounded from down the hall and through the door. "I love you too, Addie!"

Jess' soft expression had the strangest thread of guilt within.

"What?" I asked.

"Nothing." She shook her head. "I find it cute how you call her Mama."

"Shut up." I hit her with the pillow she held. "But speaking of parents, when are yours coming back from Europe?"

Jess sighed, curling into a ball on my laurel-printed duvet. "I have absolutely no idea. They come back for one week at most before they're off again. It's exhausting."

So that was the reason behind her expression; she missed them.

"At least you get the apartment to yourself, right?" I mentioned, mostly in order to cheer her up.

"Good point." She flipped over, beaming. "*And* it's like we're getting a glimpse into our apartment-sharing future."

I mirrored her reaction, squeezing her leg. "I can't wait until that day finally comes." My phone buzzed in my jeans' pocket. I quickly peeked at it, deciding to answer later.

"You're smiling, so clearly it's a text from Michael," Jess observed. "I still can't get over the fact you and he both liked each other at the same time and didn't do anything about it. You guys are pretty much the dumbest people ever."

My lips pressed into a thin line. "Well *thanks a lot* for that keen assessment."

"I'm not wrong." She shrugged. "Does this mean you guys are a thing now or…?"

"I have no clue," I confessed, wondering about it myself. "He admitted he liked me, sure, but… Jess, I don't know. The universe is playing a trick on me, I can feel it." She threw a pillow at me, and it ricocheted, hitting my Florence + The Machine album. "Don't hit Florence!" I gasped, rushing to fix the most important piece of music memorabilia I had in my room. "What did my beautiful, talented baby ever do to you?"

"Stop changing the subject," Jess snapped. "Chances are Michael's going to be your first boyfriend and you're over here self-sabotaging like always!"

"You're getting ahead of yourself." I returned the copy of *Sense and Sensibility* that my mom had borrowed to the shelf above my desk. All of my books were either cramped there or sitting in the bottom drawer of my dresser, just like my dad's.

"Michael *likes you back*," Jess reminded me. "Half the battle's won." She stopped inspecting the dark curl in her hand. "You, my friend, have the L-word. It's all over you."

"What?"

She sat upright on my bed. "Dara, are you dumb? A word starting with an L and ending with an E?"

"Leprosy?" I wondered, determining the sound to be similar enough. "Lice? Don't have either, I'm afraid."

"You know I hate it when you quote *Ice Age* in serious conversations!"

"Then you shouldn't have set me up for it." I stuck out my tongue at her.

"You should've just answered the question."

"I'm pretty sure we've had this discussion already, Jess. I'm not in love with him. You know how I feel about that."

Romantic relationships had never been a priority for me. Love was like walking to a cliff and purposely jumping off; sure, there was a chance you would grow wings, but it was slim. The most probable outcome was you would jump, fully expecting to fly, only to end up crushed at the bottom, alone, disappointed and half-dead. Reading about love was so much better. You could invest yourself in that because, although it felt real, it wasn't, and therefore caused minimal damage.

"Has anyone ever told you you're a tad avoidant?" Jess quipped.

"You did, just now." I checked my phone and showed it to her. "Hey, don't you have to be at Jeremy's?"

"Shit, I'm late!" She hopped off my bed to grab her stuff strewn across my room. "And this counts as you being avoidant, by the way." She flew into the corridor, hurrying down the stairs, and I trailed after her, holding her car keys. "Are you going to tell Frankie about what happened? You're going to his in five anyways so might as well." She finished tying her shoes, and I dropped her keys into her hand.

"I'm not sure if I will. I have to figure things out, so I'd rather keep it to myself for the moment." Opening the door, I waved to Mrs. Stafford across the street who was sitting on her porch with her terrier Chocopuddin'.

"Hey, Mrs. S!" Jess greeted over the *beep* of her red BMW.

Mrs. Stafford waved back. "Do you girls want to stop by? I've finished making cookies and my grandkids aren't coming over until six."

After grabbing a container of oatmeal chocolate chip cookies, I said goodbye to both Jess and Mrs. Stafford, and made my way to Frankie's. Not a few minutes into my walk, I slowed at the familiar eeriness creeping up my spine.

Paranoia dragged my attention away from the street in front of me, and I whirled around, scanning the area and the faint shimmering air.

No one and nothing was here other than a couple of cars. Dismissing my overthinking, I continued onwards. When I arrived at Frankie's, I found him outside in his front yard, speaking to a man with copper hair. I knew every single person Frankie hung out with—and yet I'd never seen this guy before. I didn't like the energy surrounding him. Finally noting my arrival, Frankie shook his head as he replied, and the denied man returned to his car, driving off.

"What was that?" I asked, stopping at the path to his front door. "That was super sketchy. Please tell me you're not doing drugs."

Frankie tried to grab the container from my hands. "Are those cookies?"

I hit his arm. "You're not getting any unless you answer my question."

"Nice to see you're concerned for my health." He indicated for me to follow him inside, so I did. "And no, I'm not doing drugs. You know my mom would go insane if I were. Like, more insane than the time we got drunk here during Christmas break."

"Ah, those were the days." I placed my shoes to the right and descended the stairs into the cozy basement. "It was a good thing Angela didn't tell my mom. She would've killed you… and me."

Frankie grabbed the remote from the coffee table and sat on the brown leather couch stationed against the far left wall, beneath the window, where we'd spent countless nights watching movies. "Remember when you woke up the next morning on the bathroom floor? Your face was still super pale and you said—"

"'I will never drink again.'" I plopped down beside him, throwing my legs over his. "I never even liked drinking in the first place."

"For someone who didn't like alcohol, you had no problem drinking half the bottle of tequila hidden in my closet."

"I mean it this time! I will never drink again," I declared. "Especially not after the headache I had the last day of Spring Break."

"Are you sure?" An impish smile spread on his face. "I have a bottle hidden here if you want."

I pursed my lips. "What *kind* of booze is it?"

The stairs on my right creaked under the weight of an incoming Angela. "I better not be hearing you guys plotting to do something you shouldn't be doing."

Frankie chuckled nervously. "No way. Us? Doing something potentially illegal? Never!"

"We were talking about these cookies," I added to help my best friend out. "Do you want some? I got them from Mrs. S."

Angela raised a perfectly plucked eyebrow, then her dark green eyes narrowed on me. I wasn't sure if she was buying what I was selling. "I'll ignore what just happened here if you give me the whole container."

Frankie's jaw dropped. "The *whole container*?"

I stood up, reluctantly handing our cookies over to Frankie's mom, and resumed my seat.

"Take our joy, you blackmailer," he whined, fake crying.

"Good doing business with you," Angela said, shaking the container and heading upstairs. "Oh, and if you're thinking about the bottle of raspberry vodka hidden underneath the couch, don't bother because I already used it to make *adult* raspberry lemonade."

Frankie threw his head into my lap. "Great! There goes our booze and cookies."

I brushed a hand through his hair. "We still have the movies, you know. Day's not ruined."

Frankie let out a "hmph" in response and scrambled to start the marathon to get his mind off his loss.

About a half hour into *The Fellowship of the Ring*, my silenced phone lit up on the coffee table, right in his field of vision. "What did Lamont want with you today?" he asked, spying Michael's name appear on my lock screen of our trio.

"Nothing really."

Frankie flipped around on my lap to look at me. "Liar."

The thing with having a best friend was that they could tell when something was going on, no matter if you told them or not. They could *always* tell.

"I heard from Nico that Michael asked you out."

"He didn't ask me out, per se." I did a double take. "Wait—why did Nico tell you?"

Frankie sat upright. "That's not what I'm focused on right now, Dara. Were you going to tell me about Lamont or were you going to keep it a secret?" I averted my gaze from his, not wanting to answer the question. He nodded once. "Nice to know that's how it's going to be."

I repositioned myself as well. "Why are you getting upset about this? I'm allowed to keep things to myself while I figure them out."

"Since *when*?"

"See? This," I gestured to him, referring to his reaction, "is the reason I didn't say anything."

"*Fine*." He turned to the TV. "Forget I said anything. Let's just watch the movie."

It took a lot to put me off watching *The Lord of the Rings*, and this happened to do the trick. "Actually," I grabbed my phone from the table, "I think I'll go home."

"Dara—"

Not bothering to turn back to look at him, I continued to make my way up his stairs, and left his house.

In the morning, I pulled on one of my favourite outfits—a pair of black trousers and a criss-crossing burgundy shirt that tied in the front—since Michael would be picking me up. I'd told him it was unnecessary because

I lived a few minutes away from school, but he wouldn't take no for an answer.

Once I'd finished dressing and putting on small golden earrings and a matching necklace, I started on my makeup. Absolutely flawless. After my normal twenty-minute routine, I brushed my hair (which happened to knot extremely easily despite it being so straight); obviously knowing today was a big deal, it had decided to frizz out completely, transforming into a ball of static. I struggled for ten minutes, using a mountain of oils and creams to smooth it into compliance.

I'd just spritzed myself with my favourite perfume when I got a text from Michael letting me know he was outside. I went to my window and, sure enough, found him sitting in his black Honda Civic in my driveway. Not a minute after I texted him back, I saw him smiling at his phone.

"What a loser," I muttered, grinning. Leaving my room, I descended the stairs, grabbed my bag leaned against the side, kissed my mom and dad on the cheek, and bee-lined for the door.

"Woah, not so fast, Addie," my dad said over his cup of coffee. He deposited his newspaper on the kitchen island and stared at me. "Who is the random boy parked in my driveway?"

"He's not a 'random boy.'" I bent to put on my shoes. "He's… a friend."

My mom chuckled under her breath, and apparently, so did my dad. "What does that mean?" he asked. "Do you know something about this, Sam?"

"I'm going to be late." My hand flew to the handle. "Interrogate me when I get home."

"Oh, trust me when I say I will, Adara Goodman!" my dad shouted as I ran out the front door.

I crossed the path to my driveway, passing by the perfectly trimmed rose bushes underneath the window my dad was watching me from.

Is he kidding?

I stopped in front of him and waved him away before going to Michael's car. When I reached the door, the eeriness from yesterday weighed on me again—the one where I felt I was being watched. Suspecting it was probably still my dad at the window, I shook it off and entered the car.

"Was that your dad at the window?" Michael asked when I'd settled into the seat.

"Yes, unfortunately it was," I answered, buckling myself in. At the click, I turned to Michael, who happened to be wearing a burgundy shirt, black jeans, and black shoes. "Is this a joke?"

"What?" he replied, stationing his arm behind my headrest and leaning to pull out of the driveway. It brought his grin even closer.

"Don't pretend you haven't noticed, okay?" I tut-tutted him. "I hope you realize how stupid we look going to school together wearing the exact same thing."

He changed gears, turned the wheel, and drove us down the street. "Why do you say that?"

"Because we look like..." I trailed off.

"A couple?" he suggested.

"A couple of clowns, maybe."

"Oh yeah, definitely," Michael agreed. "Not what I meant, but still accurate." He cleared his throat, causing an obvious rise of tension in the car. "But, being serious for a second, I mean, we are together? Aren't we?"

I was masking my true emotions quite well, or at least I thought I was. I wasn't going to pretend to be mature and claim I hadn't imagined this moment because, honestly, I had. The thing was, I hadn't expected him to answer so directly. I knew we were, for lack of a better word, *something*; however, I didn't think we'd actually defined anything just yet.

"I mean, I don't know," I began, and glimpsed Michael's face drop in the mirror. "I don't know if I could be with someone who rips off my style. Might be a real deal-breaker."

A look of relief washed over him, followed by a laugh. "Oh no," he drawled, "how will we ever get through this massive betrayal?"

"I have no idea." I hid my smile by looking out the window, but it disappeared completely as soon as I saw Frankie leave his house to walk to school.

His eyes skimmed over the car, widening when they found me in the front seat. A snide, disbelieving chuckle escaped him. Guilt clawed at my chest, and even after passing him, I couldn't understand the reason behind it. Was I being horrible?

Michael set his hand on my thigh. "Hey, what's wrong?"

My mind went blank, releasing whatever hold the feeling once had over me. The blood rushed to my face. "Nothing."

He nodded and removed his hand; I grew disappointed, suddenly wishing I hadn't said anything. "You can put some music on if you want," he said, passing me his phone from the cup-holder. "The code is 1-2-1-8."

Tapping the number in brought me to his music. He'd been listening to Bad Bunny before arriving at my house. "Aww, I love Benito."

"You have taste."

"Duh." I rolled my eyes and played *Te Boté.*

"Also," Michael added, "if you wanted, one of these days, we could play soccer after school at the park in front of my house, or one near yours. Whichever is closer for you."

I arched a brow at him. "Are you asking me on a date?"

Michael beamed. "We'll have a real dinner one first, I swear."

The song finished right as we pulled into Newton North's parking lot. When we got out of the car, a major sense of déjà-vu hit me; it was like in *Twilight* when Bella showed up to school with Edward for the first time, only instead of staring and whispering, people glowered as well. While walking through the halls, as if there hadn't been enough rumours already, I overheard fragments of conversation, each more or less saying the same thing: how I'd ensnared this 'out of my league' guy into a relationship, how someone probably paid him because there was no way he'd voluntarily be with me, how he was just trying to get me to join the soccer team.

Anxiety flooded my body, and every glare I received from the people passing us continued to fuel it. I couldn't even begin to imagine how much this was affecting Michael as well. "Michael… I'll just… um," I put some distance between us, "I'll see you later." Shame bowed my head. I couldn't even look in his direction when I said it, couldn't turn to him when he'd called after me. I just kept walking to my locker. Once I got there, I fumbled with the lock, swung the door open, and hid myself behind it, trying to breathe. Yesterday, Michael said he wouldn't listen to what people would say about us, about him, about me, but he hadn't realized *this* was what would be waiting for him. He was probably seriously reconsidering his decision by now.

Why in the Hell did I think this was a good idea? I thought, shoving my books into my bag and zipping it up.

When I shut the locker, I jumped back, startled at finding Michael on the other side. “What the ass, Michael?”

He leaned on Frankie’s locker. “You didn’t actually think I was going to let you get away with that, did you?”

I clamped the lock closed. “I’m going to be late for class.”

His mouth fell into a straight line. “The bell didn’t ring yet.”

“Fine. I’m going to be early, then,” I said, manoeuvering around him. The less people who saw us together, the better. It was a stupid way of protecting him, but what else could I do?

“I can see what you’re doing,” he said over his shoulder. “Are you embarrassed to be seen with me?”

I stopped dead in my tracks.

Was that really what I made him think? If ever, I would’ve thought it was the other way around. “No, I’m not embarrassed at all. It’s only that earlier there was a lot going on…”

“Does it look like I’m going anywhere to you?” The way he’d phrased the question was an answer in itself. “I told you something yesterday, Dara, and I meant it.”

“Things are different once they happen.” I avoided looking at him, staring at my feet, my nails, anything and anywhere but at him. “I thought you might’ve changed your mind.”

“Dara, look at me.” Michael’s hand found mine. “Please.”

I tore my gaze from my feet. He was the first person to really look at me, look deeply into my eyes after the incident with Lenia. And if I was being honest, I couldn't help worrying.

"Adara, I wasted almost a whole year because I believed I had no chance with you," he began. "You're smart, talented, beautiful—and if you think for a second that a few stupid rumours are going to get in the way of how either of us feels for one another," he squeezed my hand in a way that was more affectionate than I'd expected, "you're wrong. I'll be right there by your side. We're in this together."

The conviction with which he'd spoken, without so much as a falter or delay, proved to me how serious and genuine and invested he truly was.

And if he was all in, so was I.

"Together, then," I agreed.

CANTO IV

The 'L' Word (Not Lice)

For Michael and I's first date on Friday, my fight-or-flight made me feel as though I was being chased in the forest by a sabretooth tiger. Jess had to come over three hours before I left the house to calm me down. Once she'd managed to do so, we spent the next hour alone choosing an outfit. She left ten minutes before Michael was due to show up, right after giving me a much-needed pep talk.

When the time finally came, Michael drove us to Cabot's, the ice cream parlour-slash-restaurant a couple of minutes away from my house where my nerves completely vanished. After we'd finished eating, I figured he would drive me home right away, but instead he left his car at the restaurant, took my hand and told me to follow him. I wasn't sure where he was bringing me at first, however I didn't mind; I loved walking at night like this.

Eventually, we arrived at the movie theatre, where he refused to tell me what we were going to see. He insisted on keeping it a secret, which only intrigued me more, especially since he went to ridiculous lengths not to let anything slip. He'd even kept his hand over my eyes while we entered the theatre to ensure I wouldn't peek. I let out a squeal once I saw the comic book opening of the film; I had a soft spot for anything *Marvel* related, and he'd bought us tickets to watch *Captain Marvel*. I'd been so excited that Michael had chosen this movie that I gave him a quick peck on the cheek.

As the night came to an end, we walked back to the restaurant for the car. On the ride home, the whispers of anxiety and nervousness grew to massive waves which barrelled through me. Usually at the end of these things, wasn't there a goodnight kiss? It wasn't that I was uncomfortable. If ever, I was embarrassed. Michael had probably kissed a bunch of people before, whereas I was seventeen and had never kissed anyone. I did *not* want to ruin my first kiss, more so since it was with someone I really liked.

When we arrived at my house, Michael exited his car and walked me to my front door, which, I had to admit, won him serious brownie points. However, the entire time, I kept wondering if he was going to make a move on me. During our small exchange of 'oh, I had a good time' small talk, he kept playing with the piercing in his ear.

Lo and behold, Michael was just as nervous as I was.

The suspense had been killing me to such a point that I blurted out, "*Are you going to kiss me or what?*"

He'd blinked a few times at the impatient shout. Instead of awkward silence, Michael and I broke out into laughter, and a lightheartedness filled the air around us. With a hand slipping around and settling on my lower back, Michael brought me toward him. As he leaned in, the lingering shyness between us dissipated. His lips met mine with a softness I'd wondered about for so long, one which enhanced the exhilaration that quickly followed. Being with him like this was the most natural thing in the world, and the feeling of him rendered my overthinking pointless. I grabbed a fistful of his shirt to keep myself tethered to him, and his wide, blushing smile afterwards stayed with me into my nightmare-less night.

And as for the nightmare of school? Even though people hadn't stopped talking about us, Michael helped me learn how to ignore them until I had blocked everything out. The novelty eventually wore off on them, and my reputation seemed to make a decent recovery, which he'd seen to as well. Apparently, he and his friends were putting their popularity to use. Michael introduced me to Nico, Omar, and Adrián, who were more accepting than I initially thought they'd be, although it could've also been because they'd all known about his crush on me and had relentlessly teased him about it. From what they'd said that day, they never believed he'd talk to me, let alone ask me out; they and Jess sure had lots to discuss when we hung out as a group, specifically her opinion of Michael and me being idiots because we didn't realize we'd liked each other at the same time. More often than not, though, she was proud to see me branch out, become more social, and not keep to myself as I'd normally have done. She made sure to encourage me as much as she could.

Frankie, on the other hand, was another story entirely. He'd been seeing less of Jess and I, gravitating to his other friends. He never said it outright, but he didn't seem to like Michael's friends. The last I'd heard from him was on April 15th: my birthday. Every year, he and Jess would send me a text. Nothing more, nothing less. Growing older had always been a touchy subject for me, and for whatever reason, certain ages held an uneasiness—a deep, internal discomfort—as well as memories I couldn't fully remember. All I could recall were shadows of that period. And my eighteenth birthday had been no different. The texts from Jess and

Frankie came in, and so did that odd sensation. My parents distracted me, as they usually did—a number of presents here and there—but on the whole, nothing big. I should have known they were up to something.

They had told Michael about my birthday (Jess played a hand in it too, I bet), and he'd invited me to his house where, in his dining room, he'd set up the most romantic dinner I'd ever seen in my life. He admitted to getting help with the food from his parents, which made sense considering he couldn't have cooked an entire lasagna by himself, and although I didn't particularly enjoy celebrating my birthday, I had loved what he'd done. The bouquet of flowers and ring he'd given me as a gift afterwards nearly made me cry; then again, it hadn't only been his gesture that made the day unforgettable. We'd fallen asleep in his room while watching a *Marvel* marathon, and I had to run out of his house at 5 AM seeing as how my mom had been blowing up my phone. We eventually finished the marathon—after *five days* since I got grounded for breaking curfew—right in time to watch *Avengers: Endgame* in theatres with Jess, who'd been waiting forever to see it like us. We were together a lot… but not with Frankie.

A small grey cloud hovered over my head, left there by my missing best friend. He rarely answered my texts when I tried to reach out, not to mention he'd always leave whenever Michael was around. The observation had appeared in my thoughts nearly every day during the past weeks.

"I hate how I haven't been seeing Frankie as much as usual," I voiced aloud as I pushed the onions and garlic into the pot lined with olive oil. Their joint fragrance filled the kitchen.

"He could be dealing with his own stuff. You never know," Michael said from his seat at the island, grating cheese.

"I'm not sure…" I trailed off. If that had been the case, shouldn't he have come to Jess and me?

"You know couples don't spend as much time with their friends because they're busy with each other, right?"

I stirred the onions and garlic. "We always spend time with our friends, though."

"I wasn't talking about us, Dara."

I turned to him. "Are you talking about him and Marianna? Are they dating?"

Michael stopped grating the parmigiano to get a jar of tomato sauce from the fridge covered in pictures and 'artwork' made by me as a baby. He handed it to me. "I heard from Nico they were."

I added the tomato sauce into the pot on the stove, then mixed in salt, pepper, basil and parsley. "Oh."

Was Frankie's lack of communication an attempt to get back at me because of how unforthcoming I was about Michael all that time ago? Or did Marianna tell him she didn't feel comfortable with his best friends being girls and he lessened contact out of 'respect'?

"Honestly, I think Frankie's jealous."

My brows furrowed. "Why would he be?"

Michael found the penne rigate pasta he'd wanted from my pantry and set it on the counter. "Dara, remember the day I first spoke to you out on the bleachers?"

"It's May. How am I supposed to remember what you said from that far back?" I pointed to a cupboard. "Could you get the pot in the bottom left, please?"

"Hey, I expect you to remember everything I told you that day!" he jokingly scolded. "It's basically our anniversary date." He grabbed the pot, filling it with water at the sink on my left.

"I remember it was the end of March and you had an *epic* crush on me."

"You had a crush on me too, genius." Michael gave me a small peck on the cheek on his way back. He set the pot down, covered it with the lid, and turned on the heat. "But have you ever considered maybe Frankie doesn't want to hang as much because it sucks seeing you dating me?"

"Ooo, someone's a little full of himself," I teased, sprinkling baking soda to cut the acidity of the sauce.

He rolled his eyes. "What I mean is he might like you… as more than a friend."

A loud, almost hysterical laugh escaped me. "Michael, Frankie is not like that, and he also happens to be dating someone. Remember?"

Michael contemplated it for a second and shrugged. "Eh, it was just a theory. His vibes that day were off." He dipped his finger into the sauce to taste it.

"Hey!" I shooed him away. "I'm not done yet."

"Needs more salt and your dad's oregano."

"Chef Michael thinks it needs more salt," I mocked, only to taste the sauce and realized he was right. It did need salt. "Why the oregano, though? You hate it."

"Correction! I *used* to hate it," he announced.

"What changed?"

"Besides the fact that your dad puts it in *everything* he cooks?" he said. "I decided to try it again for you. The third time I had supper here was when I realized how good it was."

"Secret ingredient." I tapped the side of my head. "Makes everything taste ten times better."

"I second that." He leaned over me to reach the top cupboard and pulled out the jar of greyish herbs. "I still don't know why it looks so dark. Isn't it supposed to be green?"

I plucked the jar from him and stirred a bit into the sauce. "It's *dried* oregano, obviously it's not bright green."

"Oh well, *excuse me*, Miss Know-it-all," Michael enunciated. "Sorry I'm not an expert in pre-dried herb colours."

"*Eres un idiota de verdad. Espero que lo sabes*."

'You're a real idiot. I hope you know that.'

He smiled at my use of the Spanish I'd been learning for him. "True, but I'm *your* idiot."

"That is also true." My lips met his, light and quick.

Michael kept his mouth on mine, drawing me to him. Spinning us around, he lifted me onto the island and stood between my legs, leaving his hands on my waist to press my body to his. An ardour lived and breathed in the way he kissed me, one that I couldn't quite place yet had felt from him before. "*Te amo*," he whispered.

Caught completely off-guard, I froze and managed to slip from his arms and from the counter. "I don't un—*what?*"

"I'm not going to pretend I didn't say what I did." Michael's initial expression of sheepishness to my reaction vanished. "*Te amo*, Dara," he repeated, this time clearer. "I'm *in love* with you."

Having no idea what to make of his declaration, I turned toward the window above the sink. I didn't want Michael to see me this shocked. No one had ever told me they loved me before. Sure, I'd heard it from my parents and from my friends, however this was completely different. I had liked Michael for *three years*. To have him say he was in love with me within a matter of months was…?

The only thing I could utter was, "How do you know?"

Michael didn't hesitate to respond. "Do you remember that day in English last year when you told Miss Koutlis you didn't want to read *Romeo and Juliet* because it was 'completely overdone'?" How he remembered my exact words, I had no clue.

I faced him. "It was overdone!" I liked Shakespeare, that was a given, but not *Romeo and Juliet*. There were much better plays to read, with Hamlet being the best. "How does that have to do with anything?"

"I didn't know a single person who didn't like *Romeo and Juliet*."

"I knew *you* liked it, though. I remember you saying you did."

"I said I liked the style of *wri-ting*," he corrected.

"Uh huh, *sure*."

"You know what?" He threw his hands in the air. "I did like it. I thought the idea of dying for love was romantic. Sue me."

"That's kind of cute."

"It's beside the point. The point is: the way you went on a tangent about Hamlet, the way you knew all of these background details not many people were aware of? You were—"

"You better not say 'different,'" I cautioned. "It makes me feel as if I'm a protagonist in a 2010s Young Adult novel." Veering toward the corner, I glared upwards. "You better not make me into Y/N."

Michael popped in next to me. "Who are you talking to?"

"My author, obviously." I waved, and faced Michael. "I'm back."

He chuckled. "I was going to say you were passionate, idiot. I'd never—"

"Don't say you've never been with anyone like me before because we both know you've never met a person as *talented, brilliant, incredible, amazing*—"

"Stop with the Lady Gaga reference, no matter how accurately it applies to you." He playfully clutched at his chest. "I'm baring my heart out here."

"Michael, you didn't even know me back then," I remarked. "How could you have loved me?"

"It was the little things. Think of it as, every day I saw you, I would fall a bit more."

"My soccer skills certainly helped, didn't they?"

"I'd be lying if I said they didn't," he admitted, taking my hand in his. "The day you told me you liked me was literally the best day of my life. And the more time I spent with you, I realized that the version of you in real life had been so much better than the version I had built in my mind."

My heart thumped in my chest, similar to my panic attacks yet… not. What *was* this? "I never knew you were so—"

"Thoughtful, amazing, fantastic, an overall great catch?" Michael suggested.

I playfully smacked his shoulder. "Such a romantic. That was really sweet o—" A splashing and hissing sound cut through the rest of my sentence.

Michael whirled toward the stove. "*Shit.* Okay, hold up. I'm fixing this, okay, don't move! I'll fix it." He grabbed a towel and lowered the heat on the over-boiling pot.

As I watched him hopelessly clean up the water, the words floated into my mind, light, yet carrying a known weight centralized in my chest.

I love him.

Every action of his since the beginning led to this conclusion; the way he'd been there to reassure me that my reputation didn't bother him, the way he'd fought the stares and the rumours and stayed by my side the whole while. Not everyone would've had the strength or patience for it. Now, I was at the edge of the cliff, ready to jump off.

"Michael?"

"Yeah? I'm finishing up over here." He salted the water, poured in the pasta, turned on the timer, and stirred the sauce.

"*Te amo también.*"

His turn was slow, his smile dazzling.

CANTO V

Unwillingly Boarding the Party Express

"Come on, Dara," Michael pleaded, nearly falling to his knees in the hallway. "Finals are over. It's June and you haven't gone to a single party."

"We went to Prom," I reminded him.

"That's not the same thing and you know it."

"This is just an excuse to see me in a dress again, isn't it?"

"And what if it was?" He leaned over, grinning. "Would that be so bad?"

I pushed him away, chuckling, and opened my locker to empty it. "What about Frankie?" I gestured to him as he made his way to us.

A couple of weeks back, before Prom, Frankie had apologized to Jess and me for his stand-offishness. He thought he'd be replaced, that the dynamic of the group would change if someone new was introduced, which explained why he had reacted negatively when he found out about my relationship. His apologizing showed his maturity in face of the situation. Obviously, I forgave him. Truth be told, I'd hated not having my best friend around.

"What about me?" Frankie inquired. He unlocked his locker, beginning to shove the books and gym clothes into his bag.

"Our dear Dara won't go to the party tomorrow—" Michael started.

"It's at Jasmine's house and I don't like her," I stated, burying my clenched hands into Michael's red vest which I'd stolen from him. "And she doesn't like me. Remember how I 'pushed' Lenia down the stairs and sent her to the hospital?" The event replayed in my mind sometimes, more than I cared to admit. Interestingly, never once did any feelings of guilt or regret rise and settle in my chest. If ever, as I lay in bed alone at night, I found myself wondering: '*How?* How had it happened? Had she slipped?' And then the whispers would crawl into my ears, fill my head and stem my breathing. The recollection of the sensation made me snap back to the present. I cleared my throat and said, "Plus, there's going to be people drinking." My eyes passed between Frankie and Michael. "You both know I don't really drink anymore and we're not even legal."

"The age thing has never stopped you before," Frankie mentioned. "Besides, eighteen is technically legal in Canada."

I arched a brow. "We're not *in* that amazing country, though, are we?"

He shrugged. "We're close, and that has to count for something, no? All you have to do is remember: 'as long as you don't get caught.'"

I pointed at him. "Do not quote my dad right now."

"Come on. A few drinks won't hurt," he said with his signature Frankie smile.

"That's what you said two seconds before we got absolutely piss-drunk on tequila in your backyard last summer," I countered.

Michael gaped at me. "You got wasted and I wasn't there to see it?"

"We weren't together back then." I tapped his cheek. "And excuse me, *Francisco*, but why are you telling me to go to this party if you aren't going?"

"You know parties aren't my scene," he answered.

I sent him a hard stare. "So, you're telling me I should go when you, yourself, are not going?"

He zipped up his bag and began to walk away. "Precisely."

"Hypocrite!" I shouted after him.

"BUZZ-KILL!" he returned.

"DICKHEAD!"

That last one earned me disapproving stares from the teachers passing by in the flow of students. I ignored them seeing as how Michael continued to plead with me. "Dara, *mi novia inteligente y guapísima y maravillosa*, can we please go to this party together?"

How was I supposed to refuse him now?

With an exasperated sigh, I agreed. "Yes, alright. Fine. We can go."

His face lit up at my response. "HA HA, *victory*!"

The loud, clanging bell rang. Michael kissed and thanked me, and we left for the final class of our Senior year. I shook my head as we went our separate ways, wondering what the Hell I'd just gotten myself into.

The rest of the day had gone by woefully uneventful. Instead of cleaning out my schoolbag of the books I'd brought home, I dragged it across the floor and left it next to my desk. I had my phone squished between my ear and shoulder as I did so, calling Jess about the party.

She answered on the third ring. "What's up?"

"My damn anxiety levels."

"You always say that." She laughed. "What is it this time?"

"I stupidly agreed to go to Jasmine's party tonight. Are you going? Please tell me you're going." I silently hoped she was.

"No, sorry, Dara. I'm actually heading into the airport right now."

I dropped into my chair. "*What?* Where are you going?"

"Europe. Italy, for a bit."

"Is… is this a real thing we're talking about here, Jessie, dearest?" I asked. "You're not lying to me while you're, oh… I don't know… already on your way to *your ex's place*?" I wouldn't have brought it up unless I thought she'd actually do it.

"To see Adam?" The disgust in her voice was clear. "Hell no."

"Then how about to see your hookup buddy from Canada or wherever you said he came from?" I guessed. "You know I don't mind that as long as you're safe."

"I'm headed to Italy to see my parents," Jess told me. "It's… kind of a big deal." Her explanation had a hesitance and tautness to it. This would be a serious visit, apparently.

"Did something bad happen? If you want, I can come meet you to offer emotional support. Or maybe call you every hour to make sure you're okay and ch—"

"No, no, it's nothing like that," she assured. "It's a special occasion, is all. I appreciate the offer, though."

"Oh, for real?" I said, somewhat relieved by the information. "Even if it wasn't a special occasion, you know you wouldn't have to apologize for that, yeah? Visiting your parents is more important than a party." I meant the words genuinely. She didn't see her family as often as I saw mine due to their work overseas. How could I be upset with her for taking the chance to visit them whenever she could?

She chuckled. "You're right."

"As I usually am."

I could see her eyeroll through the phone. She regained her upbeat air. "But speaking of the party, why aren't you more excited about it? It's your first real one!"

"I went to—"

"Prom *doesn't* count," she interjected.

"Okay, but everyone from Prom is going to be there and you know I hate when loads of people are around me."

"I do know that."

"And you know because you're the same."

"Yes I am," Jess confirmed. "Just think of the bright side. You're not going to be alone at Jasmine's. You're going with Frankie and Michael, aren't you?"

"No, only Michael and maybe some of his friends. Nico, Omar, Adrián, the usual suspects. Frankie thinks he's 'too cool' to show up to a high school party."

"Yup, sounds like something he'd say." In the background of our call, a woman announced a boarding flight to Rome. "Oh, that's me. I have to go catch my plane but have fun! Live a little, drink a little, and please, please, please tell me if you and Michael have sex so I can bring you back a celebratory gift for your first time."

"I hope you realize I've been with Michael for only three-ish months," I reminded her, glancing at the calendar on my wall. "I don't want to move too fast. I want to wait for the right moment."

"Ah, yes. You're a romantic. It's true."

"Not Byron or Shelley," we said in unison.

I laughed. "Anyways, I hope everything goes alright with your parents and please be careful on your trip. I love you."

"I will. I love you, too."

The disconnected call tone sounded, and my lock screen reverted to the picture of Frankie, Jess, Michael and I at Prom. Apparently, I'd gotten a text from the two. Directly above the notifications, the time showed 6:30 PM.

"*Shit!*"

If I didn't start getting ready right away, I was definitely going to be late.

Speeding to my dresser, I frantically searched for an outfit to wear. This would be the first time besides Prom that Michael and I were attending a party together, and a juvenile part of me wanted to show I wasn't the same girl I'd been at the beginning of high school.

I hated myself for thinking that.

My mom knocked on my open door. "Addie, honey, what are you doing?" She stepped over the piles of clothes strewn on the floor. "The news didn't announce a tornado warning."

"You should do stand-up, Mama; that would've rocked the octogenarians." I shook my head, moving to my closet. "I'm going to a party with Michael and I don't know what to wear."

She laughed—genuinely *laughed*—at me. "You? A party?"

I braced my hands on my hips. "What's funny? What's the joke? Do I have 'textbook introvert' written across my forehead?"

"Yes. Have you met you?"

"I'm not amused, Ma. I can be very *social* in *social situations*."

"Fine, fine," she granted. "Just make sure you're back by, let's say, around one in the morning, alright?" Usually, she would have set my curfew two hours earlier.

I blinked once. "So *late*? Damn, what do people even do at these sorts of things?"

"Is it that hard to believe people like to have fun?"

I stopped rifling through my hangers and slowly turned around. "Who are you and what have you done with my mom?"

"You've done well these past months, Addie. I think you deserve to let loose." No trap, no sarcasm. The expression on her face showed all the signs of pride. My heart warmed at the sight. "And if you're stuck on what to wear, wear the dress I bought you last year. You know the one?"

"I don't know…"

"Is black not your favourite colour anymore?" she commented, and left the room.

My mom was right. Black had always been my favourite colour and was my go-to in any clothing choice. Recently, I'd expanded to lighter shades of blue and yellow as well (since I remembered spotting one of Michael's hoodies in my drawers). I'd debated going for a pop of colour but decided on the dress my mom had recommended, a shimmery charcoal black, whose material was thicker than the sheer sleeves I almost tore while trying to put it on and whose ruched style accentuated my curves. To adjust the overall length to reach my knees, I pulled on the strings that ran down the middle of the fabric and tied them into a neat bow. I loved that feature, especially considering I was above average height and cut-offs were typically ridiculously short on me. And although my alterations caused the sweetheart neckline to plunge a little too deep for my liking, I only had to change into a better bra, and *boom*! Problem solved.

Note to self: never underestimate the power of a decent bra.

Reaching for my black Stan Smiths at the bottom of the closet, I stopped mid-motion, rather choosing to wear heels. Since he was tall to begin with, I didn't have to worry about towering over Michael, not that he'd mind if I did. After putting on my heels and small golden hoops at my ears to match, I started on my makeup. Every product I owned lined the vanity according to how I applied them. When my base was complete—porcelain foundation, concealer, setting powder, and blush and bronzer to bring some life back to my cheeks—I smoked out the brown and black liner on my eyes, applied a dark, bloody-red lip, and dabbed gold shimmer on my cheekbones and inner corner. I curled my hair in loose waves and used nearly an entire can of hairspray to set it in place; otherwise, my hair would deflate in a matter of minutes.

Now finished, I took a step back, almost shocked by how good I looked when I put in actual effort. No, strike that. I looked great to begin with; I simply looked extra-great now. With a satisfied nod, I went to where my phone was charging to read Michael's text from before.

i'll be at urs by 9. can't wait to see u.

My eyes flicked up to check the time. He was going to be here in fifteen minutes.

I ran around my room, performing final touches on my makeup (the setting spray) and adding more hairspray to my hair (but not so much that it would become crunchy). I quickly sent a picture to Frankie of what I was wearing. As it delivered, I jumped three feet into the air from the abrupt ringing of the doorbell.

Michael.

I grabbed his ring from off my nightstand and slipped it on. By the time I'd left my room, he was already in the house, talking to my mom in the entryway. I descended the stairs, and his focus diverted to me. "Close your mouth," I said, reaching him. "You're going to catch flies."

"Dara… Fuck—I mean—shit!" He stumbled with his words, waving and attempting to censor himself in front of my mom. "No, sorry, I didn't…"

"Do you need a minute?"

"No—I mean, yeah, actually I do." His hand found mine, and he twirled me around to get a look from every angle.

My mom stifled a giggle while returning to the kitchen where she'd been cooking for my dad. "So cute," she mused, and I smiled at the comment.

Michael's eyes never left me. "This dress on you is amazing."

"I wasn't sure about it at first," I glanced at myself, "but then I said, 'screw it,' and good thing, too, because I look hot."

He pressed a delicate kiss to my temple. "I'd have to agree with you on that."

Pulling away, I jutted my chin to him. "You don't look too bad yourself."

Michael's hair fell in light waves, middle-parted and half-messy but not so much as to hide his earring. He'd chosen to pair his dark wide-leg jeans with a beige T-shirt beneath an undone black button-up, which suited him extremely well. And of course, nothing would be complete without his black Nikes.

"Now it's you who's staring," Michael teased.

"I have eyes, can I not use them?"

Before we could extend a hand for the door, my dad walked in, back late from work once again. His eyes, sunken from grading papers, flicked from me to Michael, and confusion crossed them. "What's going on? Where are you two going? Is it date night?"

My mom appeared from the kitchen to answer him. "Addie and Michael are going to a party, my love. I told her to be home by one. Come in, come eat; I made inferno-buffalo wings."

My dad dropped his briefcase, and it was *not* from hearing that my mom had made his favourite food. "One, as in *one in the morning*? No, no, that will not do at all," he declared, shaking his head. Had my parents' roles suddenly been reversed? What was happening? "No daughter of mine is going to an underage drinking-drug party!"

I winked at him. "As long as I don't get caught, remember?"

"I take that back! Those were different circumstances!"

"Kamael, darling, Addie is old enough to make her own decisions," my mom said. "Michael will be with her; you have nothing to worry about."

My dad approached her, lowering his voice to barely a whisper, however I could still hear him. "She's not going, Sam. I have a strange feeling."

"It's only one night," she whispered, caressing his arm. "What could happen?"

My dad's face softened. He rolled his eyes and pointed to me. "I want you home by *twelve*."

"One," my mom repeated faster.

"Twelve thirty."

My mom stood her ground. "*One.*"

"One thirty!"

"DONE!"

"*Shit.*" He wiped a hand over his face, realizing she'd tricked him. "You sly woman, you."

Michael and I slowly retreated from the entryway and doorframe to the path outside. "This was really weird, so we're going to leave now," I said. "*Ciao!* See you later."

At an urgent tapping on his shoulder from me, Michael ran to his car. I hurried after him, laughing. We hopped into his Civic, and I waved goodbye to my parents, who stood in the window, as we left. Where my mom seemed happy I'd be going out tonight, my dad… hints of fear flashed behind his eyes, but a fear of what? I pushed away the thoughts of what it could be.

CANTO VI

I Should Have Stayed Home

On our way to Jasmine's, Michael kept one hand on the wheel and the other on my knee as he always did when we were in his car, never failing to calm my nerves and make me feel safe. That held true now as well. It managed to ease the edge that had refused to leave after I'd glimpsed my dad's expression in the window at home.

We arrived at the party in twenty minutes, finding it already in full swing. Shadows of partygoers passed through the illuminated windows of the massive house, and the music emanating from inside boomed loud enough that Michael and I had heard it from a block away. Fairy lights had been strung from every visible tree and were being used by many guests as backgrounds for pictures.

For Prom, I'd stayed at the venue with Michael for barely two hours. I'd made an effort to go, yes, but we'd both decided to bail early, which meant hardly anyone saw us other than our friends. This party was not the same in the least.

Tightness expanded in my chest as I looked around. *Why are there this many people?*

Michael placed his hands on my tense shoulders, massaging them. "Come on, let's go inside. You need to loosen up."

I inhaled a deep breath to settle the churning in my stomach, gave him a smile and nodded. He led me inside, and I had to prevent my jaw from slacking. Crown moulding decorated the borders of the walls, doorways, and polished tile floor, and a massive staircase running along each side of the entrance hall met at the second level, the deep brown wood carpeted with beige wool. They were the kind of rich folk who had two different dining rooms and a—wait… was that a chandelier?

A giant chandelier hung from the ceiling right above the centre of the entryway swarming with people.

Michael steered me to the vast kitchen where a bucket of fruit punch (most likely ninety-percent tequila, rum or vodka) sat on a granite island. "They have this huge house and they can't afford a decent pitcher?" I whispered.

He laughed. "Get yourself a drink. I'll say hi to some people and be back so you won't get crowded." He pecked my cheek and was off.

While waiting for him to return, I decided to scoop a ladle of 'fruit punch' into one of the red cups stacked on the counter. Since I wasn't in a rush, I kept the drink in my hands with my phone, sipping every now and again. There weren't too many people around me; I was glad Michael had brought us here first rather than—nope. Spoke too soon.

A group of guys in the corner were staring at me. Not subtly, either.

One of them, whose name I wasn't sure of, leaned over to his friends. "Who's the girl who came with Lamont?"

"Don't know," his friend replied. "I think he dumped that psycho chick…What's-her -face?"

Deep breath. Deep breath.

Making a scene this early on in the night was not the way to go. I needed to take Jess' advice and have fun. I looked into my cup, contemplating the idea that drinking would solve everything.

"It's a good thing he dumped Adara, though," Jeremy, the idiot test-cheater, said. His eyes wandered from my feet to my neck. "This girl is way hotter than she was for sure."

And *there* was my tipping point.

I drank my cup's contents in two gulps and started in the boys' direction.

"Woah, woah!" Michael appeared, stopping me. "What's wrong? Where are you going?"

I informed him what I'd overheard and tilted my head toward the guys in the corner. "I'm going to teach them a lesson."

"I got you." Michael turned to them, aggravated. I wanted to tell him I could handle it, but he continued: "Why don't you four shut the fuck up? You're lowering the IQ of the entire block every time you speak. And just a little heads up, if I so much as hear Adara's name come out of your stupid faces again—"

"I'll beat the shit out of you," I finished for him. At their doubtful laughter, I neared them. "Do you really want to try me? You heard about what I did to Lenia. I'll do much worse to you, and that's a promise."

At the mention of the incident, the guys paled, gulped, and scurried off. I didn't particularly like using the threat to get them to take me seriously, but at least it did the trick.

Michael veered to me. "You didn't have to do that, you know."

"I'm a big girl," I said, heading for a refill. "I can deal with my own problems."

"I know you can handle yourself, Dara. It's just… I didn't think you'd want to."

"Honestly, it was only a matter of time until someone said something," I muttered over the rim of my filled cup.

"I wanted tonight to be different, to be perfect for you. It's your first party…" Michael trailed off, disappointed, and took a mouthful of his drink.

His reasoning brought a small smile to my lips. "Well, look," I held his hand, "the party's just started for us, right? So why don't we make the most of it?"

He beamed, and his mouth found mine. "Yeah."

"Let's go dance," I said against him as a new song began.

"Dancing? Are you drunk already?" he joked, breaking away from me.

I shook my head. "Not even close, now *come on*." Tugging on his hand, I led him to the adjacent room.

Multi-coloured lights flashed around the space, which radiated warmth from the swarm of people dancing and drinking, too distracted to notice we'd joined in. Not to mention I had drunk enough to care less about those surrounding me. Free from the gaze of others, I was given an overwhelming boost of confidence and started dancing to the blaring music. Meanwhile, Michael did nothing but watch me with a grin.

Since he was frozen there, stuck in a trance, I decided to give him an incentive. I spun around and danced closer.

He levelled out with my ear. "What are you doing, Dara?"

Shifting toward him, I smiled and slid my hand down his chest. I was feeling rather suggestive tonight. "I'm dancing."

He returned the expression. "There are people everywhere."

I faked innocence. "I'm not doing anything."

My incentive worked. Michael pulled me in closer, his arms snaking around my waist to hold my body firmly against his. The hand he flattened at the small of my back rubbed in soft motions. Over his shoulder, I spotted a girl looking at him. She pushed her long hair aside, and the warm, tight curls of her bangs fell right above her impossibly sapphire-blue eyes. The colour was brightened by her turquoise dress, which simultaneously enhanced her beige skin. Her stare and beauty caused me to become extremely self-conscious.

Michael noted my discomfort. "Hey, what's wrong?"

"That girl down there is staring at you."

"She could be staring at you for the same reason."

"I doubt it."

He glanced at her, then shrugged. "What's it matter? I'm here with my girlfriend."

"I don't think she'd car—"

Without so much as a hint of hesitance, Michael's lips claimed my own in a manner that would have dispelled any potential confusion concerning the state of our relationship. The temperature in the room rose, although being surrounded by a crowd had nothing to do with it. I'd started off by teasing him, but Michael only proved he could outdo me. Within five minutes, we'd left the dance floor, going in search of an empty bedroom upstairs.

When we found one, I shut the door behind us and locked it. Michael's mouth drew to mine again and we grasped at each other, frantic and urgent, wanting to remove the barriers between us. I took off his shirts, and he backed me against the door, his hips grinding on mine. Like I'd planned on doing earlier, I slid a hand down into his undone pants and fully wrapped it around him. He buried his face in my neck, sucking at the skin beneath my ear as I started to move my hand. Groaning, he hiked my dress upwards.

Michael ran his hand along the band of my underwear then lowered into them, stroking me in circles before slipping a finger inside and alternating. His name left my mouth in a quick rush of air at the feeling. He'd started off slow and moved faster based on my verbal instructions. A moan formed low in my throat as the sensation made my legs tremble.

Once his hand withdrew, I tapped his arm, struck by second thoughts about where we were inevitably headed. "Wait, let me go get a bottle of booze," I said, adding a smile afterwards like some kind of reassurance. "It's still a party, isn't it?"

He seemed as though he wanted to ask a question, but settled with "very true," and went to sit on the bed.

"I'll be back in two seconds, I promise." I unlocked and opened the door. "Don't move." Descending the stairs to the kitchen, I grabbed a bottle of tequila from the counter. Alcohol wasn't called 'liquid courage' for no reason. I removed the cork with my teeth and drank a mouthful, wincing at the burning liquid entering my body. I looked up from the bottle and squinted when I glimpsed a familiar face. A blink returned my vision to normal. I had drunk so much in such a short period of time that I believed I'd seen Frankie. He wasn't here; Michael was. Waiting for me. I returned to the room with the tequila in hand.

I can do this, I can.

Right as I opened the door, turquoise flashed in my vision.

The girl I'd seen earlier was on top of Michael on the bed, her mouth pressed to his.

The bottle in my hand dropped to the floor with a *crash*. The tequila spilled and spread, leaking into the wooden planks. The girl turned to face me, her green eyes smiling.

Michael looked up at me, feverish. "Dara?"

I stumbled out of the room, hurried to grab my phone from the kitchen where I'd left it, and then pushed everyone from my path on my way out the door.

"*Hey*," someone snapped. "Watch where you're—" his eyes widened as he saw my face, "—going…"

It was the man I'd spotted across the school field all those months ago.

From this close, I realized the hair that fell to his shoulders wasn't plain black but the colour of pure obscurity, blending into the night sky almost seamlessly if it weren't for the lights that flickered and outlined the wavy strands. His mouth was set into a scowl, and a frigidity iced his gaze and froze his jaw, accentuating its sharpness. He was haunting and beautiful—and I was drunk and needed to go home. I quickly apologized and continued toward the street, trying not to fall over in my heels; I came to a halt at the sidewalk, dizzy, my breathing harsh.

"Dara!" Michael ran out after me, fixing his shirts. "Can you stop for two seconds?"

"No, because if I do," hurt snuck into my voice, "I'll have to keep seeing another girl's lipstick all over your mouth."

He sighed, and the scrunching of fabric informed me he'd wiped it off. "Dara, honestly, don't be stupid. I wouldn't cheat on you."

"'Don't be stupid'?" I scoffed, whirling around. "That girl—"

"She kissed *me*, Dara!" he shouted.

A number of people turned their heads toward us.

"Come on. This is clearly a big misunderstanding. It's fine." He advanced to take me into his arms.

I raised a hand, stopping him before he could get close enough. I didn't want him touching me right now. "No."

"What do you mean '*no*'?"

"I… I need time to think." Everything was blurring together. I recognized I was being irrational, that this was the alcohol and my insecurity talking. Time would clear things up for both of us.

"What is there to think about?" He must've registered something unbeknownst to me in my own expression because his features shifted suddenly, and he let out a condescending laugh. "Are you… are you breaking up with me over a small thing like this?" He held onto my arm, preventing me from leaving. "You're making a mistake. You're throwing us away because you're acting insecure and jealous and stubborn."

"Michael, we've each had a lot to drink. Let's not have this get out of hand," I said through gritted teeth, ripping my arm from his grip and walking away from him. "I'm not talking to you anymore tonight; I said I needed time to *think*."

"Dara, can you quit being such an asshole and just listen to me?" he exclaimed.

My entire body locked in place. A splitting headache ravaged my insides with an incomprehensible pain that clawed at my bones, begging to escape. I rounded on Michael and grabbed him by the shirt. "*Say that to my fucking face*."

"Adara, I'm sorry. I didn't mean—" His focus lifted from where I'd grabbed him to meet my eyes, which had been burning through my skull. Utter horror replaced the apology and regret that had once transformed his face. "*Mon—monster*," he whispered.

Stunned by what I thought I'd heard, my hand sprung open, releasing its hold on him.

"They were right, they were all right about you," Michael said, breathless and recoiling. "Get away from me!"

No, I hadn't imagined it.

Michael had truly called me a monster.

I'd expected it from everyone else, but not from *him*. Not from someone I loved. Not from someone who'd claimed to love me.

Michael had once promised he would never hurt me—that he'd never listen to what people said about me…Yet here he was. Acting exactly like them. *Confirming* what I'd fought against.

I begged myself not to cry when the tears stung my eyes—begged to do anything else. A voice in my head answered the plea, smooth and sinister. My sadness warped and expanded into a raging viciousness, infusing my next words with venom: "I hope you burn in Hell, Michael Lamont."

He didn't seem to register it fully. His sole focus was on getting away from me.

The people outside who'd been staring at us whispered between themselves; a number had pulled out their phones to film my outburst. To them, I really *did* look crazy.

I looked like everything they said I was.

"You can all go fuck yourselves!" I shouted, lifting my middle finger up behind my back while leaving. I returned home on foot, having no other choice since Michael had driven me to the party to begin with. I flinched at the thought of him, at the thought of what he'd called me.

And the saddest part of it all was that, despite everything, my stupid, shattered little heart still loved him.

By the time I reached the house, my feet were sore and burning. My shoes had been removed by the third block I'd walked, and my makeup had been running down my face since the first. I would've gone straight to Frankie's, however I decided against it. The last thing I needed was for him to say 'I told you so' right now. What I really needed was to throw myself into bed and sleep this entire night away.

I fumbled with the spare key to unlock the front door and went straight to my room, throwing my phone onto my bed.

He said he wouldn't hurt me. I peeled the dress off my body and tossed it to the furthest end of my closet, along with the ring he'd given me. *The person who swore to never believe what anyone said...*

I scrubbed any evidence of sadness from my face in front of the vanity mirror using makeup wipes. When I finally glanced up, I reeled backwards, inhaling a sharp breath to prevent a cry.

My eyes had gone black, irises the very colour of darkness. Barely any golden-brown flecks were left.

He called me a monster...

My fist collided with the mirror. The shattered bits cut into my skin and yet, I felt nothing. I wasn't sure how long I sat on my bed, staring at my reflection in the shards. All I knew was, at one point, I started to fade.

My eyes snapped open as I plummeted through an endless chasm, tearing through layer after layer of darkness. My feet hit the ground, harsh and brusque, and my ankles received an impact that reverberated throughout my body. I simultaneously knew and didn't know where I'd landed, trapped in a meddling combination of places I had seen. The most vivid detail would be the highway. Dimly lit in the night, cracked, and completely empty except for a solitary black car driving directly toward me. In my mind, I ordered it to stop.

It came to a halt at my feet.

"Get out," I said.

The driver did as they were told, exiting their car without turning off the engine or closing the door. I motioned to the railing where an overpass had appeared. They climbed onto it immediately, emotionless and unable to fight my hold.

The order came from my lips in a voice I couldn't recognize: "Jump."

He looked back once.

Michael.

Panicked, I ran in his direction to prevent what he was about to do—what I had *ordered him* to do—but the distance between us stretched into infinity.

Fear radiated from Michael when I finally managed to approach him. The name he'd thrown at me hung unspoken in the air yet roared in my head, over and over and over again as a reminder.

Monster.

"I hope you burn in Hell," I whispered back, and pushed him.

I hope you burn in Hell.

I hope you burn in Hell.

CANTO VII

Darkness Falls

A loud knock woke me to a sweat-drenched pillow. I combed back the cold, wet hair matted to my face and reached for my phone on the night-stand to check the time: 3:30 AM. I rolled over and stared at the ceiling, knowing who would be at the front door. And if it truly was Michael, if he dared show his face to me now, I was going to kill him.

Less than five minutes later, my parents entered my room in their pyjamas, listless yet tense.

"If that was Michael, you can tell him to take a long walk off a short pier," I said. "I don't want to see him."

"That's not why we're here." My mom released a tremulous breath. Her eyes wandered over the Polaroids pinned on the string above my desk; a framed photo of Michael and I sat below.

Note to self: get rid of all evidence of him later.

"Princess, darling, the police are here to see you," my dad said.

I sat up in bed with a start. Why would the police be at my house at this hour? Was it the party? I was underage. I'd been drinking illegally. Could they have known that? There'd been one rule: don't get caught. And I'd gone and messed it up.

My mom reached for my dad's hand and signalled for him to continue.

Something was very wrong.

The last time I'd seen my parents this concerned—this *afraid*… they'd found out what had happened to Lenia.

I grabbed my pillow and hugged it close to my chest.

"Michael's body was found at the bottom of the I-90 overpass," my dad informed me as delicately as he could. "The police are saying he jumped."

The entire room stilled. Time suspended itself.

I had threatened to kill him if he showed up at my house.

I had threatened to *kill him.*

And now I would never see him again.

I looked to my shaking hands. The stuffing littered my palms and legs, torn out of my pillow, and the purple velvet fabric hung in tatters. I jerked away from it.

"The officers are downstairs," my mom revealed. "They want to speak to you. Apparently you were the last one to have interacted with Michael."

"H-how do they know that?" I faltered. "How did they know I was the last one… the last one he spoke to?"

"Eyewitnesses at the party you went to confirmed it."

There was no need to panic. The police would provide logical insight into what had happened with Michael. I took three deep breaths to steel myself, and said, "I'll talk to the cops."

Cold nipped at my bare feet as my parents and I made our way downstairs. The police were stationed in my dining room past the kitchen, spreading photographs across the table.

"Adara Goodman?" the officer with the moustache standing in front of the window asked. The tag on his pocket showed the name 'Redd.'

"That's me," I said, and sat down where he'd gestured.

"Do you recognize the person in these photographs?" the other officer asked. Her name tag said 'Martino.'

I brought the photos closer and wiped my eyes to make sure I was seeing clearly. Blood soaked the scene, painting the gravel, grass and border in shining crimson. And in the centre of it all… a boy. *Michael.* His trachea protruded from his broken neck, and his arms twisted in unimaginable directions, whereas his legs were snapped beneath him.

Just like Lenia's, my conscience hissed.

I blinked away the voice and focused on the photos. My attention gravitated to Michael's face, to his lifeless and glassy caramel-coloured eyes.

How many times have I looked into those eyes?

His hair was matted with blood.

How many times have I run my hands through that hair?

His mouth was frozen as if he'd hit the ground still screaming.

How many times has that mouth said my name? How many times have I kissed him?

Never again.

"*Yes*… yes, I know who this is," I somehow managed through the waves of sickness rolling through me. "It's Michael Lamont… he's… he *was* my boyfriend."

"Do you recognize the area?" Martino asked, and I replied I did and it was near the I-90.

"We have a few more questions," Redd pursued. "We have reports claiming that you and the victim had an altercation before leaving the house of," he squinted at his notepad, "Jasmine Mackie. Witnesses also claim you—"

"I was under the impression this was a suicide," I said, growing defensive. "Not a murder investigation."

"It's not. This is only standard procedure," Martino said. "We review all the information, compile a list of suspects based on eyewitness—"

"Well, I was home," I announced as though they'd asked for an alibi. "Ask my parents. I came home at precisely 1:05 AM."

My parents confirmed they had heard me enter the house at that time from their room.

The officers conferred with each other for a moment, addressing themselves to me afterwards. "We're going to need you to make an official statement," Martino said, collecting the photographs and storing them in a file folder.

I wiped at my face. "Are you forcing me to make one now? Or are you going to let me do it when I'm ready?"

"Now would be preferable, seeing as how the events before Michael Lamont's death are still fresh," Martino said.

I wanted the cops out of my house as fast as possible, so I complied. I wrote my statement and had it read to me to ensure I had 'accounted for every detail.' Evidently, I had left a couple of things out. Actually, I had basically lied to the police about more than just a 'couple of things,' worried I would incriminate myself in some way. It was already enough that I'd begun suspecting myself for Michael's death, no matter how improbable it might've been; I didn't need the police suspecting it either.

"Are we done here?" I asked the officers once I'd given them my statement.

"We'll be in touch," Martino said, leaving with Redd in tow.

When the cop car left the driveway, I trudged back to my room. "Please leave," I said to my parents when they appeared at my door.

"Addie, Princess, talk to us..."

"*Please go.*"

My parents walked away without another word, and I shut the door behind them. Tears streamed down my cheeks as my eyes wandered across the pictures I had of Michael. Running to my desk, I ripped the Polaroids from the string they were clipped to. I grabbed the framed selfie of us on our first date, throwing it on the floor. The glass shattered like the rest of my composure.

The books on my shelves became projectiles hurled at the wall, each leaving dents where they collided. Papers flew around my head, falling slowly. A scream pried itself from my throat, echoing sore and pitiful and grieving, as though my voice believed it could cling onto Michael and convince him to come back.

My legs wobbled beneath me, and I fell to the ground, leaning against my desk to hold myself upright. I hissed at the glass shards biting into my hands, littered around the picture of Michael and me.

Even now I could see him in that moment, saying ridiculous things I couldn't help but laugh at. And as for the others, the hundreds of small images of us? His voice seeped from every one, telling me he loved me, but soon warped into accusations.

Guilt clawed at my conscience.

I gathered our pictures, sped downstairs and swiped a bottle of whiskey from the kitchen along with a lighter from a drawer. Outside, I swallowed a mouthful of the alcohol to burn out the ache tightening around my throat and heart, doused the shreds of my memories I'd cast into the garbage can, and brought the lighter close. Fire engulfed the past, which crackled and turned to ash, ascending into the livening sky.

And at the centre of the flames, Michael burned.

My eyes darted around, rapid and wild, in the early morning, spurred by the prickling at my nape. After speaking with the police, I'd grown more alert, more paranoid that someone was watching me. None of my neighbours were awake yet, but if they had been, no doubt I would've looked suspicious.

No one is watching you, I told myself, and returned inside, exhausted.

Shutting my bedroom door, I slid down its back until I reached the ground. I tucked in my knees, cradling them to my chest like a child, and tried to bury the sounds of my sobs. It was of no use. Michael was gone, and the last words we'd said to each other before…

Before he died.

There could be no consolation. *None*, not when the words pointed their bloody finger in my direction, murmuring in my ears, malevolent and unrelenting.

My fault, my fault, my fault.

I dragged myself from the floor and stood at the window to watch the sunrise, hoping it would distract me from the monotonous repeat in my head. The sun rose in a dull haze, its rays shining over the neighbouring houses and onto morning dew-coated lawns, glittering gold and silver. From the corner of my eye, I caught a flash from across the street.

Nobody is watching you.

Fatigue flooded my bones, and my bed behind me opened its arms to my collapse. I stayed curled in them, in my hatred of myself for the next few days. Every picture of Michael was deleted from my phone that I shut afterwards. I didn't speak to a single soul, didn't leave my bed unless I had to go to the bathroom, didn't eat more than a spoonful of anything because I couldn't keep it down. The majority of the food my parents placed outside my door, meant to help me, was thrown out at the end of each day.

On the sixth day, I finally reopened my phone to eighteen missed calls from Frankie.

I wanted to see him.

When I'd told my parents Frankie would be coming by in an hour, they said they'd give us some time alone. No doubt they were thankful I would finally be talking to someone instead of holding everything in. They didn't tell me where they were going exactly, however I had overheard bits about a seminar concerning Satanials, which was likely a presentation by my dad's colleague at B.U. Before Frankie arrived, I managed to shower since I hadn't taken one in a while; I hadn't been able to do any basic task, and that only succeeded in making me feel worse. But now, I regained some motivation. Once I finished cleaning up, I threw on fresh clothes—black sweatpants and a loose tee. I'd just polished off a container of leftovers from the fridge when the doorbell rang.

Frankie waited on the other side of the door. His air was different, although I couldn't place why. Honestly, I wasn't surprised; I hadn't seen or spoken to him in days, after all. At my motioning, he came into the entry hall. Despite the temperature, he wore a blue hoodie, a favourite of mine since the colour enhanced his eyes.

"Shoes on or off?" he asked, just like he did every time he walked into my house.

"I don't know why you continue to ask me that when you know the answer," I replied, closing the door.

Frankie removed his black Stan Smith shoes, the ones we'd bought together a year ago, and left them next to mine. "You said you wanted to talk, so let's talk," he started. "The whole school knows about Michael. Actually, I'm pretty sure the entire state knows by now." He quieted, fiddling with the string of his sweatshirt. "You… you missed the funeral."

I shifted on my feet, not speaking a word. I couldn't have gone, not with everyone watching and judging and blaming me. I couldn't have gone because I wouldn't have been able to handle it. Seeing Michael's body get buried, wanting to throw myself in there with him…

"What did Jess say?" Frankie asked from the kitchen where he'd disappeared. "Have you told her?"

"Jess went out of town before…" The rest of the sentence refused to leave my lips. "Her phone's not on and I haven't exactly been speaking to anyone for the past few days."

"She's going to be surprised when she comes home."

"'*Surprised*,'" I enunciated, ambling toward the kitchen. "That's one word for it." If I had told Jess about Michael, I had no doubt she'd rush back here for my sake. I didn't want her to do that, not when she was in Italy to visit her family. Frankie could help me fine on his own. "I'm fully aware I've been taking this hard and if I don't work through it, I'll slip deeper into… whatever this is."

"That's why you invited me over?"

"I wanted to see you," I said. "To feel a little bit better. You make me feel better."

Frankie's gaze softened. "That's basically a best friend's *job description*." He rummaged around in the cupboards until he happened upon a bottle of apple and spice flavoured Jack Daniels. "Let's do this. Alcohol heals wounds, doesn't it?"

"It disinfects." I plucked it from his grasp and drank a few mouthfuls. Apple, cinnamon and clove hit my taste buds, along with a familiar burn. I shuddered at the aftertaste.

Frankie took his own mouthfuls of the whiskey. "When are your parents coming back? I don't want your mom to find us like this."

I shrugged. "We're good as long as we don't get caught, remember?" I pointed above us, smiling half-heartedly. "Don't judge. It's really messy."

We left the kitchen and climbed the steps to the room I hadn't been able to leave for longer than a few minutes without inducing a panic attack. I opened the door for Frankie.

He observed the destruction around us, whistling, hopping from one open space on the ground to the next to lie on my bed. "I've seen worse."

He was putting it mildly.

Books were strewn across the floor amongst pieces of glass from the broken picture frame. My desk was void of pens and papers, every drawer emptied and hanging on its hinges. My clothes lay in unfolded piles here and there; I couldn't bring myself to get rid of Michael's, so I'd shoved them to the far end of my closet with the dress and ring I'd worn the day he died.

"I'm sure you have," I said, forcing a chuckle. It came out as inauthentic as I had hoped to prevent. To cover up the awkwardness, I reached across the bed I sat on for the bottle in Frankie's hand.

Frankie held it away from me. "Dara," he said, his tone gentle, "you don't have to pretend with me. You know that, right?"

"Yeah, I know." I reached for the bottle again.

He moved it further. “Tell me what’s going on with you.”

Tired, I rested on my knees. “It’s just…” my fingers twisted a lock of now-dried hair, “if I told you everything that was going through my mind right now, I think you’d want to send me to an asylum too.”

“I wouldn’t.” Frankie’s deep blue eyes settled on me, and a sudden tremor followed. “Are you cold, Dara?” he asked, setting the bottle of whiskey on my nightstand. “Here, take my hoodie. It’s your favourite, anyway.”

Before I could object, he’d already begun taking it off. The fabric clung to the indigo tee beneath, and the bottom of his stomach and v-line peeked out. Despite his shirt being relatively loose, the sleeves were tight around his arms, which weren’t as toned they used to be. He’d been gaining muscle.

When did this happen?

Frankie tossed the hoodie to me. I caught it but didn’t put it on since I hadn’t been cold.

He sat at the top of my bed, reclined against the backboard. “Come here.”

I crawled to him, into his extended arms. They draped around my shoulders, holding me to his chest. His hand brushed my spine, up and down and up again, beyond soothing. My eyes lifted to him. I had always found him cute, ever since I’d first met him, but I’d never noticed how handsome he truly was. The slope of his nose, the dark lashes which framed the most stunning blue-grey eyes I’d ever seen, that one curl of his blond hair that fell over his forehead no matter how much he tried to push it back, the subtle scar above his lips...

What on Earth am I thinking? This is Frankie.

He noted my stare. "Dara, your eyes..." He lifted a finger to outer corner of my left one.

Shame and disgust forced me to avert my gaze. Michael had taken a good look and called me a monster, same as Lenia before him. Frankie might see the exact same thing next.

Thumb skimming my jaw, Frankie turned my chin so I faced him. "They're dark like the night sky."

As I scanned his features for traces of a lie, I discovered none… and I couldn't manage to remember what I'd invited him here for. All I could think of was the overwhelming need to be near him.

Frankie's mouth was warm against mine, sweet and tasting of apples and cinnamon. He wasn't startled, no matter how unexpected this was, rather reciprocating until he broke away to remove his shirt. I did the same and then pulled him on top of me. The softness of his hands roaming over my triangle bralette toward the rest of my body, combined with the thrill of him kissing me precisely where I wanted before I could tell him, left me reeling. He reached for my waistband, undid the strings, and slid down my sweatpants to reveal my matching black underwear. He brought his face back to me and began pushing down his own pants.

A staggering crack split my chest.

What was that? Wait… what am I doing?

My heart throbbed.

Michael. What about Michael?

I shoved Frankie away and jumped out of bed, collecting my clothes. "What the Hell was I thinking?" I whispered, re-dressing myself.

"*Shit*, Dara." Frankie stood and buttoned his pants. "Things completely got out of hand."

Sarcasm coated my words. "*You think?*"

He frowned. "Hey, don't blame this all on me."

"I wasn't. Trust me; it was my fault just as much as yours." And the alcohol's as well, but I didn't add that in.

Frankie grabbed his shirt from the floor, shrugging it on. "Look, we can forget about it if you want."

I had almost hooked up with my best friend. How was it possible for me to forget that? "I don't think it's possible for us to forget about it, Frankie..."

"What does that mean for us, then?"

"I'm not sure."

His voice dropped with his expression. "Do you not feel the same way about me as I feel about you?"

What? Was this the reason he'd broken up with Marianna right after we'd reconciled all those weeks ago?

I shook my head. "This… no, Frankie… My boyfriend *died* less than a week ago, and here I am kissing you. You're my *best friend*."

Things had completely and utterly screwed themselves up between us. When Frankie had stopped hanging out with me during those months I'd been with Michael, was it because he'd been jealous? Had I missed him due to our friendship or because I hadn't been apart from him since the moment I'd moved to Newton and I depended on him more than I'd believed?

Frankie had been there for me for years.

Whenever life got hard, he was never far away.

And if he did have feelings for me, these past few minutes were the perfect occasion to convince him I felt the same way.

He crossed the glass-ridden floor. "Tell me you don't feel anything," he said, and kissed me again.

"Frankie…" I withdrew from him. "I'm so sorry. I can't do this."

He looked down, cheeks flushed with red. "Did I mess everything up between us?"

"No, you didn't," I said, a half-truth. "But I think it would be best for now that you left."

"Yeah." He nodded. "I understand."

I swiped his hoodie from my bed and handed it to him. "Don't forget this."

"Keep it. It's your favourite, remember?"

"Alright." A small smile tugged at my lips and put it on.

"Promise me you'll call or come over if something's wrong, okay?" He wrapped me in a comforting hug. "You know I'm always a couple of houses down if you need to talk. *Only talking*, though. Just to clarify."

I chuckled and returned his hug. "I know, Frankie, I know."

We parted afterwards. From my bedroom window, I watched him get on his bike and leave my house. When he was no longer there, I stayed where I was, trying to figure out what had happened. Did I have genuine feelings for him, or was this my own loneliness and vulnerability speaking? If it had been Jess in his place, would I have reacted the same way? The 'yes' appeared in my head sooner than I'd have liked.

There was no use in continuing to dissect every single thought that came to mind. My overthinking had the beginnings of a migraine written all over, so I stopped it from progressing any further by grounding myself in my surroundings.

The street was surprisingly quiet today. Usually, the neighbourhood kids would've been playing outside for a while, however no one was here. The grey clouds rolling in might be behind that. Them and the fog.

Wait… when had the fog come in? The street had been clear a few minutes ago.

In front of Mrs. Stafford's house, a figure stepped out of the mist.

No, not a figure.

A *man*—the same man I'd seen across the field the first day Michael had spoken to me and the one I'd bumped into while leaving Jasmine's house.

Not possible.

Provoked by panic, I rushed downstairs and through the front door, only to discover—nothing.

Nothing but the street and the fog.

I put a hand to my scorching-hot forehead. "That's it. I *really* need to stop drinking."

CANTO VIII

Dreams or Visions?

A brown-brick house with black shutters decorating white windows loomed ahead, illuminated by flickering lampposts. The sickly tree to the right had begun to shed, littering the front lawn with withered yellow and orange leaves. Beside it, a grey car was parked in the driveway alongside another.

This was Frankie's house.

Through the window on the left, a distressed Frankie sped across his room, throwing anything he could grab into a bag. Where was he going in such a rush?

Suddenly, his head jerked up, panic flashing—no, screaming—in his eyes. He opened his window and looked to the east. All colour drained from his face, but his terror remained. In my disembodied form, I followed his gaze, and from the end of the street, out of thin air, faceless individuals appeared in the night, swords glinting in their grasps.

They charged into the house, searching for him.

Frankie crawled out of the window, perched on the ledge, and moved across his roof to climb down the drainpipe to escape. His feet hit the grass with a soft *squelch*.

I wanted to shout at him. To save him.

One of the men caught him, covering his mouth to prevent a cry. Engulfed by darkness, he next re-emerged in shards of dim light, slumped on the soiled ground, bound in chains to a stone wall. Bruises splattered his skin, and pools of blood coated the floor beneath him.

"*Find me*," he begged.

Horror seized me.

His voice echoed in my ears as a whisper. "*Help me, Adara.*"

I awoke with a scream and a cleaving sensation tearing apart my chest. Was I still asleep? I couldn't tell. I fumbled with my phone to check the time, remembering the trick I'd learned long ago: you could never read time in dreams.

3:33 AM.

I was awake.

Blinking away the remnants of my dream and wiping the sweat from my face, I reached to turn on the light on my nightstand. Afterwards, I got out of bed, heading to my broken mirror. My eyes hadn't changed from their new dark colour.

My dad barged into my tidied room, pyjamas and hair a mess; I jolted at his abrupt entrance, still rattled. "Addie? Princess, what's wrong? I heard you scream." His eyebrows furrowed as he noted the broken mirror I hadn't been able to fix. "Has it always been like that? What happened?"

I shook my head. "I only had a bad dream, is all."

"Was it the same one you always have?"

I wanted to downplay what I'd seen, but the memory of it stayed in my mind, vivid and frightening. "No, it was different this time."

"Different how?"

I didn't want to worry him. Hell, even I was worried about what I saw. Frankie's fear pounded through my veins as though it had been my own. So, I lied in part, telling my dad about the real dream I'd had the morning Michael died instead. "It… it was a memory of a dream… about Michael from the day he..." I wrapped my arms around my body to stop it from shivering.

"Darling, you're shaking," my dad said, stepping closer. He set a hand on my shoulder to try to soothe me. It didn't help. "What about Michael?"

"In my dream, I was the one who pushed him off the overpass."

My dad quickly retracted his hand. "Samantha?" he called out.

Silence.

"*Samantha!*"

After some commotion, my mom ran into my room, hastily tying a pink robe around herself that matched her slippers. She brought me into her arms and stroked my hair. "Oh, what happened, Addie?" She glanced down, and her eyes widened as she noticed the new colour of mine.

"She's had another dream," my dad told her.

"She always has the same dreams, Kam. It's fine." My mom found a blanket when she felt how cold I'd become and adjusted it around me. "She's just a little shaken up."

"Samantha, it was about Michael."

"And?"

"Adara said she was the one who did it, that she saw herself push Michael off the overpass."

Just then, I realized I might've made a mistake by admitting this to them. I should've kept my mouth shut.

My mom had paled completely. "We need to tell her, Kam," she urged.

"Tell me what, exactly?" I inquired, sitting at the end of my bed. "What aren't you telling me?"

My mom wrapped her arm around my dad, moving to a corner of my room. "We have to be honest, to explain, especially now because of her eyes," she continued despite my question. "Have you *seen* them?"

"Yes, of course I've seen them," he returned in an equally hushed tone.

"It used to be under control."

"For a while, anyway."

"With the Lenia girl's accident and Michael's death, this isn't a coincidence."

"Hello?" I waved a hand back and forth to claim their attention. "You guys are talking as if I'm not even here."

"I knew it'd only be a matter of time before it settled," my dad kept saying. "It's almost fully manifested now, seeing how it's caused her to—" he cut himself off, dropping his voice to a whisper, "*kill him.*"

"What do you mean *kill him*?" I exclaimed. "I said I killed Michael in my dream. That's all it was. A *dream.*"

My mom shifted toward me. "Sweetheart, what was the last thing you said to him, to Michael, before he died?"

"We—" I searched for the proper words. "Well, we had an argument. I was hurt. He said some things… horrible things…"

"When was it that you noticed your eyes, Addie?" my dad asked. "That you noticed they changed colour completely?"

"It wasn't me who noticed it first." My grip on the blanket around my shoulders tightened. "It was Michael. It's just—I'd been so *angry*… my eyes were burning through my skull—" I shook my head at the reminder of the feeling. "He took one look at me and… he called me a monster."

The word fell from my lips with a profound defeat. "The last thing I told him was..."

"What was it, honey?" my mom prompted. "What did you say?"

"I said I hoped he burned in Hell."

My dad's face grew dark. "Why didn't you tell us? You should have said something!"

"*Kam*," my mom hissed. "She's scared enough as it is. Shouting at her won't fix anything. What's done is done."

"Did I do that to him? Did I... did I kill him?" Tears rose in my eyes. "What's happening to me? A-am I going crazy?"

My dad calmed himself and sat at my side. "You're not going crazy," he said, holding my trembling hands. "You have a gift. One you can't control yet, and that's okay."

"A gift?" I scoffed and rose put distance between us, leaving the blanket at my place. "I *murdered* Michael. I put a girl in the *hospital*." A light of realization halted my pacing. "Wait, I've done this before, haven't I? But I couldn't remember exactly what it was. This... *this* is the reason we've moved so much?"

"Darling, we can explain," my mom said. "Please, let us explain."

My chest shuddered from hyperventilation. "I've *killed* somebody. How have I managed to *kill someone*? What happens if the cops find out I did it? I can't go to jail. I won't go!"

"Sweetheart, you need to calm down," my dad instructed. "You're going to faint."

"No," I snapped. "I am *going* to jail! I shouldn't have lied on the police statement—"

"You lied on the statement?" my mom blurted.

"She didn't have much of a choice, now did she, Samantha?" my dad remarked. "You won't go to jail, Adara. You have an alibi for the time of Michael's death. Hopefully the police will rule on suicide like they'd planned."

"Hopefully? '*Hopefully*' he says." I twirled a strand of hair around my finger, close to tearing it out. "I swear I'm losing my mind here."

My parents shared a look that said things were only going to get worse from this point on.

My dad's study had always been off-limits. A few years earlier, I'd tried sneaking in to take another one of his books, but he'd caught me and gotten so mad that I never went inside there again.

When I walked in now, after all of those years, a lot had changed. Sure, there were the same two distinct Boston University flags, however they were overshadowed by the numerous decorations of mythological beings and markings on the walls. A wooden burgundy desk lay in the middle of the room, right in front of the bay window whose seat held multiple dust-covered volumes. On the floor, once hidden behind a carpet, was an inverted five-point star, surrounded by strange symbols.

"Don't judge us too harshly, darling. We did this for you. And what we're going to tell you doesn't change the fact that we love you with everything we have," my mom assured. "You know that right?"

"You guys are scaring me," I said, sitting across from my dad. "What's this about?"

My dad inhaled a deep breath. “Let’s start with your mother and I.”

“You’re not getting a divorce, are you?”

“No, honey,” my mom replied. “Go on, Kam.”

“I’m not really a professor,” he began. “That’s only how I’ve presented myself since I’m not from around here. Samantha is, however.”

“So you’re telling me you weren’t originally from Boston? From where, then? Montreal?” I joked to lighten the tension in the room. It didn’t take.

“What he’s trying to say, sweetheart,” my mom took over, “is I’m from the Realm of the Living and he’s not.” She paused, looking to my dad for his approval to continue. He nodded. “He’s a Satanial, which means he serves under Lucifer.”

I laughed. “That’s funny. He’s a sort of Satanist, or what?”

“Well, yes and no. He’s not a human attempting to summon a minor spirit or daemon.”

“There’s *no such thing*,” I stated. “This isn’t a Ghostbusters movie.”

My dad tipped his head to my mom. “I can take it from here.” He faced me. “Samantha’s right. I’m not from the Realm of the Living. I died centuries ago and come from a place beneath the Earth itself—”

My breathing slowed. The blood pulsed through my body in a dull, repetitive thumping which rang in my ears.

“I am Rijaik Kamael, ex-Satanial serving under Lucifer, the Emperor of Hell.”

CANTO IX

Something Wicked This Way Comes

My brain couldn't wrap around what had been said. Stuff like this didn't exist in real life. Logically speaking, it wasn't possible. "That—that makes no sense."

"*This* is the sigil of Lucifer and his Satanials." My dad stood and pointed to the engraving on the floor of his office. I stayed where I was, frozen to my seat in shock. "See the inverted five-point star? That's Lucifer's main marker. The symbols around it are the signs of the Satanials. They represent our creed, of souls and daemons alike…"

Daemons?

"…written in an ancient daemonic language forged long ago by Lucifer, the first fallen angel…"

My dad comes from Hell. My dad died centuries ago.

"…the sigil says '***Harach Lazahr Nurach Sangol Aritum***,' which roughly translates to—"

The translation came as easily as breathing: "'Damned are we, the Hateful and the Wicked.'"

How did I know that? I must have read it somewhere, in one of his books or notes.

I wiped at my face, laughing at his attempt to distract me. "This is all very cute. It's basically the Mickey Mouse Clubhouse but for non-existent paranormal creatures."

"Adara, this isn't a joke and it's not a lie either," my dad said. "You can understand one of the oldest and most complex languages known to Hell."

I got to my feet. "I don't know how you expect me to believe this. It sounds like the worst horror movie ever. It's only normal I don't believe you! None of these things *exist*. Look around your office." I gestured to his books. "Everything you've said is some kind of elaborate bedtime story. That works on children, and I am not a child anymore."

"Yes, you aren't a child anymore, Addie," my mom said, now positioned at the door, "which is one of the reasons why we have to tell you the truth. We can't keep it from you any longer. Honestly, it's a wonder we've been able to do so until now."

I folded my arms over my chest. "A thesis stays a thesis until it's proven. Chemistry taught me that; if this were a Chemistry class, I'd fail you both."

"You want proof?" Impatience riddled my dad's voice. "Fine, I'll give you proof."

My joking air vanished. "What?"

He moved me away from the symbol in the middle of the room and grabbed a letter opener from his desk.

"Kamael." My mom said his name in warning.

He ignored her, set the tip of the dagger to his forearm, and dragged the blade along his flesh. Black blood rushed out of the cut instead of red, running into the lines of the symbol carved into the floor.

"***Esomonus Asmodei ksiaze dimoni dyrreth pragaras.***"

I summon you, Asmodeus, Daemon Prince of the Second Circle of Hell.

His once-shut eyes snapped open to reveal a deep red around the brown iris. The bloody opener clattered to the ground.

"Kam!" my mom shouted. "That's enough!"

I waited, bouncing on the balls of my feet before clasping my hands together and heading for the door. "Very interesting special effects trick, and I appreciate you wanting to distract me from my problems, but," I feigned a yawn, "I should really be goi—"

The smell of metal and smoke hit my nose as the summoning circle began to glow an intimidating crimson. A sound ripped through the air, and a quaking from the foundations of the earth shook the house.

From the centre of the circle, a massive tear in the fabric of matter appeared. And out of it stepped a person.

"What the…?" I gaped at the figure in front of me, and my lip curled. "*You!*"

It was him. That man… The one I bumped into at Jasmine's party. The *exact one* I thought I had seen across the street not long ago.

My dad blinked twice. "You know who this is?"

"I felt like somebody was following me around," I replied. "I thought I was going insane!" In comparison to the current situation, I'd been extremely sane then.

"It seems Lucifer ended up sending Asmodeus to monitor you, after all," my dad commented.

My neck jutted out. "Um, excuse me? '*Monitor?*'"

The Prince's ruby-red eyes found me. Although he had the appearance of a relatively young age and wore semi-modern clothes, based on this new-found information, it was an elaborate lie. He was older than the Earth itself, older than my dad.

When he noted my glare, he sent a smile my way—vicious and ominous beneath the layer of false introduction, freezing the very blood in my veins. “Kamael, to what do I owe the pleasure of this summoning?” he asked, turning toward him. A strange accent tinted his voice. “I happened to be in the middle of something.”

“Samantha and I have begun to explain Adara’s… heritage,” my dad hesitated to say. “I assume you’ve been made aware of recent incidents.”

The Prince observed me as though I was the least interesting thing he’d ever come across in his eons of existence. “She seems to be taking this surprisingly well,” he remarked to my parents. “It’s not every day one discovers their father is down below, being Emperor of the Damned and all.”

What?

Despair grasped at me with greedy claws, cutting my breath into shallow gasps and my vision into fading flashes. “Wha—Wait… you—you aren’t my actual parents?”

Asmodeus veered to my ‘dad,’ who’d fallen into a chair and buried his face into his hands. “You hadn’t told her yet, I’m assuming.” He shrugged, indifferent. “One less task for you to complete, I suppose.”

Mustering my courage, I marched into the summoning circle, straight up to the ‘Daemon Prince.’ My fist landed on his jaw with a resounding *crack*. My mom, if I could even call her that, tried to stop me from leaving. She reached for my arm, but I brushed her off and ran out of the house. Her breaking voice invaded the night, pleading for me to come back. My bare feet hit the pavement, and the brisk air turned into a full-blown gust as I sped up.

The street that had once been so familiar to me began to blur by tears, anger and betrayal. I envied every single person sleeping comfortably in their own homes, completely unaware of the world that had been revealed to me.

My parents had been lying to me since I was a child. My real father was… *no*.

With a mind of their own, my feet led me to Frankie's. He'd once said that if something was wrong, I should go see him. Angela would probably answer the door, yet not get mad at me for waking her at almost four in the morning. I'd run into Frankie's room, into his bed with him, and would tell him about had happened. He would make me feel better, same as he always did, assuring all would be fine.

But that was a fantasy. There'd be no chance he'd believe me. Honestly, I didn't even believe me.

I'm still sleeping, I thought, and shut my eyes. My arms wrapped around my body and I dug my nails into the skin. Pain would pull me out. *I'm still sleeping. Wake up. Wake up!*

My eyes opened to a pair of scrutinizing ruby-red ones. I forced myself not to flinch, and voice not to waver as I said, "You're going to get the Hell away from me before I scream."

Asmodeus' expression darkened, sending the moon to cower behind the clouds. "Are you threatening me?"

I'm not afraid. I am not afraid of him.

"You not only hit me in my perfect face, but now you *threaten* me?"

"And now I've just told you to fuck off," I said, and a brief flash of confusion crossed his 'perfect' face. "*Fuck. Off.*"

Irritation and contempt brimmed in his tone. "How incredibly charming, Princess."

"Don't condescend to me, pretentious prick." My hands balled into fists, trembling from disbelief and from fury. "And don't call me that! Only my dad is—" I stopped myself, simultaneously holding back tears. The man I grew up with wasn't my father. He was an imposter. "K-kamael used to call me that."

"He's not dead, you know," Asmodeus corrected. "Well, technically speaking, he *was*. Still *is*. Look, it's complicated. He has a better explanation and more patience than I do, so go on home."

"*No*. I'm not going back there." I looked in my house's direction, wincing. "I don't know who those people are… if I can even *call* them people."

"Go. Back. Home."

"*Suck. Holy. Water*," I retorted. "I'm not going back. You can't make me."

"Yes, Highness, you'll find that I can." The severe sincerity of his tone implied he'd bring me back in a body bag.

He won't kill me. He can't. He was sent to monitor me.

I crossed my arms and stood my ground.

Asmodeus rubbed his temples. "You're going to freeze out here, then? Is that it?" I held his gaze. "You're a real piece of work, aren't you?"

"And you're a real fucking treat yourself," I returned, nodding.

He sighed, exhausted and exasperated. "You can't stay out here alone."

"Yeah, actually, I was thinking of building myself a little nest right in the centre of the street," I deadpanned. "*Obviously* I'm going to a friend's place."

"If what Kamael told me about your dreams is true, you shouldn't be around anyone."

"You don't know anything," I told him, "and you don't need to be here either. Feel free to go on your merry way back to whatever hole you escaped from."

"Unfortunately for us both, I'm under orders to be here." He circled me slowly, inspecting. Appraising. "I was supposed to watch over you to see if your abilities developed, and they certainly have."

"Cool, hope you get a bonus for that. Have a terrible life." I started leaving, planning on crashing at Jess' place while she was away. Maybe after I got there, I would wake up and it would be the end of this nightmare. "I'll wake up. I will."

"You're already awake, like it or not," came Asmodeus' response from overhead. Two blackened wings kept him suspended in the air above me. "Now come on."

"I told you I'm not going home," I repeated, walking faster.

"And I heard that loud and clear, Highness, so grab my arm," he extended it, "and take a deep breath. This'll only last a second."

"I'm not going anywhere with you!" I swatted him away and ran.

A rift ripped open the air a few metres in front of us.

I screeched to a halt. "*Oh, what in the fu—*"

Asmodeus grabbed onto me and launched us into the obscurity of empty space. The breath drained from my lungs until I could no longer feel my limbs, and just when I thought I was going to suffocate, I hit the floor. My vision replaced itself with each gasp of air I took in. Asmodeus, however, was standing above me, faintly amused.

"What are you looking at, shit-for-brains?" My back and legs cracked as I rose. "You could've *killed* me."

"Please." He rolled his eyes. "You're exaggerating."

My hand itched to break his nose. No, I needed to save my strength. "What even was that?" I massaged my neck to get rid of the kinks. "A wormhole?"

"Something along those lines, although I think the Living—or humans, mortals, et cetera, in layman's terms—call it 'teleporting.'" He produced a strange pair of keys from his pocket to unlock a single black door. "Here, we call it ascendiating. Not that you would understand."

"What I *can* understand is you kidnapped me!"

"I'm watching over you," he corrected. "That's my job. I wasn't going to leave you by yourself in the middle of the night."

"I said I was going to a friend's place," I reminded.

"And I remember mentioning you couldn't do that."

"So you decided on kidnapping me instead?"

"It's not *kidnapping*," Asmodeus repeated, irritated. "I brought you here to keep an eye on you since Samantha and Kamael can't."

"No one needs to 'keep an eye on me,' so let me go. If you think I'll just sit still, I swear you have another thing coming."

He groaned. "Enough complaining. It's like speaking to a damn five-year-old."

"It's a *kidnapped* five-year-old, *thank you very much*, and she's about three seconds away from tearing your wings off and beating you with them!"

Asmodeus realized he hadn't retracted them. In an instant, they folded in on themselves, disappearing entirely. "Good luck trying."

I suppressed the urge to slap the expression from his face. If I was going to put my energy into anything, it was going to be toward something productive, such as figuring out where I was; then, I could leave on my own.

Orange-gold veins spread through the marble floors of what appeared to be an apartment building, slithering as though alive, and no doors were visible on the eggshell-white walls except for the one Asmodeus had unlocked. From where I stood, a lone elevator of sorts waited at the end of the hallway. I didn't recognize this place at all.

"Hurry up." Asmodeus had opened the black-walnut door. "Unless you want to stay outside, which, by all means, feel free to."

My shoulder skimmed his arm (hit him on purpose) as I crossed the threshold into the apartment. He sent a glare my way that I returned. Obviously.

The interior of the apartment mirrored the hallway with its similar floors, although parts were carpeted. The entirely black furniture on the left contrasted with the white walls on which priceless paintings and photographs hung.

I flinched when I noticed a man with snow-white hair sitting on the couch, reading. "Great! You're finally here," the man said to Asmodeus in the Hell-language my mind translated. He rose, dusted off his fitted slacks, and returned his book to the horizontal bookcase beneath a TV.

Asmodeus' brows knitted together. "How the Hell did you get in? It's impossible to ascendiate into this apartment."

“I picked your locks,” the man answered in the most natural manner possible. “I thought it was obvious.” He shifted on his heel, the gold pins of his loafers gleaming as they caught the light, which matched the cufflinks on his white shirt. His hair was slicked back, revealing a diamond-shaped face and the same red eyes as Asmodeus’, only the man’s were the colour of blood. He was almost as beautiful as Asmodeus too. “I’ve been waiting on you for *weeks*. Where have you—” The man paused when he noticed me and switched to the language he’d detected. “Oh… well, hello there, doll face.” He kept his eyes on me but directed his question to Asmodeus. “Are we sharing?”

“No,” Asmodeus replied, tensing up at my side.

“Keeping her for yourself? I thought that was my area of expertise.”

A dark blush crept up Asmodeus’ neck. “*No*. It’s not like that.”

The man grinned. “Are you sure?”

“What happened to Wesley?” an annoyed Asmodeus asked, shifting the focus to something else. “Why don’t you go play with him and leave the woman alone.”

This interaction was simultaneously awkward and hilarious. I did nothing but stand there while they spoke, watching the stoic Asmodeus falter. Why didn’t he just explain who I was? Was I such a big secret?

“Ooo, you’re so possessive.” The man chuckled. “And don’t worry. I won’t be telling anyone about *this*.” He pointed between Asmodeus and me.

It might’ve been the way he’d said it, or maybe the words held a deeper meaning that was lost on me in the moment, but in any case, it had struck a chord with Asmodeus. His mouth had set into a firm line, jaw clenched. “*This* isn’t anything,” he clarified.

A jovial beam split the man's face. "Yes, yes. You know I'm only joking." He sighed, then told me as an aside, "There really isn't anything more fun than annoying the Hell out of your siblings. Honestly, there isn't."

Siblings?

Asmodeus' brother strolled to an armchair, sprawling in the seat. "And for your in-for-ma-tion, Az, Wesley is moving out of my place as we speak. He didn't realize I needed more than what he could give me, and he called me by your name once while we were in the middle of fuc—"

"Is that why you're here, Leviathan?" Asmodeus interrupted.

Leviathan? Like the daemon Leviathan? I wired my mouth shut. *Keep calm. There's no need to panic.*

"No, but it would've been nice to bond over our taste in men." He eyed me. "And women."

Asmodeus shook his head, not bothering to respond.

"I was here about a painting, but we can talk sometime later." Leviathan stood, waved to me while passing by, and leaned over to Asmodeus while opening the door. "I'll leave you to your 'company.'"

Asmodeus clapped him on the shoulder. "You need to work on respecting boundaries, Levi."

"Haven't you heard? Family doesn't know the meaning of the word."

"Don't use that as an excuse."

"And *you* don't do anything I wouldn't do," he said in a sing-song tone. A grin broke onto his lips. "Actually, scratch that. Do *everything* I would do."

His laugh was cut off by the door Asmodeus had swung shut. Afterwards, he strode into the living room to fix the chair Leviathan had sat in.

Hoping to gain information, I asked, “Is your brother always like that?”

Asmodeus pressed a hand to his temple. “More or less. I’d change the locks in this place, but it seems he’s taken up lock-picking as a hobby.” He quickly added, “Not that that’s any of your business.”

“Alright then, grumpy. I’m just trying to make decent conversation since I’m being held here against my will.”

“I’m starting to rethink this idea,” he muttered to himself.

Oh, is he now? Let’s play ‘How Many Questions Can I Ask Until the Daemon Prince Goes Crazy?*’*

“Are you guys related to Lucifer in some way?” I asked. “Since you and Leviathan are brothers and Princes, are you Lucifer’s brothers as well or his sons?”

Asmodeus pulled a face. “His *sons*? Circles, no. My brothers and I are not related to Lucifer in the slightest. Our stations in Heaven were completely different.”

A strange sort of relief washed over me. If Asmodeus had been my brother or uncle… that would’ve been weird, and I wasn’t in *Game of Thrones*.

“Brothers with an ‘s’ as in plural?” I inquired. “How many are you?”

“Eight, if I’m including myself; one for each Circle of Hell. You’ve already met Leviathan,” he rolled his eyes, “unfortunately.”

Honestly, Leviathan wasn't as scary as I thought he'd be. He seemed cool—ignoring the obvious fact that he was a Daemon Prince from Hell. "I like him," I said. "I think he's funny."

Asmodeus' lips thinned. "Only you could meet a Daemon Prince and find him funny."

"Do I sense jealousy, Asmodeus? I hear it's common amongst siblings."

"I'm not jealous of anyone."

I laughed. "You sound like a child."

"*You're* the child," he snapped.

"I'm actually eighteen, which legally makes me an adult," I informed him. "I guess there's a grey area when it comes to you, though. You're, what? A million years old yet still pulling tantrums? Not a good look." Asmodeus wanted to give me another quip, however I interrupted him by continuing my game of 'How Many Questions Can I Ask Until the Daemon Prince Goes Crazy?' "So, including you, there are eight Daemon Princes. I thought there were nine Circles of Hell, if Dante's work is somewhat accurate."

"There are," Asmodeus said through gritted teeth. My questions had begun to annoy him. Good. "Lucifer resides in the final Circle of Treachery."

Sounds fitting.

"Why are you eight called Dae—"

"We're called Daemon Princes because we oversee our own unique legions of daemons that inhabit our specific Circles of Hell," Asmodeus explained before I could finish. "We're bound to them as angels who fell while following Lucifer at the Dawn of Time. Are you happy now? Have any more questions?"

My game worked well enough. And as of now, I had no more questions. "I'll think of something, don't you worry," I said, and started walking around his apartment, passing him.

The black couch Leviathan had initially been on stretched in front of a TV hanging above a horizontal bookcase. Matching armchairs bordered a pristine black coffee table, and a black dining room table with monochromatic chairs sat behind it. A shaded, cathedral-like glass wall ran parallel to the entire setup, and part of me wondered what was on the other side. At the bookcase, my fingers ran along the spines of the volumes lined up within: *Faust*, *The Lord of the Rings*, *Wuthering Heights*, *Persuasion*, *Frankenstein*… I reached for *The Picture of Dorian Gray* when I saw it separated from the rest.

"Could you not touch my things?" Asmodeus scolded from the armchair. "It's considered rude."

I stifled a laugh and picked up a book. "*Romeo and Juliet*? Really?"

"It's not mine," Asmodeus informed me. "It's Levi's. He keeps his things here even though I've told him not to."

"Uh huh. For sure."

"Not that I need to justify myself to you, but I didn't enjoy the play when I first saw it."

"At an Opera House or something?"

"No, not 'at an Opera House or something,'" he mimicked. "I was there when Will wrote the play itself. Who do you think gave him the idea to kill Romeo and Juliet off? To be honest, I was going for something a little different but he *had* to have the final say. You'd never believe how obsessive he was, which was good in some cases, and bad in others."

Asmodeus had *met* William Shakespeare. He had *talked* to him. He was *there* when *Romeo and Juliet* was written. Given the implication in his words, he'd probably done more than that, but I was interested all the same.

"How did your ending go?"

"You wouldn't like it," Asmodeus said, sitting where Leviathan had. "I'm sure you love the ending as is. Everyone does."

"Don't start assuming things about me. I never enjoyed the story to begin with, so give me your ending. I'll tell you if I think it would've been better."

Asmodeus' focus stayed on me, prepared to discern a lie. "Romeo stayed in exile for a few months, and by the time he returned to Verona, Juliet had been married off to a man her family approved of."

"Kind of anti-climactic," I commented.

"Romeo goes on a rampage clouded by obsession and betrayal," he continued. "He kills Juliet, her husband, their child, and finally himself."

"That's brutal," I remarked, "but I assume it was meant to be a critique of crimes of passion committed by a crazed, 'scorned' lover who believes he's owed something?"

He nodded. "Precisely."

"I like it better than the actual ending since it comments on societal issues," I admitted, returning the book where I'd taken it. "Dying for love is stupid. A terrible investment of time, really."

"Well, that's something we can both agree on."

"Just to be clear, *this*," I gestured to us, "does not mean we're getting along. This isn't the beginning stage of Stockholm Syndrome, which has been disproven, technically."

He covered his eyes with a hand. "For the last time, I didn't kidnap you!"

"Sure, dude. Whatever you say."

He removed his hand from his face. "Did you call me '*dude*'?"

I hid the smile appearing in response to his reaction by finishing to look through his collection of books, as well as his extensive library of movies. Turning on my heel, I came to a stop facing the sleek, black countertop kitchen attached to the same wall as the entrance door. "What's with the kitchen?" I asked, jutting a thumb to it. "Do you even eat?"

"I can eat mortal food; however, I don't need it to survive," Asmodeus answered. "The kitchen is merely for aesthetic purposes if Azazel isn't here to use it."

I raised a brow. "Another brother?"

"Naturally."

I hummed. "This place isn't bad. I half-expected you—"

"To live in a mangy cave riddled with bones and shit?"

"To be fair I did say 'hole,'" I reminded him.

"This 'hole' has running water and a television."

I pointed to the flatscreen. "Yeah, I can see that."

"Where do you think the science behind it came from?" he replied as if it was common knowledge.

"*Elaborate.*"

"It was Azazel's idea," he replied. "He's the creative one of the family, but I'd never admit that to him."

I actually laughed at his joke. At least I thought it was a joke. I couldn't be sure since he seemed serious. "What? Did Azazel also invent phones?" I asked, sarcastically.

"Some models."

I blinked. "*Huh?*"

"Other inventions include but are not limited to the following," he began counting on his hand, "double-chocolate chip cookies, trench coats and newsboy caps, coq-au-vin and the wine in it, margherita pizza, *limoncello* and *grappa*. He's expanded into apps recently; a video-sharing one has gotten quite popul—"

"Okay! Enough. Thank you *very* much for that life-altering information. It explains a few things." I raked a hand through my hair, wondering how many of the things I owned were Hell-fabricated.

Asmodeus' eyes roamed over me and lingered, serving as a reminder that I was in his home wearing no shoes, a tank top and pyjama bottoms. Suddenly embarrassed, I folded my arms over my chest.

"What's wrong, Highness?" he asked, sarcastic instead of concerned. I repositioned my arms, trying to cover more than I already was. "Don't flatter yourself." He stood, scanning me. "There isn't all that much to see."

I gaped, offended. "You're about to see a whole lot of my foot up your uptight as—"

"You look tired," Asmodeus interrupted, pushing me to a room in the right wing of the apartment. "You should get some rest, in *silence*."

"You piece of shit, don't touch me!"

The door on the left swung open. A white-framed bed with black sheets lay in the centre of the barely illuminated grey room, and the same shaded glass as in the main area served as the wall on the furthermost side.

A black dresser lay across the bed and a vanity was stationed to my immediate right. The door past the dresser led to what I assumed to be a bathroom.

"If this is going to end up like a cliché fanfic where there's only one bed and we have to sleep in it together, I'm going to kill you," I threatened.

"I'll remind you I'm *immortal*, so you won't be killing me anytime soon." Asmodeus shooed me inside. "And this is the *spare* room. My room is across. Don't bother me unless you're in a life-or-death situation, and don't think of leaving either. You're not exactly in Boston anymore." He disappeared into his room, shutting the door afterwards.

I slammed my own door close, then fell onto the bed with a disgruntled scream. I'd barely slid into the covers before exhaustion dragged me under.

CANTO X

Asmodeus, Daemon Prince of the Second Circle and Bane of My Existence

"W*ake up!*"

I awoke with a gasp, clutching at my chest. Asmodeus' hands encircled my arms, shaking me from my sleep. I pried him off and sat upright. "*Why* are you yelling, and *why* are you touching me after I've already told you not to?"

A frowning Asmodeus backed away slightly, moving to the further end of the bed, far enough to keep a safe distance. "You were screaming, Adara," he said with such gentleness that I flinched. This was the first time he'd called me by my actual name, not Princess or Highness with the usual disdainful tone.

"I was?" When I went to wipe the haze from my eyes, my hands returned dampened by tears.

"I heard you from my room."

"I'm fine," I dismissed.

"Adara, it sounded like you were being tortured."

Embarrassment burned in my face. Screaming in my dreams while sleeping in a stranger's house, how classy of me. "I would've been okay," I said, trying to downplay my reaction. "You could've let me be."

"I would have if you hadn't been in the middle of a seizure," he returned, tone clipped.

A seizure?

"Your body went into shock to protect itself. That's when I went to wake you up," he explained. "What were you dreaming of? You were yelling for Kamael and Samantha."

"I… I don't know. The memory disappeared as soon as I came to." I wracked my brain for a semblance of recollection. "I think I was upset with them? I don't really remember the specific reason… and I—I might've done something, but I can't be sure what." A frustrated pounding numbed my head. "It's over now. It was a dream."

Asmodeus cleared his throat, standing. "Right." His expression, once tinted by concern, had returned to stone. "Don't go screaming again. I didn't agree to," he gestured to me, "*this*."

"No one forced you to."

"Yes," he maintained. "They did."

Despite having said multiple times I was fine, in truth, I wasn't. Not in any sense of the word. The weight of my forgotten dream pressed on my shoulders, filled with an indescribable agitation that dragged its nails across my spine, digging and piercing the flesh beneath; and into those wounds seeped a profound loneliness. I had no one to ward off this unrest, no one to reassure me I was okay, that this would pass soon—although even if they did, it'd be another lie. As much as I didn't want to ask, I was terrified and paranoid, and *he* was the only one here.

"No."

"'No' what?" My brows furrowed in confusion. "You don't even know what I was going to ask."

"Yes, I did, and the answer is no." Asmodeus left, shutting the door behind him.

Ignoring the nagging feeling of disappointment at his answer, I settled in bed to fall back asleep. A shiver crept into me, prompted by the coldness biting at my extremities regardless of the blankets I was wrapped in. After staring at the ceiling for however long, desperate to calm myself, I shut my eyes to prevent the tears from falling and kept breathing, no matter how erratic. Nothing helped. *Nothing helped.*

The door clicked open and footsteps sounded on the floor. The covers lifted. The left side of the bed lightly sank as Asmodeus slipped in beside me.

I managed to face him, my voice small. "What are you doing, Az?"

That exact question appeared behind his eyes. "Don't make me regret this." I sank deeper into the covers, and my feet accidentally brushed against his. "Circles, Adara." He placed his hand on my forehead, immediately recoiling. "You're freezing."

"It's alright." I covered my ears with the blankets as well. "I'll be fine."

He huffed and pulled me toward him. The only reason I let him do so was because I didn't have the energy to fight. I half-expected him to be freezing like I was, but found him abnormally warm. His chin settled over my head, and before I knew it, I fell asleep, focused on the sound of his breathing and the scent of dark amber and mahogany.

I didn't know at what time I woke up. All I knew was that the spot beside me was cold, which meant Az must have left after I'd fallen asleep. It didn't matter. What *did* matter was that I'd been able to get some semblance of rest and stop a panic attack.

I made my way to the bathroom conveniently located five feet away in the dark. As I washed my hands, I caught sight myself in the mirror above the sink. My under-eye bags were almost as shadowed as my eyes themselves. Thinking it might help, I hopped into the shower on my right and rinsed away my horrendous night. Once I'd wrung out my hair, I returned to the room. The lamp had been switched on, and a simple black button-up, jeans, socks and jacket lay on the newly-made bed.

Whose clothes are these? Whatever. They're better than PJs.

After dressing, I headed to the main area, and found Az in the kitchen, having made coffee in an expensive-looking machine.

"You took your damn time in there." He turned around, filled cup in hand, scanning what I wore. "Much better."

I ignored his jab at my previous clothes. "Seems Daemon Princes drink coffee like humans, huh?"

Az shrugged. "It tastes good." He didn't bother blowing on the undoubtedly scalding coffee. He sipped it as it was and licked his lips right after. "Do I make you nervous, Highness?"

I dropped the strand of hair I'd unconsciously been fiddling with. "Not at all."

"Are you sure?" He set his mug on the counter. "That's not what I saw."

"You saw me checking if my hair was still wet, Ass-modeus."

His expression shifted to one of mocking. "What happened to 'Az'? I distinctly remember you calling me that a few hours ago."

What a hypocrite.

"That was a moment of weakness," I informed him.

"I figured," he drawled.

I bristled at the implication. "Do yourself a favour and drop it."

"I don't have to listen to you." The fabric of his shirt stretched as he reached for his mug, revealing a nasty scar near his lower neck.

"How'd you get the scar?" I jutted my chin toward him.

Darkness descended, shrouding his features, and he immediately abandoned his coffee to adjust his shirt. "None of your business."

"No need to get so defensive, Ass-modeus. You're the one who didn't want to drop the topic of conversation. I'm just changing it."

"*Stop calling me that*," he snapped, striding to his room.

I'd been left alone with nothing but the scent of coffee to keep me company; it seemed like the only normal and constant thing so far in light of all these recent 'changes.' I swiped Az's mug from where he'd left it and took a sip. My focus drifted across his apartment, halting on the opaque glass wall. I deposited the mug onto the coffee table and pressed my hand against a section of the glass between the traceries, causing the shade to disappear.

The apartment sat at least a hundred feet in the air, likely atop a cliff. A bare wasteland coated in reddish-brown dirt lay below and beyond, with mountains protruding from the ground in the distance. Massive bluffs dropped to endless pits glowing a sickly orange-gold hue, replacing the rays of the non-existent sun. Individuals clad in uniforms walked along the edges of the pits, where beneath the surface dark bodies writhed in pain, their faces warped into harrowing screams.

"Before you ask—"

I whirled around, startled.

"—the essence from the fire and those souls flow into the marble this place is built with." Az had reappeared, dressed entirely in black from the fitted, long-sleeved shirt, belt and trousers to the leather boots on his feet.

The sole pop of colour came from the gold rope pendant chain he fixed at his neck, as well as the small hoop earrings peeking through his hair; a ruby hung from one.

"This is what you meant when you said we weren't in Boston anymore." My attention returned to the window. "We're in Hell, I take it."

"The Second Circle of Hell, if we're being accurate."

"You mean Lust?"

His brows rose. "Yes, precisely."

"No need to sound surprised. I'm not uncultured. I've read Dante's *Inferno* from the Divine Comedy."

"*Inferno* doesn't exactly do the Circles of Hell the justice they're owed."

"I mean, that's pretty obvious since the guy didn't go to Hell while writing the work. And if you're so upset up about it, as I can see you clearly are," I pointed to the vein throbbing in his neck, "maybe you should do something."

"I have better ways of spending my time."

"That kind of sounds like an excuse."

"Circles help me," he muttered through a tired sigh.

I figured now wouldn't be the best time to ask how he felt about Milton's *Paradise Lost*. Still, it was fun watching him regret his life choices. I flashed him a forced but proud smile. "Tell me, does this place have a cool name or is it something sad like *Circle numero dos*?"

"First of all, that wasn't even full Spanish."

"I never said I was fluent," I pointed out.

He rolled his eyes. "Second of all, yes, this place has an *actual* name."

"*Il secondo cerchio*?"

"That's the exact same thing but in Italian." He levelled a flat look at me. "Are you going to annoy me in every language?"

"In every language I know," I corrected. "How about *Le deuxième—*"

"Don't bother. This is *Arxala*."

CANTO XI

Dante's Introduction to Hell was Better

I looked out to the fires, to the flames glowing near the surface of the massive chasms brimming with souls. "I thought Hell was supposed to be cold."

"Only *Lartah*, *Griviek* and *Varmir* are cold," Az informed me. For someone who lived in such a warm place, it didn't appear to have affected his otherwise glacial demeanour, seeing as he stopped talking, retrieved a book from his shelf and sat in the armchair to continue *The Picture of Dorian Gray* from the place he'd left off, marked by a red ribbon.

"So, I'm just going to stand here and do nothing, then?"

"I'm only *partially* responsible for you," he reminded me. "Unless you're ready to return to your house, be quiet and don't bother me."

"Seems like you're responsible for a lot of shit," I grumbled, and plopped onto the couch. "Emphasis on 'shit.'"

"Really?" Slight amusement tinged his expression. "I would *love* to hear this."

"Are you kidding?" I scoffed. "Did you happen to forget how you tactlessly revealed the identity of my biological father? Which, I should add, is technically the entire reason I ended up here?"

"Oh. It's this again?" Az rolled his eyes. "I didn't know Kamael hadn't told you—"

"You didn't apologize."

He sat forward, his neck straining as if he'd misheard what I'd said. "Excuse me?"

"That doesn't count as an apology. Do you know what an 'a-po-lo-gy' is?" I enunciated.

"You clearly misinterpreted this situation. That's not how this works."

"You acted like a complete ass toward me. I should get an apology. It's only fair."

Az continued to observe me, searching for I wasn't entirely sure what. My nails dug into the skin of my palms in response to the weight of his scrutiny and judgement. His lips parted, but pressed back together immediately. His mind and mouth disagreed with each other, arguing on whether or not he should speak. "I've never apologized to anyone for the actions I've committed, and I won't be starting now."

"But I'm not anyone, am I?"

"I let you stay here. That should be enough for you."

"Not out of your own volition, you didn't," I mentioned. "Therefore, that doesn't count… not that it counted for anything to start with since you grabbed me out of *my* own volition in the first place."

"Why are you still going on about th—" I reached for the coffee I'd placed on the low table and drank it. Az looked from the mug in my hands to the counter where I'd taken it. "Did you steal my coffee?"

"Is this… is this yours?" I took another sip, swished it around in my mouth, swallowed and shrugged. "Huh. Kind of tastes like mine."

"*By all the unholy Circles*," Az muttered to himself. He set his book on the table and returned to the kitchen. "What has my life come to?"

"What was that?" I asked over the rim of my mug, wanting him to repeat himself. It might rub salt in the wound.

"I said you can have my damn coffee."

"Yeah," I nodded, "exactly what I thought."

While Az finished up the preparation of his new coffee, his mention of me returning home replayed in my mind. I didn't have the slightest idea of what I'd do. I had to go back; I knew that. Not right this second, of course. I wasn't ready. But soon enough, I'd have to. I'd need to have a conversation with my par—whatever they were, as well. For now, though, I didn't want to think about it. Instead, I preoccupied myself with other matters. And with the limited information I had pried out of Az about the Nine Circles—which I assured him I'd eventually resume doing—it wasn't that difficult. The more I learned about them, the less daunting they'd appear.

My question broke the long silence: "Your brother lives in one of the Circles, too, doesn't he? You mentioned Leviathan wasn't your only sibling."

Az returned to his armchair. "Why do you want to know?" He swapped his coffee for his book on the table. "Am I not entertaining enough for you that you need to ask about my brothers?"

"As much as I enjoy this awkward silence compared to our typical exchange of insults, I'm wondering if the rest of your brothers are like the gorgeous white-haired version of Castlevania's Alucard I met or if they're like…" I observed Az to find an accurate comparison for him.

Az blinked, and his book dropped into his lap. "What do you mean 'gorgeous'?"

"Shh." I waved him off. "Don't talk. I'm still thinking. Actually? Feel free to give some suggestions. I'm leaning toward Prince Caspian meets Jon Snow, but—"

"Prettier?"

"I was going to say a staggering asshole."

Az's mouth fell into a hard line. He picked up his book and continued reading. "No, I'm not playing into this, so you can stop with your immature comparisons."

"I really hope they're like the Alucard version," I muttered, resting my chin in my palm. "Pissy Caspian sucks."

"Don't call me that. I'm not talking about them anymore."

"Why? It's an interesting topic and we were having such a fun time."

"Correction: *you* were having a fun time. Besides, my family is my business."

"Oh, come on. You're not making it very easy to figure you out, are you?"

Az's eyes finally flicked up from his page, narrowing on me. "'Figure me out?'"

Only now did I realize how it sounded. "Don't get ahead of yourself. I meant 'figure you out,'" I gestured to *Arxala* behind the glass, "as in Hell and Company."

"No."

"*Please?*"

"*No.*"

If he didn't want to tell me… "In that case, can you call dear Leviathan over here?" I asked. "Maybe he'll be more talkative. I mean, he certainly was before."

Az glared at me. The muscle in his jaw had begun to twitch, and a dark vein appeared on his neck. It seemed I had hit another nerve.

I should start a Bingo.

"If you're not comfortable with that," I resumed, "then maybe you should rethink your answer."

Az shut his book, fuming. "*Do you ever stop talking?*"

Good. I liked making him regret bringing me here.

I gave him a sweet, sarcastic smile. "You answer my question and I might."

"Fine! *Fine*. If it'll get you to be quiet for five seconds, I'll do it."

Honestly, I wasn't sure whether to be offended that he'd agreed so quickly in the way he had, or proud that I'd managed to break him.

"We've established you've met Levi—"

"Hotter Alucard, yes," I said after swallowing another mouthful of coffee, "go on."

"There's Beelzebub, Azazel, Belphegor, Astaroth, Belial and Mammon," he said, offering no other explanation. The room grew cold when he spoke the final name. "Is that enough of an answer for you?"

Az's brothers were actual daemons, the types you'd learn about from books and movies. What else had I expected? For Az to have said something different?

"Not really," I confessed. "I thought I'd get a whole rundown. Background info, funny stories… normal family lore, you know? Unless you guys don't have that."

"We're the furthest from normal," Az said. "And again, it's not your business."

"But you agr—"

"*Enough!*" He slammed a fist on his armrest. My questions had finally gotten to him. Family was where he drew the line. "Be quiet or I'll shut you up myself."

A sharp pain struck my chest.

"What?" Az scoffed at my wince. "Have I wounded your fragile ego?"

"Something isn't right." I stood up and fell down just as fast.

"And you know this because…?"

"I need to go home," I told him. "Now."

"Finally! It's about damn time." Hopping to his feet, he strode to a closet, shrugged on a long jacket, and shoved a pair of boots into my arms. "Put them on and let's go."

I refrained from making a sarcastic remark. It wasn't a priority at the moment. I had to go home. Something was very, very wrong.

I hastily did up the laces of my boots and left the apartment with Az. Now standing in the same corridor as when I'd arrived, I grabbed onto his arm and we were sucked into the dimensional vortex once again.

Six seconds later, my feet hit the pavement in front of my house. It was still night; however, a few days had passed since I'd last been here, apparent by the garbage at the end of the driveway. Through the limited, flickering light from the streetlamp, I found no real abnormalities. My house looked exactly as it had when I'd left it: the rose bushes remained undisturbed, the cars were parked in their usual places, the curtains at the windows were drawn halfway shut—

An inhuman howl rang through my ears.

Az passed me a knife with a golden hilt. "Take this."

"What am I supposed to do with a knife?" I snatched it from his hand and threw it into the grass.

"*Hey!*"

"What happens if there are robbers with *guns*? Ever think of that, genius?"

"It was the only thing I had for you," he hissed. "You don't know how to use your powers yet, so it was the next best thing."

"I'm not sure if you've noticed, but we're not in the 1600s," I hissed back. "I wouldn't know how to use a knife either."

"It's not hard to use a knife."

"Against a *gun*?" I returned, and Az rolled his eyes. He'd started walking to the front door when I blocked his path. "Are you dumb? First rule of detectiving: you *never* go in by the front." I headed around the side of the house to open the fence. "We go in from the back."

"'Detectiving' isn't a real word," Az commented.

I raised hand, stopping him in place. "Shh."

"What? What is it?" He glanced around. "Did you hear something?"

"No. I just wanted you to stop talking."

"This is ridiculous," Az said, and marched to the patio door. He stepped away when he realized it wasn't locked.

We always locked our doors. *Always*.

"That's never a good sign," I remarked. "*Especially* in horror movies."

Az slid the door, opening it fully, and I followed close behind. An eerie quiet filled the house even though a howl was heard not too long ago. We crept past the dining room into the kitchen where nothing appeared out of the ordinary. At least, I'd thought that until I noticed the broken dishes and small puddle of a black substance on the floor, shining in the bare shards of moonlight.

Az bent, stuck his fingers into the liquid, and brought them to his nose to inhale the scent. "This is Kamael's."

CANTO XII

Uncontrollable

The uneasiness building inside of me was steadily increasing—and by 'steadily increasing,' I meant it skyrocketed. "Have I mentioned that I have a very bad feeling about this?" I told Az, staring at the black puddle on the floor. "Because I do."

He wiped his fingers and silenced me with a low 'shush' when movements echoed from another section of the house. We directed ourselves to the source of the noise, slow and careful not to alert the potential perpetrators.

Past the kitchen, in the living room, Samantha raised a sword, its point aimed at a scaled beast.

Panic seized control of my body. "Mom?" I shouted. For whatever reason, the sound of my voice claimed the beast's attention, and its outer shell retracted, gaining shape. "*Dad?*" The black blood gushing from the cut in his shoulder stained both his haggard face and torn clothes. I started toward him, pushing aside my terror. "Dad? What's—"

A sad smile touched his lips. "Sweetheart, I love y—" His words were cut off when his head was. Samantha's sword had swept in an arc, stealing the life and final declaration from the man who'd raised me.

Roaring silence rang through my ears.

Samantha raised her chin, revealing the clear line of her husband's blood splattered from brow to chin. As she remained standing over his decapitated body, it soon began to dissolve, to break apart into pieces and fade away. Her deep green eyes flashed. She held the sword to her throat and sliced it open, giving way to a sick, red waterfall. She crumpled to the floor, and her body seized in the spilling blood. Her blonde hair was loose for the first time in years, now coloured crimson.

Everything had unfolded before my eyes like a scene from my worst nightmare.

A nightmare.

My nightmare.

I had done this.

My legs gave out beneath me. The solitary thunderous thumping of my heart filled my senses and muted the surroundings.

I killed them. I had killed my own parents.

My trembling hands reached for my mom. "Mama, I'm sorry…" Tears dripped down my cheeks into the pool of her blood. It shimmered on the sword as well, along with the black of my dad's. Nothing else was left of him. "I'm… I'm so sorry…"

It's my fault they're dead.

The two words repeated themselves in my brain.

My fault, my fault, my fault.

A cry, jagged and agonizing, crawled from my throat. The room exploded into shadow. Glass shattered and screamed, and wood groaned and cracked in the swirling darkness of the violent storm. My bones rattled within me, prying apart to stab and pierce my heart again and again until I could no longer feel it beating in my chest.

What have I done?

A hand found and squeezed my shoulder; it managed to clear the shadows but not my grief. "Adara, you have to let go," Az said, trying to pull me away from my mom's corpse.

I shrieked and held on tighter. *I'm sorry, Mama. I'm so sorry.*

"We need to go," he urged as the police sirens wailing in the distance grew louder with each passing second. "You need to let her go."

The darkness that had disappeared soon returned, reforming around my body in a cloak of obscurity.

I love you, I told my mom. *I'm going to fix this. I promise.*

"Adara?" Az's eyes widened. "What are you doing?"

With a silent request, I sank into a grim abyss.

My feet touched ground, and the familiar feeling of suffocation slowly retreated. The sense of confusion hadn't, however.

No, no. This is a dream.

Since I had no phone or watch to check the time with, I held up my trembling, blood-splattered hands to count my fingers. In dreams, you always had extra fingers.

One, two, three…

They were all here and accounted for. This wasn't a dream.

I inhaled a shaky breath. "Az, are you—" He wasn't next to me. In fact, he wasn't anywhere near me. "Az!" I called out. "ASMODEUS?" All that could be found in my immediate surroundings were the grey-brown rock walls of an underground cave.

How had I gotten here? Where even was *here*?

My mind flooded with a million questions, ones I couldn't possibly answer. Ones I didn't have answers to. And then, in an instant, everything came collapsing onto me: the reality of what I had done, knowing I'd killed my parents, but also my frustration and anger toward this uncontrollable curse that had claimed their lives and festered inside of me.

The last time I saw my parents flashed behind my eyes. I had run from them. They had died thinking I was mad at them, that they had lost me.

They died thinking I didn't love them.

I sank to the floor. My head fell into my hands, and shame and grief and sadness combined into a single emotion that carved what I'd become into my skin:

MURDERER. MONSTER.

What am I going to do now? What the fuck am I going to do?

Part of me wished Az was here, but he wasn't and I wouldn't accomplish anything by sitting around. If I landed myself in this place, I could get out on my own as well.

Az's voice echoed inside my head: *Adara? Adara, can you hear me? Where are you?*

I jolted, spinning around. *Az? Where are* you*? How can you speak to me right now?*

Daemons usually communicate by speech. You have the ability to communicate that way and with telepathy; Lucifer can do the same thing. He can open a mental connection between himself and any soul or daemon he wants to speak to. Now, tell me where you are, he pressed. *Describe your surroundings. I'll come find you.*

I'm not sure, I admitted, walking further. *I'm underground, in a cave with some sort of black sludge on the wall.*

I know where that is. Don't move.

How did I get here?

You ascendiated. You had to have been thinking of going to Hell or else you wouldn't be there.

I was in Hell?

I paused when I spotted a light emerging not far away. *Hold on. I can see a light at the end of the tunnel on my left. I'm headed there.*

Wait for me; we'll go together, Az instructed. *Do not move, you hear? And do not enter the—*

The communication between our minds broke. Since his warning made no sense, I continued down the tunnel until it ended, opening to a massive domed formation where other passageways scattered around the walls led as well. Pointed rock barbs hung from the ceiling, covered with odd roaming black specks. I squinted to make out what they were, only for my eyes to widen immediately after.

Hideous creatures swarmed overhead, moving with a predator-like grace.

I forced myself to look away, to ignore what I'd seen looming above. Metres before me, the ground fell away into a chasm; the flames licked at the air, drowning the souls of the screaming undead beneath. From the centre of the fiery void rose an obscene structure of black obsidian glass, formed as a collection of spiked pillars.

A castle.

The jump to the platform would be too far. I wouldn't be able to land there; I needed to find another way. Racing along the path, I happened on a bridge made of similar material as the castle, although before I could get close enough, a legion of daemons marched out of a tunnel in the eastern side—an army of sharp teeth, horns, claws and splintered bones.

I ducked behind a jutting rock for cover, observing the mass being led into the castle.

This is like real-life Lord of the Rings but a thousand times worse.

To ensure the daemons would have fully disbanded inside, I waited a few more minutes in my hiding place. Not long after, I sprinted toward the bridge, nearing the towering cluster of pillars. No light emanated from within. A greyish hue bled from the structure, ominous and imposing.

Az? Az, can you hear me?

Adara? I'm here. Where are you?

I'm about to go into the castle.

You found it? Don't move! Do you hear me, Adara? You don't move from that spot until I meet you.

It seemed pointless to listen to him seeing as I could be caught here, out in the open. But inside?

I slowed when I reached the large doors of the blackened glass castle. My hand had barely lifted from my side when a voice came from behind, stopping me in my tracks.

"Dara?"

I turned around. "*Michael?*"

CANTO XIII

Familiar Faces

There could be no mistaking him. This was Michael. The one I'd fallen in love with. Without another thought, I threw myself into his arms. "You have no idea how relieved I am to see you."

For a moment he held me back. Not soon after, he stiffened and pried me off.

"What's wrong?" The step I took away from him proved he wasn't the same at all.

His once familiar caramel-coloured eyes glowed lifeless, and a red ring encircled the iris. He wore a uniform of tough black fabric with a bronze symbol glinting over his heart: the inverted five-point star of Lucifer. The mark of a Satanial.

Fear coated my tone like tears had my cheeks. "What happened to you?" The initial emotion painted on his face transformed, replaced with anger. "I don't… I don't understand. How—"

"Don't pretend like you give a shit."

"How can you say that?" I murmured, hurt. "I loved you, Michael… I-I *grieved* for you. Ever since you died, I couldn't leave my room, I couldn't stop thinking of you, of u-us, of how I'd *lost you* and how I wished I—"

His hands balled into fists. "*Then you shouldn't have sent me here!*"

My voice vanished, stolen by him. By his accusation. My body petrified, overrun with confusion and dread. He wasn't making any sense.

"Do you remember the last thing you said to me?" Michael asked.

I stayed silent as past guilt rose up again.

He came closer. "You told me to go burn in Hell," he whispered, then withdrew. "And now here I am." He spread his arms, glanced around himself, and looked back to me. "Welcome to *Pravus*, the Ninth Circle of Hell."

Not only had I killed him, but I'd actually sent him to Hell.

"Michael," his name came out as more of a plea, "I didn't mean it." I might've been upset, but enough to have meant to kill him? No, absolutely not. "That night… it was a complete mess. You know I'd never—"

"Oh, but I think you did mean it, otherwise I wouldn't *be here right now!*"

I flinched at his shout even though I knew I deserved every bit of his rage. "I'm sorry, I really am." My apology sounded brittle and pathetic. "You have to believe me."

"It's too late for that now, isn't it?" Although he'd been furious seconds ago, his words didn't reflect it now, rife with sadness. *Defeat.*

The expression clawed at my conscience, adding to the bleeding cuts I'd left there myself. Unable to handle the pain, like a coward I tore my eyes from him, wiped my face, and focused on the glass doors barring my way inside.

"Don't bother," Michael said. "You won't be able to open them unless you have—"

I held my hand over the handle-less entryway, and it swung open with a great *thud.*

Michael frowned, bewildered. "You… you shouldn't have been able to do that. Only Satanials have the power to—"

A blaring yell of my name interrupted him.

Coat billowing in the wind he created, Az strode toward us, appearing as though he was about to murder me, find me in the afterlife, and murder me again. "I told you to *wait* for me! Instead, you went against my orders, you didn't listen—" He brought me into his arms. It wasn't a hug, exactly, so much as it was him checking I wasn't hurt. In any case, we were close enough.

What. Is. Happening?

At the sudden realization of what he'd done and the small distance between us, he backed away.

"What's this? Were you worried about me?" I asked. "How touching."

"*¿Quién chingados es este?*" Michael demanded.

"He's… um… you see" —I half-laughed, although it sounded more like a sad exhale— "it's an interesting story, actually."

"Yeah, yeah. I can tell you were really torn up about my death, Dara." Michael scoffed. "Luckily Mr. Tall, Dark and Handsome was there to cheer you up, huh?"

Az's lip curled. "Know your place, Primae. You can't speak to her like that."

"How else should I talk to her?" Michael said. "She killed me. She's a murderer."

I winced at the burning that arose from the crime branded into my flesh. My lips quivered at the rush of humiliation and the stinging of my eyes. I couldn't bring myself to argue against what he'd called me. He was right. I was a murderer.

"Bow and apologize to her," Az commanded through gritted teeth.

"*Bow?*" Michael's laugh had no humour in it. "Fuck off."

"This is your final warning."

"Who do you think you are?" Michael returned.

A twisted smile cracked on Az's face, crazed and terrifying. His wings unfurled in dark angelic glory, extending and expanding like a tar-coloured cloak. "I am Asmodeus, Daemon Prince of *Arxala*, the Second Circle of Hell, one of the first to have Fallen from Heaven to follow Lucifer."

Michael gulped. "I d—"

"*I'm not finished*," Az snapped, and Michael's mouth closed. "Adara is the sole child of the Emperor of Hell, and as such, you *will* show her the respect she is due."

Michael's eyes grew wide, drawing to mine against his will. I could only imagine what was going through his mind, what he'd think of me now that he knew the truth. How corrupted had his image of me become, if it even still existed?

"Forgive me, your Highness," he reluctantly said to Az, having been forced to a knee. "I wasn't aware who either of you were. I… I deeply apologize for my behaviour."

Az's air of satisfaction disappeared when he turned to me on his way indoors. "Disobey me again and I'll throw you to *Praeteritus*," he said, tone low so only I could hear, and vanished into the castle, leaving Michael and I alone.

Michael stood, head bent.

I folded my arms over my chest. "I'm sorry about him." I didn't understand why I was apologizing for Az's actions. "It wasn't your fault you weren't aware."

"Your Highn—"

"Please don't call me that." I stared at my feet, unable to look at him. If I did, the tears would definitely escape. "I… I won't bother you again." Following Az's lead, I went inside and did my best to compose myself.

Ornate pillars topped with blazing fires illuminated the interior of the wide entry hall. The flames danced up the vaulted ceiling and pointed arches, which flickered with orange, red and hints of blue. Corridors led to the right and left, bordered by sconces.

Az waited at the foot of a grand staircase, an upward spiral wrought of obsidian openwork. "Took you long enough," he said. "Was that not the reunion you had hoped for with your dead boyfriend?"

A slap across the face would've been gentler than his callousness.

"*Aha-ha-ha.*" I sent him a tight, mirthless smile, and shoved him from my path, starting up the stairs. "You're a fucking piece of shit."

Az came after me, trailing at my heels. "What are you doing?"

"Getting away from *you*," I spat.

"You have no idea where you're going," he commented, half in derision, half in reminder of his station here.

"I don't need you. I'm bound to stumble on some daemon or another that can bring me to my father." At first, I wanted nothing to do with Lucifer. However, considering the recent events and circumstances, I didn't have much of a choice anymore. "Or…" I stopped at the landing. "I could open a mind connection, bring him to me."

Az pointed to a pair of golden doors to our left as he arrived on my right, "He might be through there, but I don't think he'll be glad you're here. He believes you're being guarded by Kamael and Sam—" He refrained from continuing with his sentence, his concern seemingly extending to them and *only* them.

We dropped into an uneasy silence, soon interrupted by the clatter of footsteps.

Michael.

On the outside, he was the same boy I'd fallen in love with. On the inside, though, he had changed, and I'd been the primary cause of it. Us meeting again had brought on a complete whirlwind of emotion: relief, guilt, renewed sadness. Despite everything, I missed him. I missed who we'd been together.

"Do you still love him?"

Az's question took me by surprise. I blinked. "*What?*"

"I know you heard me. It's a simple yes or no."

How could I answer that when the underlying complexity was impossible to unravel? So much had happened in such a short time—to Michael, to me, to him *because* of me. Az could never understand, and I didn't need him to.

"It isn't any of your business," I responded, defensive like he'd once been.

Az's chin lifted. He wanted to say something—a rude remark, I'd bet—but decided against it, leaving for the throne room. "Wait here. I mean it," he said, and slipped inside, shutting the doors afterwards.

By then, Michael had reached the landing. He stood next to me, awkward and uncomfortable. "I know you probably hate me right now," he said, breaking the tension of our silence. "I'm sorry, Dara." His head hung in shame. His hand went to his ear, dropping when he realized his earring was no longer there. "I acted like an absolute dick before. I got mad seeing you after… after…"

After his death, my mind finished.

"I deserved it, your anger," I murmured. "And I don't deserve an apology, not after what I… did to you." My sleeve came to dry my tears. "No, I don't hate you, Michael. I hate *myself.* More than you could ever imagine. It's… it's been gutting me from the inside out." Finally, I looked at him. "I don't know what's happening to me, and I'm terrified. I'm so scared, Michael."

"Hey." He held me in his arms. "Earlier, on the bridge, the very first thing I thought was how happy I was to see you," he confessed. "But then, I remembered my death and tried to convince myself I hated you for what you did. I tried to ignore the voice in my head that called your name, that wanted me to fall into you like I had a thousand times before. And I just… I couldn't do it. You do deserve an apology because my conscience knows I can't hold you accountable for what you clearly had no control over. And I see you regret what you did."

"My regret doesn't excuse my actions, or w-what I am."

Whose daughter I was—and the monstrous implications of it.

"We can't change the past, but what we can do is try to make the best of the present together." Michael's arms tightened around my shoulders and back. "I was scared too at first, then remembered I know you, Dara, who you truly are." His hand slid to my nape. "I love you. I never stopped," he whispered, achingly honest. "*I never stopped.*"

At last, Michael fell into me like he had a thousand times before, just as I did with him. Familiarity lived beneath the surface even though it wasn't entirely the same, changed by his state and by mine; nevertheless, I would take Michael however he came.

"I'm going to fix this," I said between our lips. "I promise I'm going to fix this."

We broke apart as soon as the doors opened. Although Az seemed surprised to see us, he didn't say a word, only gave me a strange look. He'd gotten an answer to his 'yes or no' question that hadn't concerned him.

"Move." Pushing past Az, I entered the throne room.

Fire flowed through the grand hall's dark marbled pillars that stretched from the glossed black floor and converted into pointed arches, mirrored in the obsidian chandeliers suspended in the centre of the elaborate ribbed vault. Before me, stairs led to a dais where a solitary black and gold throne struck out against the blood-red tapestry of the Satanials creed-inscribed symbol.

Harach Lazahr Nurach Sangol Aritum

Four daemons lurked on the platform, towering beasts whose burnished skin appeared melted from their bones. Rows upon rows of sharpened needle teeth gleamed in their lipless mouths, and their slitted eyes on their misshapen heads narrowed upon my approach.

And there, sat on that black and gold throne, was a man.

He stopped talking to the daemons at his side, his focus veering in my direction. "Hello, daughter."

CANTO XIV

Me and the Devil (He Doesn't Like Me)

I didn't know what I'd been expecting exactly, but this was *not* it. Lucifer wasn't some kind of creature with horns poking out of his head and a pointed tail, and he didn't have a pitchfork or red-coloured skin either. He looked like a man—like the one I'd seen in my dreams for years with the black and gold eyes.

My *father* had tormented me since I was a child.

Dressed in a pristine white suit trimmed in snaking gilded thread, the sole red on him came from the reflection of the surrounding fires on his golden hair, which hung loose and straight to his elbows; its shine came second to the light that emanated from his very being. His voice, eloquent and soft yet imposing, carried off the walls, filling every corner of the room. "I was quite surprised when Asmodeus informed me how you had ascendiated here without permission."

When Az arrived at my right, I shot him an irritated glare.

"It's not every day that you see someone learn such a complicated technique with ease," Lucifer continued, offering a smile as enigmatic as the emotion in his gaze. "Then again, you are the daughter of one of the most talented beings to ever have lived."

"Funny," I remarked, attempting to appear the least bit impressed or intimidated by him. "Last time I checked, my father wasn't Gordon Ramsay."

Michael snickered from my left, which he tried to pass off as a cough.

"Evidently you've learned sarcasm from the Realm of the Living," Lucifer observed. "Now," he set his elbows on the armrests, blanketing part of the throne's façade with the train of his long, wide sleeves, "what brings you to my humble abode, daughter?"

I smiled. "I wanted to meet you."

"How thoughtf—"

"Again… *sarcasm.* I didn't actually come here for a father-daughter reunion. Frankly, I don't care that you're my father, even though I probably should, considering you're the literal Devil." To an extent, I did care, but I wouldn't admit that.

"I prefer Emperor of He—"

I waved a dismissive hand. "Yeah, no. I don't give a shit."

Lucifer's initial sort of lightheartedness vanished. "I don't believe you realize who it is you're talking to—"

"Once again: I. Don't. Give. A. Shit."

The daemons near Lucifer shifted. Hearing me disrespect their overlord, or whatever name he wanted to use for himself, must've really gotten under their skin. Or lack thereof, I should say.

"Adara," Az cautioned. "Calm down."

"No, I will not 'calm down,' Asmodeus," I returned, mimicking him. "I'm not here for pleasantries."

Lucifer signalled for his daemons to stand down. "Tell me, daughter, why are you here?"

Rage simmered beneath the surface of my fraying composure. "It's nice and all that you acknowledge me as your child *now* when that hasn't been the case for the past *eighteen years*."

"Is that what this is about?" His head angled. "You're upset I wasn't there for you?"

I laughed. "I couldn't care less about your 'absence.' What I care about is that *you fucked up my life!*" My yell and its loathing and resentment resounded in the hall.

"You'll have to be more specific," Lucifer said.

The grief and remorse that were entwined around my parents' death resurged. And with it came the fear—fear of myself and of what I had done. In truth, I was also afraid of what Michael would think of me. He'd said he loved me before. Would that be the case after I confessed my most recent act? I had no clue, and I also had no other choice.

My voice was taut, though not free from the emotions I wanted to keep buried. "I killed my par—Samantha and Kamael. Or whatever this *thing* is inside of me did."

Michael tensed at my side.

Lucifer's similar reaction lasted less than a second. "What of it?" His fingers thrummed on his rests. "What exactly do you wish for me to do?"

"I didn't ask for this." My hands lifted as if to display the power which had emerged from them—which had caused the faint crimson droplets, dried and draining, on my skin. "You're the one who made me this way, so here's what's going to happen. You're going to take it back and undo what I did. To my mom, to my dad," I cast a sidelong glance to the boy I loved, "and to Michael."

Lucifer's laughter boomed. "You cannot simply come down here and start making demands. Oh, no. You, my dear," his eyes sharpened on me, "are in *my* realm, *my* home. As such, you will abide by *my* laws. Consider yourself a—" he searched for the proper words "— new addition to Hell and to *Pravus*."

Now *that* I hadn't anticipated. I'd half-expected him to send me away. To turn me down. Not trap me here. "What do you—"

The rumbling of a pillar to Lucifer's right disrupted my protest. A section of it liquefied and reformed into a daemon similar to those at the dais.

"What is it now?" Lucifer demanded. The daemon approached him, whispering into his ear. His irritation cleared while it spoke, and a smile split his face. Whatever the daemon had told him must've been good news.

"***Yernah Nelor. Nirthe es irte osmen.***"

Follow Nelor, Lucifer had said to the daemons around his throne. *Speak of this to no one.*

They obeyed his command, leaving his side; once having reached a certain distance, their bodies melted, absorbed into the floors and pillars of the room.

"Is that it?" I wondered, upholding my sarcasm to mask my consternation; I didn't want to find out what Lucifer would do if he discovered it. "I'm a bit disappointed. Isn't this the part where all of the inanimate objects burst into spontaneous song and dance?"

He wasn't amused by my comment. "On the contrary. I believe I have a solution for your little… what should I call it? *Predicament.*"

"Which is…?"

"On second thought? Nevermind." He inspected his pristine nails. "I don't think you'd be interested. It would be much too out of depth for you, daughter of mine or no."

"Don't pretend you know the lengths I'm willing to go to," I warned, indignant. "I'm here, aren't I? So why don't you stop baiting me and tell me what I have to do."

Lucifer's brow rose along with the corner of his mouth. "Very well. You want something? You have to earn it like every other Satanial here. Fortunately, there happens to be one such way: The Sixes."

I waited a moment for him to launch into the details. When they didn't come, I said, "This is the part where you do the whole 'exposé' thing and explain to me what The Sixes are. Or is that not how you do things down here?"

Lucifer pursed his lips, gripping and releasing his armrests. "The Sixes are a series of Stages which my Satanials can go through, all in pursuit of gaining a transaction from me. Should they pass, I grant it to them."

"This sounds an awful lot like what people say about you in the 'Realm of the Living,'" I commented. "You hand out a deal for a price."

"It's a tad more different and complex than that, my dear." His reply hinted at my obvious lack of knowledge. "Mortals are alive. They sell their souls for a deal. For Satanials, I already own their souls. The Sixes were set in place as a way for my soldiers to win them back."

"What's the point of that?"

"For collective entertainment and learning," he answered, grinning. "What else?"

As I was about to ask for further clarifications, Michael held onto my wrist. "Your Grace, if we could have a second?" He bowed and escorted me to the first pillar, far enough from Az and Lucifer.

Confused, I asked, "What's going on, Michael?"

"Dara," he began with a silent plea, "I understand you said you would try to fix what you did, but this isn't the way to do it." He took my hand in his. "It isn't worth losing your life. You're special, Adara. If you die here, you'll be trapped in the void separating the Circles for years—centuries, maybe—before reforming and being stuck here *permanently* like me."

Was I prepared to risk myself for this? For my parents, for him?

No matter how I looked at it, I was already trapped and The Sixes were my best chance—a chance for me to undo what I had done, to fix my mistakes, to fulfill my promises, to *repent.* And so I found myself returning to Lucifer with Michael, and stating, "I'll do it."

Despair eclipsed Michael's once relieved expression and seeped into his whisper. "You don't have to prove yourself by dying, Dara."

Whatever response I could've given dissipated when Az entered the conversation. "And how's that going to happen, exactly? The Sixes are for Satanials, and the last time I checked, you weren't one." He turned to Lucifer. "She has no discipline, no experience, no training, nothing. What is she going to do? Annoy her way through her Stages?"

"Thank you for pitching my application to the 'Satanials Training Program' so positively." My smile didn't conceal the enmity behind it. "I love the amount of confidence in this room."

"Since you seem to have quite an opinion on this," Lucifer told Az, "why don't you handle the issues you've raised?"

Az's face fell. "*What?*" He stepped forward. "Why?"

"You said it yourself. The Sixes are for Satanials. It stands to reason she be trained as one of them."

"But why by *me*?"

"Because she is still my daughter and I won't have her trained by just anyone. Therefore, you and y—"

Forced laughter echoed in the hall, originating from Az. He put an abrupt end to it. "No, no, *no*. I did what you asked before." He pointed at Lucifer. "I refuse to be stuck supervising again. Give her to someone else."

My hands pressed to my chest. "Oh no, honey." I pouted. "How will I ever survive without your constant assholery?"

Az stared at me, incredulous. "*I beg your pardon?*"

"Yeah," I nodded, "you sure as Hell should."

Michael addressed Lucifer: "Your Grace, if I may—"

A snow-white head emerged from a door to Lucifer's left, interrupting him. "Yes, yes, I know I'm late," Leviathan said, looking as fashionable as the first time I'd seen him. "I wasn't aware that I was supposed—Oh!" He switched languages. "Michael's here too!" Once again, Leviathan noticed me later than usual. "Well, hello there, doll face," he crooned. "What is your gorgeous self doing this far away—"

"Levi," Lucifer cautioned. "Be quiet."

"Luce, come on." Leviathan continued his observation. "She looks rather good today, doesn't sh—"

"*Leviathan*," Lucifer hissed. "Return to flirting with Wesley or every other Satanial, and leave my daughter be."

"Your… *daughter*?" Threads of alarm wove into his tone. His wild eyes passed from me to Lucifer and back again before settling on Az. "Why didn't you tell me, Az?"

"That's Luce's business," Az answered. "Not mine."

"But she's so…" Leviathan lingered on me, offering a swoon-worthy smile. He then shifted to Lucifer. "And you're so…" He trailed off, expressionless.

"*Leviathan.*"

"Don't get me wrong, you're attractive as well in your own way, but we haven't really had that discussion yet, you know?"

Lucifer sighed, exasperated. "I'd very much appreciate it if you would shut your trap."

"Understood." The white-haired Prince laughed and gestured that he'd zipped his lips.

"Lamont." Lucifer snapped his fingers. "What were you going to say before this *mess*," he glanced at Leviathan, who smiled proudly at him, "stumbled in here?"

Michael clasped his hands behind his back and stepped forward to speak. "I was going to offer to take charge of Adara's training since Asmodeus declined." Az scoffed, and Michael veered to him. "Do you have something to say?"

"Yes, in fact, I do," Az replied. "You've been here for a whole of, what? Five minutes? And you believe you can 'take charge' of Adara's training?" He gave a condescending chuckle. "You probably cried the moment you'd begun yours."

Michael's initial reaction to Az had faded, and a new-found boldness replaced his intimidation. "You don't know anything about me, so why don't you—"

"I know enough," Az interjected, grim as the grave, "just like I know what you did before arriving here, as well as the things you said." His focus flitted from Michael to me.

"This has nothing to do with you, Asmodeus," I warned. "*Back. Off.*"

Confusion flashed in his gaze. "But we were having such a fun time," he riposted, and I scowled at his quoting of something I'd once said.

"You're one word away from having your blood on the floor," Michael told him.

"If it were up to me," Az continued, ignoring my warning, "I would've left you to *rot* in *Balnara*."

Michael laughed once. The red circles around his irises blazed.

Az set his hands on his hips, nodding in derision. "What are you going to do?"

Michael reached for his leg; a curved dagger soared through the air, skimming by Az's shoulder and leaving a thin cut in his coat. Black glass cracked as it embedded into a pillar. "Next time, it'll be more than a *scratch*."

The effortlessness of his throw, the rasp of his voice when he spoke the threat… I couldn't help remarking how attractive it made him look and how wrong that was for me to think.

Cheek in hand, Lucifer watched all unfold from his throne with an entertained smile, in no rush to stop anyone.

Az touched the rip in his coat, and a lifeless laugh escaped from his lips. In an instant, Leviathan ran to restrain him as he advanced on

Michael with a terrible fury burning in his ruby eyes. "Get out of my way, Levi," Az demanded. "This ridiculous Primae won't get away with—"

Leviathan grasped him firmly by the arm, whispering something into his ear which seemed to have calmed him down.

Meanwhile, I kept a hand on Michael's shoulder. *Don't let Asmodeus get to you*, I sent into his mind.

His shock at the sound of my voice in his head faded after a couple of seconds, and he retreated from the confrontation.

"I do love a good fight every now and then. It keeps things interesting," Lucifer said, clapping once. "Now, if you would have allowed me to finish before pulling your little tantrum, Asmodeus, I was going to inform you that your brothers could assist you with Adara's training if they wished, as your abilities each have their unique merits. *However*, I'm warning you," he pointed fingers at both brothers, "if I overhear so much as a whisper that you are doing something you shouldn't be, I will banish you to *Praeteritus*."

The look Leviathan sent Az prevented him from arguing. "We can train Adara, Luce; it's no problem. We won't do anything we aren't supposed to," Leviathan assured. "*Praeteritus* isn't fun at all, quite frankly a waste of time. Would be a shame if we were stuck in that loop for the next ten thousand years, right, Az?" He elbowed his sulking brother.

"Yes," Az grumbled. "It would be a waste of time."

"I'm fine with Leviathan," I told Lucifer. "I'll have to pass on this absolute *ray of sunshine*, though." I jutted my chin at Az.

"It's too late for that, Highness," Az said.

"I don't care. I don't want you."

"Well, you don't get to decide," Az retorted. "Your father does."

I flipped him off. "Well, *you* can shove it, Ass-modeus."

He sighed. "Real mature, as always."

Leviathan choked down a laugh. "Did she… did she call you Ass-modeus?"

Whirling to Lucifer, I gesticulated to Az. "You can't honestly expect me to stand being with *this* for longer than two seconds without trying to kill him." I wouldn't feel anything if I did; no guilt, no regret.

"Kill him with kindness?" Leviathan asked, almost hopeful.

I straightened my back, folding my arms over my chest. "I said what I said."

"Levi's going to be there to make sure *I* don't kill *you*," Az amended.

"*See?*" I whipped a hand out at him. "He has it out for me; I'm at a clear disadvantage."

Leviathan interposed himself between us. "I will be there to ensure the 'no killing' of each other."

Michael proposed himself again. "I can still do it, Your Grace."

"We've established you can't," Az dismissed. "Think it through, Luce. How is Adara going to focus on the task at hand with loverboy over here distracting her, not to mention his lack of qualifications?"

I spoke up. "I don't thi—"

"You make a fair point, Asmodeus," Lucifer acknowledged. "We'd not want her to fail right away, now would we?"

"I'll ask Zaze and Beel to help if they have time," Az informed him.

Lucifer shook his head. "Not Azazel, he's otherwise engaged. Lilith is in *Agarath* with hi—"

"Lilith?" I blurted, unable to control myself. "You mean the mother of daemons? The first female daemon?" I'd learned about her from a book I'd grabbed at home when my dad wasn't looking.

At home... my dad...

"People call her that even now?" Lucifer slouched in his throne, irritated. "You accidentally create your own type of daemon one time and everybody believes you're the ruler of daemons."

"So, she doesn't control all daemons, then?"

"Obviously not." He straightened, emanating authority. "*I* am the Emperor of Hell."

I sighed. "Great. Here we go again..."

"*I* am the one who controls the daemonic hoards born from the very darkness between the layers of Hell, created from the sins of mortals!"

"That sounds like an unnecessarily long way of saying 'no,'" I commented.

"I miss Lil a lot," Leviathan said, pouting. "It's been so long since I last saw her."

Lucifer abandoned his sovereign-crusading, or whatever that display of his was, to answer Leviathan. "She'll be glad to see you again." He gave Az a look and added, "You as well."

Although I wasn't thrilled by the prospect of Az training me, at least I'd be actually preparing instead of being thrown to the proverbial wolves. Plus, Leviathan would serve as a mediator, and I trusted him more than Az. "As riveting as this tangent was, do we have a deal?" I asked Lucifer. "I go through The Sixes and you fulfill my demands?"

He tipped his golden head. "Indeed."

"Okay, so how is this going to work? When do I start?"

His black and gold eyes settled on me. "Three."

"Three… what? Hours? Days? Weeks?"

"Two."

I looked to Michael in a panic. "What the Hell?"

"*Dara?*"

"One." Lucifer snapped.

I rushed forward. "*Michael—*"

The ground opened beneath my feet, devouring me whole.

CANTO XV

At Rock Bottom—*Literally*

Pitch black consumed my vision. The only indication I had that I wasn't free-falling through an abyss of nothingness came from the crunch of gravel beneath my feet. No warning, not a single one, and here I was, at the bottom of a *hole*.

I inhaled deeply and loosed a long exhale, eyeing the small light shining a few metres above. "It's okay. This is okay," I said aloud. "All I need to do is climb this… high wall… which I don't know how to do…"

School taught you a great number of things you'd never use again once you entered the real world, and it just so happened that rock-climbing was one of them. Unfortunately, there were no harnesses here and there certainly weren't any fun-coloured rocks to grab onto. I didn't have the skills for this. I had no upper body strength and no love for advanced cardio. I could barely see the damn walls.

"Fuck this!" I punched and kicked around me. "Fuck! Fuck! FUUUUCKKKK!" My palms met the walls, and I felt for breaks I could exploit.

There weren't any.

Claustrophobia had never been an issue for me before, but the proximity between my body and its tight surroundings was starting to pose a serious problem when panic was thrown in the mix. I placed my hands on opposite sides of the circle I was trapped in and tried to find a kind of anchor above me. When I did, I grabbed on and jumped. Every time I reached a couple of feet off the ground, I'd fall and have to restart.

Attempt after attempt, fall after fall, the more I failed, the more I began to familiarize myself with my seemingly invisible cage. I'd removed my jacket and positioned it in the area I knew the best to serve as a reference point.

My fifth try came and went, and I couldn't help feeling like the hole was growing deeper, that the light was moving further and further away from me. I set the terror of being stuck in this place aside and began my sixth attempt.

Faulty gripping stones were smooth, so the ones with the grooves were those I had to hold onto.

I shook out my arms, cracked my neck, and prepared for the climb. "Come on, Adara," I told myself. "Come on now."

Leaping up once again, my feet remained on either side of me against the walls. My hands shot out, gravitating to the anchors with the grooves. If I didn't find them fast enough, I could lose my balance and strength and would have to restart. I couldn't afford it, not with the light slowly distancing itself.

My deduction had been correct: the grooved rocks were sturdy.

As I drew closer to the light, my arms began to slacken, and the muscles in my legs burned as they upheld me. "I should've… worked out more," I panted. "Those annoying… gym bros… were right all along. N-never skip leg day."

Distracted by my outspoken thoughts, I reached for another rock, its surface smooth against my fingers. I barely managed to pull myself up a foot before it broke. My arms and legs extended as I fell. My hands ran down the jagged walls, and I dug my nails in until I'd halted. A broken gasp escaped my mouth while I replaced my body. My weight was turning against me. My arms couldn't take any more, and my palms stung like they'd been impaled with hundreds of small needles.

I sucked in the tears begging to be released, telling me to let go. "*No.* Stop being… so… weak," I groaned. The last thing I wanted was to fail the First Stage of The Sixes. It would definitely put a damper on my plans—and my eternity. "Think about the light."

The light. I was so close to it. A bit more. That was all I needed.

"Come on." I took two breaths and threw whatever energy I had left into my arms and legs. "Come… *on*!"

And I climbed. I moved from grooved rock to grooved rock until, finally, my pained hands grasped the edge of the opening. I popped my head out into the grey surface.

"Hello there, little Anti-Christ," a voice said.

I shrieked.

My fingers slipped off the edge.

At the last second, a pair of arms caught mine to haul me up. I laid on the stone-layered floor, gasping for air, my stomach ready to empty itself of its contents.

"I'd ask you if you were alright, although I can clearly see you're not," the voice remarked. Where had I heard a similar accent?

"That's—that's very," I gulped down more air, "observant of you." Turning onto my side, I was met by… checkered Vans? The stranger's shoes peeked out from beneath baggy khaki cargo pants in which he'd loosely tucked an equally baggy white shirt. He dressed like someone my age.

The stranger lent me a hand. “I didn’t mean to startle you.” His vibrant bronze hair claimed my attention almost immediately—and then there were his eyes. Currant-red and curious. Another of Az’s brothers. “You would be Luce’s daughter, yes? Never thought I’d say that.”

“Trust me,” I dusted myself off, “no one’s more disappointed than I am. He may be my biological father, but that’s about it as far as relations go.”

“I’m Mon.” His light beard framed his stunning smile. “Or Mammon for full, however I don’t use it as much.”

I returned the introduction: “I’m Adara.” I motioned around myself. “I assume you oversee this place, wherever ‘this place’ is. I feel like I’m in a dystopian movie. No offence.”

Multiple holes speckled the stone floor in the wide grey expanse, most of them sealed by a strange, almost breathing polymer. Near the one I’d been pulled from sat an extremely out-of-place living room with—atop a Persian carpet—a lamp on a wooden stand and a large armchair on which a laptop lay closed.

“None taken. And yes, this is my domain. You’re currently in the Bores of *Helvinat*,” Mon answered. “No doubt Luce thought it would be appropriate to start the First Stage of The Sixes in the Sixth Circle of Hell.”

Apparently Lucifer had an obsession with the number six. I couldn’t say I was surprised. Bad things happened whenever sixes were around.

"Honestly, I wasn't aware I'd be having someone brave The Sixes here, least of all Luce's own daughter," Mon continued. "It came as a surprise when he told me you would be in the Bores."

"You're not the only one." I rubbed my arms to soothe the pain lingering in my body. Speaking of surprise… "Alright, I have to mention it. What's with that?" I pointed to the setup near him.

"I figured I'd continue writing my book while waiting for you to get out."

Although I tried to hide how stunned I was, I failed. "You're a writer?"

"No need to sound so astonished." He laughed, lighthearted and airy. "You'll soon find not everything is what it seems down here. And yes, I suppose you can say I dabble with writing."

"Have you written many books?" I asked, genuinely curious.

He considered his answer, pursing his lips and looking upwards in thought. "Around two thousand and… I want to say twenty?"

"*Two thousand and twenty?*" I repeated.

"When you've been alive as long as I have, you've lots more material to work with." His setup disappeared at a snap of his fingers.

"*Woah.* How did you do that?"

"It's part of my abilities," he replied. "I can summon things and send them away as I please. Would you like anything? A drink, perhaps?"

As great as that sounded, my stomach was checked out for the foreseeable future, so I declined; I wasn't in a mood to throw up whatever I ingested.

"Maybe later then, though as of now, we really ought to get going. Your father should know you passed the First Stage." Mon crossed the stone floor and contoured the holes to the cloudy, sand-like wall behind him. With another step, he stuck to it, standing perpendicular to me. "Are you coming, little Anti-Christ?"

"I'd appreciate it if you wouldn't call me that," I told him. The nickname made terrible thoughts swirl in my mind. "And I'm not exactly Spiderman. I tend to walk on horizontal surfaces."

"Adara, I *am* on the horizontal surface."

"What do you—" His next snap left me falling toward him, and my landing threw sand into my face. "I don't think I'll be putting your Bores on my 're-visit' list." I got to my feet, coughing.

"Not a favourite, I see," Mon commented, and started guiding me down the narrowing path to a solitary metal door. "However, this is only a small part of Heresy. It's not always this gloomy, believe me."

While passing through the Bores, trapped bodies jumped and clawed at the polymeric covers, fighting to escape. Shrieks echoed in the static air when the forms plunged into darkness. A light smile came to my lips, and I scurried after Mon. Once we crossed the threshold, the door shut itself behind us. Mon left his palm hovering near the surface until large chains slithered over and locked themselves in place.

Afterwards, he shifted to me. "I trust you've ascendiated before."

"Not exactly," I confessed. "I did once by myself on accident."

"That's alright. We'll do it together, then." His wings emerged from his shoulder blades, the tips of his feathers burned at the bottom. They wrapped around, enclosing us within, and a steadily spinning sensation filled my head.

All of a sudden, the feeling stopped. When Mon retracted his wings, we found ourselves standing on the glass bridge leading to the castle in the centre of *Pravus*.

I stormed into the throne room with Mon close behind. Lucifer hadn't moved from his seat of power; he was talking and laughing with Az and Leviathan as if everything was all fine and dandy.

"Doll face!" Leviathan exclaimed as he saw me. His gleeful expression rapidly changed when he noticed mine. "*Uh oh*."

"I wasn't expecting you to have gotten out this soon, daughter," Lucifer admitted. "Mon, if I discover you sent a ladder down for her, I'm going to be quite upset."

"I didn't," he answered. "She climbed out by herself."

"That means you successfully completed your First Stage, Adara," Leviathan said, clapping. "Congr—"

"Thanks. I hope I get a heads-up for the next ones instead of being *dropped into the middle of nowhere!*" Anger poured from me in blistering waves, directed at Lucifer alongside my shout. "What happened to the so-called 'training'?"

Az, seated on the dais' steps, frowned. "That is, regrettably, still happening."

"You didn't need training for this," Lucifer claimed.

"I know you haven't been part of my life *at all* but, just to let you know, I don't rock-climb recreationally."

"You passed," Az said, once again not contributing anything useful to the conversation. "I don't see the point in complaining."

"Nobody asked you, Ass-modeus," I sneered.

Mon snickered. "I believe I will be using that nickname from here on out."

"Try and I'll finish burning your wings," Az threatened.

"Pissy as always, I see," Mon remarked. "Some things never change."

Leviathan pointed at the two. "Both of you cut it out. I don't want to do this again."

Based on what I'd seen of him before now, Leviathan intervening like this seemed out of character. Given the looks of his brothers, and his own exasperation, he'd done this multiple times. The tension between Mon and Az rendered the atmosphere in the room cold and unforgiving.

"If my presence is no longer required, I'll be on my way," Mon announced, his tone tight. He nodded to me once in parting and headed to the doors.

"If you're planning on returning to *Helvinat*, you might want to let your High Order know you'll be in *Pravus* for a while," Lucifer advised. "I'll need to consult with you for a couple of Stages." Since Mon didn't answer, Lucifer sent Leviathan after him. Then, he turned his focus over to me. "Now to answer your concerns: for the remaining Stages, you will be receiving notices before they occur. Under most circumstances, I wouldn't have done this; however, due to your lack of training, I've made an exception."

"How generous of you," I drawled.

Ten daemons appeared from the pillars to my left, tall and skeleton-like.

"That's all for the moment," Lucifer dismissed. "Asmodeus, can you put her in some quarters in the Guest Wing? I'd rather she not bother me."

He's the gift that keeps on giving, huh?

"Great. I'm a servant now too, am I?" Az stood and descended the stairs. "Let's go."

I stepped out of his path and followed as he directed us out of the throne room and through the halls of dark glass. "What's got you this pissed?" I asked. His scowl wasn't the most subtle. "Can't just be because of me."

He didn't answer.

"Mon really got to you, didn't he?"

"Mon?" Az scoffed. "Did he tell you to call him that?"

"Yeah, he did. He's pretty cool. He has this whole thing going for him. For one: he dresses well. For two: he can summon stuff out of thin air. And for three: he writes. How awesome is—"

Az's features curdled with each word I spoke.

"Okay, *what* is the deal with you guys?" To say I was curious as to what had happened between them would be the understatement of the year.

"Nothing."

I motioned to the way we'd come from. "Well, the tension back there was through the roof."

Az screeched to a halt, rounding on me. "It is *none* of your damn business. Keep your nose out of it, and we won't have a problem."

I nodded in challenge. "Oh, but it was fine when you were prying into my relationship with Michael, is that it?"

"*Adara?*" I'd barely had the time to turn around. In a second, I was wrapped in Michael's arms. "You made it." His body relaxed around mine, relieved. "You have no idea how worried I was."

"I'm here." I ran my hand down his hair. "I'm still here."

Unsurprisingly, Az ruined the moment. "Don't you have somewhere to be, Lamont?"

I'd almost forgotten he was present until he spoke.

"No, as it turns out, I don't," Michael answered, parting from me. "Mammon and Levi relieved me from my post since Adara had passed her First Stage."

"Aren't you fortunate," Az muttered.

Michael ignored him. "Where are you going, Dara?"

I side-eyed Az. "Lucifer's making this one bring me to my 'quarters.'"

"I can take you," Michael offered.

"I'm perfectly capable of doing it myself," Az said.

"You didn't even want to do it in the first place," I reminded him.

"Perfect! Then I'll take over," Michael said.

A muscle in Az's jaw twitched. "What don't you understand by Lucifer made me—"

"Okay, you know what? I don't care who brings me," I interrupted. "Now can we go?"

Michael severed the strange staring contest he and Az were engaged in, and started in the direction in which I'd previously been headed. More hallways similar to the one I'd been travelling down with Az appeared, only to break into others to the left and right. From what I could see, most of them had no end.

"This place is a maze," I said to Michael as we turned to the right.

"I know. I got lost the first time I was brought here," he admitted. "Silas made me memorize a floor plan so I wouldn't get lost again."

"Who's Silas?"

"He was in charge of my Satanial training when I was brought to *Pravus*," Michael replied, hesitant. "He's the High Order, the Rijaik."

"Ah." I had no High Order job description; all I knew was that my dad had been one.

Although I'd said I didn't care who would bring me to my room, I had begun to rethink my answer. Instead of leaving like I thought he would, Az had followed us.

Can you go away? I sent into Az's mind while Michael continued speaking. *Stop following me.*

I'm not 'following you,' he answered. *I'm going to my room too.*

A dry chuckle escaped me; I covered it with a cough when Michael gave me a confused look. *You have your own room here?* I returned. *What? You and Lucifer have sleepovers? You guys braid each other's hair?*

Hardy-har-har. How ever did you find out?

Michael came to a stop in front of a door. "And we're here. Dara, this is your room." He veered to Az, and said, "I'm pretty sure you can find something useful to do with your time. Perhaps a calming facemask to help with those frown lines."

I laughed at Michael's comment even though it wasn't fully accurate. Az did frown and scowl and glower a lot, however there was no mark of it on his face, smooth and cold as carefully sculpted marble.

"Your association with her doesn't give you complete immunity," Az told him, giving me a cursory glance. "You would do well to remember that."

"And *you* would do well to go away," I interjected. Opening the door behind myself, I ushered Michael into the room and entered right after. "Bye-bye now."

From the other side, Az shouted, "Training room when you wake up, Adara. Don't be late!" His footsteps faded with his retreat.

Finally, Michael and I were alone.

"Mind giving me a tour?" I asked, hoping he would stay with me for a little while longer.

Recognizing that, he advanced, extending an arm to the left. "As you can see, we've entered into your very own private lounge."

An upholstered couch with a high, ornamented back lay in front of a pseudo-fireplace crafted of the same material as the castle itself but boasted gilded detailing near the opening where flames flickered without wood. The elaborate bronze clock on the mantle, between two candelabra and below a giltwood mirror, didn't tick, seemingly having trouble keeping the time.

Michael ran his hand over the couch's embroidered maroon velvet. "This was taken by Mammon from Henry the 8th in 1510 along with the table at its back."

I burst into laughter at his auctioneer imitation. Whether he was being serious or not about whole 'Henry the 8th' bit, I had no clue; either way, seeing him like this was nice. Familiar.

Next, Michael led me through the door on my immediate left. "Here's the bathroom."

"There are running showers and toilets here? Isn't everyone dead? How does—" I abandoned my question. "Shit, Michael, I'm sorry. That was so insensitive."

He shrugged. "I'm kind of used to it at this point." He went to sit on King Henry's couch. "These rooms are mostly for Daemon Princes and, well, Princesses now, I guess. You're more alive than Satanials, anyways. Substantial bodies and all."

I took the spot beside him. "Seems as though there are a lot of logistics to being in Hell."

"Honestly, yeah. I was lucky that Belphegor and Lucifer got me out of *Balnara* before *Pradzios*." A light shudder ran through him.

"What's that?"

"Another logistic. It's a term used among Satanials and daemons to describe what happens to a soul as soon as it reaches its designated Circle," he explained. "*Pradzios* means—"

"The Beginning?"

He nodded. "The process souls go through where they begin the stages of eternal damnation. Essentially, they re-live their most recent sins up until their death. Once it's over, they're tortured and drown in their own nightmares forever."

That wasn't at all *terrifying*. It was only for the rest of their existence…

"Why did Belphegor and Lucifer pull you out?" I wondered. "Do you know?"

He shook his head. "They didn't explicitly tell me why, but I'm starting to think, on some level, your father did it for you and it's why I'm in *Pravus*."

Highly doubtful. My father hadn't cared enough about me to tell me the truth of who I was, let alone save a person I loved from eternal damnation. He had an ulterior motive. I could feel it.

"And now you're a Satanial," I continued. "I'll be honest, I don't necessarily understand what that means."

"Satanials are less than the Living yet more than the souls," Michael clarified. "What happens is souls are chosen by Lucifer to represent him. If you're chosen, it means he saw a desirable quality in you that would make you a perfect soldier for the Circles."

So there had been an ulterior motive; Lucifer had seen something in Michael. The question remained as to what it could be.

"Why would Lucifer need soldiers?" I asked. "Is he planning a war of some kind?"

"When I arrived in *Pravus*, I asked Silas the same thing. Just because we're in Hell, it doesn't mean there's no order. Satanials have multiple ranks, each confined to their own specific tasks and obligations. There are High Orders, or Rijaik, Primae and Zemas."

"What's the difference?"

"The High Orders are the highest ranking Satanials," he answered. "They report directly to Lucifer straight from their Circles and operate under their respective Daemon Prince, filling in as leader from time to time. The Primae—that's my order, by the way—" Michael pointed to the bronze mark on his uniform, "report to the Rijaik. We're also in charge of keeping daemons in line—even though they have their own hierarchy—and overseeing the Zemas execute their tasks while working alongside them."

"And the Zemas?"

"They torture souls, ensuring they feel the full weight of their sins as punishment."

"Do… do *all* Satanials torture souls?"

"Mostly the Primae, Zemas and daemons handle it. The High Orders tend to not do it as much because of their responsibilities with organization and delegation according to their Daemon Prince's commands. Daemon Princes, though? They do it as they please; it's how they are."

I tugged on the hair wrapped around my fingers. "Did you torture a soul?"

Michael gave a solemn nod. "It's the test that determines if you're ready to be accepted as a Satanial. If you refuse, you return to the soul being tortured. Thankfully I don't do it much… the torturing and stuff. I usually assist Silas or make sure the other Satanials are doing their jobs."

My voice came out small. "I'll have to do that, won't I? It'll be one of The Sixes."

"I'd be lying if I said no. The Sixes aren't set Stages," he informed me. "They vary with every Satanial who tries to pass through them."

Despite not wanting to, I had to ask. I had to know the odds. "Do a lot of Satanials pass? Do they usually… make it? To the end?"

"The last Satanial who tried was from *Varmir* over a hundred years ago, I heard. Khue reached the final Stage." Michael paused, unsure whether or not to resume.

My hands dropped into my lap. "And?"

"It'd been so gruelling that her soul just… dissolved, and she wasn't able to reform in *Praeteritus*."

I shouldn't have asked. I should've stayed ignorant for as long as possible.

"That rarely ever happens, though," Michael added to reassure me. "Most Satanials who go through The Sixes fail and go back to serving."

"W-what happens if I don't pass them?" I whispered. "I made you a promise. My parents… I made them a promise too."

"Then at least you would have tried, Dara." Michael squeezed my hands. "They'll know that. *I* know that. And as for now," his eyes met mine, "you're here with me and that's all that matters."

The way he'd spoken the consolation, the look that crossed his face when he'd told me I was all that mattered… Our circumstances had drastically changed, yet our old pattern hadn't. The memory and hope of us hadn't gone when Michael had.

My name left him, brimming with remorse and sadness, and his thumb brushed against my cheek. "I can't even begin to explain how much I regret what I said to you, the things we said to each other… from before…" His shame could've been a fourth person in the room, sitting by my own. "I was weak and scared, and I should've known better. You're not what you think you are." Michael wiped away my tears, born of my relief at his words. "I'm sorry for everything, Dara. I am."

"So am I, Michael," I murmured.

His red-circled eyes settled on my shadowed ones, so different yet shining as they had that day in my kitchen when he'd given me his heart. Despite knowing what I had done to my parents, despite what I'd done to him, and despite my corrupted blood, he still loved me.

I placed a light kiss on his mouth, and withdrew slightly, memorizing his features. "I never thought I'd be able to see you again, to feel you again." My hand drew to his chest where his heart should've been beating, curling at the strange sensation whispering in my ear.

Michael's lips touched mine. "*Te extrañé*, Dara."

"I missed you too."

CANTO XVI

Sometimes I Wish I Could Sink into Nothingness

Whatever pieces of myself that had shattered at Michael's death gathered, placed in their designated compartments by his own hands. What else could I care about right now when he and I were this close again, when we could erase my mourning together?

The noise in my mind quieted, exchanged for the memories of simpler times introduced by him, by us. And so, I kicked off my boots and made quick work of his jacket, tossing it to the floor. He reached for the hem of my shirt, pulling it over my head, and a puff of dirt—courtesy of my First Stage—rose into the air when it landed on the ground. My hand slipped to his neck, drawing him toward me as I reclined onto the couch. I kissed the tip of his nose, followed by the corner of his mouth. Michael angled himself to complete our joining, his desire agonizing. And how agonizing was it for me at the reminder that what I touched now, what this emanated from, was his soul.

Michael laughed into me, and I breathed him in. "You might actually be late for training."

"Then I'll be late," I replied, indifferent. The sight of Az's face if I walked into his training lessons late flashed in my mind—his stupid, statuesque, allegedly perfect features warped with disappointment and irritation.

Good, I thought. *He can choke on it.*

Michael's hand dipped between us, unbuttoning my jeans. A gasp stole from my lips when his fingers slid into my underwear, and he grinned against my mouth. I hurried to push down his pants.

Highness, would you mind not opening this line while fucking your boyfriend? Az said. *It'd be very much appreciated. Oh, and you better not be late for training.*

A stunned yelp caught in my throat, and I froze. Michael retreated, and I sat upright, clutching at my face burning from mortification. I'd unintentionally opened the communication between Az and I while Michael was—*oh no.*

Way to kill the mood.

"Dara? What is it?" Michael asked, concerned.

I fake-massaged my shoulder. "I hurt my back pretty badly earlier in the Bores." They'd both been genuinely hurting, although the pain had faded since then.

He swore. "Did I hurt you? I didn't mean to."

Shit. I felt terrible lying to him like this, but I could've never explained what had actually happened.

"Don't worry about it. I think it'd be best if I rested, though." I fixed my jeans, found my shirt and put it on. "Plus, I have training tomorrow or whenever I wake up—time is weird here—and I know it kind of sounded like I didn't care, but I actually do. I can't be caught as unprepared as I was for the First Stage, so... *yup.*"

Michael moved to the edge of the couch, returning his feet to the floor. "No, yeah, of course I completely understand. This is a big deal." He stood to fix his pants, grabbed his jacket to cover his bare chest, and kissed my cheek. "I'll let you rest."

I wanted him to *stay*. I wanted him to talk to me until I fell asleep, to listen to his voice as I did when he used to sneak into my room from my window.

I held onto his forearm, murmuring, "I don't remember telling you to leave."

He smiled. "You want me to stay?" At my nod, he hugged me, pressing his lips to the top of my head. "Then I will."

As my arms wrapped around him, welcoming his familiarity, an unknown feeling weighed on me. A missing piece amongst those we'd gathered. Michael was a Satanial now, I recalled, and we were in Hell together, both of us not exactly human anymore.

Michael and I passed through the arch to the left of the entryway leading to an alcove where a wide bed sat on a crimson carpet trimmed in gold, similar to the tassels on the black curtains draping from the canopy and those on the roll pillows laying on the brocaded duvet. The flames in the sconces mounted on the patterned walls strengthened when we entered, reflecting off the gilded mirrors hanging on either wall atop a commode—ornamented with vases and statuettes—and a vanity, alongside landscapes of what I could only assume to be the Circles.

I lay on the bed, flipping toward him and drawing nearer. "Do Satanials sleep?"

"The dead don't rest," he answered.

But he could. If I passed The Sixes, he wouldn't need to be this anymore. Everything would go back to how it once was.

I rested my cheek on his shoulder. "Are the others not going to wonder where you are? Your dismissal from your post won't last…"

"It doesn't matter," he said, sighing. "*Estoy dónde quiero estar.*"

Eventually, I nodded off to the sound of Michael's voice, disappearing into a dreamless sleep for I wasn't sure how long. By the time I'd woken up, Michael had gone, both from the bed and my rooms.

As if on cue, the front door clicked open and he walked in. "Hey, you're finally awake. I thought you'd sleep forever."

"So did I," I said with a laugh. My eyes drew to folded fabric in his arms. "Whatcha got there?"

He held up a uniform similar to the one he wore, tossing it to me. "I passed by the supplies' storage to get something for you to train in, obviously."

I thanked him and went to change. While dressing, reluctance coursed through me at knowing I'd have to deal with Az after what he'd heard between Michael and me. This wouldn't end well, I could feel it.

Once I'd zipped my uniform, I glanced at myself in the mirror above the commode. The shiny black symbol of Lucifer and his Satanials shone on my chest, over my heart, and knife sheaths were sewn into the outer-thigh portion of the pants. Would I have to use knives to train? It hardly seemed necessary.

After tying my hair into a loose braid, I found Michael on the couch. He handed me my boots. "I'm worried," I confessed, doing up the laces beside him.

"Don't be. This is just training." He got to his feet. "It's like when you used to help me study. Do you remember?" I nodded and mirrored him.

"You learn the material and then apply what you've learned to a given situation. In this case, it would be your Stages."

"Tell me you're staying with me," I pleaded, burying my face into his neck as I hugged him. "Only for this session."

Disappointment tinted his tone. "I tried convincing Silas, but he'd received orders from Lucifer already. He's assigned me a position with the *Yrirmah* daemons in the lower *Paxtara* faction."

"I'll pretend to know what that all is," I said. "If you can't stay with me, could you at least walk me to wherever I'm supposed to go? I don't think I could make it there by myself."

"Yeah, sure. It's on my way. Come on." Michael and I left my rooms, and he led me through the castle halls, down the winding staircase, past the front doors, and out into the smothering heat of *Pravus*.

"Where is it we're going, exactly?" I asked once we'd crossed the bridge, heading into the across tunnel.

Michael nearly disappeared into the dark. "*Pravus* Satanials have their own training grounds," he explained. "The room hasn't been used in a while, though. Apparently, I was the first to be trained in about sixty-five years. It's probably completely off-limits now since you'll be using it."

The right wall of the corridor fell away, revealing a cave whose rock barbs protruding from above and below loomed, rows of teeth in a gaping maw. Shouting uniform-clad bodies surrounded multiple circles established across the unlevelled space; within these were the fighters, some wielding swords and knives, and others pure brute force.

I slowed at the makeshift ledge. "What is this place?"

"This is part of *Yranta*," Michael answered. "Essentially, here, Satanials and daemons can challenge one another for the best positions and souls to torture in *Pravus*. It's a tradition of sorts that Lucifer and Silas have allowed." He pointed at a larger circle with more spectators where a Satanial faced off against a horned daemon. "Kira Kano's fighting Labolas again. I'll definitely be seeing her in *Paxtara* after this. I seriously don't know why Labolas keeps trying. He always loses against her."

We continued on our way, encountering Satanials with black symbols on their chests, same as I had; they nodded to Michael while passing by, acknowledging his rank.

"Those were Zemas Satanials," he mentioned, "if you were wondering."

We turned into another tunnel, arriving at a set of doors made of material similar to that of the castle which Michael opened for me. The training room's right wall spanned at least fifty metres, lined with swords, axes, maces, knives and targets, whereas wrought iron stairs on the left climbed to a balcony overlooking the main training area. At the far end, in front of a sizable lancet window whose obsidian tracery above formed grinning grotesques, Az observed the combat circles. He'd exchanged his cut coat for a long-sleeved turtleneck, loose and tucked into his pleated trousers cinched at the waist by a belt, its buckle gold like the pendant around his neck and his small hoop earrings, partly visible through his hair; he'd tied it into a small bun at the back of his head, however a few wavy strands had escaped, resting on his expressionless face.

"Lamont!" a woman called from the doors. It was Kira, the Satanial who'd been fighting the daemon. "*Paxtara* isn't going to look after itself, you know."

Michael faced her, remarking, "Labolas lost again."

"I'll tell you all about it on the way," she promised, laughing. "It was more interesting than the last time, and I'll let you guess who I'm torturing for the next thousand years. Hint: it's a *Pope*."

Michael nodded. "I'm coming." He turned to me. "*Nos vemos luego*, okay, Dara?"

Az's attention bearing down on me sent every muscle in my body to tense, and Leviathan wasn't here yet. A trenchant silence stretched.

"Don't leave me alone with him," I pleaded in a whisper, eyeing Az over my shoulder.

"Levi is going to show soon. You'll be fine." Michael kissed my cheek in encouragement, but the gesture gave me no sense of comfort. "I'll come get you when you're done."

Before Michael left, Az greeted Kira. She bowed her head, then flashed him a flirtatious smile. I would've rolled my eyes if he hadn't descended the steps to meet me. "You arrived late."

"How can I possibly be late if I don't know how time works here? Besides, that eighteenth-century clock in my room doesn't work."

"Perhaps you'd be on time," Az began, poised for a strike, "if you didn't waste it having sex with your sanctimonious dead boyfriend instead of taking this seriously."

Embarrassment twisted in my stomach. "I *am* taking—"

"Look, I don't care *what* or *who* you do in your free time, as long as you remember there's a reason you're here. Oh, and," he spared me a glance, "don't make me hear about it, no matter if you're thinking of me while he's with you or not."

I shook off my fluster to reply, "I am taking this seriously, as I was saying, and if I was having sex—with someone who loves me, by the way—I certainly wouldn't be thinking of you."

Az approached. With every step he took toward me, I took the same amount in reverse… until a pillar beneath the balcony halted my movement. "Well, your mind wouldn't have linked to mine unless you were." He levelled his head with my ear, close enough to hear my blood slow. "That, and I certainly wouldn't have heard your weak moans."

"Hello, my beautiful people!" Leviathan greeted, strolling through the training room doors. When Az rapidly withdrew from me, his brother asked, "What's going on in here? Have I interrupted something?" A suggestive grin grew on his face. "Do I sense sexual tension?"

"Ew." I grimaced. "The only tension here is between me and the wall of weapons I'd like to test out on your brother."

Leviathan laughed. "That's the first time Az has gotten a reaction like that, that's for sure."

"How, oh *how*, will he ever recover from such a devastating blow?" I ignored Az's glare burning at the back of my head to add: "I was starting to think you wouldn't show, Leviathan."

He halted in front of the wall of weapons, scanning each section. "*Ugh*, don't call me that. It's what your father calls me when he's mad at me."

"Alright… uh... Levi?"

He beamed at the use of his nickname. "Much better. Now how about—"

The patter of footsteps entering the room de-railed his train of thought, originating from a newcomer. The handsome man's curly, near-black hair was pushed in a side-part, barely reaching past the shoulders of his beige coat. His lack of uniform—evident by his flowy black button-down, jeans and ankle boots—and red eyes indicated he was another of Az and Levi's brothers.

"Oh, look who it is, mates," Levi said to Az and me, faking a British accent. "Back from, what? The thousandth trip to England, innit bruv?"

"Ha ha, very funny, you arse. Not like I've heard that one before." His reply revealed traces of a British accent. "Now what's all this I heard from a *Renjahj* daemon about Wesley breaking into your flat?"

CANTO XVII

Knives, Sin City, and Andy Warhol

W*hat?*" Levi ran a hand through his hair. Then, he snapped his fingers, suddenly remembering, "I forgot to change the passcode. I'm so stupid."

"Nobody's arguing with you on that," Az said.

"Yeah," Levi nodded, smiling in a mocking and exaggerated manner, "shut up." He pointed to his other brother. "Is there anything else, Asta?"

The Daemon Prince's brows knitted together. "They also mentioned some bit about Wesley taking your favourite painting?"

Levi gasped. "Not my *Caravaggio*!" His wings unfurled in one smooth motion. Where Az's were a cloak of otherworldly darkness and Mon's appeared plush except for the burned sections at the bottom (courtesy of Az, apparently), Levi's black feathers were silky and glistened with each turn. He extended a hand to the window at the end of the room. Not a second later, a rift opened within it. Clearly, he and Az shared the same method of ascendiating. "I'm going to deal with this. I'll come back soon, but Asta, take my place in the meantime, alright?"

Before his brother could answer, Levi's wings propelled him forward into the dimensional portal, which closed once he'd gone through.

"That was cool," I said to no one in particular.

Az shrugged, aloof, and went to meet Asta, whose full name I assumed was Astaroth. In a shocking turn of events, Az *hugged* him. An actual hug occurred in front of me. Considering how he acted around Levi and with Mon, this was a rare display of affection I didn't realize he was capable of.

"How long's it been since we last saw each other?" Astaroth asked.

"Since Vegas in '91." An endearing smile brightened Az's face, illuminating his haunting beauty in a way I suspected I would never see again.

Asta laughed and clapped Az on the shoulder. "Those were good times." His wine-red eyes shifted to me afterwards. "Oh, where are my manners? Hello, I'm Astaroth, Daemon Prince of *Varmir*, the Seventh Circle of Hell."

"What a mouthful," I joked.

"It is, isn't it? I prefer Asta. And you must be Adara." He offered a warm, welcoming smile and hugged me. "I've heard quite a lot about you already."

Although his embrace caught me off-guard, I returned it. "Nice to meet you, too. What have you heard about me so far, if you don't mind me asking?"

Asta and I broke apart. "I wasn't aware Luce had a daughter. It would appear he only told a select few." He eyed Az momentarily, without any detectable resentment. "I also heard about what happened to Samantha and Kamael. My deepest condolences."

His sincerity rang hollow against the very worst of my thoughts. "I don't deserve them; I'm the one who killed my parents in the first place."

"It was an accident, Adara, caused by your lack of information, that's all," he reassured. "You're incredibly brave and dedicated for doing this—

" he gestured around the training room "—willing to be trained as a Satanial to go through The Sixes for them. These Stages aren't famous for being easy."

"Yeah, I've heard that. What kind of daughter would I be if I didn't at least try, though? I know they weren't my biological parents, but they raised me and loved me as their own." At the threat of resurfacing memories, I blinked away the tears stinging my eyes and chuckled afterwards to lighten the mood. "I hope the training will be easier in comparison."

"Right," Az said. "The key word here is 'training,' and since we don't know when Levi is returning, Asta, you're helping."

"Brilliant." Asta rubbed his hands together in anticipation. "What are we working on?"

"Oh, you're going to enjoy this one." Az neared the wall of weapons, selecting three knives; he sheathed two and tossed the last to me.

At me, more like.

My rapid dodging left the knife to hit the pillar at my back. "*Hey!* Free etiquette lesson for you: normal people don't randomly toss knives at others."

"How fortunate we're not normal nor people, then."

"Ah-ha-ha-ha, you're *hilarious*." My hand gripped onto the hilt, pulling the knife from where it was embedded. The black blade shone, hinting at the red filigree in the unique metal. "How is this going to help me? I don't underst—"

"Of course you wouldn't understand. You've been here for hardly five seconds," Az interjected. "It just so happens that this," he pointed to the knife I held, "is how the majority of Zemas Satanials torture their souls and it's one of the first skills they learn down here."

My mouth went dry. "Torture a soul?"

"Don't worry about that yet," Asta said. "For now, we'll teach you the basics. How's that sound?"

"I think that'd be alright," I said, albeit still worried.

"I'm fine with it as long as she can beat any of the Satanials out there once we're done here." Az tilted his head toward the window, where past it lay Hell's soldiers battling for positions throughout *Pravus* and its districts.

"Wait a minute." A nervous laugh fell from my lips. "Who said anything about doing that?"

Az looked around, then back to me. "I did. Right now."

"I'm a little concerned, you know, considering the fact those Satanials have way more experience than me."

"And your point is…?"

"I'll get *crushed*," I told him. "It'll be humiliating."

A shit-eating grin spread on his mouth. "It likely will be."

"You want to see me fail, don't you?" I accused.

"I mean, it might be entert—"

Asta's loud claps cleaved our argument apart. "If I could have your attention, please! We ought to return to the task at hand, oughtn't we?"

"Yes, we should," Az agreed, leaving, "and since you're the expert, I'll let you take it away."

With his back facing me, I flipped him off. Using *both* hands, knife and all.

Asta said nothing, simply positioning himself in front of the last of the targets nailed to the first half of the pillars supporting the balcony. "What do you intend to do in the meantime, Az?"

He stationed himself on the stairs. "I'll sit, observe, and offer input every now and again."

I stood next to Asta, mumbling, "Sit and judge, more like."

"I heard that," Az said.

Asta removed his beige jacket and tossed it at his brother. "Catch!"

Az caught and waved it about. "*Hey!* I am not a coat rack."

"Could've fooled me," Asta countered, teasing. "Now, Az, mate, I'm going to need you to hush it up. You're disturbing me. Coat racks don't speak."

I snickered, muttering, "*A coat rack.*"

Venom brimmed in Az's eyes as they flicked to me. "You're going to regret that."

"*Oh no.*" I lifted my free hand, purposely shaking it. "Look, I'm so scared. I'm shaking!"

"You know, I quite like her," a grinning Asta commented.

Az didn't need to reply to his brother on my subject when his grimness spoke louder.

Asta claimed my attention. "Alright, Adara, let's get into it, shall we?"

"Aren't you getting a knife?" I noticed he didn't have one.

He chuckled softly, then swung his right arm. The sound of unsheathed metal sang, and a steel dagger appeared from his forearm, falling into his palm.

My jaw slacked. "*No. Way.* That is the coolest thing I've ever seen!"

"You're easily impressed," Az remarked from where he sat, patronizing.

"Not by your shit manners, I'm not," I replied.

Asta playfully rolled his eyes. "Az, stop being such a wet blanket and let the lovely girl compliment me, would you?"

Az stared at him, brow arched. "'Wet blanket?', 'Lovely girl?' Whose Gran did you steal those from?"

"Look, I can make a mean cup of Earl Grey," Asta answered, unaffected by his brother's quip. "I'd say I'd fix you one, but Adara and I in the middle of something right now, so do me a solid and shut your pie hole, please. Much appreciated." He flipped the knife in his hand.

I pointed at it. "How did you do that? The knife-arm-thingy."

"Perks of having these kinds of powers." He handed his knife to me; I accepted it, sliding the one Az had thrown at me in the holder on my thigh. "I prefer the knives to the daemon form any day."

I blinked. "One more time: '*daemon form?*'"

Asta confirmed it. "With the passing years in Hell, those who fell with Lucifer began to develop shapes contrary to our celestial forms, reflecting the very creatures we walked amongst and ruled over as a punishment for our 'betrayal.'"

My initial curiosity dissipated at the underlying threat of his innocent answer; the possibility *I* might have a daemon form terrified me beyond comprehension. For my internal darkness to translate to my exterior… People had already called me a monster when I appeared human.

Rather than ask for more information as I probably would've done in usual circumstances, I steered the conversation to continue with the lesson, desperate to distract myself. Asta obliged and started me off relatively easy by focusing on target practice.

At least, I *tried* to focus, but still unsettled and unfamiliar with what I was doing, my knives kept hitting the wooden bracings of the pillars instead of the target.

"I haven't seen throwing this horrendous since that time we went to Vegas, Asta," Az mentioned. He hadn't moved from the steps, watching his brother and me with his chin in hand.

"She's not gotten used to it yet, is all," Asta said. "And I remember that holiday quite differently than you do, I reckon."

Az half-laughed. "I'd be surprised if you remember any of it at all."

"I don't know if I should be offended or not," I said, accepting the next knife Asta produced. The one from my holder was currently tip-down, stuck in the wooden floor.

"I meant no offense," Asta said.

Sensing an opportunity, I said: "You can always make it up to me."

"How so?"

"If I get this knife in the centre of the target" —I pointed to it— "you guys tell me about this *incredible* Vegas trip. Deal?"

"You haven't gotten one remotely close to the target," Az reminded me.

My gaze flicked between him and Asta. "You boys should have nothing to worry about then, right?"

Asta looked to his brother. "We have a deal," he agreed.

We shook on it.

"Perfect. Now go ahead and take a seat."

Asta did, settling in next to Az, who leaned over to whisper, "This should be interesting."

Oh, I was counting on it. My curiosity was a powerful motivator, but not as powerful as my spite. And I planned on having Az eat his words. To do this properly, I had to clear my mind entirely and go through the steps Asta had taught me.

First was my stance, for which my back needed to be straight and the rest of my body relaxed. My right foot was put forward and the left placed slightly behind.

Second step was arranging my grip. I held the knife like a hammer and kept my thumb on top of my other fingers.

Third step was aiming. I envisioned the knife's tip meeting the objective before pointing the blade upwards and taking a deep breath. Once I was focused and sure of myself, I loosed the knife.

The metal wobbled from sheer force as it hit the target's dead centre.

When I turned, Az and Asta were gaping, although only the latter was impressed. I ambled over to the steps, sitting in front of the brothers. "So, how was Vegas in the nineties?" I inquired, tone sickeningly innocent.

Az couldn't wrap his brain around what I had done. "I—how did you… this isn't—"

"A deal's a deal," I reminded him.

"She's right, Az. We did agree to it." Asta leaned back, flourishing a hand. "Go on."

"Why am *I* the one who has to do it?" Az protested.

"Think about it, mate. It'd make no sense for me to tell a story I'm scarcely able to remember. Not to mention you," Asta poked his brother, "were the least sloshed. It's only logical that you tell it. *However*, I will jump in if I happen to recall any details. Fair?"

Admittedly, I had low expectations when it came to the probability of Az going through with this, especially since he was notoriously private about 'his business' and his family (or mostly about Mon, it seemed), yet he sighed loudly and said, "I'll preface by saying I might not remember every single detail either because that *entire* trip was a complete blur. Essentially, Belial persuaded Beelzebub, Asta and I into going to Vegas with him this one year as a vacation of sorts. It didn't take a lot of convincing for Beel since he loves the make-or-break of gambling."

"Az and I stupidly went because we thought it would be fun," Asta added.

Az? Fun? I find that hard to believe...

"We're not an hour into being at Caesar's Palace and we're already babbling and not walking straight," Az continued. "Asta's drank half of the bar—"

"I lost count after my third pint, I believe," Asta commented.

Az tapped his shoulder. "And you decided to show off your knife-throwing skills in the middle of the bar. The Living thought you were a performer from *Cirque du Soleil* who came to the hotel. You'd been aiming for a... stuffed ram's head, I think... but it ricocheted and hit an Elvis impersonator."

"In his *arse*!" Asta shouted, bursting into a fit of giggles. His laughter encouraged my own. "I remember that! What was it we did afterwards? Was it Belial almost marrying the stripper? What was his name? Jourdan?"

Who would've thought? Daemon Princes were, to an extent, quite human too.

"That came later." Az's brows furrowed. "Beel was on his twelfth shot, I was finishing up another whiskey and then Belial…" His eyes livened. "That was when he got *the idea*."

Thoroughly entertained and intrigued, I urged, "What idea?"

"A fully inebriated Belial thought it would be a good idea to convince Beel to get a tattoo."

Asta buried his head in his hands. "Oh no. This part I could never forget no matter what." He raked back his curls, looking to Az. "Should we be telling her this?"

"Tell me what?" I sat up straight. "Now you have to say it. You can't leave me on cliff-hanger."

Asta pointed at his brother. "If you tell her, I am not to blame, or if Beel finds out, I shall deny everything."

Shaking my clasped hands and pouting, I begged, "Please tell me, Az."

For a fraction of a second, his eyes widened. He consented. "Belial convinced Beel to get tattooed by his favourite artist: Andy Warhol."

My shoulders sank. "Wasn't Andy Warhol dead by the 1990s?"

"He was, but Beel wasn't aware of it, was he?"

"You guys didn't…"

Az's hand found his chest. "*I* didn't do anything." A hint of a smile touched his lips. "Belial's powers are centralized around shapeshifting, you see, so he transformed into Andy Warhol. Beel lost his mind. He couldn't believe 'Andy' was going to tattoo him."

"And he didn't notice anything strange at all?"

"That's the best part," Asta said, breaking his vow of silence on the matter. "He was so off his face that his empath abilities weren't working properly."

Az faced Asta. "What happened to you not talking about this topic?"

"I won't say anything else after this, I swear. Do continue."

Az's doubtful expression came and went, and he resumed: "Since Beel wasn't able to sense 'Andy's' feelings, he had no idea it was Belial in disguise. By then, we'd started placing bets to see how long it would take for Beel to figure out what we'd done."

I motioned between him and Asta. "You placed bets on your own brother?"

"We place bets on everything," Az informed me. "Belial wagered Beel wouldn't notice until we returned to Hell, but I said he would definitely notice when he came to in his hotel room."

"And?" I prompted.

"Asta and Belial had come my room to talk about it when Beel burst in wearing only a towel. That's when I knew I won," Az said, and Asta slapped a hand over his mouth to stop himself from laughing. "Beel whirled around, pointing to his lower back. We'd thought it was hilarious the night before, but in the morning, all of us sober? It was better than we could've ever imagined."

"What tattoo did Belial give him?"

With an absolute straight face, Az answered, "A Campbell's soup can with the label reading 'Belial's Bitch.' Beel hates him for it to this day."

A sideways smile came to Az when I reeled, cackling. Here I was, in *Hell* no less, laughing at a Daemon Prince's story about something Jess and I would one hundred percent have done to Frankie. I hoped I would be able to see them again.

"Does Beel still have the tattoo?" I wondered, stemming the uncertainty surrounding my future.

Az nodded. "He does."

"Shouldn't it have healed over somehow?"

Asta's head angled. "You're wondering how a tattoo done by a shapeshifting Daemon Prince stayed on another Daemon Prince's skin, who also happens to have powers?"

"Fair point." My eyes drifted from him to the window where Levi's rift had opened; he'd been gone for a while now. "I'm going to assume Levi isn't coming back."

"Oddly enough, I was overly invested in his and Wesley's relationship," Asta admitted. "I had wagered they'd last around a decade. Mon thought the same, too."

"Hey, I've met him," I said.

The room, once warmed by memories and laughter, plunged into glaciality at the mention of Mammon.

Acrimony curved Az's brows and mouth, hardened his gaze. "Storytime is over and so is your break." He got to his feet. "We're starting with the next lesson." He clapped a few times to garner my attention. "Let's go, Highness! I'm not staying here forever."

"Jeez, fine," I grumbled. "No need to be rude about it."

Asta hopped up, offered me a hand, and we moved to the centre of the room together.

"What's up with him?" I whispered.

"Mon and Az don't get on," Asta answered in the same whispered tone. "Don't know why. Neither of them will tell me anything about it."

Strange. He and Az seemed close, so why would Az keep this from him? Why did Az and Mon hate each other as much as they did? Was it something Mon had done? Az's hostility rendered the idea unlikely.

I considered my theories over and over again during Az and Asta's teachings of how to distinguish between an opponent's attacking or feigning stances. Asta's mention that we'd be moving onto actual fighting snapped me from my daze, albeit first, he outlined a summary of defensive moves—how to block and turn an opponent's weight against them, for example—as well as offensive tactics. We practised each, one by one, and even got around to sparring.

Of all the times we practised—twenty-three times if I was being accurate—I managed to win *once*. During the twenty-fourth attempt, I managed to hit Asta, but only because he'd stopped mid-move, having received a communication from Lucifer requesting his presence. And so, we wrapped up our sparring match early.

Less than a second after Asta, the interim mediator, had gone, my initial discomfort returned. Once again, I was alone with Az. "I'm warning you now," I aimed the knife in my grasp at him, "you do anything stupid and I won't hesitate to stab you."

"Very charming, Highness." He flicked the blade away with a finger as though it were a fly, not a weapon. "It's a tempting offer, however, I have better ways of spending our time together."

CANTO XVIII

Anything Can Be a Sheath if the Blade is Plunged Deep Enough

For the better part of the last fifteen minutes, I had been following Az through the tunnels dug into the rock with no clue as to where we were going since he refused to share that information with me. I eventually pieced it together when he led me down rock-hewn stairs packed with dirt.

We were headed to *Yranta*. To the combat circles.

The passageway fed into the cavern teeming with shouting Satanials and screeching daemons. Some of the screams sounded victorious and others… less so.

I tapped Az's shoulder. "You know, this really isn't necessary."

He brushed me off, replying over the clamour, "There's a purpose to everything I do, Highness. I did say you were going to regret laughing at me."

"I thought you were kidding!" To be honest, I thought he'd forgotten about his threat as well.

"Evidently I wasn't." He strode through crowds of Satanials who bowed low at his approach, setting aside their avidity and retreating to clear a path to one of the smaller circles at the far end of the cave.

I stayed close behind, ignoring the stares of souls and creatures alike, until Az stopped at a circle. His threats rang in my ears. "You're not seriously going to make me do this, are you?"

A hand pressed against my lower back, and Az shoved me through the final wall of bodies into an open fight circle where two Satanials were battling, knives in hand.

"*No, no, no.*" I turned around, but Az's firm grip on my shoulder prevented me from running.

"Rasa!" he called.

A pale woman with raven hair chopped clean to her chin stepped forward at his summons, walking toward us along the perimeter not to disturb the end of the current fight.

"There you are, Kano," Az said in the language of Hell.

Kano… So, she's related to Kira. Sisters, maybe?

"Who have you brought me this time, Asmodeus?" Rasa replied in the same language. "A new Satanial in the making?" Her red-rimmed eyes examined me, lingering on my uniform. "She must be quite special for you to be training her yourself."

"She's many things, however I wouldn't necessarily use 'special' to describe her," Az said.

I bit the inside of my cheeks to prevent myself from directing a torrent of curse words at him. I had no intention of potentially worsening my situation.

"She'll be fighting in the next round," Az informed Rasa in English, "not to win a position, though."

Was he not aware I could understand him when he first spoke, or did he know perfectly well and simply wanted to make a fool out of me?

"Understood." Rasa gave a bow of her head. "Are you coming, hon?" she asked, motioning me forward. "You're not going to get anything done standing around."

I flinched. "I-I'm not read—"

Az pushed me again, this time harder, right into the centre of the circle.

"Ammar!" Rasa barked. "You're up!"

A tall and muscular soul cleared the border, whirling a dagger in each hand. The black symbol on his uniform indicated he belonged to the Zemas tier of the Satanials. He didn't speak, only nodded to Rasa in acknowledgement.

A nervous chuckle escaped me. "Look, buddy, there's been a misunderstanding," I said, slowly retreating. "I'm not supposed to be here right now, so if you could take it e—"

Ammar advanced in the blink of an eye, slashing a dagger around as he tried to grab at the symbol on my chest.

I managed to dodge his next attack, which had almost sliced open my cheek. "Dude, *what gives*?" I shouted, my arms shooting out. "Did you not hear what I just sai—"

One of Ammar's blades met my right arm, piercing the fabric and skin beneath. I yelped at the sting, rearing and stumbling away from him. While I cradled my injury, assessing the damage, the crowd roared, chanting his name.

This was *insane*. I had less skill than my opponent and even less experience.

How the Hell am I supposed to fight against the dead? I sent into Az's mind.

Capture the sigil on his chest and you'll win, he answered. *It's simple.*

I scoffed. 'It's simple,' he said. This wasn't *anything* like capture-the-flag.

And what if I don't? I asked. *What if Ammar gets mine first?*

Standing across the circle with his hands braced on his hips and Rasa watching attentively at his side, Az looked down his nose at me. *You'll lose*, he said. *Think of it this way: imagine your opponent is someone you hate. That should motivate you.*

Fugitive strands from my braid clung to my forehead. I ran my sleeve over my face, sponging up the sweat but leaving a smear of cold blood behind. Ammar had his back to me, basking in a premature victory and high-fiving Satanials. That pride… who did it remind me of?

Thanks, Az. You gave me a great idea.

Incensed, I reached for the knife sheathed at my thigh and sent it flying into Ammar's left shoulder. He yelled and fell to a knee, leaving his weapons to clatter to the ground. While he attempted to rise, I sprinted for him. Leaping onto his back, I removed the knife from where it was lodged, using it to stab his neck again and again. My free hand shot out to snatch the symbol on his uniform. Feeling my injured arm snake around him, he dug his fingers into the wound and I half-sobbed at the pain. Ammar threw me from him with all his might, and I barrelled across the floor. Both the knife and my breath were knocked from me as I landed on the compacted dirt. A cry caught in my throat at the throbbing in my arms and aching in my legs. Ammar collected his weapons from the ground, starting in my direction with a triumphant smile.

A laugh cut through my ragged and uneven breaths. Ammar stopped mid-stride, his confusion yielding to panic when he glanced at his chest to find torn fabric. "Looking for something?" Fighting a wince, I lifted the sigil in my hand. "Looks like I… like I won."

An impressed Rasa clapped from behind Ammar. Az stayed motionless next to her, and somehow, Levi was beside him, covering his mouth in shock.

Rasa beamed. "Unholy Circles. That was absolutely *amazing*." She veered to Az. "Are you sure this was her first time?"

Ammar aimed a grimace my way, then pushed through the crowd which had begun cheering for me.

"I leave for a few hours and this happens?" Levi motioned to the combat circle. "Why do I always miss the fun stuff?" He shook his head, disappointed.

"Congratulations," Az said to me. "You passed the Second Stage."

What Second—*no* fucking *way*.

A burning, white-hot rage thundered inside of me.

Tossing the sigil aside and launching to my feet, I marched out of the circle and paused by Az. "If you were wondering who I was imagining back there," I began venomously, "it was *you*."

My shoulder slammed into Az's as I entered the throng of Satanials, headed to the training room where I hoped Michael would be. When I arrived, though, there was no sign of him. And so, my anger won. I broke anything and everything I could get my hands on. Kicking, throwing, punching, shredding… it didn't matter.

Az's deprecating voice emanated from the entrance. "Care to explain what the Hell is going on?"

A humourless laugh bounded off the walls, halting when I faced him. "Do *I* want to explain? How about you do some explaining, Asmodeus? You weren't going to tell me that I was walking into my Second Stage at all?"

Az folded his arms over his chest. "Are you finished?" His indifference only continued to fuel my rage and hurt.

"*No, I'm not finished!*" I shouted. "What would've happened if I had failed, huh? Ever thought of that?"

"I suppose we'll never know, will we?" Az said. "But at least now *you* know to mind my warnings."

All of this… because I was an inconvenience to him?

My hands balled into fists. I wanted to beat the rotten life out of him. I wanted to do to him exactly what I'd done to Ammar.

"Adara?" Michael appeared at the doors. "What happened?"

"Spur of the moment Stage Two, that's what," I answered.

Concerned, he passed right by Az to get to me and discovered the cut on my arm. "You're bleeding?" His focus snapped to Az. "You didn't give her a heads up like Lucifer told you to do?"

"It must have slipped my mind," Az lied.

Heat poured from Michael, adding to that of the hatred flaring from me. "*Do you realize what you could've cost her?*"

Chaos brewed behind Az's eyes. "Cost her or cost *you*?" he countered. "And I'll tell you the same thing I told her. She passed. There's no point wondering 'what if?'"

Anguish pried apart my ribs, tore at my flesh, broke my voice. "How can you not understand the gravity of what you've done? You claimed I wasn't taking this seriously, but here you are purposefully sabotaging me. I'm doing the best I can even though I'm being killed inside by *myself*. This is my *life* you're screwing with—my *future*—as well as those of the people I love. And you could have ruined it all *for what*? The satisfaction?"

Succumbing to my fury, I snatched the knife from Michael's leg and launched it at Az's head. Blindsided, Az ducked at the last second, barely evading the projectile, however his shock wasn't good enough. I meant to take another of Michael's knives, this time to carve Az's face off and toss it at Lucifer's feet, but Michael hauled me onto his shoulder and carried me from the training room, kicking, screaming and swearing.

While Michael and I walked back to the castle and to my room (after he'd succeeded in calming me down), we discussed what took place during my Stage, including our mutual disdain for Az. "Let's forget for a second that Asmodeus almost screwed everything up," Michael eventually said. "The bright side is you passed your Stage. I'm really proud of you, Dara."

I returned the smile he gave me. "Thanks."

"Alright, now that that second is over, if Asmodeus pulls something like this again or hurts you in any way, I'm going to kick his ass."

"If things ever reach that point, I'll do it myself, but I appreciate the offer." I needed to be the one to make Az bleed. Michael, on the other hand, might have more to lose in Lucifer's eyes as a Satanial if he crossed a Daemon Prince.

Levi emerged from the corner of the hallway Michael and I were nearing, so I called out his name.

"Oh hey, doll face. Hey, Michael." He waved. "Have you two seen Az? I have to talk to him. I thought he'd be here, but no luck."

I suppressed the curling of my lip. "Last I saw him, he was in the training room. He might've left since then."

"Shit." Levi rubbed his neck. "Alright, thanks, anyhow," he said, passing us. "Congratulations on passing your Second Stage, by the way. I didn't have the chance to say it earlier."

I extended a grateful smile. "Thanks." After he'd gone and we'd resumed our walk to my room past the turn, I remarked to Michael, "This is the second time Levi's called you by your first name."

"Yeah? What's wrong with that?"

"Nothing. It's just that everyone I've met here so far calls you by your last name."

"We're on a first name basis," he clarified, opening the door to my room for us once we'd reached it. "Silas had been training me when I first got here and Levi happened to pass by on his way to *Paxtara*. He hung out for a while, helped me a little too."

"I bet he was hitting on you the whole time." The conclusion wasn't completely unfounded; I had noticed the small spark in Levi's eyes whenever he saw Michael or me.

Michael laughed and shook his head. "He has a naturally flirty persona, is all."

"Funny you should mention that when you're genuinely incapable of noticing when someone's flirting with you."

"I am not," he argued.

"Are too."

"No, I'm not."

Removing my jacket, I threw it onto the couch, not caring if my blood would stain it, and sank into the cushions. "Remember that one time we went to Cabot's at the beginning of May?"

Michael paused in front of the fireplace. "What of it?"

"The waitress was flirting with you the entire time we were there."

Michael clasped his hands in front of his mouth. "Adara, she was flirting with *you*. It was so obvious. She refilled your water when it was already full as an excuse to talk to you."

"Are you sure?"

"Yes!" Michael exclaimed.

"That doesn't count because I can never tell if girls are flirting with me or they're just being friendly. My statement still stands for you. Like there was this—"

"Dara, you're the one who doesn't know she's being flirted with."

"Oh, yeah?" I crossed my arms. "Name me a—"

Michael launched into his evidence: "There was the time we went over to my cousin's house and he wouldn't stop telling you that you could 'do so much better' than me and he'd save you a front seat for his next football game so you could see 'real talent.'" He made finger quotations.

I stifled a chuckle. "I'm not counting that either. He was *thirteen*."

"And?" Michael said, and I raised a brow at him. "*Fine*. There was also the time we went to the movies and the guy at the booth ignored me completely and wrote his number on your ticket, you remember? What was his name? Andrew or something stupid like that? *Oh!* Oh, and my soccer game at Learning Prep in June. The captain of their team winked at you—"

"Okay!" I burst into laughter. "Let's agree to disagree."

Wistfulness bloomed in my chest at hearing Michael mention how we used to get ice cream at Cabot's and walk to the cinema to watch whatever movie had been recently released, how he would invite me to his games and I'd cheer him on while he played. And in the open arms of his references lived the memories of us going to his house after he'd win or lose and accidentally fall asleep in his room, us sitting on the sand in the light of the setting sun at the beach, or lying on the grass in my backyard, stargazing.

Now here we were in Hell, and the past watered the seeds of my grief and frustration and remorse. We were supposed to do so much more with our lives, experience so much more than we had.

A chance still existed, glimmering in the distance.

I would fix everything. I owed it to him.

Michael's return from the bathroom snapped me from my daze. He took the seat beside me, wiping the blood which had crusted on my skin with a wet cloth. "That's weird." His head angled.

"What?"

He removed the cloth from my supposed wound, revealing a small whitish, near-invisible scar. "Does it still hurt?"

My brows furrowed, mirroring his confusion. "No, actually." I hadn't realized it had stopped its throbbing or bleeding. "But thank you for helping me." I pressed a kiss to his cheek. "Do you have to go back to *Paxtara*? Will you stay with me? Please?"

"*Me quedaré contigo.*"

CANTO XIX

Glimpses of the Past

My body sensed that Michael had left while I slept. However, when I woke up, he had returned and was lying next to me. I snuggled closer to him, hoping to get a few more minutes of rest.

The person banging on my door had different plans.

I groaned and buried my head into a pillow. Michael patted my back twice in consolation, leaving the bed to deal with it.

The door creaked on its hinges as Michael opened it. "What?" he grumbled.

The reply didn't reach my ears.

"Still asleep. She's recovering," came Michael's curt reply. Then, seconds later, "She'll get up when she's *ready*."

Shoving my sheets aside, I stumbled into the main room. "I'm awake." I yawned. "I'm good to go…"

Michael veered to me when I appeared, a gentle smile at his lips. "You're not dressed, *amor*."

"I am." I wore exactly what I'd been wearing when I went to sleep: my bralette and uniform pants. Blinking away my sleepiness, I discovered Az in the corridor, clad in the blackness of his soul, whereas Michael stayed in my room, gripping the door.

Resentment and revolt ripped from my bones, cloaking me. "Considering the circumstances," I managed, "I will be going to put on the rest of my uniform."

"There's a new jacket in the commode," Michael told me.

"Much appreciated. You can close the door now."

Michael slammed it shut in Az's face, cutting off whatever the Daemon Prince meant to say. "Dickhead."

A head of snow-white hair at the wide window caught my eye the moment I entered the training room. Relief crashed over me. "Levi!" Thanks to him, I wouldn't have to be alone with Az again. The ground would be soaked in blood if I had my way.

He veered in my direction. "Ah, doll face!" Beaming, he rushed over to hug me. "Hello, gorgeous."

"What's with you and Asta giving her hugs?" Az wondered from the stairs.

Levi released me but kept an arm around my shoulder. "We're not like you, Az. We actually enjoy spending time with her... even if it's predominantly spent preparing her for potentially lethal Stages."

"True," I granted, "but at least you make things a little less bleak, and you won't work against me, right?"

"Why would I?" Levi's smile faltered. "What kind of question is that?" He followed the line of my seething gaze to Az. "Alright, am I missing something here? I can sense serious hostility."

"I guess you can say I'm feeling a bit on edge, is all." I avoided expanding on the subject any further.

"Okay?" Levi's dark brows knitted together. His mouth opened as if he meant to ask for clarification, but he shut it directly, determining this could become a bigger issue and take away from what we were here for. "I should apologize for not helping you with training before your Second Stage, doll face. The Wesley-incident took longer than I expected."

"Don't worry about it," I assured him. "You're here now, and you got your *Caravaggio* back, yeah?"

"I did! And I will be here as long as you need me," he declared, then lowered his voice to add, "Unless Mr. Grouchy kicks me out."

"I might if you keep calling me that," came Az's caution from behind. He'd left his spot, drowning us in his shadow.

"If you want to preserve your sanity, I would ignore him," I told Levi.

"Good one." Levi chuckled.

I clasped my hands in front of myself. "So, what are we getting up to during this session? Do you have a plan?"

"We're focusing on your powers," Az answered in his stead.

Dread surged from the pit in my stomach. "*What?*" I shook my head. "No way. There's no chance in Hell."

"You don't have a choice."

My forced, empty laugh echoed. "You're telling me I have to use the powers that killed Michael and my parents to get them back? Are you insane? I came here to *undo* what I did, not get deeper into this mess."

"You'll need them for upcoming Stages," Az informed me. "It's an inevitable fact."

Although a part of me suspected this could happen, I had refused to believe it, actively avoided the thought, convinced myself I wouldn't need to use them—but the truth remained clear: it was always an unspoken possibility, and I'd continuously pushed it off in vain, hoping for an outcome that had never existed.

I would have to call on the darkness, on those volatile shadows which poisoned my veins and fed sinister whispers to my mind. If I granted it freedom, what would it do to me? Would I be able to trap it again, or would the already unstable barrier keeping it at bay disintegrate?

I had promised, though; I would fix everything, *no matter what*, even if it meant risking what little control I possessed. My sole consolation came from the deal I'd struck with Lucifer: if I beat The Sixes, he would take it all away—my actions and this curse.

The paranoia that had seized my body receded, and I uttered, "Fine. Continue."

"First and foremost, it's important to inhabit a certain headspace," Levi started explaining, determined to be helpful. "It is all about *mindset.* You need to be aware of what you have; your ability is a part of you, a living, breathing element. You need to know how it moves and how it reacts in order to use it properly. What is it exactly that makes your power emerge? What triggers it?"

I considered his question, twirling a lock of hair around my fingers. "Well, at first, it would only affect people if they looked directly into my eyes."

"All the time, or every now and again?"

I shook my head. "When my emotions were strong enough. Usually, in the moment, all I could feel was… anger."

"That's a good start." Levi nodded, proud. "Az told me shadows came out of you once, before you arrived in *Pravus*."

A lump lodged in my throat. "Yeah, what about it?"

"We're going to use that trigger to coax them out of you again," Az said, and Levi agreed with him.

The mere mention of the method sent distress to pound in my skull, in my ribs, in my legs. "I—*no*. Not that," I managed, swallowing hard. "W-we need to find another way."

"How come?" Levi asked.

I wrapped my arms around my body; my nails dug into the sleeves of my uniform, into my biceps beneath, now stinging. "The thing that triggered my 'shadows' last time was really, um, painful for me. I… I don't think I could go through it again."

"Your trigger doesn't necessarily need to be that specific memory," Levi said, which relaxed me to an extent, like his touch on my arm did. "We'll figure out another way, and when we do, we can teach you how to control your powers. Who knows? They might be triggered when you're under a sort of immense stress."

The idea that I could learn to control my powers offered an additional semblance of comfort.

"There is no other way, Levi," Az said. "She needs to use that trigger."

"I don't *need* to do anything," I stated.

"Yes, you do," he countered.

"Why are you pushing this, Ass-modeus?"

"How about I give a demonstration?" Levi suggested. "It won't be the exact same thing, but I think it could help." I smiled at him, grateful, and he went to position himself in the centre of the room. "The first step is to clear your mind of outer distractions." He closed his eyes and inhaled a few breaths. "Step two is to focus on a specific memory or an intention, something you know your powers would emerge for."

"In your case, Levi, it would be to show off," Az drawled.

Levi grinned in reply and returned to the task at hand, remaining motionless for a couple of seconds. "For step three, Adara, you need to feel the power flowing in your veins, in your blood." His body began to vibrate. "And then step four…"

Levi split into seven different bodies, all of whom looked like him, down to his pinstriped, cloud-grey suit.

"That's *awesome*!" I marvelled. "Which one is the real you?"

"Figure it out," the Levis said altogether.

Az sighed from the pillar he leaned against. "It's obvious."

The Levis rolled their eyes. "It should be to you; you're my brother."

"This is useless," Az said. "We need to be teaching Adara about her powers, not yours."

"You should've asked Asta for help, then," the Levis jeered.

"I *did*. He left for *Varmir* with Luce."

The Levis touched their hearts and laughed. "You wound us."

During their interaction, I'd inspected each Levi individually. "This one," I said, stopping and pointing at a 'clone.' "This is the real you."

"How are you so sure?" A cheeky smirk spread on the Levi's mouth.

The multiple I stood in front of now had radiated a different energy than the others, odd as that sounded. "I feel it," I answered.

The other Levis disappeared, leaving only one: the one before me.

"Ha, I knew it!" I clapped my hands, and Levi took the opportunity to high-five me.

"Your father struggled to determine which was the real me at first," he revealed. "There was this time where he got mad at me for reasons I can't remember…"

"Levi," Az warned.

"I say that because Luce *always* gets mad at me, and I don't keep track of everything." Hands on his hips, he cast his eyes upwards, absorbed in thought. "Actually, on this particular occasion, I might've wanted to go to Earth to see how God was doing with the whole 'let there be light' thing…"

"Levi."

"And I multiplied myself so I could sneak out and Luce wouldn't find me..."

"*Levi.*"

"Let me tell you, the funniest part of it all was what happened once he *did* find me. You'll never believe it, but I was in—"

"Levi!"

He turned around to an impatient, fuming Az. "What? I'm in the middle of a story."

Az pointed to the doors. "*Get out.*"

Levi pouted. "Why? I'm not—"

"You've been a distraction since the beginning *and* you're wasting time by filling her head with ideas that won't work. Now *leave.*"

"What gives you the authority to do this?" I questioned. "I want him here."

"It's a good thing we don't operate based on what you want," Az rejoined. His glare shifted to his brother, sharpening. "I won't ask again."

The two stared at each other for a moment, locked in a battle of wills, however Az's intransigence persisted, his resolve formidable. What could Levi do but buckle?

"*Fine*," he reluctantly consented, lifting his chin, "you grouchy-ass tyrant." I grabbed his arm, pleading for him not to go. He patted me on the back, eyeing his brother. "Good luck with him." With that, Levi stomped out of the room like a scolded child.

I shot Az a disapproving look. "He was helping."

"He was distracting you," Az corrected. "We can't afford any distractions, especially now."

I gestured between us. "So this is a 'we,' huh?"

"Quiet." Az held onto my shoulders, repositioning me in the centre of the room where Levi had displayed the steps to using his power. "What works for others won't always be what works for you."

"But Levi said—"

Az snapped his fingers. "Can you not interrupt? You have the attention span of a five-year-old."

"Do you want me to throw a tantrum like one too? Because I can make that happen," I threatened.

"Circles help me," Az whispered to himself, exasperated, before resuming with his previous thought. "Let's say, for example, you're in a Stage—"

"I use a knife, same as I did on Ammar. Stab, stab." I imitated the movement. "Problem solved." Imagining my opponent being Az made me laugh, and I motioned again.

"Damn it, Adara! This isn't funny."

"*So-rry* for trying to lighten the uptight mood you're effusing."

A muscle in his jaw twitched. "I am *not* uptight."

"Pardon my French, but you're so uptight that if I shoved a lump of carbon up your ass, I'd have a diamond within the next few minutes."

Az's face went blank, though impatience simmered close beneath the surface. "Are you finished?"

"Oh, no. I have more, but continue your lesson, I guess."

He massaged his temples with a hand. "You have no knife," he said. "You *summon* your shadows. That's what's going to happen."

"How?"

"You know the answer."

My resolve wouldn't bow when opposing his. "I said it once and I'll say it again: I am not using my parents' death as a trigger, Asmodeus."

"You don't have a choice, Highness."

"*Stop saying that*," I demanded. "Levi mentioned there were other ways. Different stressors—"

Az waved that off. "Forget what Levi said. We're doing this my way."

"No, we aren't," I stated. "I'm going to try my own way." Which was precisely what I did.

The next unknown number of hours consisted of my following Levi's steps to summon my shadows, obviously substituting the parental-murder-death part for other memories, even going as far as thinking about what I'd done to Michael. Az offered input… and by 'input' I meant he was berating me since I couldn't conjure the smallest wisp no matter how hard I tried. A gruelling exhaustion shackled my mind, my body, my energy, induced by the sheer force it required to merely *attempt* to summon something.

"I told you your way wouldn't work," Az repeated.

Panting, I slumped to the floor. "How much longer do I have to do this? Every bone in my body hurts. And I'm starving."

Az shook his head. "That's not important right now. We're going to do this for as long as possible until you can get it right—which includes using your trigger. My job is to train and prepare you. Your inability to follow instruction is hindering that."

"It seems your 'job,'" I got up, ignoring the pain to level out with him, "is to be an absolute asshole." I clapped twice. "You're doing so well. Keep up the fantastic work!"

The red in Az's eyes flared. "*Use your trigger*."

"Eat shit, Ass-modeus."

Why couldn't he understand how hard it would be for me? Did he not consider how much further it would break my already precarious sanity if I re-subjected myself to my worst nightmare come true? Or had he considered it and simply didn't care?

The flapping of unfolded wings drifted into my ears. Az hovered above the ground, flying to the balcony.

"What are you doing?" I asked, confused.

Stationed at the railing, Az extended his palm to the area below. "You want this to be over? You don't want to use your trigger?" The air in front of me shimmered, enveloped by a growing mist. "I'll give it to you myself."

The mist began to form something.

No, not something. Someone.

Samantha.

My mom stood in front of me with my dad not far behind. Their bodies glimmered, the outlines reflecting and refracting the firelight of the torches.

How was this possible?

The thumping of my blood in my ears silenced every manner of sound, including Az's voice from the balcony. All I could focus on was them. My parents and how they'd come back, how much I had missed them, how I needed to apologize for my actions.

But this wasn't the time for that. Their positions before the glass window weren't like those they'd assumed in our family pictures.

She was going to kill him. My mom was going to kill my dad, then herself.

I'd let their deaths happen once; I wouldn't stand by now.

I raced to stop her, to save them. Not six feet later, I slammed into the air, tumbling across the floor. Despite the pang in my shoulder, I rose immediately, bewildered by what had halted me. When I tried again, my hand met an invisible barrier. My fists banged against it, desperately trying to break through.

I punched, I clawed, I kicked to no avail. Paralysis soon took hold, rooting me in place as Samantha raised the sword over Kamael's head.

This was what Az *wanted.*

This was all his fault, all his plan to force my shadows out.

My eyes *burned.*

An indescribable pressure compressed the pieces of my broken heart, of my devastated beliefs, curious to see how much more I could endure. A sluggish presence slithered through my veins, shocked into a million particles that moved like blood, coursing and pumping in a thunderous rage.

A manic smile warped Samantha's face as she swung down, relieving Kamael of his head. Her sword found its way to her own neck.

An agonizing scream tore from my throat. Darkness burst from my body, decimating every sliver of light. The sheer strength from my shadows' movements evolved into a tempest, churning around in a riotous storm of fury and anguish and despair.

My knees buckled beneath me, striking the hardwood. When the obscurity cleared, daggers of crystallized shadow decorated every visible wall, protruding and gleaming; they began to leak, slowly amassing to return to their home in my veins.

I can't breathe.

Why couldn't I breathe?

Each inhale entered half-formed. My lungs screamed and ribs pierced my insides. My hands flattened against the ground as I attempted to centre myself, to remember the techniques I'd employed when I was younger. Tears rolled down my face in scorching rivulets, yet through the haze, I found Az's boots; he'd flown from overhead and landed three feet from me. "How could you?" I whispered through partial breaths. "*HOW COULD YOU?*" A sob broke past my quivering lips. "You made me re-live my parents' death… for what? As an incentive to summon a *shadow*?"

Az's voice sounded miles away. "I did what I had to do."

"*No.* You did it because you could." Salt filled my mouth—salt and sorrow and shame. "Do you enjoy seeing me like this? You enjoy seeing me weak and defeated?"

"Is that what you think of me?"

"*I think you're sick, Asmodeus!*" Wiping at my eyes, I pushed myself from the floor and rushed to the exit. Reaching the doorframe, I halted and turned. "There is something rotten inside of you."

For a second, a shred of emotion flickered in his features. No, I was wrong. Instead, they had hardened and twisted, beautiful but terrifying. "You know what? I have *nothing* to apologize for. This is what you signed up for, and this," his wings expanded, showcasing their dark angelic grandeur, "is how I was created."

"And oh, how the mighty have fallen," I lamented, as false as he was. In the next instant, I'd spun on my heel and stormed out, accidentally bumping into someone on the way.

"*Woah*, are you alright?"

"I'm fine," I snapped, and continued past the stranger.

"Az, what did you do?" the stranger asked as they entered the training room.

I didn't look back. I kept going, running through the tunnels until I reached an opening. My legs gave out, and I collapsed against the wall, terrorized by an onslaught of scattered thoughts, seized by erratic breaths, invaded by glacial shudders.

"Adara, is that you?" A scuffing of boots on dirt revealed a blurry Michael, who crouched in front of me. "Dara, what's wrong? Are you having a panic attack?"

The words died on my tongue. My hearing warped, then my vision went.

CANTO XX

To Kill a Daemon Prince

The canopy's faint outline took form with every blink of my heavy eyes. Groaning, I sat upright in my room in the castle and pressed a hand to my aching temple, the only physical pain that remained. Michael had brought me here, I remembered that much. Seeing as he was missing, I must've been unconscious for a while; he could get away with missing a few of his duties due to his association with me, but not all, and it was in neither of our interests to let anyone know I'd fainted.

Swinging my legs over the side of the bed, I hopped to my feet, free of their boots, and headed to the bathroom, undoing the fastenings of my jacket. The light flared to life when I entered, as did my horror when I glimpsed my reflection in the mirror.

The capillaries around my black irises were inflamed, swallowing the white in a crimson similar to the strange flush which spread along the area above the collar of my jacket. Pulling it aside revealed tendril-like splotches slithering across my skin. Alarmed, I removed all of my clothes, discovering the marks covered my whole body.

Who stared back at me? Who was this… this *creature*?

Averting my gaze, I slipped into the shower to chase away my shivering, but no matter how hot the water was, I felt no warmth. No relief. The monotony of the droplets striking my skin encouraged the seeming silence to be filled by recollections of my screams. In the next instant, I was sitting, curled into a ball under the steady flow of water and memory and misery.

My parents' biggest mistake wasn't lying to me; it was having allowed me to live.

I should have died. It should've been *me*.

A knock came at the door. "Dara? *¿Estás bien?*"

My head whipped in the direction of Michael's voice. I rose, shut the water, and exited the shower, grabbing a towel hanging on the wall rack. "Yes," I lied, "I'm fine."

"I'm sorry I wasn't here when you woke up. Silas summoned me to assist him in the planning of another sub-level of the boro—no, it doesn't matter."

I quickly wrung my hair and dried off. "It's alright, Michael. I understand. I'm not upset." Wiping the steam from the mirror revealed an absence of the rash in my eyes and on my skin.

"Was someone else here before me?" Michael wondered.

I popped my head out, clutching my towel. "No, why?"

"Strange." He returned from the decorative table with clothes—*my* clothes from home.

Home.

"That is strange." Incapable of deciphering what it could mean at the moment, I accepted them and the boots he'd brought, ducking back inside. I didn't know who had brought them, why, or if I would receive any more, so I washed my dirtied belongings in the sink and hung them on the rack to dry. Once I finished dressing, I opened the door and Michael tumbled in back-first. My short chuckle registered as foreign to my brain.

"Well, shit." He stayed on the floor, grinning. "I got you to laugh." I helped him up. "You look better. That panic attack really did a number on you, huh?" He removed the strand of hair trapped beneath my collared sweater. "Do you want to tell me what happened?"

A sharp stabbing arose in my chest. "I… um… I saw my parents."

Michael gaped. "What? How? But they're—"

"It wasn't really them," I explained. "Az—Asmodeus created a sort of… illusion, I guess… so I could summon my shadows."

"And he chose *that*?" His eyes snapped to the door, and his fists shook at his sides. "I'll kill him!" He stormed out of the room faster than I could register.

It wasn't hard to determine where he was headed: the only place he expected Az to be by now—whenever *now* was. I arrived at the training room in time to see Michael throw open the doors and hurried after him.

He marched right up to Az, snatching him by the collar. "You forced her to watch her parents die? What the fuck is wrong with you?"

"This doesn't concern you." Az pushed Michael away. "Adara, tell your boyfriend to back down before he hurts himself."

"You're an egotistical, arrogant piece of shit." Michael began to shake, though not from fear. "I'm going to laugh when you're bleeding on the floor." Frenzy shone in his eyes, now fully red, and blade-like teeth snapped out of his mouth. His arms dislocated from their sockets, collarbones protruding from beneath his skin as it tore itself apart.

Worried, I ran to his side. "What's going on?" My hand met his rearranging shoulder. "Michael?"

At feeling someone touch him, he pushed me aside with tremendous force, and I collided with the bars on the stairs. My vision went fuzzy. An incessant pounding struck at my head as though my brain expanded to crush against my skull. The lungs screaming in my chest begged for me to breathe.

My fingers drew to the top of my head, returning wet. My eyes strained. *Blood.* "W-wha…" The pulsing and nausea made it impossible to focus. I couldn't utter a coherent sentence.

Az had watched the scene unfold, frozen in place, but his attention soon shifted to Michael, baleful. Without hesitation, his fist landed on Michael's face.

Crack.

Michael's neck spun on itself, his broken nose leaking black. With a petrifying cry from him, the torn skin gave way to a pile of tatters from which grew a mass of deep red. Three heads sprouted from the collecting body, each with four wholly maroon eyes. A pair of immense leathery wings unfurled from the ten-foot-tall creature's back, half-obscuring the barbed tail swishing behind.

Michael had a *daemon form.*

The daemon version of Michael charged at Az; he slipped under Michael's legs, his jacket fluttering, but in doing so encountered the barbed tail. Over and under he dodged to avoid it, never landing a blow of his own, though not for the lack of opportunity.

I crawled in their direction, calling for a stop to this. Az halted mid-step. Michael didn't.

His tail collided with Az, tossing him against the wall of weapons. Az fell to a knee with a groan, pressing a hand to his abdomen. The daemon Michael appeared to sneer. Az stood, the pain clear in his restricted movements despite his attempts to conceal it. His wings sprouted from his back, one placed on the floor and the other held out skyward. The daemon flew for him and, with one bat of Az's wing, was propelled across the room at an angle, smashing into the window.

Setting aside my dizziness and nausea, I rushed to position myself between the two.

"*That's enough!*" The intensity of my shout shook my senses awake. My shadows had inadvertently come out, holding both fighters apart.

The daemon convulsed and shrank, morphing into Michael. "Dara, I'm so sorry. I didn't mean—"

"I know you didn't," I said, retracting the restraints from him and Az. Michael was otherwise unharmed, and although Az seemed fine, the look in his eye and the subtle sweat accumulating on his brow betrayed the fact he was hurt. Badly.

He deserves this... but I should've been the one to do it.

I walked away without sparing him a second glance. And yet... I couldn't leave. Not like this. And so I found myself spinning on my heel to return.

"Dara, what are you doing? Did you forget what he did to you?" Michael's hand on my shoulder stopped me. His eyes flicked to the blood on my forehead. "It was an accident, Dara. I swear, I didn't mean to hurt you." He pointed at Az, whose shirt had darkened beneath his jacket. "It was *his* fault!"

"Keep in mind I told you he was an asshole," I got out, "not 'hey Michael, go fight Asmodeus for me.'"

"I know you didn't, bu—"

"Exactly. I didn't. I don't need you to step in every single time because you think I can't handle myself!" True as that was, it wasn't my main concern.

"What else was—"

"Come here." I took him by the arm, leading him away from Az. Or at least out of his earshot. "*Necesito que confíes en mí. Sé lo qué estoy haciendo, lo juro.* Now act annoyed." He did as I asked him, maintaining his affront. Satisfied, I added, louder, "Look, just leave me here to settle things with him on my own" —I cast a look at a disinterested, silent Az— "and we'll talk about this later."

And we'd definitely have to; this clearly hadn't been the first time Michael had entered his daemon form, and never had it crossed his mind to tell me it existed.

Michael gaped in disbelief, shaking his head and muttering to himself on his way out. Almost immediately after he'd gone, Az's front disintegrated. He leaned on the wall for support, but his weight turned against him. He crumpled to the floor, pressing onto the injury Michael had caused.

Ignoring my splitting head, I approached him and knelt down, my hands hovering over his.

Az pushed me away. "I don't need your help. I can do it—" he groaned "—myself." The lengths of his blinks increased with his waning consciousness.

"You can barely stay awake, Asmodeus." I examined his shirt, where the fabric had significantly darkened in comparison to earlier. "You're losing a lot of blood."

"No, I'm okay…" His eyes closed again… and stayed that way.

"Asmodeus?" I tapped his cheek. "Az, you need to wake up."

No response.

I hit him hard enough for my hand to leave a dark mark across his face, which did make me feel slightly avenged.

His eyes snapped open, the ruby colour alarmingly drained. "*What?*"

"You passed out, dumbass! Are you seriously going to say you don't need my help now?"

Az shook his head, yet hesitation lived behind his wavering gaze. I removed his coat, careful not to cause him more pain. When I lifted his shirt, he winced, clenching his teeth. Black blood gushed from the spike planted in his oblique, cloaking the exposed area. I used the interior of his coat to clear part of the stream. The first swipe revealed scars much like the one I'd previously seen on him that time at his apartment after I'd woken up from the sleep he'd helped me slip into.

"How bad is it?" he asked, unable to see the wound himself; if he tried, the injury would no doubt worsen.

"You want the truth?"

"Obviously. Why else would I have asked?"

"You look like you debuted in a slasher film as 'bloodied corpse.'"

"Not the time for jokes, Adara."

"Hey, I'm allowed to say whatever I want after what you did to me."

Az grimaced. "This… isn't… helping."

"Fine." I moved closer him to get a better look. "There's a small barb stuck in the muscle. It's embedded deep."

"Shit." Az tossed his head back. "Alright, I'll just do it myself." He sat up and shoved his fingers into the open wound. Blood rushed out faster.

"Are you dumb?" I pulled his hand away, ice-cold against my fingertips. "Why would you do that?"

"I need to remove the spike!"

"*Well don't do it like that!*"

"How else am I supposed to do it?" His skin began to change form, knitting back together. The barb was too far in for me to reach with my hands, lodged in between his muscle and bone, but leaving it in would mean considerable internal hemorrhaging. Now, this made no difference to me (in fact, I'd love knowing he'd be plagued by pain for eternity), but to him? Serious problem.

"I'm going to try something on you, okay?"

He baulked. "You're going to test something on me *now* of all times?"

"Yes. Do you trust me?"

"Do I trust you *experimenting* on me? What do you think?"

"Az!" I looked into his draining eyes. "*Do you trust me?*" He nodded, and a profound satisfaction emerged at my victory. However, I wasn't finished yet. "Before I do this, you have to swear you won't tell Lucifer what Michael did to you." If Lucifer discovered Michael had started a fight with a Daemon Prince, he'd undoubtedly be reprimanded. Severely. At least now I could ensure his protection.

Az's lips parted in disbelief. "Are you… extorting me?"

"Come on, Az. Who do you take me for?" I smirked. "Clearly I'm making you a deal here."

"I don't know whether I should be offended, or…"

"Proud?" Following the suggestion, I leaned toward him. "That would make two of us. So, what'll it be? Pain or an agreement?"

His focus on my reaction passed to his abdomen, then back to me. "I swear I won't say anything."

"Smart choice. How rare for you." My hand hovered over the injury, and I called on my spite and determination for the strength to enact my intention. Warmth spread through my arm slowly at first—so slowly I hardly noticed it. Not a second later, shadows poured from my palm, crawling into the gash. Az inhaled a sharp breath at their entry and at the persistent bubbling of blood in the self-healing cut.

Please.

An object gravitated into my palm; reeling in the darkness, I discovered the spike there. Beneath the black slick, Az's skin had healed over completely. He passed a hand over the scarred area and leaned off the wall. "That burned."

"*Sorry,*" I drawled. "Did my saving your life make you uncomfortable?"

"You didn't 'save my life,'" Az repeated, covering himself. "You removed your boyfriend's daemon barb from my side through extort—an *agreement.*"

"Oh, I didn't just save your life?" I displayed the barb. "How about I stab you again and leave you alone?"

Az rose from the bloodied floor, grabbing his coat. "I'll have to pass on that offer. I've had enough stabbing for today."

"I think the words you were looking for are 'thank you' or 'I appreciate you helping me, Adara.' Any of those would be nice."

Az extended a hand to me; I slapped it aside to get up on my own, but before I could leave, his fingers wrapped around my wrist, gently tugging me back to him. "You're right." The firelight caressed his softened features. "Thank you, Adara." His eyes, no longer the drained, lifeless red they'd once been but a vibrant ruby, drifted to my hairline, just like his hand. The thumb he brushed on my healed cut quieted the aching ravaging my head. "Does it still hurt?"

"No."

"That's good," he murmured. Unspoken words lingered on his lips, pleading to be acknowledged.

CANTO XXI

Forgive Us Our Trespasses

Confusion spread across Az's face when I stumbled backwards. The spike slipped from my grasp, clattering on the ground, and I headed for the exit as fast as my feet could take me.

"Adara?"

"No… I—I have to go." Over and over, I told myself to pretend like that had never happened. What was wrong with me? Was I stupid or had I completely lost my mind? How hard had I hit my head? Was I suffering severe side effects of a concussion?

"Adara."

Despite not wanting to, I turned. "We had an agreement, and I repaid you for your one kindness at your apartment. *That's it.* I haven't forgotten what you did to me and this," I pointed to him, the bloody floor, and my head, "definitely doesn't change a thing. Now, if you'll excuse me, I have better things to do—and I'm *literally* in Hell."

I needed to talk to Michael.

Az stepped toward me. "Adara, I—"

My defensive hand stopped whatever nonsense he meant to spew, and I continued to the exit. "Save it. I don't care."

"Adara!"

The aggravation of him calling my name finally boiled over. "*What*, Asmodeus*?*" I rounded on him. "What more can you possibly have to say?"

"*I'm sorry*," he blurted.

My breath lodged in my throat. "W-what was that?" Had I misheard him, or had he genuinely said what I thought he had?

A dark blush settled on his cheeks as he spoke the words again, struggling. "I said… I said I'm sorry for what I did to you."

He had never apologized before. He'd once told me it was something he never did and never would do, not to anyone.

Did he think this would accomplish anything? Did he honestly believe that, just because he'd shown a sliver of remorse, I should forgive him?

"You're sorry?" My laugh echoed off the walls, half-incredulous, half-forlorn. "If it wasn't enough that you almost ruined my chances for the Second Stage, you decided to *force* my shadows out of me! You used the *one thing* I told you not to: my worst nightmare become reality." My gaze stayed on him, tense and sharp and biting as the silence between us. "Why did you do it?" I demanded. "I want the truth. *Why did you do it?*"

"What in the Nine Circles happened here?" came Levi's voice from the doors behind me.

Az tensed. "Training," he lied, breezing past me to leave.

"Stage Three is starting soon! Aren't you coming?" Levi shouted after him. Az didn't bother answering. "Alright." Levi's attention fell to me next. "Um, no offence, doll face, but you look rough."

I looked down at myself—at Az's blood staining my hands. "Yeah, none taken."

Once I'd successfully scrubbed off Az's blood as well as my own, I changed into my uniform and tied my hair into a tight braid to remove it from my face. Thankfully by then my headache had vanished.

"Do you know what Stage Three is going to be?" I asked Levi when I came out of my room. I wanted to get as much information as I could before heading into this thing.

Levi led me out of the Guest Wing. "Az told me Asta left during the training session we were supposed to have together, so I'm assuming it has to do with that."

Not having the slightest clue of what was to come or where it would occur unnerved me more than I cared to admit. "Where are we going, then?"

Levi had been guiding me to the throne room. No, the great serpentine staircase. "Luce wants us at the bridge."

I descended the steps at his side. "Couldn't you have ascendiated there?"

"No one ascendiates in or out of this castle besides Luce," Levi replied, "and you, I suppose, since you're related." He opened the doors, welcoming the suffocating heat.

"How come no one can ascendiate in or out?"

"Luce has this spell of sorts on it. He likes to be notified about all comings and goings. That, and it's not exactly necessary. Ascendiating is more useful for travelling between Circles, Realms, stuff of the like."

While Levi had been explaining, I spotted Asta and a luminous Lucifer further on the bridge, speaking to each other.

"Is Az not coming?" Asta asked when we reached them.

"I'm not sure," Levi answered. "He had a bit of an acc—"

The doors opened again and Az appeared. Water dripped from his dark hair and earrings, evidence he'd recently left the shower. He fixed the golden pendant around his neck, visible due to the first few buttons of his shirt being undone. A number of scars peeked from behind the fabric. Where had he gotten those? Did they have something to do with Mon?

Az met up with us on the bridge, though kept his distance from me. "Who had what?" he asked Levi, flattening the lapels of the new coat he donned atop his bloodless clothes.

"You had a change of clothes," Levi said, motioning to him. "Are we good to go?"

I played with the end of my braid. "You know, I think I left the oven on."

"Giving up already?" Lucifer wondered, amused. "Here I was expecting more."

I dropped my braid. "That'd be convenient for you, huh? No, actually. I'm not giving up, so let's get on with it."

"Very well." Lucifer faced Asta and tilted his head to me. "Asta, if you would."

Asta nodded, and his wings unfolded. The dark, velvety feathers curved around me, the frozen-coloured tips grazing my ankles. "I hope you don't get ill while ascendiating," he joked.

I appreciated his attempt to take a notch off my nervousness. Soon, the spinning sensation I'd experienced with Mon in *Helvinat* began, and my eyes reflexively shut. When they reopened, I was no longer surrounded by Asta's wings; I sat on a cold stone chair three feet above a dark, reflective surface. Curious as to what it could be, I prodded at it with the toe of my boot.

Leaden ripples undulated across the mysterious liquid, stopping at the base of seven short stone pillars that encircled me; Lucifer waited upon the centremost, with Levi on his left and Asta to his right. Az chose to stand next to the latter.

The distance separating us had to be around a hundred metres. If the Third Stage was to make it to one of the remaining pillars, I highly doubted I could.

"The rules of this Stage are straightforward." Lucifer's voice skated across the surface. "Stay in your seat."

It sounded simple enough; I'd been nervous for no reason. I relaxed in my chair. "Do I not get any bathroom breaks?"

Levi and Asta laughed.

Without warning, Lucifer's arms lifted, and a quiet, disturbing smile warped his features. "Enjoy, daughter." The water—more sludge than liquid—followed his motion, soaring into the frigid air. A tendril grazed my arm and I recoiled at its vicious bite freeze-burning my skin. The waves moulded against the walls of an invisible dome, imprisoning me.

Then, darkness reigned.

An anvil replaced the brain in my skull and a hammer struck it over and over again, setting my head to throb. Shaking the feeling away did nothing. I had no clue if my vision had been affected either due to the lack of light. If there was some, maybe—

A ray broke through the wall of black, intensifying. My hand covered my eyes, but when I lowered it, the darkness had disappeared. All I could see now was… my house?

The maple tree to the left, the red door, the trimmed rose bushes lining the front beneath the windows, the cars in the driveway, my room on the second story visible past the curtains… even the low buzz of mowing lawns and the rhythmic ticking of sprinklers in the distance were the same. I instantly sat upright when figures emerged from the front door, walking along the stone path.

"Hello, darling," my mom said. "We missed you."

My dad wrapped an arm around her waist, smiling at her and at me. The bags under his eyes had disappeared and his brown hair had grown out like he'd always wanted. He looked so relaxed. So *happy*.

A broken sob stole from my smiling mouth.

My mom opened her arms, her blonde hair dancing in the gentle breeze. "I know you're not too old for hugs."

"What are you doing here?" I asked.

"We're bringing you home, Princess," my dad said, gesturing to the door. "I've just made your favourite." The smell of lasagna consumed my senses.

"I—" A hesitance rooted me in place.

My mom frowned. "What's wrong? Did you not miss us?"

Tears welled in my eyes. "I… I did. I *do*." More than anything. More than life itself.

My dad beamed. "Then what are you doing all the way over there, sweetheart?"

"Come with us, honey," my mom beckoned. "It'll all be over if you come with us."

Was this a dream? I couldn't tell. My fingers spread over my legs. One, two, three… until ten. That meant I was awake. I was truly and completely awake. And I missed my parents. I missed my life. I wanted to go to them, to tell them I loved them and I was sorry.

My foot advanced to go to them, but slowly returned. That same initial hesitance rooted me where I was. As much as I had longed for this, it didn't feel right. A high-pitched ringing filled my ears when I tried to recall what had happened before now. I couldn't remember how I'd gotten here or what I had done then either. The more I looked around at my house, my street, the more everything felt wrong. This was very, very wrong.

"It's not them," I whispered.

My mom's brows furrowed. "Do you not love us?"

"They're not really here," I said through regulated breaths. "It's not really them."

My house disappeared in a blur of shifting colour.

In the blink of an eye, I'd been brought to my living room, my stone chair placed where I'd stood the night my parents died.

My mom's face drained of colour as her hand extended to the floor. "Do you not love us anymore?" she repeated, a sword gravitating into her palm.

My dad knelt in front of her. "You can stop this," he told me. "Please." Terror and heartbreak glistened in his eyes. "Please, stop this."

Stuck on the edge of my seat with nothing but the rush of blood pulsing in my ears, my shadows begged—*pleaded*—with me to be released.

This is a test. This is just a test.

I gripped the chair's freezing armrests to prevent myself from moving. "I'm sorry," I said to my parents. A solitary tear rolled down my cheek. "I'll see you soon, I promise."

Despite having witnessed this event firsthand and having experienced it again recently, its violence would never fail to torment me, to tear at my soul. Even so, I didn't avert my gaze. I watched, unblinking and unmoving, as my mom severed my dad's head before killing herself.

The scene fell away, and I wiped the evidence of my sadness from my face in time for an inscrutable Lucifer to reappear along with the Princes. I immediately searched for Az. His constant solidity—his set jaw and mouth, his critical gaze, his knitted brow—had softened into stinging poignancy.

"I must confess," Lucifer began, contemplative, "I had believed this one would have been the end of your journey." His disappointment didn't lie with the outcome alone. "It appears I'll have to adjust the difficulty of the remaining Stages."

Where Asta brought me back to *Pravus*, Levi and Lucifer departed to find Mon. I didn't know where Az had gone; he'd disappeared into the castle before I could so much as say his name.

"Do you know where Az's room is?" I asked Asta as we crossed the doors into the entry hall. A squadron of Satanials originating from the left-hand corridor encountered us first, evidently bowing to the Daemon Prince of *Varmir* and not to a nameless Zemas.

Asta nodded in greeting to the Satanials, then started up the serpentine steps, "Can I ask why?"

"I have to talk to him about something. Training stuff."

He waggled his brows. "Eager for the next Stage, are we?"

"I'm absolutely buzzing," I deadpanned.

"He ought to be in the Guest Wing where you are." Asta and I directed ourselves there once we attained the landing, but where I would turn left for my quarters, Asta went to the right, tapping my arm. Less than five minutes later, we stopped at a door relatively close to my room. "If he's not here, come join Beel and me in *Paxtara*. All you need do is ask any Satanial and they'll bring you."

"Okay, thanks," I said. Asta hugged me goodbye. Once he was relatively out of sight, I knocked on Az's door; from across, rustling and footsteps sounded. It opened slowly, too slowly for my taste, so I pushed it open myself. Strolling in without invitation, I headed for one of the gilded black armchairs similar to the velvety couch in front of the false fireplace opposite the entrance. "Nice room," I remarked. Across from where I sat, past three pillars, lay the bedroom—although what intrigued me most was the rectangular box a little further left atop one of the many baroque accent tables.

"Why, hello to you too, Adara," Az said, his tone flat. "No, please, do come in. Make yourself comfortable." He shut the door.

"Hi, and alright, I will. Thanks." I rested my feet (my calves, really) on the arm of the couch beside me.

Az pushed them off and brushed the fabric. "Mind telling me why you're here?"

I set my feet on the carpeted floor. "Well, I came to Hell by accident. You should know that; you were there."

"Here as in stalling in *my room*," he specified, and my lips thinned at his observation. "I half-expected you to be on your way to find Lamont to tell him the good news."

We still needed to talk, that was true. "I'll do it later."

Instead of taking a seat on the couch, Az left for the odd box, opening it. A mini fridge? Glass clinked when he produced a jar filled with floating grey ripples, which he handed to me when he returned. "Here."

"Ah. A chilled jar. *Thanksss*." I accepted it, hesitant. "Has anybody ever told you you're a great gift-giver?"

His head tilted. "This isn't a gift, Adara. This is a soul."

My face twisted. "Like the things outside?" I inspected the ripples. "Why are you giving me this not-gift, exactly?"

"This soul is from *Varmir*, which means it needs to be chilled. Violent souls always taste better, in my opinion. Those in my Circle are a close second."

"*Taste?* You're saying that you…" I stared at him, "You *eat* souls?"

Az swiped the jar from me, unscrewed the lid, and took a sip. "Do you want some or not?" He'd once mentioned he didn't need mortal food to survive; this must've been why.

"I'll pass on your *Vintage à la Violence*." Although I refused, the scent made my stomach grumble.

"Adara, you need to have a bit of this," Az insisted. "You're going to starve at this rate if you don't."

"I've survived this long without consuming souls," I replied. "I think I'm good."

"That's not possible. Kamael must've found a way for you to eat them, otherwise you'd most likely be dead."

My dad hadn't done anything of the sort. When could he have possibly—

I stilled.

The seasoning he'd always put in my food. He said it was *oregano*.

The revelation that I'd been ingesting souls since infancy made my stomach churn. The thing in Az's jar had been part of a human once.

Shrinking, I shook my head. "I don't want any of your human-smoothie."

"It's not a human anymore." He pressed the jar into my grasp as he pressed its importance. Cold nipped at my palm, but the warmth spreading on the back of my hand answered in challenge. "Come on, Adara."

As far as I knew, there weren't any *Jollibee's* in Hell, and I wasn't going to let starvation be the reason I failed the Sixes. Bringing the jar to my nose, I sniffed the content, then drank. A small gulp was all it took to chase away my hunger and deep-seated exhaustion.

"And?"

"It's not the worst thing in the world," I answered, returning the jar to him.

He swallowed a mouthful and replaced it in the fridge, ripples curling against the glass.

I'd been consuming souls since childhood because I was partly from this Realm, but what would've happened if a regular human had ingested some?

"Az?"

"Yes, Adara?"

"Theoretically speaking," I inspected the end of my braid, "what would happen if, let's say, a human ate souls?"

Although confused, he said, "It would depend how many times—"

"Could it make the person develop a daemon form when they died?" A light urgency threaded into my voice. "If they went to Hell, would they have a daemon form?"

"Not exactly," he answered. "Daemon forms are rare, which is why souls who possess one exclusively occupy the role of Rijaiks (if it's not filled by a daemon) and partially that of the Primae. Normally, souls shouldn't turn into daemons unless…"

My pulse jumped. "Unless what?"

"Well, unless they've already come into contact with one."

CANTO XXII

Revelations

Guilt leaped into my throat, impossible to swallow down. Az's words replayed in my mind on an endless loop—but so did the realization of yet another consequence of my existence. It amplified. *Shrieked.*

"Adara? What is it?" Az asked.

"I—" My chest shook, and my nails dug into the armrests. "*I* turned Michael into a daemon. It wasn't enough that I sent him to Hell, but I turned him into a daemon."

In an instant, Az had crossed the room and gone to a knee before me. "Adara, you didn't. You're not a daemon; Kamael was an ex-Rijaik who served for hundreds of years. If ever, that's the most likely possibility. Encountering a daemon is a condition—a spark. There needs to be a significant sin—a fuel—to engage with it in order to produce a daemon form in a soul."

"Michael met my dad *because* of me. And I killed them both!" I laughed to fight the urge to cry, to scream. "Michael is here because of me, and my parents are dead *also* because of me."

"You had no idea about the powers you had or their extent, Adara. You can't blame yourself for things that were out of your control."

I pressed the heels of my hands to my eyes. "I've heard that before, and it's no longer a good excuse." It was a temporary fix which had run its course.

"It's not an excuse, nor a temporary fix that's run its course. It's the truth." He removed my hands from my eyes. "And did you forget how you volunteered to face The Sixes for them, to undo it all?" A pause followed, so he could formulate what he wanted to say. "These Stages aren't easy—Circles know *I* haven't been—but you're still here. You're still trying. Your will is strong and so is your resolve to fulfill your promises. It's one of the things I respect and admire the most about you."

Now *that*, I hadn't expected. Not his admission and acknowledgement, not the gentle earnestness of his voice, Hell, not even the sincerity bleeding from his expression. This wasn't a sort of validation I needed; I wasn't in search of it from him or anyone else, for that matter. His accountability and respect, on the other hand? That meant more to me than I cared to admit.

"I wouldn't have passed today if it wasn't for you," I told him. "After the Stage, I understood why you were so adamant about using the memory of my parents' death. Why didn't you tell me you were preparing me for the Third Stage?"

"Lucifer forbade it," Az answered. "He had my brothers and I take an oath after the Second."

"Then how were you able to show me—"

"I found a loophole: passing the memory off as though I was teaching you about your powers would lead you to release the emotions from your system during training rather than in *Varmir*'s Mirror of *Luctae*. And I needed to do it when Levi wasn't there; if he said anything, even accidentally, it wouldn't end well for him with Luce. As for you, well..." He fell silent a moment. "The Second Stage... I wanted to teach you a lesson, yes. I despised how I'd been ordered to monitor you for months instead of being in my Circle, in my home. But your reaction to, and the potential ramifications of, my actions?" His gaze lifted from his hands flexing over mine, nervous. "I had to compensate for them somehow, so I did. I didn't *want* to hurt you." The addition came as a whisper. "I hadn't expected or considered I might be pushing you to a breaking point. I didn't... I didn't enjoy watching you shatter under the weight of the trauma I forced you to re-experience. For that, and everything, I am sorry."

What was I meant to say to this?

"I appreciate you doing this, Az," I managed through my shock. "I think I owe you an apology too. I thought you created that illusion on purpose to hurt me. I made you out to be depraved, said there was something rotten in you, and you didn't correct me. You were ready to let me believe it."

He exhaled a long breath. "There was nothing to correct, really. Look where we are, Adara. We're not exactly Saints down here."

"Az, you can be one of the 'villains' while having honourable intentions. The two aren't mutually exclusive. Oftentimes, it's simply a matter of perspective."

His brows lifted. "That's a very philosophical observation. I hope you'll apply it to yourself as well. You may be Lucifer's daughter, but you're also a decent person, even if at times you don't believe it."

Like before, Az's words gave me the strangest comfort. "I think we should start over. I'm not saying become best friends or anything, but maybe just..."

"Just be civil enough not to want to kill ourselves whenever the other talks?" Az suggested, a smile pulling at the corner of his mouth.

I suppressed the smile wanting to appear when his had. "Something like that. A mutual understanding?"

He shook my hands. "Deal."

I left Az's room feeling lighter than before. Now, my only opponents would be Lucifer and the Stages themselves.

"Adara? Isn't that Az's room?"

I jumped at the sudden noise in the corridor, clutching at my chest. "Don't sneak up on me like that!" I shouted, slapping a chuckling Mon on the shoulder.

"I was on my way to find you," he said. "Why were you over here?"

"I needed to clear a few things up with your brother after my previous Stage. We kind of had an argument before it happened."

"I'm not shocked. You should be careful around him." His tone then was ominous.

"What's that supposed to mean?"

"Nothing." Mon shook his head, looking at his shoes, and shoved his hands into the pockets of his slim cargo pants. "Never mind."

He was hiding something—him and Az both.

"Okay?" I said, albeit still skeptical. "You said you were looking for me? What for?"

"Your Fourth Stage." He cocked a brow. "Why do you look confused?"

I didn't hide my disbelief. "Two *consecutive* Stages? Is that even allowed?"

"Considering Luce makes the rules, I'll assume it is." He motioned for me to follow him from the Guest Wing.

"Do you know what the Stage is about?" Given where we were headed, now it truly would be taking place in the throne room.

"I do. However, I can't tell you. If I did, I'd break the oath I took," he answered, referencing what Az had earlier.

"What happens if you do?"

"I'd most likely be sent to *Praeteritus* for the next hundred thousand years or so."

What?

Az had made it seem as though the loophole he'd used wasn't a big deal, yet if it wouldn't have worked, he'd currently be in *Praeteritus*. He'd risked being imprisoned in the void between the Nine Circles for millennia to help me.

Mon touched my arm. "Are you okay, Adara?"

"*Huh*? Yeah, of course." I dropped the end of my braid that I'd unconsciously been twirling and realized we had arrived at the throne room.

He gave a nod and opened the doors. I entered with my head held high even though I didn't know what awaited me. All I knew was, if I passed this, I'd be one step closer.

One step closer.

I was really glad Az had insisted I drink the *Varmir* soul now.

"Did you only just decide to have me complete two Stages consecutively?" I asked Lucifer, the question completely rhetorical. "You do know that too much of a good thing is a bad thing, right?"

He was alone in the grand hall, at his throne. At the bottom of the dais' stairs sat a metal table decorated with intricate patterns, a Satanial symbol carved into its base. "I see these Stages haven't affected your ability to form sarcastic and unnecessary commentary."

"What in the Nine Circles would happen if I lost such a special gift? I'm sure we'd all be devastated."

A contemplative look crossed Lucifer's face. Despite concealing my outer reaction, on the inside, it unnerved me. "I had Mammon here help me with this Stage. You see, I had to start expanding my scope, thinking of new ideas."

"Nice to see I'm encouraging your creativity," I remarked.

"I've also enlisted the aid of a few… how should I put this? Unwilling volunteers."

He snapped his fingers, and six Satanials mobilized from the side doors, each of whom held a hooded, screaming body soon positioned in a horizontal line near the metal table. Fear pervaded the throne room.

The hoods were ripped from the bodies. Some trembled, eyes frantic and flummoxed.

These weren't souls.

Lucifer motioned to the humans. "These are the Living who signed a contract with me. I granted them what they wanted and received their souls in exchange. In full honesty, I intended on collecting them later but changed my mind for the purpose of this Stage. Why not make this fun for everyone?"

I hid the hesitance in my voice the best I could. "What do you want me to do?"

"This Stage of yours will be different from the last ones."

"In what way?"

"That would be the purpose of this demonstration," he answered, and gestured for Mon to approach. He left my side, nearing the table, and summoned twelve cups from the air. Floating above the metal surface and reflecting the firelight, each was identical in make, filled with the same clear substance.

"I'm going to assume this isn't water," one of the women said, her Greek accent thick.

"Oh, but it is, Anastasia, dear," Lucifer responded. "It just so happens that a number of these cups will contain a special ingredient."

"It's been summoned directly from the frozen depths of the *Trajadian* Trenches in *Griviek*," Mon added.

"The rules are simple," Lucifer said. "Drink from the right cup, and you may keep your soul and live."

"What if we don't?" the woman in a sharp suit next to Anastasia asked.

His black and gold eyes flitted to her. "So wonderful to see you again, Angelica. But come on now. You're an intelligent woman. What do you think will occur?"

A man in expensive clothes threw himself onto his knees at the foot of the stairs. "*Please*," he begged, lip quivering. "I don't want to die."

"I didn't force you into signing a contract, Alexander. You *chose* to sell your soul for money and power. This is your own fault." Lucifer's nose crinkled with the curling of his lip. "Now get up. Your tears are ruining my floor."

Alexander stood reluctantly, shoulders hunching as he choked down his sobs.

"Will we die?" a man with grey hair and a French accent asked. "If we choose the wrong cup, will we die?"

"You'll find out soon enough, François." Lucifer smiled. "You all will."

With a wave of Mon's hand, the table came to life. The metallic patterns rose and formed a large clock, set at twelve minutes. Twelve minutes, twelve cups and six participants. Lucifer hadn't said it explicitly, but statistically speaking, the Living had a fifty percent chance of picking the right cups if half were poisoned. The man named François observed each individually, searching for a difference between them with the help of a red-haired woman, seemingly unbothered by the time. The woman named Anastasia shifted on her feet, gaze passing between the table and Lucifer. In the spur of the moment, she grabbed the closest cup to her and drank from it. She was the first to do so. Only two minutes had elapsed.

She blinked a few times, pressing a hand to her chest and loosing a shaky breath.

She survived.

François took Anastasia's glass, showed it to his partner, and gave her logical explanations and possibilities as to why the woman had survived. He passed his hand over the table, tracing out a pattern, and proposed the answer was found in how the cups were arranged. Anastasia's had been at a point of the star that the twelve formed along the metal markings. Angelica listened in on their conversation while they determined that, since one point had been taken, only four were left on the original five-pointed star. Quickly, she checked how much time was left on the clock:

two more minutes had gone. She grabbed a cup at the point of the star and drank from it.

She survived.

Four people were left. Four people, three points.

The red-haired woman looked at the clock's hands showing it was coming up on five elapsed minutes. She reached for the cup at another point and drank from it.

Now, there were two points.

Alarmed by the remaining men charging forward, François ran to claim one of the final cups at the point of the star across the table, right when half the total time had gone. The last two men wrestled to the floor, fighting the other for the final cup. The man with a scar on his face beat Alexander, his beringed fist returning bloodied with each punch. The reverberating clink of metal hitting the glass floor gave them pause.

François collapsed. His body seized, and with every shake, the more foam leaked from his mouth. When the seizing stopped, the light in his eyes followed.

"Might want to hurry yourselves, gentlemen," Lucifer prompted. His golden head angled toward the clock, which showed ten minutes had passed out of twelve.

The man with the scar shoved Alexander aside, vying for the final point of the star even though the theory had been disproven. A bloodied Alexander had no choice but to select a cup at random. They both drank at the same time. They both met the same fate as François when the clock struck the end of twelve minutes.

Lucifer congratulated the women who'd lived, proceeding to burn each of their contracts. Once complete, the pillars to their left cleaved apart to reveal an image forming between the cracks, a gateway to the Realm of the Living. The women left without another word, almost running toward their way out.

"It's your turn now," Lucifer then said to me.

The cups replaced themselves over the table, and the hands of the clock reset to the start of twelve minutes.

The irregular thumping of my pulse swelled in my ears as I looked at the three dead bodies littering the floor at my feet. Any hope I had of passing this Stage was slipping through my fingers. "But… but it's not possible. There's no way I can do this."

"I did tell you I would start making your Stages more difficult," Lucifer reminded me. "I kept my word, Adara."

I gesticulated to the bodies. "You'll let me die like them? You'll let me *die*!"

"You say that as though I won't see you again." Lucifer laughed, light as a breeze. "Don't worry, daughter. We will see each other in a hundred thousand years. Perhaps then I'll keep you as one of my Satanials."

This was it. I would die here. Why did I expect anything different?

A father was not a dad.

Mon's expression revealed nothing—nothing except the question hiding behind his eyes: would I pass, or would I fail?

The cups hovering above the table refilled, and the hands on the clock began to move.

Think, Adara. Think!

The 'star-point' theory hadn't worked. Well, it had up until a certain point. I reviewed what I knew as fast as possible. The women alone had survived. What did they all have in common? I wasn't going to survive only by being a woman; that would be too easy. Anastasia had been the first to drink from her cup after only two minutes. Angelica followed after another two, and the red-haired woman drank only a minute later. François drank at the halfway mark.

I glanced at the clock: nearing three minutes. I hit my palms against my head, pacing back and forth, beset by dread, by dismay addling my mind. Time was ticking away. The clock's metallic hands hung above me, invisible knives suspended by fraying threads.

Tik… tik… tik…

Wait. I stopped in place.

I laughed. It had been so obvious: everyone who'd drank from a cup before the halfway mark had survived.

As the time approached five elapsed minutes, I grasped at whatever cup I could get my hands on. I finished its contents fully before six minutes. A handful of seconds passed.

I was still standing. *Breathing. Alive.*

Mon's engrossment traded for surprise. His attention shifted to Lucifer, whose head tilted to offer me a smile veiled in a commendation as transparent as the sleeves of his flowing white robes.

I needed to show him I wasn't affected, that he hadn't stopped me despite his efforts. "This wasn't exactly a Satanial-type Stage, now was it?"

Lucifer's hair might have been golden, but his threats were silvery. "The next one will be, I assure you. Mark my words."

A pride I hadn't felt before soared inside of me as I left the throne room. I had passed my Fourth Stage, one I'd thought was impossible. Less than a couple of minutes ago, Lucifer had been prepared to let me die, yet what he hadn't prepared for was my catching on to his recurring theme.

"Adara!" Mon arrived at my side, fixing his striped shirt ruffled by his jog. "How did you figure it out? The Stage?"

"I don't know if you've noticed, but Lucifer has a small obsession with the number six."

He considered my response. "I never thought about it that way." His focus drifted around us and down the corridor.

"Are you looking for something?"

"I'm headed to *Paxtara*," he said, not answering the question fully. "I'd ask if you'd want to come, however, I think it's safe to say you'd enjoy some rest."

"You guessed correctly. I know for a fact that as soon as my head hits a pillow, I'll be out like a light." I began walking again. "Unless another Stage gets sprung on me."

Mon laughed at my joke. When we turned the corner together, Az appeared from the hallway I'd left earlier. I called out his name, wanting to talk to him. He turned at the sound of my voice. A frown immediately formed as he noticed his brother next to me.

"I'll see you around, okay?" I told Mon.

"Remember what I told you," he whispered, alluding to the warning he'd given me about Az. He gently squeezed my shoulder and eyed his brother before leaving in the opposite direction.

After he'd gone, Az asked, "Did something happen?"

"Yeah, a Fourth Stage."

Despite the distance, he reacted the same way I had once I'd found out. "*You had another Stage?* When?"

I pointed in the direction of the throne room. "Just now, actually."

He walked toward me, waving a hand. "No one told me you were having your Fourth Stage."

I met him at the halfway point, stopping at the window overlooking the western part of the chasm surrounding the castle. "Mon was the only one there. Well, him and Lucifer," I amended. "And there were humans too, eventually. I don't know if that counts since they're not from here."

"The Living? Why were they in the throne room?"

"They were being used as a sort of demonstration for what was, by far, the *worst* game of roulette I've ever played. It was a whole production with a clock and twelve cups and an ingredient from the Traja-lala trench or something."

Az's eyes widened. "The *Trajadian* Trenches?"

I tapped my nose. "That's the one. It turns out all the cups became poisonous after six minutes."

"You haven't even built a tolerance to that kind of Hell-poison yet," he responded, baffled. "Lucifer could have killed you. You could've been imprisoned in *Praeteritus* for who knows how long."

Was he worried about *me* going to *Praeteritus*? What a hypocrite.

"Me?" I gave a forced laugh and slapped him on the chest. "You'd be there too, you ass!"

On instinct, his hand drew to the spot I hit. "*Hey!*"

My voice dropped to a harsh whisper in case anybody was around. "Were you just not going to tell me your little 'loophole' could've sent you to *Praeteritus*?"

Az's throat bobbed. "That's irrelevant. It's not what we're talking about right now."

"Answer the damn question. Were you going to tell me?"

He avoided the question again, this time turning away from me in the process. "I truly don't understand why you're so worked up about this."

"You could have *died*."

"And? It doesn't matter." The way he disregarded his own life made me want to tear my hair out—and beat the shit out of him simultaneously.

"'*It doesn't matter?*'" I followed after him and grabbed his shoulder, forcing him to look at me. "It matters to me, Az!"

"Why?"

The intense burning in his eyes when they met mine rendered it difficult to formulate a decent sentence. "Because… because it does."

"'Because' is not an answer."

"Why do you care if I was sent to *Praeteritus*, then?" I countered.

My question caught him off-guard. "I asked you first," he said, crossing his arms over his chest.

I groaned, exasperated by his stubbornness. "You're a real piece of work, you know?"

"I remember saying that about you once."

"We're not getting anywhere with this. What happened to our mutual understanding? I thought it meant we'd be on the same page and, at the very least, start being more honest with each other."

"I'll answer your questions when you answer mine."

"Because I *care*, Az, okay?" I blurted, fed up with the ridiculous back and forth. "After learning what you did, I care that you could've lost your life because of me. As much as I wanted to kill you before, I don't want to be responsible for your death. I've killed enough people as it is."

"That's precisely the reason I wasn't going to tell you anything!" Az swore at the volume of his exclamation. He wiped a hand down his face, pinching the bridge of his nose. "You already blame yourself so much, Adara. I didn't want to add to it, if that's even a possibility for me; I haven't exactly deserved your empathy."

Did he think so little of himself despite shedding part of his aloofness, taking accountability, and placing himself in a position of vulnerability through his honesty?

"Even if I had died, beyond the pain, a hundred thousand years is nothing to me because I would return to my rank—I could return home, but you?" The remainder of his implication stood in the silence, perceptible to us both. Another stood at its back, concealed.

I stood there, speechless. As of recently, he'd been surprising me more and more. Would that be the case for his next answer? "What aren't you telling me?"

His lips parted, preparing to reply, but not a single word left him. All he did was glance at his feet before walking away.

"What happened to answering my questions when I did yours?" I yelled at his back.

Az looked over his shoulder. His mouth moved, however no sound reached my ears.

CANTO XXIII

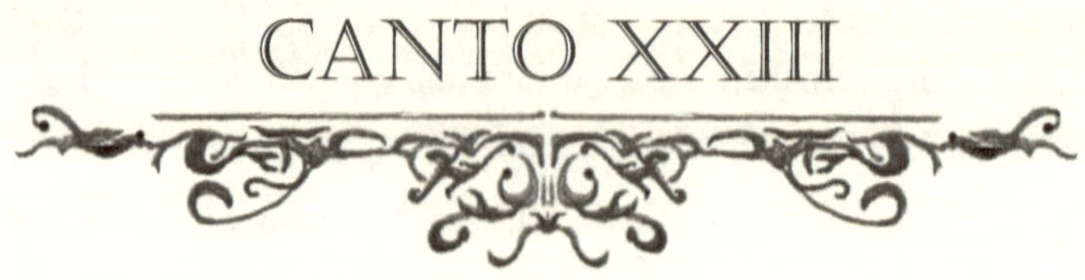

The Darkness Within

I continued through the now-familiar hallway toward my room, absorbed in thought, courtesy of earlier events. Two Stages within mere hours of each other plus the conversations I'd had with Az? It had been stressful to say the least.

When I finally reached my room, I discovered Michael leaning on the door. “I've been looking for you,” he said. “We need to talk.”

Shit. I had told him I would find him later, after his and Az's altercation, but I'd completely forgotten after my Fourth Stage. “I know. I'd have found you sooner somehow, but I finished two Stages one after another. Kicked while already down kind of situation.”

“Was that before or after you came out of that asshole's room?” He didn't bother asking how they went or if I was alright. “Did you handle things like you said you would?”

“Alright, what we aren't going to do is use that tone,” I began. “I got Az to agree not to say anything to Lucifer about your fight, which is why I stayed behind in the training room. Afterwards, I wanted to settle his issue with me, but I didn't have enough time because my Third Stage interrupted us. That's when I went to his room. Long story short, Az apologized and we came to an understanding for the remaining Stages.”

Michael frowned. “What are you doing, Dara?” he said as if I’d done something wrong. “This isn’t the time or place to start making friends, especially with ‘Az.’ I get you’re stuck with him, but you can’t trust him. You should be careful.” He sounded suspiciously similar to Mon.

“Who told you I came out of Az’s room?” I inquired.

Michael’s mouth clamped shut.

“Michael. Answer the question. It was Mammon, wasn’t it?”

Michael nodded.

“Circles help me,” I whispered. Why on Earth would Mon do that? He’d warned me more than once, and here he was warning Michael as well. What did he know? Why did he need to involve Michael?

There had to be more to it. There *had* to be.

“Why does it matter who I heard it from?” Michael returned. “The point is: you can’t trust Asmodeus.”

“Instead of undermining me, he’s helping me now, Michael. So, I do trust him. And if he helps me, he’s consequently helping you too.”

“You’re saying that like he wasn’t forced to train you in the first place.”

“I won’t deny that, but things have changed since then.”

“Yeah, I’m *sure* they have.”

If I told Michael how Az had helped me pass the Third Stage, it would put all of us in danger; and by pretending not to know what Az had done, I could safeguard the legitimacy of my competing in the Stages. “You don’t have to trust him; you just have to trust me, alright? I know what I’m doing.”

Michael’s skepticism mildly cleared. “Alright,” he consented, rubbing my arm. “I wanted to apologize again for what happened in the training room. You know I'd never raise a hand against you. I needed you to get away before I Changed; I didn't want you caught between Asmodeus and me. Clearly, I underestimated my strength."

I tipped my head to my room. "Come in; we can talk more there." He did, following at my heels. I removed my boots at the door, cast my jacket onto the couch, and left for the bed where he soon joined me. "I know you didn't purposely hurt me. I'd assumed it was an accident because it might've been your first Changing, however the fact you didn't seem fazed by it made me think otherwise."

"No, it wasn't the first time," he confessed.

"Why didn't you tell me you had a daemon form?"

Michael's lips thinned. "Well, there wasn't any use. I don't see it as a part of me; I see it as a means of survival here. Deep down, I know who and what I am, and nothing can change that, just like you know who you are."

I wished I shared his convictions, his beliefs, his hope. He might've known who I was, but I had no idea anymore. We could agree on his still being Michael; and I would take him however he came, daemon form or no.

"Besides, once you pass The Sixes, it'll be as though it never existed," he observed.

I hesitated at asking the next question. "And do you know why you developed it?"

He nodded once. "Encountering daemons isn't completely uncommon, Silas says. If it hadn't been Kamael, it'd have been something else. As for the sin…" His brows knitted. "It was how I treated you. How I broke my promise. My anger might have landed me in *Balnara*, but my betrayal secured me a place in *Pravus*, I'm starting to think." No blame tinted his voice.

When I woke up some time later, I discovered Michael had let himself into my quarters, recently returned from his post. "Hey." I smiled, glad to see him. "What are you doing here?"

"I overheard some things." He shut the door at his back. "I came to give you a heads up that your Fifth Stage is starting soon."

Fifth Stage? Lucifer was placing these closer and closer together. How was I supposed to go through this one so soon, especially with having barely done any training since the last?

"Did you happen to overhear what it could be?"

Michael shook his head. "All I know is it's taking place in *Pravus*, in the *Yrantanian* caves. Someone's going to take you there soon. I'm not sure who, though."

"Okay, thanks for letting me know. I appreciate it."

"I have to get back before they notice I'm gone." He kissed me. "Good luck, Dara."

"Thanks." After he'd gone, I put on my Zemas jacket and boots, tied my hair into a high ponytail, and waited for whoever was meant to get me. Despite convincing myself I would be fine and shouldn't panic, I jolted when the knocks echoed throughout the room—the three, slow, consecutive knocks signifying the arrival of the Stage that Lucifer had promised he'd make harder. And this time, I believed him.

I'd expected Asta to be at the door or maybe Levi.

A familiar golden sigil pendant greeted me instead.

Az.

Something in his air had changed, but I couldn't exactly put my finger on it. Once I did, I had to force myself not to stare, not to ask about the long lateral scars adorning his newly exposed forearms. Since when did he wear clothes showing more than a sliver of his neck and wrists? Sure, he'd pushed up the sleeves of his black ribbed sweater, however this was the first time he voluntarily revealed himself like this.

When he said hello, I didn't answer, still bothered by how our last conversation had ended. Contouring him and leaving my room, I started down the hallway, headed to the front of the castle; I'd been to *Yranta*, a part of it anyways, so I didn't need Az to lead me there. We walked in silence filled only by the sound of footsteps clacking on the glass floor and passing Satanials.

"What's with the silent treatment?" Az eventually asked.

I began descending the staircase. "I thought you'd be happy I've finally shut up."

"Yes, I've been throwing a giant celebration with fireworks." He reached for my shoulder. "Adara—" seriousness settled in his saying of my name "—what is it?"

"Fifth Stage stuff," I lied, pushing his hand away and continuing down the stairs. "There are knots in my stomach, that's all. I'm not in a talkative mood."

No matter how hard I tried to bury it, he caught the subtle shift in my tone. "What happened to our mutual understanding? Being more 'honest with each other'?"

I halted, unable to stop the laugh from leaving my mouth. I hated how Az quoted my words back to me, especially while being hypocritical about it himself. "You truly want to know?" I faced him, tilting my head to where he stood. "You didn't answer my question during our last conversation."

"I did. You simply didn't hear me."

"Yeah, which was really cheap of you," I pointed out.

"You should've specified."

So much for that 'starting over' bullshit. Frustrated, I lifted my hands in surrender. "Forget about it. Forget I said anything. I don't have time for this." I descended the rest of the steps and crossed the entrance hall to open the doors.

"Do you even know where you're going?" Az shouted, rushing to catch up.

The *Yrantanian* caves were, evidently, not where I'd visited. "No," I confessed, grudging. "Where are we going?"

Az signalled me to the middle of the glass bridge, pointing to a tunnel in the side of the fiery chasm surrounding the castle when I arrived.

"Is there some kind of ladder or an invisible staircase?" I wondered. "A lava slide, since there's no water?" A quick unfolding noise came from behind, along with a light gust of wind. "I don't like flying."

"What's so wrong with it?" Az's wings bristled as he approached. "You aren't afraid of heights, are you?"

I hesitated but didn't fight him when he positioned my arms to hook around his neck and lifted me from the ground. A shudder rippled through my body at the look I cast over the edge of the bridge. "I'm not afraid of the height," I said. "It's the falling part that bothers me."

His half-bare arms wrapped around me, tight and secure. "There's nothing to worry about."

"I swear on the Nine Circles, Az." A threat laced my words. "If you drop me, mutual understanding or no, I'll punch you."

He shrugged in acknowledgement. "Fair enough. Do you want a countdown?"

"Are you joking? How old do you think I am? Do I want a countdo—"

Az propelled us downwards. I screamed, clutching onto him for dear life. My eyes pinched shut, and I buried my head into his neck, his golden chain surprisingly cool against my cheek.

Only when I felt Az land did I reopen my eyes and remove my arms from around him. "Thanks," I said, embarrassed by the way I had screamed, "for, you know, not dropping me."

"I barely had to carry you considering the fact you almost crushed my neck hanging onto me." He proceeded to massage it.

I chuckled. "Sorry about that. And about your sweater too." I fixed the collar and smoothed the wrinkled fabric. Az tensed beneath my palms. "What's wrong?"

"Nothing." His hand lifted to mine, thumb brushing against its back as he removed it from his chest.

I cleared my throat and, hopefully, the bizarre thought which had come to mind. "Maybe we should…" I pointed in the direction we were supposed to be headed.

"We should go," he said, and ventured into the wide tunnel.

Following relatively close, I could almost see him shaking his head through the dim lighting. The further we walked, the louder the chants and shouts grew until they turned into roars, signalling our arrival. Az paused at the opening and peeked inside. I copied him, suppressing a gasp when I saw where my Fifth Stage would be occurring.

Satanials lined the platforms protruding from the walls in the daemonic theatre. Sharpened rock spikes hung from the ceiling, glowing a menacing orange, red and blue from the fires encircling the area. A tunnel higher up in the rock, metres above the ground, led to a stone balcony on which Lucifer, clad in ivory, stood with Asta, Levi and Mon. Behind them, Michael spoke to a blond Satanial I'd never seen before, who had a gold symbol glinting on his uniform. He must be Silas, the Rijaik, my dad's replacement.

My focus drifted to the very centre of the cave. My stomach dropped. Every array of knife was laid out on an inclined metal plank, a butcher's tools.

And there, invisibly bound atop a mark etched into the floor, was a soul.

I had antagonized Lucifer after the last Stage by saying it hadn't been Satanial-like enough. He'd warned me that the next one would be. He'd kept his word. I needed no instructions from my father; I understood what I had to do.

This was the final step in Satanial training: torture a soul.

Ducking into the tunnel, I slumped against the wall, shaking my head.

"Adara?"

Helplessness gripped my throat, laughed in my face, mocked me. "I can't… I can't do this. Whether that thing is dead or not… I can't do it. I am *screwed.*"

"You're not." Az set his hands on my shoulders. "You can do this, Adara. You're so close."

I wiped my face. A shaky breath parted my lips. "I need you to lie to me," I instructed. "I need you to tell me what I'm going to do isn't horrible."

"I can't."

Disappointment, fear, guilt—each of them ran through me at once, threatening to force me to my knees and destroy my resolve.

The reassuring squeeze Az gave my shoulders brought me to stand upright, prompting my focus to return to him. "Listen to me, Adara. A small piece of advice?"

"Are you allowed to give me this advice?"

"I'm not *not* allowed." He glanced at the soul. "Try to look past it. Look *inside*. See what he's done—his sins—then draw your own conclusions. Your opinion might change." He offered an encouraging smile and left.

What Az said consoled me to an extent, though not fully. I jumped up and down in place, shook out my arms and, in turn, any nerves as well.

I could do this. I *would*.

Deafening shouts thundered when I exited the tunnel and entered my Fifth Stage.

"Ah, here she is! Our new *potential* Satanial!" Lucifer's voice encompassed the cavern, cleaving through the noise. He addressed me directly. "Is this 'Satanial' enough for your liking?"

"I guess." I shrugged, masking my true emotions. "Wouldn't have guessed you were the *Gladiator* type, though."

"It was my idea for the *Yrantanian* Caves!" an excited Levi exclaimed. "I thought it would add a little something extra to the overall ambiance."

Although it wasn't exactly under the most ideal circumstances, he was proud he'd helped.

"It's infinitely better than a dungeon," I granted. "Thanks, Levi."

He beamed, then poked Mon in the arm several times. "See? I told you she'd appreciate it."

"Stop that," Mon said, flicking him on the shoulder. "Don't you have anything better to do? Such as going yachting?"

Levi set his hands on his hips. "What are you talking about? I'm not going yachti—" He noted his navy suit and nautical striped shirt. "'Going YaChTiNg,'" he mimicked. "Hilarious. I'll have you know this is *Ralph Lauren*."

"That doesn't make it look any less like you're about to hop onto a boat with a bottle of champagne for a ride off the coast of Monaco," Mon quipped.

"Lads, can we not do this now?" Asta asked, ever polite. "You're causing a scene."

Sure enough, every Satanial had quieted, staring at the Princes. Levi sent his brother a false smile and told Lucifer to continue with what he'd been saying.

"There's no need for you to talk," I informed Lucifer before he could utter a word. "I know what I have to do."

"Then, by all means," Lucifer extended a hand to the soul, "proceed."

I think I'm going to pass out, I sent to Az, who'd just reached the balcony. He positioned himself as far away from Mammon as possible. He'd taken to standing near Michael over his brother, and that was saying something.

Breathe and remember what I told you.

I wish I'd had more time to develop those kinds of skills. Now, I had no choice. I was going to have to improvise. And honestly? This was the worst time to do it; I had no contingencies for if it backfired.

To suppress my uneasiness, I inhaled a deep breath through my nose and exhaled through my mouth. I subtly nodded to Az.

The ground crunched beneath my boots as I made my way to where the soul was bound. Turmoil threatened to paralyze me, but I pushed past it, reminding myself of my goal, of who and what I was doing this for.

From up close, the soul wasn't burned like the few I'd encountered. It appeared so… human.

Look inside, I instructed myself.

A presence moved within my veins, sluggish and scorching, to concentrate itself into my eyes. Familiar sensations sparked one after the other: the splitting headache, the burning sensation, the stiffness—those I'd feel before I hurt someone.

Look inside, I ordered.

My limbs lost all feeling, and what remained shot toward the soul.

My vision went black for a second, soon adjusting to the limited light. Fire-drenched rock no longer surrounded me. I was in… a basement?

A ray of light issued from beneath the door at the top of a staircase. The hinges groaned, and a knife-wielding man stood in the frame: the soul I was meant to torture, ungnarled and mortal. From behind me, whimpers bounded off the walls, intensifying as he descended the stairs. When he flipped on a light-switch, atrocity emerged.

Three women, their clothes ripped in the worst possible places, were chained to rusty, filthy cots. Panicked looks flitted from one woman to another, their faces bearing sweat and blood and bruises. The man unlocked a blonde woman's shackles, grabbed her arm, and dragged her back up the stairs. From across the door, her screeches merged with the harrowing cries of the remaining women.

I had seen enough.

Summoning the entity that had brought me here, I forced myself to withdraw from the soul's memory.

At first, I'd been hesitant about the prospect of torture. Now, those knives at my side gleamed with a brighter appeal. But that would be too easy. The shadows within me had a different plan, encouraging the approach that had flashed in my mind.

The ugly and mangled body fought against its invisible cage, gnashing its stained teeth through stringy muscles.

Willing the symbol on the floor to vanish, it did, and the invisible walls disappeared with it. The soul wanted to charge forward, to attack, yet it barely made it a step from its departed prison. My searing eyes had set on it—on that scum, that lowlife who deserved the pain I intended on delivering.

Then, it started screaming. *Wailing.*

Each cry fed into the rush of power raging inside of me. Every last one serenaded the darkness roiling within to do more. To do *worse.*

Punishment. Punishment.

The image had already formed in my mind, waiting. All it would require was a single order.

And so I gave it.

The shadows bled from my palms to convene around the soul, weaving and threading around its ankles and wrists as caliginous chains.

Manifesting themselves into the vision, they extended, suspending the soul in the air low enough that I could continue what I'd set out to do.

I didn't need the provided knives when Asta had supplied ample inspiration.

My shadows hardened and crystallized in my hands, forming daggers whose serrated edges burrowed into the junctures where the soul's arms and legs met its body when I loosed them. The darkness twisted in slowly on my command, exacting a howl of agony from the soul and a laugh of unbridled satisfaction from myself.

"Is anyone else really turned on right now?" I heard Levi ask no one in particular.

Asta sighed, shaking his head in disapproval similar to Mammon, who stared at him as though wondering: "Why do you speak?"

Lucifer, on the other hand, rounded and cuffed Levi on the ear. "Spare us your lechery, or else I will have Asmodeus send you to *Arxala* to spend time with the souls there."

Levi rubbed where he'd been hit. "My bad." He chuckled. "I forgot you were here for a second."

My gaze shifted to Az. The shining in his eyes, the smile of absolute pride enlivening his features—they made my pulse race more than torturing this soul did. Returning to it, I sent my shadows to wrap around its neck and tighten every time it struggled against me. With a dagger in hand, I would take this a step further. The soul's jaw dislocated from the sheer force of its screams, its eyes terrified when I set the tip of the dagger onto its worthless body.

At the very core of my being, I understood *this* was what I was meant to be doing. This feeling… I wished it would never go away.

When I finished, I stepped aside to show what I'd done. Satanials shouted, chanted their creed. Their symbol lay engraved in the soul's chest with my dagger in its centre.

Then, I gave my last order: a final touch.

With an immense pull outward, my shadows tore at the impaled junctures until the soul shattered, its dismembered parts scattered on the floor. All that remained was the head, hanging upside-down by the remaining shadow chain.

Pleased with my work, I directed my attention to the balcony. While everyone there exuded respect—*Lucifer included*—Michael didn't.

I recognized that look...

Lucifer's voice flourished like the light of dawn over the horizon, drawing me from my mind. "Well done, Adara. Very well done."

A compliment. Rather than being upset I'd beaten another of his Stages, he'd given me a *compliment.*

He extended a nod of approval and called Silas, the High Order, to his side. "Someone will have to clean that mess up."

After the Rijaik relayed a command to Michael, he disappeared into the tunnel with Lucifer. Michael made his way down the stairs to the other Satanials gathered at the base—Primae, according to their uniform symbols. He passed by someone I didn't recognize headed to speak to Az on the balcony.

Meanwhile, I went to meet Michael. The members of the group he'd joined each congratulated me, including Rasa who was there as well. "Michael, could I talk to you?"

"I'm kind of in the middle of something right now, Dara." His answer was unusually clipped. And since when did my name have that edge to it?

"It's fine, Lamont," Rasa said. "Meet up at the post with us once you're done; we'll have one of the Zemas clear the area." She smiled at me before leaving with her group. "Good job again, hon."

I thanked her and turned to Michael. "What's with you?"

"I don't know what you mean." Michael didn't look at me when he replied. His mind was elsewhere. He was *here*, right in front of me, yet I found myself completely detached from him. No… no, that wasn't it. Observing him for a few seconds longer, I realized that that wasn't the case. In reality, it was the other way around. I felt a detachment: *his* from *me*.

I swallowed the lump in my throat. "You're acting weird. I thought you'd be a little more… happy… I don't know."

"Happy about what?"

"Are you kidding?" I pointed to where I'd been standing. "Did you not see what I did?"

"Which was what, exactly?"

"*Passed* my Fifth Stage?"

"That's not what I saw, Adara." A glance around us left him withdrawing into another tunnel in the rock walls.

"What do you mean?" I followed after him; we weren't finished with this conversation. "It was a Stage, Michael," I stated. "I did what I had to do."

"That's the thing." He veered to me. "I understand you had to do it, but—"

"But, what? What's the problem? You had to do it too, no?"

"It's different." The light of the distant fires caught onto his changing expression. "They were two completely separate situations."

My patience was thinning. "*How?* How is it different?"

"Because I didn't *want* to do it! I didn't want any of this!" he yelled, and I recoiled from his sudden outburst. "I understand you were forced too, except for you… you started off doing it for the Stage, but then… I saw the look in your eyes, Adara. You were enjoying it." He'd hurled it like an accusation, dripping with judgement. "You liked seeing that soul suffer."

I decided to be truthful; if not with him, then with who? "So what if I did? That soul deserved it. You didn't see its final sin, Michael. I did."

"It doesn't matter; it's messed up!" he exclaimed. "You *carved* into it and tore it apart!" A smile broke on my lips as I recalled the memory. "*What the fuck, Adara?* What is wrong with you?" Fright and horror flashed across his face. "You were supposed to be against this, remember? You were supposed to want to get rid of your powers, not use them!"

The reminder snaked around my body, and I retreated into the battleground of my mind. What was so wrong about dealing out a punishment which was completely deserved? What was so wrong with using my shadows to see it through? This had been the first time I'd felt fully connected to them, where I had started to control *them* rather than have them control *me*. That had always been the main challenge—my powerlessness when it came to their sway. But now? The discovery that they could listen to me? That dropping the barrier between us and allowing them to flow unimpeded instead of constantly struggling against them brought me a profound internal peace? That was greater than anything I could have imagined.

How long had I lived in fear of myself, of the force raging inside of me? Caged and starved for years, it had seized any and every opportunity to escape. It had lashed out from the weight of my shame and neglect and disgust.

All it had wanted was recognition and acceptance.

I was *done* being scared. I would demolish the barrier. If I could master my power, why give it up? Why would I want to surrender what I could do, the way I could feel, with my darkness?

Maybe my dad had been right. Maybe this had been a gift all along.

He would be proud of me for this and so would my mom. They loved me knowing what I was from the start. They *loved* me.

"I'm exhausted, Michael," I said with a sigh. "I'm tired of fighting against myself and denying what I have, especially when all that does is harm me. When I welcomed my darkness, I felt right. Whole. Not lost. Not unknown to *myself.* As though I was exactly where I was supposed to be, doing what I was meant to. If admitting that makes me the villain, fine. I'll be the villain."

Michael took a step back. I knew what he was thinking, and, in the faint light, I could see it in his eyes.

I couldn't stop myself from flinching. It felt like an eternity since I'd seen it, however the look was the same: the one he'd given me before calling me a monster. And it *hurt.* It hurt just as much as the first time although he didn't say it out loud. More, even.

I'd shown him who I was, who I'd discovered in the shadows, and he wanted nothing to do with her. All of those promises he'd made turned to ash in our hands, along with whatever remained of us.

To hide my grief and pain, to outrun the sharp stabbing in my chest, I began leaving the tunnel.

"Where are you going?" Michael called after me. "Come on, I didn't say anything, Adara!"

"Were you planning on saying you'll love me regardless?" I fought the tears prickling at my eyes. "How you'll accept me for who I am, not who you want me to be? Do you actually love me, Michael, or do you believe—if you don't convince yourself to, if you don't convince *me* of it—that I'll leave you in Hell?"

Now, he really said nothing. And in the nothingness, I recognized how little he truly knew and understood me.

Every part of me hoped he'd understand, hoped he would accept me however I came. How stupid was I to think that? To believe he would see me in the same light after learning the truth? Why did I ever think he could love me like this?

Darkness and all?

CANTO XXIV

Stepping Into My Own

I had managed to wipe and swallow my tears by the time I'd re-entered the location where my Fifth Stage had taken place. Weaving through the departing Satanials, I climbed the stairs to the balcony to meet with the Daemon Princes who hadn't left yet. Az was nowhere to be seen, and neither was whoever he'd been talking to. I believed it might've been the stranger I'd bumped into while rushing out of the training room a while ago.

"Back so soon, Adara?" Mon remarked.

"I was," I glanced around, "looking for you, actually."

"Oh, really?" He grinned. "Whatever for?"

"The drink you offered me after my First Stage. I'd prefer something strong."

"Coming right up." He nodded and summoned a small shot of a clear liquid.

Thanking him, I tossed it back. *Tequila, my old friend, how I've missed you.* I flipped the glass onto the balustrade. "Give me another one."

"By the Circles, doll face." Levi popped in as I drank the second shot. "What happened to you? Is that tequila?"

"Nothing," I lied. "And it is tequila. I'm in the mood to celebrate. I've made a breakthrough."

"So we saw," Asta said, joining the conversation and hugging me. "I personally thought what you did was brilliant. Very mediaeval-like."

"I was feeling historically inspired, partially thanks to Levi because of the set up."

"You're welcome," Levi said, cheerful as ever. "It's unfortunate Belial couldn't be here, though." He directed a question to his brothers. "Have any of you talked to him recently? I'm supposed to be heading to *Balnara* soon for Phel."

"You volunteered to go, didn't you?" Asta presumed. Levi couldn't hide his smile. "You need to leave William alone, mate."

"Who's William?" I asked.

"William is Belphegor's High Order-slash-boyfriend," Levi answered. "In my opinion, he is one of the hottest Satanials we have. Very much my type, but sadly Phel's already Claimed him, which really sucks because—"

Mon snapped his fingers to gain Levi's attention. "Stay on topic."

"Right, yes. I was wondering if you've heard anything from Belial. I know Lil is coming back soon as well, it's just that she and Zaze have been on radio silence for a while."

"Lil's on an assignment from Luce, although, I haven't the foggiest idea what it is," Asta said. "And Zaze… I reckon he's helping her."

"Belial isn't coming," Mon said. "Apparently there were some new souls he wanted to 'personally welcome to Hell.' I'd say it was an excuse for his anti-social self not to attend."

"Attend what?" I inquired. "My last Stage?"

"Exactly. You're coming up on the big Six." Levi lifted the same number of fingers. "That's no small feat, you know."

"Something tells me I'm going to need a little more than improvisation for that one," I replied with a chuckle.

"Well, your 'improvisation' gave me great inspiration for my book," Mon said. "It helped cure my writer's block. I need to jot everything down before I forget." He tapped my shoulder in farewell and I thanked him again for the drinks. Levi followed soon after to head to *Balnara*.

Considering how unprepared I'd been, my Fifth Stage had turned out pretty well. If I hadn't looked inside the soul to glimpse its past, I had no idea what would've happened, what I would've done. I was curious as to what else I was capable of—and there was one way I'd figure it out.

"I'll never get over how many damn tunnels there are in this place," I commented to Asta. He'd offered to accompany me to the training room when I'd mentioned wanting to practice using my shadows for the final Stage.

He laughed. "You're lucky I was here, otherwise you'd be halfway to *Paxtara* by now."

I returned his laugh. "I don't doubt it." Since he and I were alone, I took the opportunity to gain insight into something that had previously sparked my curiosity. Seeing as it concerned Az, and he and Asta seemed to be close, I thought it could be worth a try. "On a completely unrelated note," I started, "can I ask you a question? You don't have to answer, though."

Asta guided me into the left branch of a forking path. "Sure. Go ahead."

"What's with the scars on Az's arms?"

"Oh. You saw those, did you?" he said after an extended moment of silence. "Usually he's covered up, if not with what he wears then with his abilities. His scars are never on display as they were now. He lets me see them only on occasion, when he wants to be comfortable or doesn't wish to expend his power, since I've resolved not to ask questions."

Although I'd never seen Az use his abilities how Asta mentioned, he did tend to cover up. I'd only ever gotten a small glimpse of the scar on his neck, and when I'd asked him about it, he'd shut me down fairly quickly… and rudely.

"Why is that? Is he ashamed of them in a way?"

"If he is, he hasn't told me. Az is quite…" Asta trailed off, searching for the right word. "*Private*. He tends to keep to himself. Doesn't trust many people."

"Does it," I hesitated, "does it have to do with whatever's going on between him and Mon?"

"I can't say for certain if the two are related. I don't know the full story about what happened between Mon and him. I reckon the only one who knows something is Lilith." Asta paused and placed a hand on my shoulder. "Word to the wise, never pressure Az to talk. Trust me. Getting him to open up is like chipping away at a block of ice with a plastic spoon. Even the most dedicated give up eventually."

But if one were truly dedicated, they'd wait until the ice melted, wouldn't they?

What a strange thought.

"Here we are," Asta said.

We halted at the training room doors. The first time I'd crossed them, I'd had no clue how things were going to turn out. I recalled how Levi had had to run back to *Griviek* because Wesley had snuck into his place, how Asta had had to step in, and how I'd convinced him and Az to tell me about their Vegas story.

"I'll be off. I'm meant to meet with Beel," Asta informed me. "He must be wondering where I am. I don't doubt he's about two seconds away from having a fit about his boots from Zaze."

"Boots?"

"Don't worry about it," he said, hugging me goodbye.

Once Asta had gone, I entered the training room, surprised to discover it was occupied by Az and the person he'd been speaking to on the balcony. My sudden presence drew his focus, and he stopped speaking, mid-sentence. "Hey," I greeted, reaching the two.

The way Az looked at me was off—observed me, more like. What was he trying to decipher or search for?

The other person's eyes passed between us, settling on Az. "Are you really having me do my own intros now?" They waved in Az's face to regain his attention. "Yes, hello! Welcome to *Pravus*. It's nice to have you back from La La Land."

Az blinked. "Ha ha. Very funny, Beel."

"Beel?" I echoed. "*You're* Beelzebub?"

"Beelzebub, ruler of *Lartah*, the First Circle of Hell, at your service." Az's brother lifted my hand and dropped a delicate kiss on it, winking at me. "Otherwise known as the good-looking one of the family."

"And good-looking you are," I agreed, and spotted Az give an exaggerated roll of his eyes. Although Beel's clothes made him appear as though he'd walked off the cover of a GQ or Rolling Stone magazine, with his satin-like trousers and crisp white shirt beneath a leather jacket, that wasn't what had struck me the most; it was the combination of his blush-red eyes with soft sable skin, and how the neatly trimmed and styled facial hair growing around his jaw aided in its definition. "You look so familiar to me."

"I get that a lot when I go to the Realm of the Living," Beel replied. "Then again, humans often get confused. Apparently, they even think Luce and I are the same beings."

I inhaled a breath through gritted teeth. "Ouch, that's crap luck."

A deep, soothing laugh flowed from him. "Honestly." I liked Beel immediately, similar to how I'd instantly liked Levi; he had the personality of someone I'd get along with very well. "By the way, I watched you during your Fifth Stage, Adara. I have to say you did an amazing job. It's crazy. You're all anybody's been talking about around here, especially…" He tipped his head to Az.

"I mean, I would assume so. Az was probably bragging about how he taught me everything I know and how I'd be completely lost without him." I poked Az in the shoulder. "Isn't that right?"

"Surprisingly, no," Beel denied. "Kind of the opposite, actually."

"Oh, *really*?" I arched a brow. "Do tell."

"Well for one, he was practically singing your prais—"

Az interrupted, preventing his brother from revealing any further information. "Adara, why don't you ask Beel to show you his tattoo?"

"Sorry, *what?*" Beel blurted. "You didn't seriously tell her about it, did you?" His mouth fell into a hard line. "Tell me you're joking."

Az shrugged. "She and I had a deal."

I nodded. "We did have a deal."

"She wanted to know about Vegas," Az said.

"I wanted to know about Vegas," I confirmed.

Beel sent Az a pointed glare. "And you just *haaad* to include my tattoo in there, huh?"

"To be fair, I'm known for being quite frustrating," I pointed out. "I would have annoyed him until he told me."

"Cute, but not an excuse. *You—*" He pointed at Az. "We said what *happens* in Vegas *stays* in Vegas."

"*You* said that," Az countered. "I never agreed."

"You guys didn't happen to invent that saying, did you?" I asked no brother in particular.

"I didn't." Az jutted his chin to Beel. "He did while he was drunk. Then a company bought it off of him years later, and Zaze is still jealous about it. It's the only reason Beel is as rich as he is."

"You know that's not true," Beel began, and from the way he was speaking, another argument was surely about to break out. However, he stopped himself and wagged his finger. "Nuh uh. I see what you're doing. Don't change the subject."

"I won't tell anyone, if that's what this is about," I threw into the conversation.

Beel smiled, grateful. "Why thank you, Adara. It's nice to see loyalty to secrecy isn't dead." He'd aimed the joking remark at Az.

I motioned to the two. "Couldn't you tell he had told me beforehand by using your empath powers?"

"They don't necessarily work that way. Hey, I can give you a demonstration if you want?" he offered.

Oh no. Airing whatever emotions I was experiencing, particularly after my falling out with Michael, didn't sound at all entertaining.

"It won't work on you because you're Luce's daughter," Beel explained, and relief instantly rushed into me. "I guess one option's left." He turned and set his blush-red eyes on Az.

Az immediately understood what his brother meant to do. "No, Beel, I'm serious. I don't approve of this."

"Think of it as payback for the Vegas story," Beel justified. "Then we'll be even."

"I don't like you," Az said with a mocking grin. "There. No need for this."

"Too late." Beel focused for a few seconds. Meanwhile, Az tensed and crossed his arms over his chest, shifting from foot to foot. "He's... angry... but that's not exactly new, is it?" Beel said to me, and a smirk formed on his lips. "He's frustrated with more than one aspect of his life. He's confused and conflicted... though about what?"

"Beel." The urgency of Az's warning revealed his brother was dangerously close to uncovering a detail he'd rather keep hidden.

Suddenly, Beel's brows shot up and his smirk faded. He'd discovered it. "*By the Circles...*"

"That's enough." By the tone of Az's voice, he believed Beel had gone too far. "You had your Show and Tell moment. It's over. We're even now."

"Yeah," Beel acknowledged. "On that note, what is it you came here for, Adara? Before we had this fairly eye-opening conversation, of course. Are we intruding on anything?"

"No, no. Not at all," I assured. "After my Fifth Stage, I was a little curious to see what else I could do with my powers. I feel like there's something… more. I just haven't exactly figured out what it is yet."

Beel glanced at Az, then back at me. "I'd help. Genuinely, I would. But have you *seen* these clothes?" He spun in place to display them. "This jacket is *ex*-pen-*sive*, and no offence, but I did not spend four hundred dollars on these boots only to get them creased."

"Four hundred dollars?" I didn't hide my disbelief. "For a single pair of boots?"

"Az can help you, though," Beel volunteered, tapping him on the arm.

"You do realize you can change and come back, right?" Az mentioned.

"In any other circumstance, I would. I'm telling you, I really would, but I was supposed to meet up with Asta literally forever ago. He's going to kick my ass for making him wait."

Az sighed. "You're making up excuses now?"

"Actually, he's not," I told Az. "Asta's the one who walked me here and he did mention something about boots from Zaze. I didn't understand what he meant in the moment."

Beel's face lit up. "Zaze bought me these sick boots from a new Gucci launch he went to with Asta a few months ago. I forgot to pick them up after going to *Paxtara* with Asta a short while back. I always lose track of time down there. Those souls are *so fun* to torment. Their pain always feels the best," he added in as an aside. "I went to visit Kira not too long ago for Pope Innocent VIII. He sanctioned the Witch Burnings, you know. Major betrayal of women."

"I was aware, yes," Az replied. "And, in that case, you're not staying with us?"

"I'm sure you're capable of handling Adara by yourself."

"You should stay with us," Az insisted.

Beel clapped him firmly on the shoulder. "Walk me out, would you?"

"It was nice meeting you," I said to Beel as he left.

Beel turned around to wink at me. "You too, sweetness!"

Az and his brother had probably gotten around to finishing another conversation since I waited in the training room by myself for a while, seated on the stairs leading to the large lancet window. I didn't necessarily mind. In truth, I was trying to process everything that had happened with Michael before I arrived here. Our breakup had stung at first, however, if I was being honest with myself, the initial overwhelming pain had subsided, almost fully gone, which confused me more than anything else. Had some part of me expected this to happen? Had I been unwittingly conditioned into preparing for him to leave me?

At the thought, I stilled. Despite all of Michael's apologies and reassurances concerning our shared trauma and regrets and my volatility, deep down, I had known. He could never love me the way he once did, not like this, not when I'd become nothing but the shadow of the pedestal he'd put the idea of me on—and it was better, *safer*, to begin protecting myself so that when the blow finally came, it wouldn't devastate me as badly as it should have. Perhaps it had been a survival instinct. And yet why were these recognitions the bringers of more sorrow?

I caught movement in my peripheral vision. Az had returned. Wiping my eyes and the underside of my itching nose, I rose from the stairs. As I approached him, I immediately noted he seemed paler than usual. "Are you okay?" I asked. "What did Beel say to you? Is it about what happened before?"

He shook his head. "No, I—it's fine. Everything's fine." He cleared his throat and his attention broke from the floor. His brows furrowed when he met my gaze, and he stepped forward asking, "Are *you* okay?"

"Yeah?" I said, confused. "Why wouldn't I be?"

"You look… far away."

"I could say the same about you," I responded. Az clearly didn't want to mention what had passed between him and his brother a couple of minutes ago. I wouldn't pressure him into telling me or into staying, for that matter. "Honestly, I'd understand if you didn't want to be here with me—"

"No, it's alright," he interjected. "Besides, I'm the one in charge of teaching you to use your *umbra*, anyway."

"'*Umbra*'?" The word was unknown to me. "What is that? A technical term for my shadows?"

"Yes, it's essentially another name for the same thing," he answered. "I know you weren't sure about using your powers at first, however, I think it's safe to say that's not the case anymore."

"Right. My main issue had been the self-imposed barrier, which is gone now. And since you're the expert and you so graciously volunteered—"

"A loose term," he amended.

“Semantics.” I waved a hand. “As I was saying, since you’re here and said you’d help, how about you teach me something new?”

“I hope you don’t mind if we go over things you already know first as a warm-up.”

“Sounds easy enough.”

Az chuckled, and for the first time, I noticed the small dimples in his cheeks. Had they always been there? Or was it because I’d only now witnessed a semblance of a genuine laugh from him? “You seem confident about this.”

“It’s because I *am* confident. You saw me in my Stage. Pretty sure that’s a step in the right direction.”

“Really?” He raised an eyebrow. “Care to make this interesting, then?”

“I’m listening…”

“How about a game?”

That piqued my interest. “What kind of game?”

“After the warm-up and once I finish teaching you, you’ll apply what you’ve learned. We go one versus one and use a point system. Whoever gets the most points by the end of the session wins.”

My shoulders slumped with my dipping excitement. “That’s all we get?”

He shook his head. “You can also win bragging rights.”

A lightbulb switched on in my brain. “You mean to tell me that if I win, I can hold this over your head forever?”

“And if I win, I can hold it over yours,” he replied. “Deal?”

I grabbed his hand and shook it. “Deal.”

This was going to be fun.

CANTO XXV

Temptations

For my warm-up, Az started me off by summoning small shadows and crystallizing them like I'd done in my Fifth Stage. If I had abilities similar to Daemon Princes—Levi had his multiplication, Beel was an empath, Az could create illusions, Asta produced knives from his arms, Mammon summoned objects at will—what other characteristics did I share with them? When Asta had first mentioned their daemon forms, my terror came from the fear of my exterior reflecting my internal darkness. I had nothing to be afraid of now. Not of perception, not of myself.

My fingers curled around the crystallized shadow in my palm. In the facets of the serrated blade, my reflection glimmered, then dissipated with the dagger. "Theoretically, could I have a daemon form, Az?"

"Is that what you've been thinking of this whole time?" he wondered, a rhetorical question. "Focus on your breathing while you summon and crystallize. It'll help you concentrate."

Regulating my breathing equally regulated the form of my shadows and the time in which they took it.

"To answer your question," Az reverted to the topic at hand, "technically speaking, the answer is yes."

"Is it because of Lucifer?"

Az fixated on my technique, quitting his pacing to observe the shadows bleed from my veins into my palms, enraptured. "That's one possibility. There could always be more."

"More?"

"Kamael is the most probable scenario," he explained. "Your proximity to Hell and its operation through him, since he was a Rijaik, could have encouraged its development, and the souls you consumed likely encouraged it further."

I looked at my arms. "Shouldn't I have transformed by now?"

Az shook his head, his loose hair—and the earrings amongst the locks—swaying. "Not necessarily. There could be another barrier within you, similar to the one you had with your shadows. You haven't reached it yet, I believe, or your need for it. My brothers and I use ours for the same reason."

"If that's the case, why didn't you use yours when Michael attacked you? You could've avoided your injury if you had."

"And miss out on the chance to be extorted by you?" Az barked out a laugh, motioning to the room in instruction. "Imagine spreading the darkness around; a well-timed surge can be used as an evasive tactic."

"Your instruction just now sounded like an evasive tactic," I remarked.

"Funny."

I rolled my eyes at him. Focusing on my breathing and the command I relayed to my shadows, they shot out of my palms to fill a section of the room. Not bad for a first try, however, it'd require a lot more concentration and effort to produce a shadow on a larger scale.

"Not horrible for a first try. Go again," Az encouraged. "Really visualize what you want to make happen."

"'Not horrible,'" I repeated. "Frame that for me, would you? Polish it too while you're there. We can hang it up next to your *lack of a response*."

Az nodded a few times. "Alright, that's certainly a choice." Rather than brush me off, he said, "As misguided and out-of-line as Lamont was, answering him with my daemon form would've escalated the problem. It wasn't about winning a battle of wills; it was about not giving you something else to worry about after everything…" pensiveness crested over his face, "which both worked and didn't, now that I consider it."

"I'll nominate you for the *Bizarre but Considerate Award* anyways," I replied. "You'll get a sticker if you win."

Az braced a hand on his hip. "No medal? No plaque?"

"We're low budget this year, unfortunately." Although I didn't doubt what he'd said, it felt as though he was withholding information. "And as for the other part you haven't told me?"

Az pursed his lips. "Luce has this rule about not letting me Change while indoors. It gets kind of… structurally unsound?"

"You break things?"

Confirming, he gestured to the window, the pillars, the balcony. "Especially in a place such as this. If I Change here, I'll never hear the end of it."

Pausing my efforts, I ran to Az, grabbed his hand, and tugged him toward the exit. "There's a *nice* big daemonic colosseum that's probably empty by now. Would be a shame if someone went to use it, huh?"

Az dug his heels into the ground, leaving me to essentially lug a large rock. "Would be a shame if someone forgot we have a game to play," he returned.

I whirled around, releasing his hand. "*Right!* Game then daemon?"

"If *you* win," he added with a fond smile, gone to sit at the top of the stairs, "then daemon. Finish warming up first."

"Yes, *go-go-go-go-go*." I pushed him to his usual place and returned to what I was trying to achieve, raising my hands, attempting to fill the room with darkness; I needed to take this seriously if I was going to beat Az afterwards. The prize called my name: bragging rights and a daemon show.

But Az seemed determined to distract me.

He leaned against a pillar, his legs spread apart so one foot sat on a bottom stair and the other lay in front of him. His hands were clasped behind his black waves, which both brought them forward to gently curl about his cheeks, his jaw, his mouth, and made the sleeves of his sweater strain against his partially-exposed arms. He mindlessly whistled a tune as his ruby eyes rested on me, not the window.

On instinct, I reached for a strand of my hair but stopped. I huffed, annoyed with myself and with him. "Could you quit it? It's distracting."

"Quit what?" he asked, continuing to whistle.

"Seriously, Az, if you don't stop, I'm going to beat it out of you," I threatened.

"Oh?" The noise halted and he dropped his arms, shifting to me. "Why don't we get into it, then?"

My stomach dropped. "R-right now? Like at this moment?"

Az stood and came to face me. "Yes now. We made a deal, didn't we?" He lifted his hands. "Unless you want to back out?"

"I'm not backing out."

"Come for me."

My shadows, once flowing freely through my veins, burst from my open palm. Az's wings swiftly unfurled; he hovered ten feet above the ground, out of the path of my attack. A smile grew on my lips.

"What are you smiling abou—" His eyes widened before drifting to his ankles—to where my *umbra* had been snaking around and tightening.

On command, my shadows yanked forward, throwing him to the ground. "One point for Adara," I announced.

Az released a violent cough, although while he was still down, he countered with a bat of his wings. The motion sent me flying back. My shoulder landed on the wooden floor first, absorbing most of the impact, and prickled as pain danced through it. The spots beginning to form in my vision cleared with my deep breaths. After they'd gone, I got to my feet again.

"That's one point for Asmodeus," he said, mimicking me.

To catch him by surprise, I immediately jabbed at him, but he'd anticipated it and caught my wrist. He brought his arms under my left one and pressed his forearm onto my triceps, hurting enough to force me to bend. If he managed to get me to my knees, he'd be in the lead. I called for my shadows, crystalized them into a jagged dagger in my unattended right hand, and sliced at his leg, which momentarily destabilized him.

Hissing, he dropped to a knee, inspecting the injury. "Did you *cut me*?"

"It's barely a scratch," I said, evaporating my *umbra*. "You're fine. And that's another point for me, by the way." When Az took the hand I lent him, he seized the opportunity and tugged me to the ground while he rose. "Rude," I grumbled. "I was trying… to be… polite."

"This isn't the time for politeness." Az bent, his hands on his hips. "Are you giving up, Highness? I can hear it now: my unlimited bragging rights—"

My swinging leg interrupted his daydreaming. I knocked him off his feet and he hit the wood with a resounding *thud.* Meanwhile, I used the rest of my energy to stand (and cackle). "I think you mean *my* bragging rights."

Az slowly got up, massaging his no-doubt throbbing head. "I should've anticipated that."

I tightened my loosened ponytail, fixed my stance, and gestured for him to come at me. An invisible mist-like substance emerged from his palm, the particles blanketing his being reflective.

In the blink of an eye, Az vanished.

"Oh, come on," I groaned. "I didn't even know you could do that!" A shift on my foot put the whole room into perspective, yet I couldn't find a single trace of him.

"Here I am," he whispered low in my ear. Every hair on my body stood on end in response to his closeness.

Spinning around to hit him, I met empty space and frustration instead. "How the Hell is this fair?"

An invisible hand encircled my arm and launched me ahead with such force I tumbled to my knees.

Az's reply echoed from every direction and none: "Who said we were playing fair?"

I screamed, slamming a fist on the floor. Last time I'd checked, I couldn't see invisible people. How was I supposed to make the invisible visible?

The invisible visible…

That's it.

Although I hadn't mastered the skill, I congregated my *umbra*, fed them my vision, *fuelled* them with my will, and commanded they swallow the light. The darkness listened, bursting from my extremities in churning black waves and crashing across the room. For a split second, an outline of a figure with wings floated near the balcony. If only I could get onto that ledge, closer to Az without him seeing me. If only I could—

My body shattered into a million pieces, thrown into a vacuum to form and reform, moving at a slithering pace, utterly unbound and unfeeling and weightless, but gathered in a mass directly above the balcony's ledge. I glanced around through my veil, concerned about what I had done and how I'd done it.

The fire of the torch across from me flickered. The shadow cast beneath it danced, whispering my name.

I'm in the shadow, I realized.

My hearing was blocked despite not being confined by a physical form. A layer peeled away as I forced the barrier separating me and the outer world to open. Az's illusion disappeared; he flew down, landed on the hardwood, and retracted his wings, searching for me in the room cleared of my *umbra*. His calling of my name grew panicked. I ordered myself to move within the shadow to near him. With his back turned to me, I shot forward.

My body regrouped in time to tackle Az. He struck the ground upon impact, with me above him. "You're *way* more comfortable than the floor," I laughed.

Az winced, his pinched eyes prying open. "Where in the Circles did you come from?"

"From up there." I angled my head to the shadows. "Seems you're not the only one who can become invisible. In conclusion: I *win*."

"You didn't 'win,'" Az stated.

"Yeah, I did. I had more points than you."

"No, you didn't." He attempted to remove me from him. "Admirable try, though."

As soon as he reached for my legs, I hunched and pinned his wrists to the floor. "*Admit* that I won."

"You didn't," he repeated.

"I have you pinned to the ground," I reminded him, tightening my grip.

He slightly lifted upwards. A hint of mischief flashed in his eyes. "I won."

Warmth radiated from him.

Oh...

I released Az's wrists, meaning to push myself off, but his fingers gently pressed into my hips, keeping me in place over his lower torso. My gaze fell to his mouth, to his parted and inviting lips. When I looked back up, I discovered he'd been staring at my mouth as well.

Before I knew it, Az had risen again—had closed the distance between us. My eyes grew wide, stunned by the feeling of the lips I'd been admiring on mine.

Az was *kissing* me.

I could've pushed him away. I should have. For whatever reason, though, that wasn't what I was doing. I was kissing him *back*. I had wanted this. I'd never realized how much, how terribly, until it was actually happening.

Az sat us up. His fingers threading through my hair snapped the elastic, leaving the locks to cascade. My arms wrapped around him and I lifted myself higher onto his lap, demolishing whatever little space remained that separated us. Az groaned out my name, and I devoured the prodigious, ardent longing bleeding from him, begging to be put out of its misery. I forgot where I was, what I was doing, *everything*. Az had scorched every thought in my mind until all that remained was the inescapable feeling of him.

"*What in the actual fuck is this*?"

My head whipped to the source and I jerked back from Az, who'd pulled his hands away from me just as rapidly.

"*Oh, shit.*"

Michael stormed out of the room, slamming the doors behind him.

CANTO XXVI

Every Action Has Its Consequences

I scrambled to my feet and ran after Michael despite not having the slightest clue how I planned to get out of this. All I knew was that he'd witnessed something he shouldn't have and I couldn't let him leave. "Michael?" I shouted down the tunnel. "Michael, wait!"

"Now I can see how it is you've been passing your Stages," he snapped when I finally caught up to him. "What was your 'understanding' exactly? You fuck him and he gives you all the answers? Was that you 'knowing what you're doing?'"

A rush of air left my mouth. I shoved him. "*Fuck you*, Michael." Luckily, my voice didn't crack with the weight of the hurt that his assumption brought. "I worked hard and suffered to get to where I am—more than you'll ever understand!"

"It's not hard to understand how naïve you are, Adara." He shook his head and an empty, lifeless laugh followed. "Your precious Daemon Prince is just using you. You don't mean anything to him."

I played ignorant. "I have no idea what you're talking about."

"Oh, you don't?" He nodded once. "Maybe you'll remember when *your father* asks you about it. That'll jog your memory."

This was not good. Not good at all.

The wheels in Michael's mind turned. "Maybe Lucifer would give me some sort of deal in exchange for this information. He might find it interesting."

Michael was planning on double-crossing me? On essentially nullifying everything I had done to win him and my parents' souls back from Lucifer?

"Lucifer wouldn't give you shit and you know it," I told him, faking confidence and repressing my rage. "He wouldn't believe you. Az and I aren't friends. We can't stand each other."

"Don't waste your time convincing me," Michael said. "Save it for your father."

"Do you realize how simple it would be to tell him about you and me and have him write you off as being vindictive toward me and jealous of Asmodeus because of our forced proximity? But don't let me stop you. Go spin whatever made-up story you want to him."

"I can see what you're doing." Michael scoffed. "Do you think I'm an idiot?"

"Yes, I do," I said with a derisive laugh. "You have to be the dumbest person in the Realms to think that I actually cared about Asmodeus. After all he's done to me, do you honestly believe I would've wanted *him*?" Consideration flashed across Michael's face, though I could tell he wasn't fully convinced. "Face it. I'm your only chance to get out of here. You need me."

"Why am I not surprised you'd bring that up?"

"You *need* me," I repeated. "Think about it. If you say anything to Lucifer, especially the load of bullshit you just concocted, it ruins both of our chances."

Michael started into the tunnel. "We'll see," was all he said. Not knowing what he'd do unsettled the Hell out of me, but my arguments were sound.

Once he'd gone from my sight, I exhaled an exhausted breath and pinched the bridge of my nose. My feet were heavy as I returned to the training room where I had left Az. The only issue was… he wasn't inside anymore. He was leaning against the doorframe, arms crossed, gaze trained on his feet.

"Az…" I trailed off when his eyes lifted. They'd frozen over, hardened and pierced me. I tried to approach him; however, he'd already turned around. I followed him into the training room and found a rift forming near the window. "Az," I warned, "you better not ascendiate from me right now."

He set his drained eyes in defiance to mine. "Watch me." And he stepped through the dimensional tear.

Without so much as a second thought, I sprinted for the closing rift and jumped in after him. A quick crushing against my chest, an intense dose of a spinning free-fall and one overbearing sense of nausea later, I landed directly into the dirt. "Why am I always landing in dirt?" I grumbled, rolling onto my back and wiping a hand down my face.

"Hey, you!" an impatient-sounding Irish woman yelled. "What are you doing on the ground for?"

"Well, I didn't exactly choose to park my face in the dirt on purpose," I answered through my pains.

"Get up and return to your post," the stunning woman ordered.

My post? What was she talking about?

My focus adjusted to my immediate surroundings as I sat upright. Reddish-brown powder dusted my chest, my arms, my legs. I began brushing it off of my body, and while turned to the left, an orange glow flashed. I'd been dropped off at the foot of a fire pit in an area I'd seen before.

I was in *Arxala*; I had ascendiated to the first place I could remember there, the one that had been clearest in my mind.

I pushed myself from the floor. "I need to speak to Az—Asmodeus. I know he's here."

"He would request your presence if it were needed."

"Look, gorgeous, I'm requesting his," I replied. "He and I have unfinished business so if you'd be kind enough to go get him for me, I'd be *very* grateful."

"Unfortunately, Zemas, you are not in any place to request to speak to the Daemon Prince without the approval of your supervisor," the Satanial said. She clasped her hands behind her back, revealing the bronze symbol on her chest: Primae, the second highest Satanial Order.

"Zemas?" I pulled at my jacket. The black symbol glinted on the fabric. "I swear, I'll burn this uniform…" Given where I stood, I'd seen this fire pit from Az's window in his apartment, which meant it was close. I marched away from the Satanial, toward the cliff in the distance. "Az! You get your ass out here *right NOW*!" I yelled at the top of my lungs, stomping. "*AZ!*"

"Get back to your post or I'll *place you* back!" the Satanial barked.

I rounded on her. "Try me. I dare you."

She summoned reinforcements, and from the spiral path appearing along the walls of the soul pit, multiple Satanials rushed out. I hadn't planned on letting things escalate, but my patience was being tested. As the Satanials assembled and approached me, I allowed my *umbra* to spread.

A gust of wind blew my hair into my face and I pushed it back angrily, combing the strands and tucking the solitary blonde streak behind my ear.

"Stand down, Aignéis. This isn't necessary," an authoritative voice said. The Satanials obeyed, assuming a soldier-like stance of ease. "You're to report to the *Zial* Plains right now. All of you."

Aignéis' attention passed to me. "And what of the disobedient Zemas?"

"I'll deal with her," Az answered.

Although reluctance lingered in Aignéis' movements, she complied either way, nodding once and motioning for the Satanials to follow her. I waved them goodbye with a grin.

When they were sufficiently out of view, Az turned me to him. "*What* are you doing? I get home and two seconds later I see you here, yelling, about to start a fight?"

"I warned you before you left," I reminded him.

"I didn't expect you to jump in after me, Adara." Az's tone shifted, leaping from calmness to anger. "Do you understand how dangerous that would've been if you weren't accustomed to ascendiating?"

"It's a good thing I was, then," I said. "Plus, you didn't exactly give me a choice. How was I expected to know you'd throw a fit and leave?"

He forced a dry laugh. "A 'fit?' Are you serious?"

"What else do you want to call it? You just up and left."

"And you should've let me. You should've stayed in *Pravus* to train for your Sixth Stage."

"But you—"

"You're perfectly capable of training by yourself. If ever, you can ask for a replacement. Here's an idea," his voice turned bitter, "why don't you return and ask for *Mon*? I'm sure he'd gladly take over for me considering how close you two are now. Or better yet, have your boyfriend do it since you've expressed your opinion of me so clearly to him once again." Az didn't bring up what I had said specifically, however, the last words were spoken through his teeth.

"Yes, of course. Why didn't I think of that?" Sarcasm rolled through my reply. "I'd definitely want to spend more time with my ex-boyfriend after everything he's said to me."

Az's eyes widened at the mention of the 'ex-boyfriend,' and in a split second, narrowed on me. "This keeps getting better and better. You two broke up and I was your consolation prize, is that it?"

"Are you joking? I'll remind you that *you* kissed *me*."

"You kissed me back," he countered. "That doesn't help your case."

"You're not even giving me a chance to explain."

"Because I don't care." He then added in, "Just like you don't."

"I was *lying* to Michael. For all those books you love reading, you think you'd know how to read a situation."

"Well, you did quite a convincing job, Highness."

I faked shock. "*WOW!* It's almost like that was the whole point."

"Yes, I'm certain it was, rather than some poorly-made excuse to lessen your guilt."

Az's stubbornness was beyond frustrating. What else could I do when he was refusing to hear me out? Talking to him now was like talking to a wall and nothing had a chance of getting past it.

My exasperation finally burst. "You know what?" I blew out my cheeks and set off into an unknown direction. "*Fine*," I muttered to myself. "Whatever." Calling on my shadows, I ordered them to fulfill my request. I had ascendiated to *Pravus* once and I could definitely do it again if I put my mind to it.

"What are you doing?" Az asked.

I lifted my arms and let them drop to my sides in defeat. "I'm going back to *Pravus* like you wanted, remember?"

He shrugged, unbothered and uncaring. "Go right ahead."

Disappointment nearly manifested on my face at his answer, mimicking the aching in my chest at how dismissive he acted. I didn't allow it to. I hardened my expression to reflect his same apathy. "Okay, I will."

"*Good*."

My voice strengthened. "*Great*."

His tone matched itself to mine. "*Fantastic*."

"*Perfect*." My shadows poured from my palms, rising in billows to surround me like they had the first time I'd ascendiated.

I had fully intended to leave. I was prepared to, yet the look that flitted across Az's face, rendered hollow and haunted and forlorn, gave me pause. He'd put on a believable front, I had to admit; however, convinced that I was leaving, his guard had dropped, and the quick flash of emotion I wasn't meant to have seen made me want to chase it away, along with how he'd looked at me and his belief of my feelings toward him: the lies I'd spun to Michael. Even if Az refused to listen to me, at least I'd know I had tried. And that was good enough for me.

"Michael was ready to sell me out!" I blurted. "He was going to sell me *and you* out to Lucifer, thinking he could get out of Hell with it. I had to improvise. I tried to convince Michael by saying—" I glanced at my shadowed boots in shame "—by saying those things about you… that I didn't mean at all." Witnessing Az shut himself off was the worst of it, especially when it had been so hard to get to where we were in the first place. "And just to be clear," I continued, "I didn't kiss you back to fill some sort of void left behind by my ended relationship." When I met Az's gaze, I hoped he would be able to see the truth in mine. "I kissed you back because I… I wanted to." The confession sent heat rippling into me, settling in my cheeks; I trusted the darkness I'd summoned blocked most of the reaction. Having finally said what had been on my mind—having *tried*—I shut my eyes and ordered my shadows to return me to *Pravus*.

"Wait." Az's hand cut through the obscurity, fingers encircling my wrist. He stood before me now. Smoky curls of darkness grazed his chin, latched onto his body. "Call your shadows off."

"You just said—"

"Forget what I said. Call them off," he repeated.

My *umbra* halted by my command and retreated into my veins. Barely a foot of separation existed between Az and me. All that linked us together were his warmed fingers around my wrist and his eyes on mine.

"What is it?"

He inched closer, lowering his head. "Say yes. Please."

"*Yes*."

The thumb of the hand at my neck brushed my jaw, and he drew me toward him. His lips passed over mine, soft as silk, yet not unrenouncing of a keen suffering. The desperate misery of his longing coiled with my own—recognizing, welcoming, accepting with outstretched arms. Mirrored. My fingers dug into his arm to hold and press myself against him.

Us, like this, right now, as we were… it served as a confirmation this hadn't been a fleeting attraction we'd felt only in the situation in which we'd previously found ourselves. It meant *everything*.

Az withdrew, his forehead touching mine and chest rising rapidly from quick breaths.

If I released his arm, I had no idea if he'd disappear or if I would. "What was that for?"

"I needed to see it for myself."

"See what?"

"If you truly meant it." This represented the same for him, his outright confessions a stark opposite of his usual reserved self.

My lips quirked despite my attempt to stop them. "I guess you kind of don't despise me, then, huh?"

"Oh, I don't know." Az laughed, mellifluous and genuine; it had to be the first I'd ever earned from him.

I hid the proud smile that was forming by resting my head against Az's chest. His arms snaked around my waist to keep me close, and my fingers brushed over the uneven bumps on his skin.

Az inhaled deeply, his exhale slow. "I… I got those in Media," he said at length. "It doesn't exist anymore, but it was a region in the present-day Middle East." The falter which had snuck into his words betrayed his certainty when it came to mentioning his scars, leaving him unsure of if he should continue.

"Az, you don't need to tell me anything," I assured.

He took the corner of his bottom lip between his teeth and separated from me, drifting to the pit we'd been standing by to sit down and let his legs hang freely over the edge. When I joined him, my hand found his and gave it a gentle squeeze to let him know I would listen but was also prepared to wait if that was what he wanted.

"I'd been staying in a town in Media for a few years," he began telling me. "I had a life there, became acquainted with people, ones I considered friends. A handful of influential nobles heard rumours about what I was from—from around, and some man who pretended himself a hero offered to help rid the town of 'the threat,'" he managed through the emotion crushing him. "My friends—who I stupidly thought I could trust after the years, who had *welcomed* me, who had made me feel alive—turned on me once they found out what I was. And yet what hurt the most was how the two who'd known from the very beginning betrayed me. They betrayed me, and the commotion this all caused?" He shook his head, pained by the reminder. "That 'hero' I told you about? Well, he was being protected by an angel. We fought; a great battle of Light versus Dark, or so he wanted it to seem. I hesitated in the final minutes, all because I had known him back in Heaven, and it cost me. I was cast out, sent to Egypt, weak. I had lost, and these were what remained." He showed his arms once more, dejected. Desolate. "It's been centuries. *Centuries*, and I still can't…"

My fingers traced the markings.

These scars weren't only a reminder of what had happened—they were a reminder he carried on his body of the ones who'd betrayed him.

He'd wanted to tell me something else, the words on the tip of his tongue but refusing to come out. Nevertheless, he had managed this much—this burden. He had pushed through to share it, still.

"Thank you for telling me," I said, setting a palm to the relics of his loss. "And I wanted to let you know I understand the struggle of non-acceptance. It doesn't matter what others think. What matters is accepting and understanding yourself, and the right people—the ones who will support you—will make you feel alive again." Az didn't interrupt the whole time I spoke, only watched me. "You're lucky because you have your brothers to help you. Asta, Beel… even Levi in all his weirdness and tendency to annoy you," I added, and Az chuckled. "And, well, you have me."

Az angled his head to reveal a look of pleasant surprise. "I do?"

"You're part of the reason I learned to accept myself, Az," I confessed. "So yes. You have me too."

If this would complicate things, I didn't know; I didn't much care in the moment.

Metres beneath the border where we sat, souls writhed in patches of fire and baths of lava. Ghostly bodies. Shells of human beings with burned and decomposed faces, black holes dug into their skulls where their eyes should've been. Lipless mouths left rotted teeth on full display. Nails were dirtied and cracked as they tried to climb up the jagged rock walls.

An idea came to mind, which I voiced aloud: "What do you say we go let all of that pent up anger out on the souls down there?" I gave a sidelong glance into the pit. "I'm sure the guy who runs this place won't mind."

Az gave an endearing smile. "Let's do it."

CANTO XXVII

Thoughts of You

After spending a decent amount of time in the pit, Az and I climbed the long spiral path leading to the surface. "You were right," he told me once we reached the top where we'd sat earlier. "I did need that."

I sighed. "I could get used to you saying 'you were right' to me. It has a nice ring to it; I'd make it my ringtone if I had my phone."

He rolled his eyes. "It's the first and last time you'll ever hear it."

"I wouldn't be so sure about that if I were you." I could've sworn I caught a glimpse of a smile from him as he turned away.

Az pointed to the cliff situated behind us, formed by the formidable mountains. "That's where the apartment is," he informed me. A wave of his hand removed a veil from the cliff-side, and, near the fringe, the glare of windows reflected at me.

"I knew I was screaming at the right one. Imagine I'd been screaming at a random daemon lair?" My face twisted. "*Embarrassing*."

Az's wings unfurled. "Let's head to *my* daemon lair, I suppose."

I opened my arms to him. "What?" I asked when his brows rose.

"You're not going to argue with me on this like you usually do?"

"Do you want me to?"

"Perhaps."

"Wipe that shit-eating grin off your face and come hold me already."

The elevator I had spotted when I'd first landed at Az's apartment had been exactly that. It brought us from the top of the cliff to the white hallway.

Az opened his apartment door, which cleared the opaqueness on the windows and allowed for the fires to illuminate the interior. "After you."

"Not inviting me to stay in the corridor?" I patted his chest on my way in. "Wow. You're such a charmer when you want to be, you know that?"

"Everyone knows this." He entered after me, removed and placed his boots to the side with mine, and headed to the couch. He searched around, found an object from between the cushions (a remote, by the looks of it), and sat, sighing.

"What are you doing?" I halted behind him, hands on the headrest.

He spread his arms. "I'm unwinding." I waited for the rest of his sentence, as I felt there was more to it. "I'm going to watch a movie."

"Really?"

"Whenever I finish reading any book, I like watching movie or series adaptations and noting differences."

"Hey, I do that too."

Az motioned to the screen portraying *The Picture of Dorian Gray*. "Do you want to watch this with me?"

"I find it weird how you've been alive for so long, literally alive when that book came out around a hundred years ago, and you're only getting to reading it now."

"Technically I've finished it," Az corrected. "Besides, you said it yourself; I've been alive for a long time. Things tend to pile up after a while. Now," his head reclined, resting between my hands, so he could look up at me, "are you going to watch this with me or not?"

My fingers itched to trace his features surrounded by night, but I pulled at the collar of my uniform that had suddenly gotten warmer. "I… I'd like to get out of this first."

"There are clothes in the first drawer of the dresser in the room you stayed in. You can grab anything from there." He reverted to sitting upright. "I'm warning you, though, hurry up or I'll start the movie without you."

"Like Hell you will." Reaching over, I plucked the remote from his grasp and ran off in search of my change of clothes.

Deciding against going to the room I'd once slept in, I snuck into Az's instead. Unlike mine, his had no window. Instead, a stunning dark walnut bookcase stretched across the furthest wall. I couldn't help myself from taking a closer look. Every shelf held at least a hundred to two hundred books, similar to those Az had in the living room, however these were much older, their spines worn as though they'd been read a thousand times. *The Picture of Dorian Gray* had been placed back here.

Az's collection wasn't limited to a single genre or language. Names in the Latin alphabet jumped out at me: Brontë, Byron, Dickinson, Sartre, Stoker, Shelley. He had Dante too? These editions were centuries old; *La Commedia* and his treatises on language were there in their *original* vernacular.

I would have to convince Az to lend them to me eventually.

As I continued running my fingers over the multi-coloured stamped spines, one caught my eye more than the rest. I removed the book, surprised at its heft. My eyes drifted to the bottom of the cover where gold lettering spelled Mammon's name, accenting the smooth dark leather binding.

Did he write this?

I flipped to the first page and started reading. The writing brimmed with flowing prose and sharp sentences—all in the language of Hell. Mon's employment point of view made the work read like Mary Shelley's *Frankenstein* or Bram Stoker's *Dracula*, with Mon in the place of Robert Walton or Jonathan Harker. The story began in a city called Ecbatana and described the deaths of seven men, each married to a woman named Sarah, who'd each been killed not long after the weddings had taken place by a creature pursuing her and terrorizing the city's inhabitants. Although I wanted to see how it unfolded, Az's voice startled me into returning the book to its place.

Searching quickly in the dresser opposite his bed, I pulled out a coal-black mock-neck, and ran across the hallway before Az could catch me snooping. After swapping my uniform jacket for the shirt, I found the fabric smelled faintly like him. I didn't know when the scent had become so comforting, but it had, and that somehow felt like everything.

Seeing as how the shirt covered a little past my hip, cutting off near my higher thigh, I removed the remote from my pants and put them with my folded jacket and socks on the dresser. I fixed my hair in the bathroom mirror, washed my hands, swiped the remote from where I'd left it, and made my way back to Az.

"*Finally*. You took my remote *and* your sweet time. Come sit do—" The glance he aimed at me lingered, roaming from my collar to my bare legs.

I contoured the armchair to arrive at the couch, tossing him the remote. "You said to grab anything. I found this shirt in the second drawer. Hope that's okay."

"Circles help me," he whispered so quietly I almost didn't catch it.

"Do you not want me to wear it?" I looked down at his shirt. "You could've just said that. I can take it off if you'd like." I shrugged and lifted the hem near my thighs, reaching my neck before Az shouted '*no*.' I suspected he hadn't meant it to come out as strongly as it did.

"I mean…" He cleared his throat. "Please keep it on."

I pursed my lips and arranged the shirt over my body. "Why? I wouldn't be cold without it. Oh, and 'there isn't all that much to see.'" He picked up on my reference; his cheeks darkened from the rush of blood. "It's what you said last time, remember?"

"*Really?*" Az said, almost in disbelief. He clasped his hands in front of himself. "What else was I supposed to say, Adara? 'Congrats! You caught me staring at you'?"

"Hm." I flipped my hair over my shoulder. "Another typical mortal reaction."

His attention reverted to the TV. "Come on. Let's watch this movie before I change my mind and—" He stopped, not daring to finish his sentence.

"'And,' what?" I wondered, stepping forward.

Az's gaze wandered over me again, deliberate, and his arms extended so that one stayed near his side and the other rested along the top of the couch. His legs spread slightly wider than before to get comfortable in his seat. It should've been an innocent action but it hadn't been. Not in the least. "Should I paint you a picture?"

"Do you have the skill for it?" I answered, and the ruby in his eyes sparked at the challenge in my voice. "Basil Hallward does, anyhow." My head tipped toward the TV, indicating the movie. "He paints Dorian's picture, remember?"

Rather than call me out on my overt taunting, Az played along, taking up the challenge. "He does." He pressed his remote, starting the movie, and pointed it beside him. "Are you coming to sit, or will you stand the whole time?"

I did sit. Incredibly close to him, in fact, on purpose. But what was meant to affect him alone didn't. The opening sequence played, however my attention was split between the movie and the thoughts of acute proximity swirling in my mind. Az moved his hand to place the remote elsewhere, and when it returned, his fingers inadvertently grazed the skin of my bare leg, leaving a burning trace in their wake. My legs squeezed together to stop the pulsing between them, and I dug my nails into my thighs, internally shouting at myself to get out of my head. And it had worked for a while. I managed to concentrate on the portrayal of Dorian Gray, who, for some reason, seemed oddly familiar to me.

My eyelids grew heavy after the first hour. I let them close for a moment, then stirred and awakened on Az's shoulder with the ending credits rolling on the screen.

"Why didn't you wake me?" I mumbled to him. "I missed the ending."

"It's alright," he said in an equally hushed tone. "Go back to sleep, Adara."

When I awoke again, I was no longer on the couch; Az had carried me to the guest room. After a few extended seconds, I attempted to fall asleep again, but the more I tried, the more thoughts flooded my mind, keeping me wide awake. My eyes opened against my will, leaving me to stare at the white ceiling to analyze those thoughts.

The common factor in each and every single one of them was *him.*

And it was driving me insane.

The sheets I'd been wrapped in from all my tossing and turning were pushed to the side as I got out of bed, headed to my closed door. I stopped myself from reaching for the handle.

What am I doing?

My hands went to my face. Exhaling a shaky breath, I turned around and neared the window, waving to remove the tint. The light from the fire pits of the barren wasteland poured through the mullions and tracery, etching circles and leaves and flowers onto the floor.

I shook with impatience, wasting no more than five minutes on the view before returning to the door, only to hold my hand on the cool metal handle.

What is wrong with you, Adara? I hit my forehead against the wood. *Stupid, stupid, stupid.*

I released a sigh and finally opened the door.

Az was on the other side in the dark hallway.

CANTO XXVIII

Be Alone With Me

Az quit his pacing. His hand fell from his mouth, which had been drawn in uncertainty, and he froze in front of my door when I appeared. The light emanating from behind me barely reached him, yet revealed the sudden softness of his features.

"Can't sleep?" Despite being the only ones in the apartment, both of us awake, my voice came out quiet.

"You could say that," Az replied. "Same for you?"

"Yeah, my mind is just—" I prevented myself from saying anything else, from admitting how my head had been filled with thoughts of him. "Busy, I guess." I shifted from one foot to the other. "Thanks for… um… taking me to bed—I mean—bringing me to bed."

"Of course," was all he said. Two words that signified the end of our conversation but kept me rooted in place regardless. No… it wasn't them. It was the mere sight of him.

The brightness of his eyes, the natural curvature of his lips, the flush of darkness on his cheeks…

I swallowed the dryness in my throat and veered away from him to hide the red I knew had spread across my face. "Alright, bye, then." I scurried back into my room, to the window to watch the fires as a distraction. My fingers reached for a strand of hair resting on my shoulder and twisted it, only to abandon the nervous movement not a second later.

Az had entered the room after me.

"I must've forgotten the part where I allowed you to come in," I commented, plucking up my courage and facing him.

He reclined on the wall not far from me, arms crossed over his chest. "I must've forgotten the part where I reminded you this is my apartment," he countered.

"Yes, well, I'm tired now so you can leave." The sentence had left me more quickly than I could comprehend, all to cover up the agitation stirred by his proximity.

"Funny," Az said.

"How's that funny?"

"Just a few minutes ago, you said you couldn't sleep," he recalled.

"I actually—"

"You mean to tell me you got tired again in that short period of time?"

"It could happen," I defended, and he arched a brow. "I mean it *is* happening. Right now. It's happening right—"

He shook his head. "No, it's not." His radiating presence, added to his accurate reading of me and to the pressure of the ongoing fight in my mind, was overwhelming.

"Alright, fine. No it's not," I muttered, hating how easily I had cracked.

"What was that?" he asked, wanting me to repeat myself.

"I said you don't look like you're going to be leaving anytime soon," I lied, "so do you want to tell me why it is you can't sleep?"

Az grew silent at my question, and his arms slacked at his sides. For what felt like an eternity, I could only stand there and watch him, waiting on the sound of his voice while he thought and rethought his answer a hundred times over, searching for the right words. "For the same reason you can't, I suppose," he finally responded. "My mind won't stop thinking."

My voice rose slightly above a whisper. "About?"

At last, his eyes parted from where he'd trained them, hauntingly exquisite.

With every step he took through the shadow and the light, bringing himself that much closer, the more certain I was he could hear the racing of my blood. And when he reached me? It halted completely.

Az lifted a hand, unsure of whether or not to continue. The small step I took toward him brought my cheek into his palm, leaving his thumb to brush beneath the curvature of my eye. "You have consumed every one of my thoughts." His gaze remained on me, unwavering in its enthrallment, in its admiration. "Every. Single. One."

Thoughts of me filled his mind just as how thoughts of him filled mine.

I could see myself in him, not some distorted version he'd created of who and what I should be, but a reflection of every aspect of what made me *me*—aspects that he understood and acknowledged as intimately as his own. His darkness found familiarity in my shadows in return, both captivated and grateful.

I allowed my lips to graze over Az's, the exact amount needed for him to melt under their touch. His lashes fluttered against my cheek as he bent to meet me, his mouth light and smiling on mine. The hands that had been pressing me to him lowered from my back to the edge of my shirt; his palms flattened against my skin beneath, warm and delicate. I pulled at the fabric and he helped to raise it over my head, leaving me in nothing but my bra and underwear. Afterwards, I reached for his hips, hesitantly lifting the hem of his shirt. I'd only ever seen him without it once, and at the time he'd been covered in blood… however, that wasn't the main cause of my apprehension. Az had been secretive about his scars to begin with, and even though he'd shared part of the story behind them, this was another matter entirely. This would be crossing many boundaries he'd spent years protecting.

"Is this okay?" I asked, withdrawing at the uncertainty I thought flashed in his expression.

It must have been a trick of my imagination since his hands came to mine to help remove this barrier. The decision had left him more physically and emotionally exposed than I believed he'd been in a long time. Long, short, large and small… scars peppered every inch of his skin—and every single inch was beautiful, much like a work of art in its own right.

My tracing of his marks induced his eyes to flutter shut, however he fought against the urge to sink into his quiet relief in favour of the one he could gain from watching me continue, from witnessing me witness him without flinching or the revulsion he might've expected to surface. Once my hands drifted from his shoulders to his chest, a dark blush spread on the highpoints of his face, intensified when I held my palm to the two scars crossing over his pounding heart.

"Are you ashamed?" I asked, not because I suspected he was, but to offer him the chance to voice the emotions he'd grown accustomed to suppressing.

"No," he answered, confirming my suspicions. "Years ago, I might've been. I might have been… disgusted, maybe, with myself. However, now…" He glanced at where my hand remained, sincere and steady.

"Now is different."

"Now is different," he repeated, almost thankful.

My hands travelled down his chest, settling on his hips. "Can I continue?"

He nodded. "Please do."

Undoing the fastening on his pants first, I pushed them down by the waistband and followed with his underwear. When he'd stepped out of them, he reached for the straps of my bra, sliding them past my shoulders before undoing the clasp at my back. He cast it aside along with the rest of our clothes.

Hooking his fingers in the band of my underwear, Az lowered himself to his knees, drawing the fabric over my hips, and paused to deposit a kiss on my stomach. His gaze wandered over my naked body on his way, as did his gentle fingers, to commit the path he traced to memory.

I didn't feel self-conscious or uncomfortable like this in front of him. Bare. Exactly how he had chosen to be in front of me.

From his kneeling position, Az glanced upwards at me. "*Divine*."

My hold, which had gravitated to his shoulders while he'd lowered, flexed against his scars. How could he speak a single word, and make it half a prayer but complete sin? How could he look at me with eyes brighter than any gem, than any fire of Hell, like Believers looked to their Saints? I was no saviour, no hero—and he knew it. He *knew*, and still he knelt, all because he understood, because sacrament was sacrament, even when sinister.

When my caresses drew to his face from his hair, he burrowed into my palm. He pressed his lips there, then to my wrist and forearm by my legs. "Can I kiss you here too?"

"Yes. You can."

And he did.

Az advanced, and my hands that had once caressed his hair returned there; but soon my strokes of encouragement became a grip in answer to his own on my hips which he used push to himself closer to me. His tongue passed over my cunt in skillful motions, and he puckered his lips to garner more of my pleasured hums and gasps. More for my sake, yes, but also for his—evident by the vehemence of his hold and of his desirous sighs.

Slowly, the tension he'd been creating within me deepened, almost overwhelming; just when I thought I couldn't endure it anymore, his shining eyes found mind, and all semblance of my composure collapsed.

Az stayed where he was a while longer, lapping up my release, standing only once he was satisfied. The light smile on his wet lips transferred to me when his mouth claimed mine, whispering of want. Willing the feeling to return to my legs, I led him toward the bed. When we reached the edge, he wrapped an arm around my waist, guiding me into a comfortable position.

This left Az to hold himself above, between my open legs, with those night-coloured waves framing his beautiful face. "Tell me now if you want me to stop."

I hadn't needed to entertain the idea. *No. Don't*, I said into his mind. *I want you.*

"I want to hear you say it." The most delicate and honeyed of pleas lived in his reply.

The anticipation of his touch and my aching from the lack of it was unbearable. "*I want you.*"

As soon as the repetition reached his ears, his mouth strategically trailed kisses from my cheek to my jaw, flitting to my neck and collarbone; then, he lingered on my chest where his tongue flattened against the hardened tip of one breast while he palmed the other.

I held onto him, brushing my fingertips back and forth on his decorated arms, although I stopped when he continued his descent along my sternum to my stomach and to the beauty mark at the juncture between my hip and thigh. All the while, his hands followed where his lips went, grazing the exposed skin and provoking a burning chill to shoot through my body. Eventually, his palms glided up my arms to my wrists, and he intertwined his fingers with mine to carry the result of our joining to either side of my head, against the pillow where he equally braced his forearms.

Az maintained direct eye contact with me as he finally moved forward. A soft grunt caught in the base of my throat at the foreign feeling. Even though the sound had been faint, light concern crossed his beautiful features. "Are you alright?"

"Never better. Keep going."

With my assurance, Az started to move again, his necklace brushing my collarbone. The slightly strange sensation I'd felt a few seconds ago began to fade, replaced by the rise of the one he'd caused when he had knelt before me. My hands clenched in his, and he responded with equal force, equal fervour.

Lifting my legs higher on his hips and angling my head upwards to him, I murmured, "*Come here, come closer to me, Az*."

Fondness consumed his expression at my request. His hands slipped from mine if only to cup my face, to frame it here, with himself, and his sigh of my name echoed into me, devastating and divine in its tenderness. He maintained the same motion, the same strength, whispering small encouragements between kisses. The pressure engulfing my body crept down the length of my spine until an unimaginable thrill arched through me in a great electrifying burst, fierce and blinding. I opened my eyes at precisely the right time to witness a blushing, ethereal Az come utterly undone as he called for me.

Once we'd recovered, he removed himself from inside me, but stayed hovering above my body; with a soft smile, he placed a gentle kiss on my chest, over my heart. I curled my ankle around his calf and slid it upwards. In one quick motion, while he was unprepared and unsuspecting, I flipped him and straddled his lower torso.

Az laughed in that way I'd been longing to hear; the affection in the sound melded into the lightness of his knuckles gliding along the length of my upper thighs. "This looks familiar, don't you think?" he remarked, alluding to the moment we'd had in the training room.

Grazing his cheek with my fingers, I let my touch drift to his dimples and his jaw. "How's this version?"

"Just as great," Az replied. His hands slid past my thighs and hips to my waist. "Tell me what it is you want."

My thumb outlining the underside of his mouth, feeling his every word, returned to his jaw. "I want what you do."

Understanding, Az proceeded to lift my hips so I could sit on him. The new position brought an equally new tension with it since I was on top for the first time. With my palms pressed to his chest, I moved slowly, raising and rotating my hips until a gratifying pang made me shudder. Whatever I was doing seemed to work for Az too—his eyes snapped shut and a half-groaned '*Adara*' tumbled from his parted lips. I bent toward him to kiss the scars near his neck, on his shoulders, above his heart; by the Circles, the force of its beating alone could be enough to ruin me. When he reopened his eyes, his hips lifted to meet mine, contributing his own motions. Extraordinary warmth pooled in the base of my stomach. I sighed at its expansion, biting my bottom lip, and when blood bloomed in my mouth, so too did it bloom in Az's. He'd lurched forward, having thought us too far, and now we shared this unholy covenant between us.

The next instant, Az sat us up like he'd done in the training room, digging a hand into my hair and pulling on it gently to expose my throat. He dragged his lips along the skin, and I moaned at his invasion and devouring of my senses. Enclosing my body in his arms, he kept one hand splayed between my shoulder blades and the other at the small of my back. He leaned in close to my heart, and I threaded my fingers through his waves from the base of his skull, all to keep him exactly where he was.

We clung to each other, desperate, as if we both feared the exact same thing: that somehow, we could disappear from one another at any second.

My release built as a raging fire in my stomach, scorching and unrelenting. Az looked up at me, repeating my name over and over again. At the last, he quivered violently and his wings unfurled from his back at a tremendous speed, which served as the final push I'd needed to completely unravel in his arms.

After staying how we were for I didn't know how long, Az pressed a kiss to my heart and held onto my waist to help me up. He hadn't registered his wings had shown themselves yet. When he had taken notice of them, however, his brows drew together and he retracted them. He then lay down, and his right arm came to drape around my shoulders to keep me close, to keep my body in contact with his.

I entangled my legs with Az's, resting my head on his quick-beating chest. "Has that not happened before? The thing with your wings?"

"This would be the first time."

I glanced up at him. "What does it mean?"

"I'm not sure," he met my eyes, "but I think it's something good."

I hummed in answer, pleased. Returning my head to lay on him, I kissed his chest and traced the two crossing scars there. He stroked my hair, inducing a yawn from me. It became harder and harder to stay awake.

Az bent to kiss my forehead. "You can sleep, Addie."

Every part of my body froze, my bones replaced by ice. A sharp pain clawed at my chest, at my memories. I waited until Az's breathing slowed, indicating he'd fallen asleep, and carefully slipped out of bed, leaving him to stir peacefully.

Addie.

Lost in thought, I wandered to the window in the living room, which bathed me in the shadow and light of flowers and leaves. Beyond, uniformed bodies surrounded the pits, looking in and shouting while patrolling the borders. I'd once stood in this very spot the first time Az had introduced me to *Arxala*, to his home.

He had called me Addie. To him, it might not have been important, but for me? It meant infinitely more. And everything was so different now.

I shivered at the coldness sweeping over me much like a blanket of snow—light but stinging. My arms wrapped around myself, though I soon realized this cold wasn't external.

The coldness dissipated when Az approached from behind and replaced my arms with his. His palms were warm as they slid across my stomach, pressing me to him. He dropped a kiss on my shoulder. "What's wrong?"

My thumb drew lazy circles over the hand on my stomach. "Nothing."

He took two deep breaths before he spoke, and when he did, an uncertainty had stolen into his voice, almost to the point of insecurity. "Are you having second thoughts?"

"Are you asking me if I regret being with you?"

From over my shoulder, Az turned his head, seemingly embarrassed to answer my question.

"I don't," I told him, "not one bit." And it was the truth. It added to the complication of things, yes, however I had no regrets.

"Then what is it?"

"Az, I'm fine."

"Why are you lying to me, Addie?"

There it was again, except this time, no sadness washed through me. The way he'd said it… I couldn't figure out what it was exactly.

"Was it something I said?" he pursued.

My separation from him spurred his concern. "I never let anyone use that name before," I confessed, focusing on my breathing. "The only people I ever let call me Addie were my parents. Not my friends, Hell, I didn't even allow Michael to call me that."

Az's face fell. "I'm sorry, Adara. I didn't know. I never heard…"

"It's fine. You couldn't possibly have known. It's a little weird hearing it again… in such different circumstances. Kind of makes me realize how much I've missed it." My shoulders sank with my sigh. "I probably sound so stupid right now."

"No, Adara, not at all. I understand what you mean. If this is what you want, then I won't use it."

But that wasn't what I wanted. Quite the opposite, in fact.

"Az, you've entrusted me with a part of yourself, one I doubt you've shared with many others." I neared him and placed a hand over the scars on his arms. "It was important to you, just as this name is to me. And I… I want to share this part of myself with you because I trust you too. I'm aware it's not the same thing, but I—"

I never finished my sentence. Az had already moved forward. His lips found mine with such profound sentiment that I could feel precisely how much significance my words held for him, and he whispered into me what I had shared with him.

Looking out at *Arxala* with Az's slow stroking of my arms, time slowed. In that moment, everything disappeared. We were all that existed.

And it was perfect.

CANTO XXIX

The Calm Before the Storm

The golden-orange glow pouring from beyond the glass into the otherwise dark room greeted me when I woke, illuminating my arms and legs entwined in Az's. We had held onto each other the whole time we'd slept, tangled in sheets.

I craned to look at him, catching him shut his eyes. "Oh no, don't mind me. You can keep admiring the view." Despite calling on his every reserve of self-control, a cheeky grin grew on his lips. "I knew you were faking." I chuckled. "You were watching me sleep, weren't you?"

"I was not," Az said, undoubtedly lying. "I was, uh, admiring the thread count of the sheets…" I stared at him, unconvinced, and he broke. "Alright, *fine*. Yes, you caught me. Congratulations, you're Sherlock Holmes."

"You," I poked his chest, "are the worst liar."

His hand came to mine, leaving it to spread over the area I'd poked. His nose crinkled as he smiled, which I'd never seen until now. *Adorable*. He'd probably have laughed that off or denied it had I spoken out loud.

I kissed his cheek and moved my lips to the other. Right as I arrived at his mouth, something rubbed against my thigh. I raised a suggestive eyebrow. "Excited, are we?"

"I can't exactly control it," Az defended. "And it's not helping that you're near me like this either."

I faked innocence. "Like what?"

"You know what," he replied, lifting the blankets off of us. He withdrew from the bed, and I realized this was the first time I'd seen his back. Fewer scars adorned the skin, but the largest were the ones of his wings on his shoulder blades.

"Where are you going?" I failed to avoid making it sound like a plea for him to come back.

"To shower." Az angled his head in the bathroom's direction and disappeared inside.

"I'll stay here, shall I?" I muttered, lying down again. My head hit the pillow and I stretched my arms out, fingers flexing on the sheets as they had on Az to keep him close to me. I reached for a strand of hair and twirled it while debating what I should do next.

My focus slid to where he had gone.

Now out of bed and across the room, I pushed the bathroom door open. Steam clouded the mirror to my right, as well as the shower. No matter how fogged the glass was, I could still make Az out through it. His palms rested on the wall facing the showerhead, the water cascading and sluicing over the curves of his arms, his chest, his side. He tossed his head back, passing his hands over his wet hair and raking it from his beautiful face.

Circles help me.

Warmth welcomed me when I stepped into the shower. I slid the door shut, reached for Az, and pressed my lips to one of the scars on his shoulder.

"I was wondering when you'd decide to show up." He turned to me. "I was less than a minute away from coming to get you myself."

"A written invitation maybe for next time." When he chuckled, I brushed aside the curl which had fallen onto his cheekbone. The water dripping down the soft angles only enhanced how painstakingly pretty he was. "I think you're beautiful, you know that?"

Dark blood rushed to his cheeks, and it wasn't due to the heat. He took his bottom lip between his teeth to stop his mouth from reacting. In the end, he couldn't help himself; that dimpled smile of his came through, bright and endearing. He answered me with a kiss. Beneath its layer of lightness waited an emotion I encouraged to surface. My thumbs caressed his flushed cheekbones, and I guided us backwards. His hands glided to my legs to wrap them around his waist.

Az pinned me against the shower wall and broke from my mouth to ask, "Can I fuck you, Adara?"

My want flared. "Yes, you can."

At registering my answer, Az slipped a hand between us to guide himself into me. He moved slowly at first until I spoke my desires into his ear. My whispered words rippled into him and his pace steadily increased, claiming gratified gasps from us both and a recognition of how much restraint he'd been exercising when we'd woken up together moments ago. His mouth and hands were still gentle on my hips, my arms, my chest, as was his tongue, which ran along my wet skin to sooth the marks his fervid lips were leaving behind.

Az's pleasured groans of my name echoed, blending and merging with my repetitions of his. My legs tightened around his waist, and my nails dug into his shoulders as he pulled me closer while moving his own hips.

The sweet insanctity of his pleas for me provoked my dissolve into rapture with a shout.

Not soon after, Az's wings burst from his back, striking the side walls.

He leaned his forehead on mine, holding my face in his hands, and I stayed there, arms hooked around his neck. My chest rose in rapid bursts, lungs absorbing the steam-laden air while I tried to replace the thoughts that had completely left me. Az didn't answer to my murmur of his name, seemingly for the same reason.

Angling his face, I said, "Az?"

"Huh?" He blinked a few times, returning to the present, and lowered me, ensuring my feet were secure on the tiled floor before releasing my waist.

"Not meaning to alarm you but," I pointed to his wings, "it kind of happened again."

They disappeared in the blink of an eye. "This is the second time now."

"Do I get a prize or unlock a new level when I reach five?"

He fought a grin and brought the shampoo to my hair. "You are so strange."

Az and I spent the next ten minutes *actually* showering. We took turns lathering shampoo into the other's hair and rinsing it out. We repeated the process with the body-wash afterwards.

"Well, that was a great shower," I said when we had finished.

He fixed a towel around me, his own hanging low on his hips. "Definitely."

"Minus the whole 'almost breaking it' part."

He wiped the condensation from the mirror. "In my defence, I wasn't aware that was going to happen."

"Again," I added.

He passed me another towel to dry my hair with, similar to his own. "You almost cost me a shower."

I sponged up the water from the dripping strands. "I'd pay you for the damage, but I don't know what the exchange rate is down here."

"Exchange rate?" He chuckled, shaking his head. "Where do you come up with this stuff?"

"What can I say?" I tapped the side of my head, right at my temple. "I have a gift." As we continued to dry our hair, a veiled thought played at the back of my mind. Had I forgotten something? This feeling always appeared when I forgot to do—*Oh*. Oh no.

"Adara?" Az noticed my sudden change in air. "What is it?"

"We…" I struggled to form the slightest coherent sentence.

"Addie, what's wrong?" Az hung his hair towel around his neck. "Collect your thoughts and talk to me."

"I'm not… I'm not going to get pregnant, am I?"

Az kept a straight face only for so long until he started laughing and didn't stop until I threw my hair towel at him.

"Why are you laughing right now?" I demanded. "This is serious!"

And it was. Very serious. We'd had sex three times, none of which had been protected. I wasn't ready to have kids. In fact, as soon as I'd been old enough to learn about the concept and my body, I was sure that having children was not for me and my opinion hadn't changed over the years. It never would. I didn't think I'd ever have to visit the topic like this, least of all with and because of Az.

Az calmed down, and said, "Don't you think if it were possible, we would've done things a little differently?"

"So let me get this clear: I *won't* get pregnant?"

"No, you won't," he kissed the damp hair on the top of my head, "alright?"

Relief blanketed me. "Okay."

"Good." Az opened one of the bathroom vanity drawers and produced a brush. "Now, come here."

I went to him and he retreated by a step to place me in front, before the mirror. He set the brush against my hair to comb it out, careful not to tug on any knots. Although we were both aware I was capable of doing this myself, he did it anyhow. His fingers tucked away strands, soft and soothing.

When Az finished with my hair, he removed the towel from around his neck to start on his own. He stopped when I extended a hand, waiting for him to give me the brush so I could do the same as he'd done for me. He gladly obliged, and I enjoyed twisting his locks into more defined curls.

On our way out of the bathroom, Az stopped suddenly and his head tilted.

"What?" My hand settled on his arm. "Az, what is it?"

He exhaled a sharp breath. Whatever he was going to say wouldn't be good. "Lucifer is wondering where I am," he told me. "I'm guessing he's going to be calling for you soon as well. Apparently, your Sixth Stage is being moved up."

My jaw dropped. I had completely forgotten about it. "*Oh shit.*"

"Don't worry about it just yet. Get changed into your uniform and meet me in the main area, alright?" Az said. He left the room right after.

I grabbed the uniform I'd removed when I had arrived at the apartment, shaking it out in case any dirt was left over, along with my underwear from the pile of clothes on the floor. I began to rifle through the drawers filled with Az's shirts in search of socks and opened the second-to-last to find a number of women's underwear sitting untouched. In the last drawer were pants and shirts.

Why does he have these?

"Addie? Are you done?"

I'll ask him later.

I took a pair of socks and shut the drawer. Buttoning up my jacket and fixing its collar, I left the bedroom and entered the main area. When I got there, I noticed his arms were exposed again. His usual golden chain hung over the black high-collared shirt, and the material hugged the top of his arms as he tied his damp hair in a half-bun. I adored when his hair was loose, but he had this certain effortless-yet-composed look to him when he tied it. Not to mention his impeccable earrings were on full display now.

He smiled when he caught me staring. "Are you enjoying the view?"

"I think I prefer you with fewer clothes," I said. "If we didn't have somewhere to be, chances are things would be progressing very differently, trust me."

"Oh?"

I nodded and pointed to the counter. "Like there." I pointed to the couch. "There." And finally, I pointed to the window. "*Especially* there."

Az swore and tugged at his straight-leg trousers. "Now is not the time to be saying that to me."

"Why?" I approached him. "Do I make you nervous?" I kissed his ear and slipped a hand to palm him through his pants. "*Come on.* We can be quick." Az turned me around and ran his fingers through my hair to gather it into a ponytail. "I thought we had places to be," I said, pleased that I'd changed his mind. "Although, I don't mind where this is going."

"As much as I would love to let you do whatever you want to me, we do have places to be. I'm tying your hair so it doesn't distract you during your Stage."

My shoulders dropped in disappointment. "Are you serious?"

"Yes, get your mind out of the gutter."

"*Asshole*," I muttered.

"No, my name is Az. You think you'd know that by now, considering how often you moaned it," he said in the most casual manner.

"You are such an ass!" I exclaimed through a disbelieving smile.

"Oh, and the Circles wept," he drawled, and went to the kitchen to start making coffee. He removed a jar of souls from his fridge and set it down. "Are you going to have some?"

I rested my elbows on the counter. "I love how you're saying that as though you're making cold brew."

"Nothing enhances energy like coffee and souls."

"Pretty sure we need it after what we've spent our time doing."

"Hey," he pointed at me, "don't start again."

I raised my hands in defence. "I'm not starting anything."

He nodded once and removed two mugs from his cupboard. "Sure you weren't."

I stopped him as he was about to prepare the drink. "You can put the second mug back," I instructed, and motioned to his.

He pushed his coffee to me. "This is becoming a regular occurrence, then."

"It tastes better when it's stolen from someone else," I told him in between sips. "It's an unspoken fact."

Az wouldn't fight me on this. "At least the souls are going to kick in when you need them most. You'll be set for your last Stage."

The last Stage. This was it. I was so close to the end, so close to what I had been working toward. And yet I had no idea what would happen afterwards if I won, if I got everything I wanted. The complications were piling up, throwing themselves into a giant knot I would soon need to untangle.

I'll cross that bridge when I get to it, I told myself. Unfortunately, I was underestimating just how quickly it was closing in.

Az swallowed his mouthful of coffee and deposited his mug on the counter. "Are you ascendiating by yourself or do you want to come with me?"

"I mean, I don't want to risk getting trapped in another dimension," I replied, and headed to lace my boots up at the door. Being trapped in another dimension wasn't an actual concern of mine anymore.

Az opened the front door and held out a hand. I placed mine in his and we were off. In a couple of seconds, we landed in the opening of a tunnel leading directly to the castle at the epicentre of Hell. The bridge was empty—no one and nothing in sight. Az and I crossed it to reach the doors, which opened when I lifted my hand to them.

Once we entered the castle, my attention drew to a blond Satanial: the Rijaik I'd seen speaking to Michael after my Fifth Stage. Silas emerged from the left wing with a group of four Satanials and three slender, skeleton-like daemons. When he took notice of Az and I's arrival, he gave the group an order and dismissed them. As they left, each bowed their heads in acknowledgement of us. The daemons, however, spent a somewhat longer time bowing in our presence than the Satanials, but they stood closer to me than to Az.

"***Irnith tellah ohlor enarteh.***"

Continue on your way, the High Order said.

The daemons obeyed, departing from the castle, and the doors shut with a *boom*. Silas shook Az's hand like an old friend would and offered me a bow of his head. Afterwards, he informed us that Lucifer waited in the throne room and personally escorted us there. With him walking ahead, Az and I were out of his field of vision. This allowed Az to stay near me. To keep his hand in contact with mine.

With the distance to the throne room decreasing, so did the depths of my breathing. It settled only when Az's hand at my side slid to my lower back. That small, singular gesture spoke volumes, conveying more than could have ever been spoken aloud. It was reassurance, yes, but also belief, trust and support.

When the Rijaik opened the golden doors, Az dropped his hand and kept a safe distance from me. Two rows of Satanials were assisting to the display, lining the long of the hall at each pillar. Lucifer was at his throne as always, the Satanial tapestry behind him still as striking as the first time I'd seen it. Mammon and Asta were next to each other on seats to the right made of black glass that had bled upwards from the ground in front of the dais. On the left, Levi sat by someone I could only assume to be Belphegor. His pronounced eyebrows shot up at seeing Az, his deep vermilion eyes happy and clear beneath them.

I scanned the gathered Daemon Princes.

Where's Beel?

"Hello again, daughter," Lucifer said as I approached. "I should inform you that, only a short while ago, I heard news from a Primae in *Arxala* about an angry and 'disobedient Zemas' with the ability to control shadows."

"Ah, Aignéis is still talking about me, huh? I didn't realize she felt that way for me. I should call her."

Levi elbowed Belphegor. "Adara is like Az and I."

Lucifer ignored my quip. "Any further insight on the 'disobedient Zemas' part in particular?" It sounded more like a demand than a question.

"She was pissing me off," I answered, shrugging. "Nothing more to it."

His gold and black eyes narrowed. "I'm wondering why it is you were there in the first place."

What should I say? I asked Az through our minds. *I can't exactly tell him we were alone in* Arxala.

Az improvised. He did his best to act as apathetic and disinterested as possible. "I instructed it. Her ascendiating was terrible."

"*Hey.*" I whirled to him, offended, adding to our story and the animosity we'd once had. "It was not terrible."

Az looked from me to Lucifer and back again. "It was," he maintained. "I'd use the word 'rough,' but that wouldn't come close to covering it."

"Here we go, alright." I nodded in mocking. "You're just upset because my method worked and yours didn't."

"Upset? Oh, *please.*" He scoffed and rolled his eyes. "Don't make me laugh."

"If you did, we'd all go in search of the bleating goat running through the halls."

"It's almost scary how similar they are," Belphegor commented to his brothers.

A voice projected from the doors: "Hold up, I'm here! Don't start without me!" Beel strode into the throne room wearing an ugly plaid pyjama with blue slippers.

Levi barked out a laugh. "What in the Nine Circles are you wearing, Beel?"

Beel ignored Levi, stopped beside Az, and punched him in the arm.

"Ow! Beel, what the Hell?" Az shouted, massaging the area.

"You didn't forget something by any chance?" Beel asked, waiting for a response Az didn't have.

"Did *you* forget something, Beel?" Mammon inquired through a snort, inspecting his brother's outfit.

"How considerate of you to join us, Beel," Lucifer said with a loud sigh. "What happened this time?"

To be honest, I was wondering the same thing.

Beel braced his hands on his hips and stared at Az. "I found it funny when I woke up in your apartment and you weren't there."

Ah. This fake story was Beel's attempt at saving our asses. I silently thanked myself for having made him read Az's feelings after my Fifth Stage; it was the only plausible explanation to how he knew about us. So, I doubled down on Beel's story and pushed Az on his other arm.

"What is with the touching?" He grabbed onto his arms. "New idea: everybody stop touching me."

Play along. Beel is saving our asses, I sent to Az.

I pointed an accusatory finger at Az. "You said you woke Beel up."

"I definitely did."

"You said he told us to go without him and he'd catch up."

"He definitely did that too."

Beel's eyes narrowed on Az, addressing me. "He didn't even knock on my door!"

Az shrugged, all innocent. "It was an honest mistake."

"I had to haul ass out of your place wearing *this* monstrosity," Beel grimaced as he gestured to the outfit he wore, "because of your 'honest mistake.'"

"You didn't need to leave *Arxala* wearing that," Az said. "You could have changed before you got here. Blame yourself, not me."

Are those actually your clothes? I asked Az.

They are, he answered. *I leave them at his place when I visit. I have no clue where he got the slippers from, though.*

"I was going to be late," Beel returned.

"You were late anyhow," Lucifer remarked from his throne.

Sarcasm brimmed in his tone. "*No*, you don't say? I wasn't aware. By the Circles, look at what I have to deal with!" Beel twirled around in his ridiculous pyjamas, then crossed his arms over his chest, petulant.

"*Gasp!* Beel wearing a generic brand? It's a tragedy!" Levi taunted.

Surprisingly, Asta joined into the teasing as well. "Beel, mate, you're getting a rash. I think you're developing an allergic reaction to anything other than high-end."

Belphegor took a different approach to the situation, shouting and cackling, "You should see how stupid you look right now!"

Thank you so much, Beel, I sent to him. *I am so, so sorry for this.*

You two dumbasses *owe me big time*, Beel replied.

Lucifer grasped at the armrests of his throne. "Wonderful! Now that we have established why Beel was late, however entertaining it was, Adara, I trust you're prepared for—"

"Does anyone have a phone with them right now?" Levi asked around the room. "A camera? A sketch-pad? Anything?"

"I do." Belphegor fumbled with the back of his light-blue jeans to produce a phone. "It's precisely for occasions like these that I keep my phone on me at all times." He snapped a picture of Beel's outfit. He burst into laughter and showed the picture to Mammon, Levi and Asta.

Beel faked a laugh, accosting his brother. "Aha-ha-ha. Can I see that for a minute?" Before Belphegor could refuse, Beel grabbed the phone from his hands and cracked it in half. "Whoops."

"You broke my phone!" Belphegor's voice had risen to an abnormally high pitch. "Do you realize how many memes I had on there? My social media followers are going to wonder where I am!"

"Phel, I promise, if you start screaming I am going to hit you," Mammon threatened. "I quite enjoy my hearing."

"But my memes," Belphegor whined.

"You should see how stupid *you* look now," Beel retorted.

"Beel, stop antagonizing him," Asta said.

Belphegor pointed at Beel. "You're buying me a new phone!"

"Says who?"

"Both of you be quiet and sit down." Lucifer didn't need to scream to assert his authority, just as the sun didn't need to herald its rising. "Leave your squabbling for another time. I want to start this Stage."

The brothers reluctantly did what they were told. Belphegor returned to his place, and a seat formed at Mammon's other side for Beel.

"What about Lil?" Levi asked Lucifer.

"You know how she is. Always wanting to make an entrance," Lucifer replied. "We'll have to begin without her." His head tilted to the Princes, signalling for Az to clear the floor.

"Good luck, Addie," Az whispered in my ear while passing me. At the seats, he assumed the spot near Levi.

I placed myself in the centre of the room, announcing, "Let's get this party started."

"Meyer," Lucifer called.

Silas, the High Order, stepped out of line. He bowed his head once, motioned for Satanials to join him, and unsheathed the blade hanging at his hip.

As a red-haired Satanial reached for the daggers on his leg, Lucifer raised a hand. "Wait a moment. I said I needed to increase the difficulty of these Stages, did I not?" he recalled. "Let's make this interesting, shall we?" He snapped his fingers at someone else and pointed to where I was. "You beat her," he began telling the Satanial, "and I'll offer you your freedom."

Michael advanced, his face blank and eyes void.

In that one second, I knew he'd made his choice.

CANTO XXX

Judas On All Sides

I'd been worried about Michael turning on me, however I hadn't believed he would, had dismissed the threat as him having spoken out of resentment. And now here we were. Whether we were together or not had no influence on the fact that I had made him a *promise*, but it seemed he wasn't interested in upholding his, or in acknowledging the implications of his decision. He'd told me himself how dangerous The Sixes were, how I could die in Hell, and I'd gone through Stage after Stage to get *here*. He knew what I was fighting for. For my parents' lives and for *his*.

He knew, yet still he chose to turn on me. And this betrayal stung more than anything.

"I went through everything to help you," I whispered to Michael, suppressing the tears threatening to escape. "*I risked my life for you.*"

"It's nothing personal, Dara," Michael answered. "I have to do what I have to do. You know that."

The despair, the *grief*, constricting my lungs, my heart, my mind burrowed, and in the darkness, it ignited into anger—into fury.

"You can always forfeit," Lucifer proposed as a viable suggestion.

"Thanks for the encouragement, father dearest." The sarcastic remark left my mouth before I could stop it.

"I'm basing this on odds, and they don't happen to be in your favour," he said with an unnerving certainty. "You'll be facing three vicious fighters."

"Malatesta and Lamont both come from *Balnara*," Belphegor agreed.

"And the last is my very own Rijaik," Lucifer added in.

Three against one?

"I can tell this will be easy," said the Primae Malatesta, the oldest appearance-wise. "Quick, even."

"What makes you so sure?" I asked.

His off-putting laugh made my blood curdle. "I can smell your fear, little girl." He held his nose high and inhaled deeply. "And your *weakness*."

The rage I had been restraining bellowed.

Weakness?

My shadows erupted from my arm at full strength, sending the Satanial spinning into the air. He landed three feet away from Lucifer with an echoing *thump*. "You're really living up to your name," I commented. "I wonder if I'll wipe out your bad temper as easily as I wiped you out just now."

Malatesta shook his head and bared his teeth, fuming.

"Let's go, doll face!" Levi cheered. "You're Levi's special champ!"

The show had begun.

Meyer barked orders to his comrades and flourished his blade, gripping it tighter. The two advanced in my direction, and my power pulsed inside my veins, aching to be released again. I loosened the reins. My *umbra* leaked from my hands, pooling to the ground before rising to swirl about me as a menacing gloom. A tremor invaded Michael's body, rearranging his bones and tearing his skin apart to reveal his growing reddened daemon form.

"Let's go, boys!" Belphegor shouted, clapping. "This just got *real.*"

Malatesta swung at me but I dodged and my fist slammed into the side of his head. "Yeah, real *stupid*," I mocked.

Az and Levi laughed from a distance.

I glimpsed Meyer steal up on me from the corner of my eye. In a quick motion, I grabbed his blade with my shadows and tossed it across the room, which left him scrambling to remove a curved knife hanging from his leg. All the while, Michael's leathery wings sprouted from his shoulder blades, his body becoming larger and larger by the second. With a knife raised, Malatesta charged forward again, determined to repay me for humiliating him.

I rolled my eyes. "This fucking guy."

He was bothering me way too much; it was annoying, really, however I would take care of it right now. My *umbra* launched from my left hand and pinned Malatesta against a pillar. On my command, they crystallized and trapped him within.

"Are you sure he came from *Balnara*?" I asked Belphegor between breaths. "I'm seriously wondering what that says about the state of management up there."

Belphegor scoffed, muttering something sounding like "snarky little Shadowbringer."

Metal flashed in my peripheral vision. Meyer swung his knife at me and I hit his wrist to deflect it. In response to his attack, I shot a dagger of shadow at his arm. It barely grazed him. He'd moved out of the way in time and jerked his elbow backwards, ramming into my mouth where my teeth cut the skin and blood met my tongue.

Belphegor jumped to his feet. "Come on, Silas!"

I summoned my *umbra* once again, ducking under Meyer's arm as he switched his knife hands to strike at my other side. While lowered, I struck his kneecap with tremendous strength. He sank to the ground, knife skidding across the floor and out of his grasp. I kicked him and pressed a knee to his chest. Looking into his green, red-rimmed eyes, I held a hand over his face and forced my shadows into him. I weathered whatever jabs he managed to land on my legs, my hip, my sides—an attempt to break my concentration and the solidity of my arms. My darkness entered through his mouth and eye sockets, enough to reach every point of his body. The tendrils crystallized while still within the Rijaik, immobilizing him completely.

A deep wail shook the glass castle.

Michael had fully Changed into his daemon form. He was all that remained.

In reaction to Michael's many heads and foaming mouths, obscurity emanated from my skin in a spreading shroud. His large leathery wings flapped, propelling him in my direction. I jumped over his barbed and swinging tail, tucked and rolled into a somersault to prevent a harsh impact on the ground. The glass floor cracked and splintered where Michael's strike had landed, where I'd once been.

A dull thumping blared in my ears at the thunderous racing of my blood. My rapid breathing stabbed at my lungs, scratched at the interiors.

I needed a plan and *fast*.

I scanned the area—the ground, the Satanials, the pillars, the arches—and clung to the first thought that crossed my mind. One second, I'd been on the floor; at the next, I watched from the shadows above. Michael's daemon form had lost sight of me.

For now, I was safe.

"Would you look at that!" Levi marvelled. "Absolutely stunning ascendiating!

"Thanks to me," Az mentioned, maintaining our lie.

"Once again, ever so humble," came Mammon's snide remark.

While Michael continued searching for me, the pieces of myself reformed and released at my order. Falling from the arches of the ceiling, I landed directly on his back, not unfelt by him given how his talons, slicing through the air, rang with every attempt to grasp at me. I ducked, I dodged, trying to avoid their trajectory as much as I could for as long as possible until I could find an opportunity. How could I, though, when his aim became scattered and unpredictable?

The razor tips caught me, cutting the uniform to slash the flesh beneath.

A scream ripped through my throat. A profound, singeing pain spread across my abdominal region where blood had begun to soak the shredded fabric.

I didn't want to hurt Michael, however he'd given me no choice. He'd made his own abundantly clear and had forced my hand. "*I'm sorry*," I murmured, forming a jagged-edged knife. Black blood sprayed when I stabbed the talon closest to me, met by my shadows seeping into the freshly made wound.

Michael's heads *howled.*

An involuntary sob escaped my lips, a reflex at knowing that I was the cause of his cries.

Between blood and darkness, I forced Michael into his original form, into the boy I'd fallen in love with. He buckled under the pressure, shrieking, and his wings gave out. We plunged from the air.

I jumped at the last minute, bracing for impact, and landed hard on the ground. My lungs heaved with the deep breaths I swallowed. Aches shot through my body with each inhale and exhale, but it was worth it. My pain had been worth it. I had beaten my opponents. I had really done—

Crash.

My head whipped in the direction of shattering glass.

Malatesta had broken out of my shadow cage and begun to Change.

"You have got to be *kidding me*!" I bent, placing my hands on my knees while I continued catching my breath and ignoring my bleeding.

Belphegor made a comment to his brothers that I didn't catch. My focus was otherwise occupied by the daemon standing in Malatesta's place, its form lean, crafted of ash with orange light bursting from the cracks and hollow sockets.

In the blink of an eye, its claws encircled my neck, digging and crushing my windpipe.

"***Nihara litarge yahrae laqut, nimah.***"

You are weak, little girl.

My feet kicked with every inch I was lifted from the ground. I reached for a shadow, any sliver I could slink into, only for nothing to come of it. My *umbra* had halted completely, frozen in my bones. Frantic, I hit the daemon's arms over and over again, fighting to free myself from its grip. The blood loss and lack of air took its toll.

My body grew numb and limp. Anvils replaced my eyelids, and I was tired enough to close them.

From miles away, Az's echoing, unknown words burrowed and sent a shock into me, a vehement spark of energy that left visions returning to dance in my mind. My once trapped shadows moved like a sombre veil to burn through my eyelids, sear my veins, and ignite. Their suppression crushed me from the inside out.

No more.

Shadow burst from every extremity in a surging, unbridled wave to engulf the throne room in darkness. The sudden impact of my violent eruption incapacitated the daemon momentarily, breaking its hold on my neck.

Fire soon emerged from the dark.

The daemon's ashen mouth opened to spew flames, meaning to find me. In a split-second decision, I recalled the shadows, consequently exposing my placement. I concentrated my *umbra* and projected the product forward with all my might.

The sheer magnitude of the strike launched the daemon backwards. To slow itself, it dug its nails dug into the polished floor, leaving scratches along its path. When it had finally stopped, the daemon Malatesta charged at me to retaliate.

I didn't move. I didn't run. I stood my ground.

A nameless sensation stung my eyes. As I set my volatile gaze on the daemon, it halted in its tracks.

A voice projected from my throat, half-mine, half-other:

"***Ahnark dradei Praeteritus.***"

The daemon dropped to a knee, its head bowed, and dissolved. Its body fell away into ash, absorbed into the ground until nothing was left of Malatesta.

"Wait, no! That's not—*What was that*?" Belphegor sputtered from where he stood. "What in the actual Circles was that?"

"It seems Adara can control daemons," Asta observed. Once he realized he'd said it aloud, he looked to Lucifer. "I thought that power lied only with you."

"Yes, this is quite interesting." A tightness invaded Lucifer's tone despite his efforts to minimize it, one that revealed he didn't know I possessed the skill either—one that said I wasn't supposed to have it in the first place.

I clamped a hand against my injured abdomen to stem the bleeding, not yet healed because of its depth, and stumbled toward the throne. As I neared the seats, the remaining Princes stood to meet me.

"You did great, doll face," Levi said, his smile distorted from my hazed eyesight.

"I never doubted you'd do phenomenally," Beel chimed in.

Belphegor glowered at me from where he'd sat, angry that I'd sent his Satanial to *Praeteritus*. I paid no attention to him. Instead, I searched for Az, discovering him by Asta, radiating relief and pride.

Mammon stood closest to me but didn't speak. He wore an odd, portentous smile while fixated on Az.

A slow series of claps echoed in the room. "My, my, that was entertaining." From the pillar closest to the throne, an exquisite woman in a tailored maroon suit stepped into the light. "And the finale? *Wow*. I honestly got chills."

"Lil!" Levi exclaimed, beaming. He, along with Asta and Beel, went to greet her. Even Belphegor left his seat to do the same. Every Prince gravitated there… all except Az and Mammon.

Lilith broke from the group, her black heels clacking on the floor as she strode to Az. "Hello, lover." She pressed her red lips to his. "Long time no see."

Wait, what?

I would've thought he'd push her away. Do something. *Anything*.

He didn't.

He reciprocated her affection, wrapping his arms around her waist to press her to him.

To make matters worse, Lilith turned to speak to me afterwards. "Sorry I missed your Stages, Dara," she said, offering an apologetic smile. "But congrats, anyway. You really were amazing."

No...

Distance and foreignness seized my voice. "*Jess?*"

CANTO XXXI

Have I Fallen For a Lie?

Jess' once recognizable curls were gone, the straightened golden-brown locks curving to her collarbones, and the lack of hazel in her eyes added to the maturity in her face, initially unrecognizable to me. Their colour had slipped into a bright scarlet red.

Jess, one of my best friends, was *Lilith*, the first female daemon.

No, this had to be some kind of sick joke. I had to be hallucinating.

"Why, isn't this a happy coincidence!" Lucifer exclaimed, opening his arms in a swell of pearlescent fabric.

How was this possible? I'd known her since I was fourteen years old; I'd met her barely two weeks after Frankie.

No.

The signs had been right in front of me the whole time.

When my parents had learned that 'Jess' and I had become friends, they'd been glad—oddly relieved, even. It made watching over me at my new school, where they couldn't be around, simpler, especially after the final incident in Colorado. She'd been the one Lucifer had sent to keep an eye on me in Massachusetts. 'Jess' rarely ever talked about her parents, and I'd never met them because (coincidentally) they were never home, which led me to believe those 'family' issues she was having where she had to leave for 'Europe' had been issues *here*, specifically the assignment with Azazel in *Agarath*. It all made sense. The time-frames aligned perfectly. However, that didn't make the information any easier to digest. All of those days we'd spent together throughout the years, every sleepover, every late-night drive, every vulnerable conversation we'd ever had—every single one of those memories had been based on a lie.

I had *trusted* her, *confided* in her… and she had been assigned to me the whole time. Had been lying to me about who she really was. Had been feeding the thoughts and fears I'd never have dared share with my parents to Lucifer.

She'd been truthful about only two things. First: Adam, the boy who'd broken her heart. He was *the* Adam. The first man to walk the Earth. And second: the person she said she'd been seeing.

Everything was happening too fast for me to process. The anguish clawing from my chest, determined to rupture, had begun to pry through my ribs.

An air of confusion settled over Lilith. "You didn't tell her about me?" she asked Lucifer, who'd been watching the scene unfold.

"Obviously not, and for precisely this reason," he replied, cheek in hand. "This is infinitely more diverting, wouldn't you agree?"

Az's voice came next. "Adara?"

I glanced at both him and Lilith… and at their joined hands. My gaze shifted to her to find concern there.

I had worn her clothes. The clothes and underwear at Az's apartment had been hers. I'd slept in the bed she shared with him.

Like lightning, the realization struck through me.

I'd been a stand-in for her. My best friend.

Waves of nausea rolled in my stomach. Instead of vomit, a chuckle escaped my mouth, which soon evolved into full-blown laughter whose constant and idiotic sound swallowed the room and my mind teetering on the edge of absolute hysteria.

The rest of the brothers looked between themselves, completely bewildered.

My hand slipped from my injury. The accumulating blood leaked onto the cracked floor of the glass castle in the centre of Hell. I laughed and laughed and laughed until my lungs brimmed with the betrayals I'd sustained.

I collapsed.

The final thing I saw was Mammon rushing forward to catch me.

"She's waking up."

"She's going to be fine, Az," Lilith said. "She's stronger than you think."

"Don't assume what I think," he replied. "I'm aware of how strong she is."

Lilith noted his sharpness. "You're not the only one who cares about her, Az. She's my best friend."

"I don't believe that applies anymore." Mammon had joined in.

Mammon?

"It does because she is," Lilith defended. "She still is to me."

My eyes cracked open, adjusting to my room in the castle. "Mon?" I uttered, my voice hoarse.

Shuffling noises were followed by him pushing aside the drape of my bed and kneeling next to me. "Hey, Adara. You were out for a bit. Gave us quite a scare."

Us.

I wanted to scoff but broke into a coughing fit instead.

"Lilith, take Mammon and go tell Luce she's awake," Az instructed.

"And what are you going to do?" Lilith asked from the foot of the bed, next to the post where he leaned. "Stay here?"

"I'm not going anywhere," Mon argued. "If Adara wants me here then I'm staying."

"It wasn't a request." Az left no room for debate.

"Mon, you know how he is." Lilith rose, contoured Az, and placed a hand on Mon's shoulder, but looked at me. "Let's not get into this, especially now of all times."

His eyes flicked between the two of us. He didn't protest. He simply nodded and left with her. The softness in Mon's gaze had explained it clearly: he would have done anything for her if only she'd asked.

I sat up in bed, passing my hand over my stomach. The wound was no longer there and neither was the pain that came with it. A small whitish scar decorated the skin Michael had stabbed.

Az arrived at my side, palm pressing on my arm to steady me. "Hey, hey. Go easy."

The pain returned with a vengeance, this time centralizing in my chest. I swatted him off. "Don't touch me," I spat, rising quickly from the bed to distance myself from him. I grabbed whatever I could find from the closest dresser to cover up.

"Addie, please." His demeanour was grave, his energy drained, and yet *I* was the one who'd bled out. *I* was the one who'd been hurt.

"*Don't*," I warned him. "Don't you *dare* call me that." I'd allowed him to use the name, having given him yet another meaningful part of myself… only for it to be ruined. He'd managed to ruin everything completely and I'd been stupid enough to have enabled it.

"So this it, then?" He folded his arms over his chest, defensive. "This how you're going to leave things between us?"

I laughed at his audacity. "There is no 'us.' Never was."

"Look, I had no idea your father had stationed Lilith to be with you in the Realm of the Living either," he explained. "Honestly, I didn't know; I never saw her myself." He believed my anger was directed at him hiding her identity from me.

I wouldn't put it past Lucifer to deceive those closest to him. Even I had barely recognized 'Jess' when I'd seen her again, however that would be an entirely different conversation I'd have with her… if I ever decided to speak to her after this. I didn't want to. I didn't want to see her. All I wanted to do was scream and cry.

"That's not what I was referring to." My hands gripped the edge of the dresser I leaned against. "Were you going to tell me you two were together, or were you planning on stringing me along for a little while longer?"

"Are you seriously asking me that?" Az asked.

"*This isn't a joke to me, Az!*" I wiped my face and eyes, half-wishing this was a dream happening in my unconscious mind. To see him standing in front of me with that same expression when I pulled my hands away was a mockery. *Reality* was a mockery. "You used me," I said, unable to stop my voice from cracking. "I was… I was just some quick lay to you," my lip trembled with the hurt breaking through my words, "all while you waited around for someone else."

Az's shoulders slumped. "That's not true. What happened between us meant somethi—"

A laugh that was mostly a sob cut him off. "Please. Enough," I said, intercepting the blatant lie he meant to convince me of. "It meant something for *me*." I shook my head, rephrasing my correction to reflect what I truly wanted to say: "For me, it meant *everything*."

He'd been staring at his boots as I spoke, not daring to meet my eyes. When he heard the last statement, his head snapped up. Az understood he'd been my first. "*Circles, Adara.* You should've told me."

"Az, I gave myself to you because I believed this was *real*." My hand involuntarily settled on my aching and bleeding heart, wounded on all sides. "Because *you* made me believe it was." The truth was it hadn't been; it had only been lust, an illusion, nothing substantial or genuine. What I felt for him, what he'd felt for me—no, what I *thought* he'd felt for me. The same sadness from before crept in once again, and agony and betrayal blended together, sinking their hooks into me. "*Wow.*" I blinked away the tears stinging the corners of my eyes and chuckled, sniffling and wiping my nose. "You actually made me believe you cared about me."

His brows drew together. "What are you insinuating, exactly?" His expression switched to one of incredulity. "That I… I somehow tricked you into feeling something for me?"

I pushed the sadness aside to get a hold of myself. "You were always good at manipulation, weren't you?" The comment equally applied to his powers.

"Oh, please." His laugh was clipped and smug. "I'll make this plain and simple for you." The words gritted through his teeth: "*You wanted me.* All out of *your own* volition."

"It was an awful lapse in judgement," I returned. "A mistake. All of this was."

"*But it wasn't to me!*" The force of his shout was enough to make the ground shake and resonate into my bones. He sighed. "It wasn't to me, Addie." The profound defeat pouring from him then almost convinced me his declaration had been genuine.

Almost.

Little by little, suffocation had built inside of me. The accumulation of falsities wrapped around my neck, tightening with every second I spent near Az. I had to leave. I *needed* to.

Without another word, I spun on my heel, left the alcove, and headed for the front door, though before I could reach the handle, mist spread and filled the room. The surroundings distorted and disappeared, rippling as though submerged underwater.

The door had gone. No matter if I continued forward, I encountered empty space.

"Az, I swear to you," I threatened, in no mood for any more of his tricks. "Let me out right now or—"

"Or what?" he said. "You said your piece, but you won't hear mine."

"I wonder why?" The reply dripped with sarcasm. "So you can continue lying to my face and hiding things from me?" I leaned in ever-so-slightly. "*No thanks*. My capacity for your bullshit has exceeded its limit."

"*My bullshit?*" he repeated in disbelief.

"Yes!" My flaring frustration and fury made me want to do more than scream at him. He had used me, had exploited my vulnerability, and gone behind Lilith's back to do it. Which other women had he hurt besides us? What other woman was left to pick up the pieces caused by his destruction and selfishn—

Wait a minute. A wisp of a thought murmured in my mind, born of a sudden connection.

Could it be? There was only one way to find out.

"It's bullshit," I resumed. "What you did to me, to Lilith… and to Sarah."

Az went rigid. "How do you know that name?" His voice had dropped to a disconcerted quiet.

My suspicion had been right, yes, yet why didn't I feel proud?

I crossed my arms before meeting his eyes. "There was this book I—"

His jaw clenched, and I could almost hear his teeth grinding against each other beneath. "*You went into my room?*"

"Mammon wrote it about you, didn't he?" I continued. It was the sole logical conclusion. It would explain why Mon had been warning me about Az and it would've also explained part of the nature behind their animosity. Mon had known something Az hadn't wanted him to, and now my determination to know the truth was greater than ever. "Tell me, the creature killing the men married to Sarah was you, wasn't it?" I said.

"Were you using her like you were me? Did her husbands get in the way of your plan so you got rid of them?"

"Why is it you're so quick to assume the worst of me, Adara?" For a second, I thought Az seemed hurt by my accusation. But I knew better. That was an impossibility for him. To be hurt meant he needed to have feelings.

"*Because you lied to me, Asmodeus!* What else am I supposed to think?" I pressed my hands to my head, hitting my temples. "He warned me. *Mon warned me*. And like a fool I didn't listen."

Falsehood faded with the endless nothingness of my surroundings. The room had returned to its original state, real, not imagined.

What I'd said had triggered something in Az. Something strong, cutting deep enough to encourage the repeal of his illusion.

"You seem to have me figured out after all." It wasn't the manner in which he'd spoken the claim that unsettled me; it was the light smile he wore. "You were right. I did kill those men. I was the creature responsible for their deaths."

I flinched at his confession, not because I hadn't known he'd done it—part of me already knew he had—but from the fact that he'd actually owned up to it, that he'd *admitted* it.

Az's anger wasn't unfamiliar—I'd witnessed many shades of it. However, this particular type was by far the worst. A frigid callousness resided in his scrutiny of me. *Hatred.* I had pushed him into telling me the truth, yes, but I didn't realize I'd been pushing him toward a breaking point as well. I pushed hard enough to see him snap.

"There's no point in keeping up the act when you've already found me out." He looked down his nose at me, his indifference almost frightening.

"I got my revenge on Lamont for disrespecting me by taking you from him. And as for you? Yes, I used you the same way I used Sarah and Lilith. I figured might as well, no? I was bored and annoyed by my duties, and you were already there, granted, a slight challenge but still willing." His gaze held mine, unwavering. "You, Adara, meant nothing to me. I felt *nothing*. I hope this satisfies your curiosity."

By the time he'd finished, a droplet landed on my arm. A tear had escaped and was sliding toward my elbow. I was crying?

I quickly dried my face. I hated being unable to control my emotions, hated the way they revealed my weakness. And I hated how Az could see it, see how much he had affected me. I'd been so naïve. So *gullible*.

How starved had I been of understanding, of affection that came from a place of complete and honest acceptance, that I'd ignored every warning, every sign that others and my mind had sent?

I threw open the door, and as I stood in the doorframe taking one last look, I finally determined who he reminded me of. It was Dorian Gray. Beautiful, but careless and selfish. Az's picture, his soul, was as scarred and flawed as his exterior.

I couldn't think of anything else.

I wanted to hurt him.

I wanted to hurt him like he'd hurt me.

My voice mimicked the emptiness of the hollows in my heart: "You are one of my biggest regrets."

When the words left and settled in the fraught space between us, the temperature dropped. No heat. Only all-consuming, numbing coldness.

And, as if I'd shot him point-blank in the chest, the ruby in Az's eyes had drained.

CANTO XXXII

Calling in a Bargain

I had made it barely a few feet away from my room, from where I'd left Az. The act I'd put on crumbled. Out of my splitting bones and thrumming veins, shadow exploded in every direction, plunging the hall into darkness. Agony pressed down on me. Crushed me. Wanted to bury me alive.

I'd been ripped awake from a dream—from a fantasy—and thrown back into reality.

This was the reality. And so was the pain that came with it.

I crumpled to the floor, clutching at my aching chest, not knowing how much more I could take. It was all caving in. *I* was caving in. And I would be buried in the broken pieces of myself.

Make it stop, I begged. *Please, make it stop.*

"Dara?"

My eyes opened, met by shadows. They retracted, slowly slithering into my veins to reveal Michael. He was crouched before me, much like he'd been at the beginning of my time in *Pravus*. How far we'd come since then.

"Are you hurt?" Frantic, he inspected me for injury. "Tell me… tell me I'm not the one who did this to you." His voice came out broken and strangled. "I'd never… I'd never forgive myself… I know how hard you worked, how much you sacrificed. I have no idea what I was doing, what I was thinking. *H-he* echoed in my head. So… so *persuasive*. The things he said, the visions he planted. I never wanted *any of this*. I messed up, Dara. I messed up big—"

To see the boy I'd loved reduced to nothing but a shell of who he'd once been killed me. Black blood had crusted on his split lip and bruises of the same colour decorated his face. He'd been beaten almost to a pulp, and I was the one who'd done it to him.

The things we'd done to *each other* were deplorable.

"We messed up so bad," I told Michael, and pulled him into a hug.

His arms wrapped around me, tight and shaking and guilty. "Dara, I'm so sorry," he whispered. "I just—I just want—"

"I know. I know."

And I did. I understood. I wasn't so blind as to absolve myself of my own faults and implication in this, no matter my personal revelations, or of the conditions that led to him being here or making the decisions he had. He'd made his mistakes, but Hell knew I had made mine. He hadn't deserved any of what had happened to him; he should've been at home, playing soccer in the park, eating his favourite double-chocolate ice cream, preparing for his gap year travelling before college.

But it could be over. It was possible now.

I grabbed Michael's hand and brought us to our feet. "Let's go."

He frowned, confused. "What's going on?"

"You need to bring me to Lucifer," I said. "I made you a promise and I'm going to keep it."

Michael had led me out of the castle and into a tunnel to the left which climbed higher and higher into the rock. When we arrived at a set of black glass doors, he stopped. "I'm not allowed in," he informed me. "It's off-limits to Satanials."

"You won't be one anymore."

"Dara, I should tell you now before we go in. Lilith is Je—"

"I know. I don't want to talk about it," I said with a defeated sigh.

He nodded in acknowledgement, and I raised my hand to the doors. They opened to a lounge surrounded entirely by dark glass, which served as a continuous window overlooking a grand chasm of souls being tortured by Satanials and daemons.

Levi stood there, watching. "Asta, come here!" He gestured for his brother. "Come look at Ashe."

Asta hopped out of his seat. "What are you on about?"

"She's going to do the thing with her tail again." Levi poked Asta, excited. A loud *boom* cut through the air, followed by thousands of shrill shrieks. "*Ah yes!* I love when she does that!"

"Didn't you two breakup a hundred and twenty-six years ago?" Asta asked.

"Yes?" Levi answered. "What's your point? Not all relationships have to end on bad terms."

Beel, who'd changed into proper clothes, must've made up with Belphegor seeing as how they'd been speaking to each other at the further end of the room. He was the first to notice my arrival and had paused his conversation when he saw Michael near me. I gave him a look, one that said not to ask any questions.

"Doll face?" I'd barely had the time to turn my head before Levi smothered me in a tight hug.

I patted his arm. "Hey, Levi."

"That's enough." Asta shooed his brother away. "Let the girl breathe, for Circles' sake." Levi did as he was told, although I could tell he wasn't very happy about it since he held his nose in the air and returned to the window. Asta smiled and gave me a lighter hug. "I'm glad to see you're alright."

'*Alright*' wasn't the word I'd use to describe how I felt.

At the complete end of the lounge, Mon sat on a couch beside Lilith, his arm draped over her shoulders. She'd been speaking to Lucifer, who was arranged on the dark red velvet settée near Belphegor.

Her attention shifted to me once my presence had been made known. Her brows knitted beneath her bangs. "Where's Az?" she asked, and Mon rolled his eyes.

Of course that would be the first thing to come out of her mouth.

Even though the mention of his name stung, it didn't sting half as badly as her having torn my heart from my chest with her own lies. "I don't know and I don't really care," I said.

Mon chuckled. "That makes two of us."

"Greaaaaat," Levi drawled, plopping himself into one of the armchairs. "Here we go again."

"It was a *joke*," Mon said, obviously lying.

Lilith eyed him. "Knock it off, Mon." Her attention returned to me. "I was only asking you a question, Dara. No need to get worked up about it."

"I gave you an answer, didn't I?" I replied, already reluctant to speak to her, but more so now because of Az. "I. Don't. Know. Go find him yourself if you're not happy."

"Okay, *look*," she started, leaning forward, "I realize Luce didn't tell you the truth about me—"

"I thought you would've liked to have the honours," Lucifer chimed in, woefully unhelpful.

"*Not now, Luce.*" Her scarlet eyes flicked back to me. "I instructed him to tell you; it's not my fault he didn't in order to satisfy whatever drama he'd planned out in his mind, so could you try toning down your hostility?"

A humourless laugh left my curling mouth. Lilith had no right to blame it all on Lucifer. She'd lied to me just as much as he had, and she'd had more than one opportunity to come clean.

"My hostility?" My balled hands opened, and the firelight in the room flickered with the growing darkness. "*I'll show you some hostility.*"

Asta rushed to put himself in the middle of the heated discussion. "Ladies, perhaps you two need a breather."

Michael held onto my arm.

"I, for one, am very interested in how this is going to play out," Belphegor said, at the edge of his seat. "Let her go, Lamont."

"I apologize, Your Highness," Michael said, bowing his head. "I can't."

It took a great deal of strength to reel in my shadows, however I was here for a reason and this argument with Lilith was wasting my time.

"I'm surprised you're here, Lamont," Lucifer commented. "I don't recall requesting your presence at this gathering."

"Evidently I'm the one who told him to come," I said.

Lucifer grew amused. "After everything that transpired during your Sixth Stage?"

"Cut the shit," I snapped. "Give me what I'm owed."

"What you're 'owed?'" he echoed with a Cheshire-cat smile. "Whatever do you mean?"

"Don't fuck with me right now," I spat. "The deal! I've gone through your ridiculous little Sixes and I *passed*, so GIVE ME WHAT I AM OWED! Undo what I did!"

Lucifer tapped an index finger to his chin, brows drawing together in momentary thought. "Unfortunately, one of your requests cannot be fulfilled at this time."

"I'm walking out of here with Michael no matter what you say," I declared.

"He wasn't who I was referring to."

Lucifer was getting on my last nerve.

"Can you stop with the riddles and just tell—" I stopped mid-sentence and swallowed the shock my throat, hoping this wasn't what he'd meant. "Samantha and Kamael?"

"Correct," he confirmed. The light around him fluttered like the Daemon Princes did, confused by the revelation.

"But… but I don't underst—"

"I believed you would've figured it out by now, what with all of the resources at your disposal." He picked a tuft off his sleeve. "Then again, once you'd agreed to The Sixes, it was too late."

"You're telling me that," my voice dropped to a harrowing whisper, "after all of this… I *can't* get them back?"

"Kamael won't be around for another few hundred years or so. As for Samantha, her gathering in *Praeteritus* hasn't been completed; I cannot simply pluck her out or speed up her formations," he explained. "Not to mention the fact that new information has arisen and needs to be investigated." He signalled to a frowning Lilith. She acknowledged it, seemingly as disturbed by the information as I was, and left the room. For what investigation exactly, I didn't know.

"What is it you're saying?" I asked Lucifer.

"For now," he clasped his hands together with a sense of finality, "what I can offer you is Michael Lamont, daemon form-less. *Only* him. That is, until the issue surrounding Samantha has been resolved and her timeline has been determined."

This continued to be news to the Daemon Princes. Lucifer didn't have access to *Praeteritus*? He couldn't pluck my parents' souls from the void?

What Lucifer had revealed disappointed me beyond anything I could have anticipated, and yet, I wasn't surprised. Deep down, I'd known something like this could happen. It had only been a matter of time before another obstacle presented itself, ready to crush everything I'd worked toward once again.

"As for your main concern?" Lucifer's attention slithered to my hands and extended his. "I'll be taking your abilities from you." His notification sounded rushed, similar to how he'd reached out to me despite the smoothness of the motion.

Was he in a hurry to claim my shadows, my power, for his own? Why would he be?

"I'm keeping them," I informed him. I hadn't been planning on giving them up for a while now. My *umbra* was a part of me, reminded me of my strength. In a twisted way, I had my father to thank for that.

Lucifer took issue with my refusal, his hands curling into his sleeves. "That is not what was agreed upon. Your powers were included in the deal."

"For all your eloquence and command over language, father dearest, I'll remind you that my *parents* were also included in our deal, but the condition can't be fulfilled. The part about Michael can be, and since he's all you can 'offer' me at this time, you can start explaining how I get him back."

Michael's hand slid into mine. The sorrow in his thankful smile told me he was equally disappointed that I hadn't gotten everything I'd been fighting for.

Lucifer propped his elbow on an armrest, and he leaned his chin on the palm of his hand.

Would he let us leave? Would he annul the deal and keep us here? No, he couldn't.

"When you've returned to the Realm of the Living, bring Lamont's soul to where his body is buried and join them together," Lucifer finally said. "Once the merging is complete, he'll be able to live again. The moment he leaves Hell, his daemon form leaves him."

The relief crashing over me remained within, untranslated onto my face. My gaze drifted around the room, to Beel, Asta, Levi and Mon. I didn't extend any goodbyes since I would eventually cross paths with them again.

"Let's go," I said to Lucifer, urging him onwards.

Inconvenienced but bound to his word, he raised his hands above Michael and me.

"***Innir Amarae Mortale dirmir.***"

The ground vanished from beneath our feet, replaced by a cavity into which we plummeted—an airless corridor of walls crafted of burning and smoking sheets that led from dark to light.

EPILOGUE

A loud shrill rang in my ears. My eyes snapped open, and I bolted upright in the middle of a street with Michael on my left. On my right, a car honked at us. "Okay, okay!" I shouted at the driver, picking Michael up by the arm. I motioned to the car. "We get it! Just go around!"

"Adara?" Michael tugged on my sleeve.

The driver honked another three times and passed by, flipping us off. I returned the gesture. "Have a *phenomenal day* too, buddy!"

"*Dara*."

I whirled to Michael. "What? What is—"

Dying orange rays of the sun setting over the trees painted the sky into a beautiful sight of pink, purple and blue. We were in the Realm of the Living, standing in front of my house on my street. In its windows, its tree, its roses, I saw my first day of high school, the first time I'd driven a car, fifteen-year-old me getting caught sneaking out of my room using the trellis, outings to the beach, family dinners… all the way to tearing open my college acceptance letter on the front lawn in our pyjamas.

"We made it," Michael said through a gasp.

"Yeah, we did." The rush of emotions manifested as rivulets rolling down my cheeks. Yes, we'd made it—we'd truly made it through it all—but that didn't kill the fear of how I'd continue on. It had been a matter of time until everything I'd buried surfaced and caught up to me. I'd kept putting off what I would do if I passed The Sixes, saying 'let future Adara handle it,' but the future was here now and I had no idea what to do.

My plan hadn't worked how I'd imagined. How I had *hoped.*

I hated to think I would return to the real world after everything I'd gone through, especially without my parents. How could I move forward? Did I have the strength to resume my old life despite what had happened? Would I still go to college? How? I'd gain student debts, get a job to pay them off, graduate, get another job and work forever?

I didn't have to do that, though. I could actually live and see the places I'd always wanted to see, do the things I'd always wanted to do. The possibilities were endless… but what was the point if I had no one left to share them with? No family and almost no friends.

Michael's hand rubbed my back. "Dara, I'm really sorry about your parents, and about Jess."

"So am I." I wiped and blinked away my tears, sniffling; when I did, I discerned a soft note of amber from my uniform. "We should get out of these clothes."

I looked to my house, apprehensive. The last time I'd been there, my parents had died. I didn't know if I'd be able to stomach going back, but we needed to get out of the open. Michael Lamont was dead, after all. I pushed my initial hesitance aside, headed for the front door and unlocked it with the spare key hidden in the fake rock near the bushes.

I prepared myself for the worse: to see my mom's body and the sword covered in her and my dad's blood.

Only… nothing was there. All was completely normal. No blood, no body, no displaced furniture, no broken wood or shattered glass. It was as though my parents' death had never happened.

I tore my gaze away, halting the surge of memories, and climbed the stairs to my room with Michael in tow. As with downstairs, it appeared untouched, frozen in a time when I'd still been oblivious. My phone sat on the nightstand, so I turned it on to see the date: *August 16th*.

We'd been gone for *weeks*?

The relentless dings of notifications became too much; I turned off my phone and returned it to where I'd taken it. Afterwards, I went to my closet to remove Michael's clothes from the far end and handed them to him.

He brushed a hand over his hoodie and pants. "You kept these?"

"I couldn't… I couldn't bring myself to get rid of them…"

A sad smile pulled at his lips. "Th-thanks."

I nodded and wandered around my room to various drawers to pick my own clothes; I needed to switch out of everything I currently wore, from my uniform to what was underneath, which had been stained with blood.

"You can get dressed in here," I told Michael. "I'm going to pop into the bathroom for a bit." I left him and went to jump into the shower. The last remnants of blood—red and black—washed away, tinging the water swirling down the drain while I remained under the showerhead. My shoulders shook from the sobs, from my abject grief and devastation. I could only hope the water muffled the sounds to prevent Michael from hearing.

Afterwards, I collected myself and dressed in the loose trousers and plain black crew neck I'd chosen. Although it was August and although I'd chosen to wear a crew neck, I wasn't warm enough. Once I'd returned to my room, I grabbed my denim jacket from the hooks by the door. When I veered, I found Michael standing in front of my vanity mirror; I hadn't noticed before, but the red circle around his irises had disappeared. He almost looked the same as he had in his earlier days.

"It's crazy how much I look like myself but don't," he murmured.

"That won't matter soon. We're going to fix it, remember?" I said, slipping on my black Doc Martens I'd stored in my closet.

He turned away from his reflection. "Right."

With that, we exited my house. I locked up behind us and directed us to the street. "Okay, we need to find out where you were buried."

Michael scrambled to the left, after me. "Where are you going?"

"I… I kind of… couldn't go to your funeral," I confessed. "We're going to see someone who was there."

I banged my fist on Frankie's door. "Frankie! Frankie, open up, it's me!" I'd told Michael to stay hidden so no questions from any passersby would be asked concerning a supposedly dead boy walking around looking very much alive.

Angela answered the door, her eyes narrowing on me. Had they always been that blue? I'd been away for so long that I'd forgotten. "Can I help you with something?" she asked, her tone expressing a large amount of irritation.

"I'm really sorry to bother you, Angela, but is Frankie home?"

Her perfectly plucked eyebrows furrowed. "Who's Frankie? There's no one by that name here. I think you have the wrong house." She began closing the door.

I shoved my foot in to stop her, pushed the door open, and started up the stairs. "I'm sorry, this'll only take a minute," I yelled, running to Frankie's bedroom. "Frankie, this isn't funn—"

The door I threw open led to a home office.

"No, no. This can't be happening." I searched everywhere for the slightest trace of him. "I don't… I don't understand..."

How could he be missing? How could it be as though he'd never existed?

My hands went to my hair, tearing at the roots and hitting my head again and again. It had been of no use. All I'd gotten from it were small whispers at the back of my mind.

The voices soon grew louder, creating a roaring commotion—and in the commotion came the singular whisper.

The dream I'd had.

It wasn't possible.

But the dreams I'd had so far had come to pass, hadn't they?

My original nightmares of the realm of flames and monsters, and the man with black and gold eyes—it had happened; I had gone to Hell and back.

The nightmare I'd had of Michael, the one where I'd pushed and killed him—it had happened.

The nightmare I'd had of my parents, even though it hadn't been clear—it had still happened.

The dream I'd had of Frankie…

Find me… Help me, Adara.

No. It couldn't be. I wouldn't believe it. There had to be another explanation.

"You're going to leave my house right now or I'm calling the police," Angela threatened from behind. She held a phone toward me, her finger one millimetre away from the call button where 9-1-1 was flashing.

"Please don't." I raised a hand in defence. "Please… just… Michael Lamont; do you know who he is?"

Her head tilted, confused by the sudden change of topic. "Yes? He's the boy who committed suicide back in June. Poor kid. Horrible thing."

"Where is he buried?" Urgency riddled my question. "Which cemetery is he at?"

Her finger retreated from the call button. "*Newton Cemetery and Arboretum*. On Main Street, I think."

I thanked her and sprinted out of the house, calling for Michael. He appeared soon after from the bushes and trees, hidden beneath his hood. "What did Frankie say?" he wondered.

"Do you know how to get to *Newton Cemetery and Arboretum*?"

"Yeah, I used to pass by it on my way to school in the mornings, why?"

"Because that's where you're buried," I answered. "Let's go."

"Dara, wait." Michael held onto my arm. "What happened with Frankie? You look like you saw a ghost."

"It wasn't a ghost," I said. "I'll tell you on the way, now come on."

And I did. By the time we'd reached the cemetery, I had finished my story and night had fallen, meaning Michael could remove his hood. No one came here at 10 PM, and no lampposts lit our way.

"How is that possible?" Michael wondered as we followed Main Street, keeping our eyes out for his grave. "Frankie couldn't have just vanished."

"I'm telling you what I know," I replied. "You should've seen her. Angela had no clue who I was talking about."

"What do you think it means?"

"There's a reasonable explanation behind this, I'm sure. Frankie got a scholarship to NYU, did you know? What I think happened is that his mom found out he went behind her back and disowned him in a way."

This theory was an attempt to convince myself I hadn't screwed up again—that I didn't somehow have a hand to play in this situation.

"Yeah, hopefully that's all it is," Michael agreed.

"Don't worry about it." I avoided the branch on the paved path cutting through the grass and trees. "Let's focus on finding your grave."

The moon had peaked in the night sky, casting a white glow on the tombstones and mausoleums we passed. We had searched for hours through every section of the cemetery along this road until, finally, I could see we were nearing Michael's grave.

I bent and ran a hand over a vine-riddled slab of stone. "We've reached the 'K' section," I whispered. "We're getting closer."

Michael didn't answer me. I popped my head up to check where he'd gone. Around a few hundred metres further, past the towering trees and through the shadows of branches creeping across the grounds, I spotted him. Abandoning my place, I contoured the rows of tombstones, interspersed with monuments, to reach his side.

Michael knelt at a relatively fresh grave, its grass nearly fully grown. The flowers lying at the base of the stone weren't withered, dropped off only recently.

His fingers traced his own name inscribed into the marble.

In loving memory of Michael Lamont

2000-2019

Beloved son and friend

"It's weird… seeing this," he said, his voice small, fragile even. "To think people came here for me… cried for me… thinking I was dead."

"It's going to be hard explaining this to everyone."

"You're right. I guess I'll have to figure it out eventually."

I attempted a joke to lighten the dismal mood: "You're not exactly famous enough to pull off this 'Sherlock Holmes' kind of death."

He laughed, a sort of short chuckle. "Yeah, I'll say I faked my death to write a theory for a social experiment or something."

"An independent documentary coming to HBO soon," I tagged on.

It seemed almost wrong for us to be here laughing together considering the certainly unusual circumstances. Considering everything that had happened to us...

I asked Michael to stand aside so I could remove his casket from the plot. I called on my shadows once again, and the dark trees looming above us rustled in the turning winds. Infusing the soil with my *umbra,* I ordered it to retrieve what I was after and felt it grip onto the wood beneath as if it were my own two hands. The ground began to move, pulsing like the very earth breathed, before giving way to a dark and glossy oak casket. I manoeuvered it to the left, minding the hole, and dropped it gently into the grass.

Michael wiped away the remnants of dirt, his fingers trembling and tapping against the hood. "Adara, I just wanted to say thanks for, you know, keeping your promise." His next words were low, and his head dropped. "I didn't deserve it… especially since I was never strong enough to keep the promises I'd made to you, to treat you the way I thought I was, with decency and an open mind and support—the way you deserved no matter what."

His reflection soothed and stung all at once.

"We've both done things we wish we could have done differently," I told him.

He gave a solemn nod. "I don't think anything's going to be as it once was."

"No, it won't."

"What are you going to do, Dara?" He looked up at me. "What are you going to do after this?"

There it was. The question I'd been dreading the most.

"I'll figure it out," I replied, offering him my best fake smile. "Don't you worry about me."

"I can't help it. We can—"

Everything had suddenly gone quiet. No more leaves rustling, not even crickets chirped. All was completely, deathly silent.

An eerie hum spread, calling to me like a beacon.

My eyes caught a quick movement in the thicket less than ten feet away.

Michael glanced around. "What is it?"

"Stay here."

"Where are you going?"

I didn't want to alarm him. "Not far. I'll be back." Leaving him to undo the clasps on his casket, I followed what I'd seen near the willow surrounded by bushes. Their branches scraped at my arms as I pushed forward, and I emerged at the edge of a small lake within the cemetery grounds. “There’s nothing here,” I said to myself. My hand covered my eyes and I shook my head. “Great. I’m back for not even a day and I’m already seeing things.”

Through the scent of pine, oak and magnolia dancing in the night breeze, hints of mahogany and dark amber invaded my senses. A quiet, breathless and incredulous “no” fell from my lips.

“You’re not seeing things.”

That voice. Those few simple words capable of encouraging the return of a pain I wanted so desperately to forget.

My blood pulsed in my ears as I turned to the water bank. I wasn’t prepared for this. Every single part of me wished to never have seen him again, yet here he was after what felt like ages and not at the same time.

The shadows cast on his face by the moonlight revealed the return of frigidity, and the white shards curved and caressed the angles of a lone, emotionless statue. Far and forbidden to touch, similar to the rest of him. The high-collared, long-sleeved shirt he’d chosen to wear covered him completely, leaving him just as reserved and hidden from the world as when I’d first met him.

No amount of analysis would be capable of abating the loathing coiling in my stomach—loathing of him, of what he’d done to me.

“What are you doing here?” I demanded.

Another rustling came from metres away. An irritated Lilith appeared, pulling leaves from her hair. “Az, what makes you so sure she’s even he—” She stopped in her tracks when she noticed me and looked to him for an explanation.

“Adara?” Michael shrieked, running through the bushes. “*Mierda! Dara?*”

I whipped around, and he grabbed onto my forearms. "What? Michael, what is it?"

Fear and distraught flashed in his eyes. "I-it's gone. My body…"

"Someone's taken it," Lilith said.

"Thanks for that, Captain Obvious," Michael snapped, not realizing who'd spoken. He did a double take. "Wait." He frowned, jutting a thumb in Az and Lilith's direction. *"¿Ellos qué hacen aquí?"*

"I was wondering the same thing," I replied.

"First Frankie goes missing, then my body disappears, and now you show up?" Michael said to them. "This can't be a coincidence."

Lilith's brows rose. "Frankie's missing?"

"Don't pretend like you care," I said, bitter about her fake concern. "It's not as though you were actually friends with him."

"Don't start with me, Dara," she cautioned. "Not now. Not when we have bigger problems on our hands."

"'Bigger problems?'" Michael repeated.

"These aren't coincidences anymore; it's a pattern," Az told Lilith.

"They have to be linked," she agreed. "*They have to be.*"

"What's that supposed to mean?" I inquired.

"What it *means*, Highness," Az began, "is that we believe whoever took your friend Frankie and Lamont's body are the same people responsible for killing Samantha and Kamael."

What? But that would mean…

I *wasn't* the one who had killed my parents?

FIN.

ACKNOWLEDGEMENTS

Right, so. Here we are. It's currently 11:30 PM on a Friday night, on the 13th of February, and I'm writing the acknowledgements for my debut, BBAD, while listening to Florence + The Machine. That said, chill out—I know the book's ending has made you… unwell—and let's get into it.

First and foremost, I would like to thank me, myself, and I. Why? Because without me, this book wouldn't exist, would never be in anyone's hands. Truth be told, I struggled for a long time to get it into the world. Years of querying, years of rejections, years of debilitating self-doubt and years of placing this series (yes, series) on the backburner while I distracted myself with new stories, new worlds, new characters. My girl Adara was always there waiting for me, though, so I figured I would return to her, let her have her moment on her birthday. Finally, it's happened. The dream I've had since I was a youngster has come true! Huzzah! So, this is for you, younger me. And for you, Addie.

Secondly, I'd like to thank my friends for all of their continuous support during this process. I can't even begin to tell everyone reading this (if y'all are, actually, reading this) how often my buddies have swiped up on my Instagram stories, commented on my posts, or even just sent me messages about BBAD, how often they've cheered me on when I felt like giving up, and how they encouraged me to take this publishing path. I'd especially like to give a shout-out to Samantha, who read the very first pages of BBAD when we were youngsters in college (sorry for killing your character off, BTW), and Sara, who was the first to read the book in its entirety and who's been reading every single one of my stories since then. Honourable mentions—other than the wonderful women in my dedication: Stef, Jenny, and Giuliana—include Grace, who's been championing BBAD since I first mentioned it to her, and Gabby, indie author Queen extraordinaire who's been there to guide me through self-publishing.

Thirdly, I'd like to thank my editor, Amanda (@amfreelanceediting on Instagram), for her copy and line edits on BBAD. Without her, I guarantee there'd be a million more typos in this book, sentences that didn't make any sense, etc, etc.

Fourthly (??? strange word ???), I want to shout-out another talented Amanda (@amandawawyn on Instagram) since she did the art of Adara in the *Yrantanian* combat circles. Absolutely stunning work, and you should definitely commission her.

Last but not least, I'd like to thank all the coffee, chips, cookies and candy I ate while drafting and editing BBAD. Your sacrifice was truly appreciated.

Addendum for when I inevitably return to this and realize I forgot to mention something/someone:

- Shout-out to my family because the money they gifted me throughout 2024 and 2025 financed the publishing of BBAD. If any of you are currently reading this, I have no wish to discuss the contents of this book with you.

Lili Mastronardi is a fiction writer from Montréal, Canada. Although her first language is French, she is fluent in English, knows (decent) Italian, and is trying her hand at Spanish. While obtaining her degree in Analytical Chemistry from Dawson College, she drafted her first full-length novel, BBAD, and finished its sequel BSAS in university after drafting a second book from a new series, nicknamed VWIP. As it stands, she has completed 7 novels. She tends to write queer female protagonists in fantastical settings who are morally grey or villainous because she believes angry, evil women are the best and deserve to showcase the extent of their rage and power. Whenever she's not busy drafting yet another book (and ignoring her phone), she's either drinking unhealthy amounts of iced coffee despite the weather, info-dumping Game of Thrones lore on anyone who cares to listen, or cooking up some pasta dish since her Italian heritage runs red as tomato sauce in her veins.

www.ingramcontent.com/pod-product-compliance
Lightning Source LLC
LaVergne TN
LVHW050919080826
845145LV00001B/131

* 9 7 8 1 0 6 7 5 1 6 3 0 7 *